SEEK AND DESTROY

|| AMERICA RISING ||

SEEK AND DESTROY

william c. dietz

ACE
New York

ACE
Published by Berkley
An imprint of Penguin Random House LLC
375 Hudson Street, New York, New York 10014

Copyright © 2017 by William C. Dietz
Penguin Random House supports copyright. Copyright fuels creativity, encourages diverse
voices, promotes free speech, and creates a vibrant culture. Thank you for buying an authorized
edition of this book and for complying with copyright laws by not reproducing, scanning, or
distributing any part of it in any form without permission. You are supporting writers and
allowing Penguin Random House to continue to publish books for every reader.

ACE is a registered trademark and the A colophon is a trademark of
Penguin Random House LLC.

LEGION OF THE DAMNED is a registered trademark of William C. Dietz.

Library of Congress Cataloging-in-Publication Data

Names: Dietz, William C., author.
Title: Seek and destroy / William C. Dietz.
Description: First Edition. | New York : Ace, 2017. | Series: America rising ; [2]
Identifiers: LCCN 2017002942 (print) | LCCN 2017007080 (ebook) |
ISBN 9780425278727 (hardback) | ISBN 9780698184428 (ebook)
Subjects: | BISAC: FICTION / Alternative History. | FICTION / Science Fiction / Adventure. |
FICTION / Science Fiction / Military. | GSAFD: Science fiction.
Classification: LCC PS3554.I388 S44 2017 (print) | LCC PS3554.I388 (ebook) |
DDC 813/.54—dc23
LC record available at https://lccn.loc.gov/2017002942

First Edition: June 2017

Printed in the United States of America
1 3 5 7 9 10 8 6 4 2

Cover art by Paul Youll
Cover design by Sarah Oberrender
Book design by Kelly Lipovich

This one is for my son-in-law, Major Dane Franta, USAF.
You the man.

CHAPTER 1

||||||||||||||||||||||||||||||||||||

No nation ever had an army large enough to guarantee it against attack in time of peace, or ensure it of victory in time of war.

—CALVIN COOLIDGE

WASHINGTON, D.C.

A thick layer of dark clouds hung low over Washington, D.C., as the Black Hawk helicopter circled the severed stub of what had been the Washington Monument—and passed over the remains of what had been the Museum of Natural History, the National Gallery of Art, and the Capitol Building. President Samuel T. Sloan had seen pictures of the destruction—but still wasn't prepared for the terrible reality of it.

Sixty meteors had entered Earth's atmosphere on May Day 2018. Some splashed down in the Pacific Ocean, where they exploded and sent tidal waves racing east and west. Others swept in over North America at 1:11 P.M. PST. One of them exploded over the San Juan Islands in Washington State. The blast was twenty to thirty times more powerful than the atomic bomb that fell on

Hiroshima, and the secondary effects included a powerful shock wave, earthquakes, and enough particulate matter to block the sun. Millions died.

But the horror wasn't over. *More* meteorites rained down. Denver and Washington, D.C., were destroyed. Sloan had been the Secretary of Energy on that horrible day—and in Mexico on official business.

It wasn't until after the arduous trip home that Sloan learned the truth: All those senior to him had been killed and, by virtue of being alive, he was president. But the country was so broken by then that most of the Southern states had seceded from the Union, triggering the Second Civil War.

And that was why Sloan had returned to the capital . . . To not only announce his intention to rebuild Washington, D.C., but to reconstruct the country itself, no matter the cost.

Army One circled the Capitol Building's shattered dome and flew west. Moments later, it passed over the courthouse, the theater where Lincoln had been shot, and the ruins of the White House. That's where the former president and the first family had been when the incoming meteor killed them and half a million other people.

The Black Hawk began to lose altitude as it swung around the State Department and swooped in for a landing adjacent to the Lincoln Memorial. Thanks to Sloan's press secretary, an ex–PR man named Doyle Besom, a large crowd was present to greet Sloan. Many of them had been hired to rebuild the capital. So Sloan heard enthusiastic applause as he exited the helicopter and paused to wave.

Like the rest of the federal government, the ranks of the Secret Service had been decimated during the disaster. But recently confirmed director Raul Jenkins was doing the best he could to reconstitute the organization—and his agents were there to protect the president from any would-be assassins in the crowd.

Cameras whirred and clicked as Sloan ran up a short flight of stairs to the top of the temporary platform. "Always run up stairs . . . It makes you look young and energetic." That was just one of the many pieces of advice Sloan had received from Besom. And most of them were correct.

Attorney General Reggie Allston was on the platform waiting for Sloan. He had closely cropped hair, dark skin, and was dressed in a beautifully tailored suit. The handshake was followed by a man hug. "You look good, Mr. President."

"But not as good as you do, Reggie . . . Where do you get those suits?"

"That's a secret, Mr. President . . . I want to look better than you do."

Sloan laughed as Allston turned to the bulletproof podium and microphone. "Good morning . . . My name is Reginald Allston, and I'm here to introduce the man many people call the Fighting President. When a renegade general seized control of Fort Knox, President Sloan fought side by side with our troops to take it back. And when our Rangers attempted to capture the oil reserve in Richton, Mississippi, President Sloan fought with them. That's how we know we've got the right man for the job."

Besom's people were salted throughout the crowd. And when they began to clap, the people around them followed suit. Allston smiled, nodded, and let the applause continue for a moment. Then he raised his hands. "But we're here to fight a different kind of battle today . . . a battle to restore the nation's capital. The task will take years. Some say ten, others say twenty, but it makes little difference. We *will* get the job done!"

The applause was entirely spontaneous this time, and quite loud.

Allston waited for it to die down before making his introduction. "Ladies and gentlemen . . . On this, the first day of this city's reconstruction, it is my honor to introduce President Samuel T. Sloan!"

Sloan stepped up to the mike as Allston moved to one side, and the crowd applauded. There were what? At least three thousand of them . . . filling the space between the platform and the long, narrow Reflecting Pool. A government-authorized camera drone swooped in to capture a tight shot of Sloan's face. Electronic communications continued to be somewhat iffy north of the New Mason-Dixon Line, but improved with each passing day. "Good morning," Sloan said. "It is a distinct pleasure to meet some of the many people who are going to—"

There were three suicide bombers. Each killed at least a dozen people when their vests exploded. And that included 60 percent of Sloan's Secret Service detail. The blasts were too far away to harm him. But they were close enough to open a bloody gap through which more attackers could charge.

The crowd had been screened. But the weapons were there all along, concealed by a thin layer of soil and marked by dots of orange spray paint. All the second wave of assassins had to do was scoop up a weapon and charge the platform. The podium saved Sloan's life during the first few seconds of the attack. Then he ducked, stuck his hand inside his jacket, and pulled out the Glock he had started to carry.

As far as Sloan knew, he was the only president who routinely carried a gun . . . And a good thing, too, since he'd been forced to use it once before. The surviving Secret Service agents had opened fire by then, and some of the attackers were down. But as Sloan leaned out to look, he saw that five assassins were still vertical and coming his way!

Sloan fired. But it seemed as though the wild-eyed man in the lead was wearing body armor, because he took two bullets in the chest and kept coming. Fortunately, the third round punched a hole in his forehead and knocked him over.

As that attacker fell, the woman coming up behind him tripped on the body, giving Sloan the opportunity to kill her, too. Then Secret Service agents flooded the stage and hauled him away. The camera drones captured the whole thing—and the footage of Sloan defending himself cycled over and over on TV. Press Secretary Besom was a happy man.

MURFREESBORO, TENNESSEE

The old warehouse complex consisted of three one-story concrete buildings, one of which was dedicated to housing a makeshift cafeteria and an exercise area—all powered by an army generator. After donning three layers of clothing, Captain Robin "Mac" Macintyre made her way down a grubby corridor to a steel fire door. Then, pulling a knit hat down over a mop of dark brown hair, Mac stepped out into the driving sleet. The temperature should have been around eighty, but because of the globe-spanning layer of airborne particulates that blocked the sun, it was thirty-seven instead.

A trail of scuff marks led Mac to what was popularly known as "the command shack." She pulled the door open and stepped into the warmth provided by a "liberated" stove. Staff Sergeant Woods was seated behind one of the beat-up desks that had been captured with the rest of the complex. "Good morning, ma'am," the noncom said cheerfully. "The major is in his office."

Mac said, "Thanks," and turned to her right. She was about to knock when Granger motioned her in. He had carefully combed hair, a slightly bent nose, and gray eyes. Mac saluted, and Granger threw one of his own. "Close the door and take a load off. I've got a job for you."

Mac wasn't surprised. In addition to the responsibilities associated with being in command of Bravo Company, Mac served as the battalion's executive officer, too. "Yes, sir. What's up?"

"The brass want us to snatch a rebel general," Granger replied.

"Okay, no problem. Before lunch? Or after?"

Granger chuckled. "After. His name is Revell. General Scott Revell. He's in command of the Bloody Bill Anderson 205th Infantry Regiment. That means he could provide us with valuable information."

Mac knew the rebs liked to name regiments after Confederate generals from the *first* civil war and, by all accounts, Anderson had been famous for his brutality. "Okay, and what makes them believe that we can grab a regimental commander? That sounds like a special ops mission to me."

"It *is* a special ops mission," Granger told her. "Your job will be to deliver the operators, provide security, and bring everyone out in one piece."

Mac frowned. "Really? We're supposed to fight our way through a regiment of troops, find their CO, and take him home? Why not use helicopters instead?"

"Because," Granger said, "you won't have to fight your way through Revell's regiment. According to one of our spies, he's having an affair with the wife of a local politician. The pol has to attend a county-council meeting each Wednesday at 7:00 P.M. And that's when Revell drops by.

"The politician's house is located about twenty miles inside reb-held territory. And, whereas the weather might keep the rotor heads from lifting off Wednesday night, your Strykers will be able to get through."

Mac knew that the Union had spies down South, just as the Confederates had agents in the North. And she knew Granger was correct . . . The weather *could* keep the helos on the ground. But driving twenty miles into enemy-held territory wasn't her idea of a good time. Of course, Granger didn't care—and neither did the brass. "Yes, sir. So we're talking *this* Wednesday? As in tomorrow?"

"Tomorrow night," Granger replied. "If that's convenient."

Mac grinned. "I was going to paint my nails . . . But if you insist."

"I do. An eight-man special ops team under the command of a butter bar named Thomas Lyle will arrive here in a couple of hours. Be nice to him."

Mac looked innocent. "I like second lieutenants. They're cute, like puppies. Is there anything else?"

"One thing," Granger replied. "And that's security. If word of this operation were to leak, you could walk into a trap."

It was a sobering thought. Mac stood. "Roger that, sir."

"Good hunting."

As Mac left the command shack, she headed straight for the motor pool, which was housed in another one-story concrete building. The structure had been bombed during the fighting, but the roof had been repaired, thanks to the efforts of Company Sergeant Mary Dodge. That meant the interior was ten degrees warmer than the outside temperature.

But Mac could still see her breath as she made her way over to the spot where Second Lieutenant Marvin Haskell was kneeling next to a Stryker's exposed brake drum. It was a Stryker RC. The "RC" stood for "recon," and the crew consisted of a commander/ gunner and a driver, both of whom were present. The gunner yelled,

"Atten-hut!" and Mac waved the courtesy off. "As you were . . . Which is to say, damned cold."

The joke produced an appreciative chuckle from everyone except Haskell. He had sandy-brown hair, a farm-boy face, and a serious expression. "Morning, ma'am," Haskell said, as he stood. "The brakes on one-one are good to go."

"Excellent," Mac replied. "Come on . . . Let's grab a cup of coffee."

The big pot was on twenty-four/seven and contained a liquid that had the appearance and consistency of motor oil. But it was located on a table where they could talk without being overheard. Mac took the opportunity to brief Haskell on the mission. She finished by saying, "We'll take one-one, one-two, and one-three. Each truck will carry four green hats plus the crew. I'll ride in one, and you'll ride in three. Any questions?"

"Yes, ma'am. What about my soldiers?"

Each platoon included four squads of infantry, one per truck. "Tell 'em to grab some extra sleep," Mac replied.

"They won't like being left out."

Mac shrugged. "Sorry, but that's how it is. And Marvin . . ."

"Ma'am?"

"Smile once in a while."

Haskell frowned. "Yes, ma'am."

CAMP DAVID, MARYLAND

In spite of the damage done to Washington, D.C., the presidential retreat known as Camp David was unscathed. Sloan and his advisors on national security were seated around the long wooden table in the Laurel Lodge conference room. It was a sobering moment because the last time Sloan had been there, it had been for a cabinet meeting. And, except for him, all the other people who'd been present were dead. Including the previous president. He pushed the thought away. "Okay, people . . . Let's get to it. You're up first, George . . . What's happening in Europe?"

Secretary of State George Henderson had brown skin, a jowly face, and was built like a fireplug. "Nothing good," Henderson replied gloomily. "Most of them suffered a significant amount of damage. And, like us, are going through social turmoil as a result. Sweden broke away from the EU, Muslim extremists took over a large section of France, and the government of Germany imposed martial law."

"That works for me," the Chairman of the Joint Chiefs said. Four-star General Herman Jones was a Marine from the top of his closely cropped head down to the toes of his extremely shiny shoes. "I'm in favor of anything that keeps the Europeans busy. Otherwise, one or more of them might form an alliance with the Confederacy."

Henderson nodded. "Fortunately, that isn't likely to happen anytime soon. Russia took some serious hits, and they're busy gobbling up all of the ex-Soviet states, plus anything else that isn't nailed down. That's going to be a big issue postreconstruction, but there isn't anything we can do about it now."

"The secretary is correct," Martha Kip agreed. She was a fifty-something blonde who had spent fifteen years in the CIA and five at the NSA before Sloan chose her as National Intelligence Director. "As for Iran," she added, "we might see something good develop there. Indications are that the Grand Ayatollah is dying of cancer— and there's a real possibility that a more progressive leader will succeed him."

Sloan was just getting to know Kip but liked her style. He turned to Henderson. "I know you're thin on the ground, but let's get ready to take advantage of the change if the Ayatollah dies, and a more amenable person takes his place." Henderson nodded as he scribbled something on a pad.

Sloan made eye contact with Jones. "How about the war, General? Do you have anything new to report?"

"General Hern has been able to hold on to every square foot of territory we've taken," Jones answered proudly. "That said, we're stalled just north of the Mississippi state line."

It was the very thing that Sloan feared. A long, grinding war that would take a terrible toll on both sides and leave the country vulnerable to external threats. In an effort to end the war quickly, Sloan had approved an airborne assault deep into enemy-held territory, where he hoped to seize an oil-storage facility and establish a foothold. Unfortunately, that effort had been a colossal failure. Sloan still had nightmares about it.

So what to do? Grind away? Or press the Joint Chiefs for a new strategy? Sloan made a mental note to speak with Jones privately. "My compliments to General Hern," Sloan said. "Please tell him how much I appreciate his efforts. We will, needless to say, continue to monitor the situation. What else have we got?"

Attorney General Allston cleared his throat. "The preliminary report regarding the assassination attempt is in, Mr. President, and the findings are significantly different from what we expected."

Sloan's eyebrows rose. "How so?"

"Based on what the FBI has been able to piece together, the assassins *weren't* rebels," Allston replied. "They were members of an obscure religious cult associated with a man who calls himself the warlord of warlords."

Sloan was well aware of the fact that while his government had succeeded in restoring law and order to many areas of the country, that wasn't true everywhere. Criminal gangs, led by self-styled "warlords," had taken advantage of the chaos to carve out personal kingdoms. It was a problem that hadn't been fully addressed because of the war. "Okay, who *is* this guy? And why does he want to kill me?"

"His name is Robert Howard," Allston answered. "He's an ex–army noncom who, according to various sources, is very charismatic. So much so that he runs his own religious cult. Based on his military experience and personality, he controls most of north-central Wyoming.

"As for *why* he wants you dead, the answer is simple . . . Howard can see the handwriting on the wall. Once the federal government is fully restored, it will turn its attention to him. And he wants to maintain the status quo."

Sloan turned to Jones. "Are we working this?"

The general shook his head. "Not really, Mr. President. Most of our assets are pointed south."

"I get that," Sloan replied, "but we need to squash this bug. Not because of the attack on me—but for the citizens of Wyoming."

Jones nodded. "Yes, sir."

Sloan turned his attention to Besom. "What about optics, Doyle? What's the flavor of the day?"

Besom stirred. "With very few exceptions, the press corps assumed that the assassins were rebels, Mr. President. So their stories are slanted in that direction. The general effect has been to demonize the Confederacy."

"So how will we correct that?"

Besom's eyes bulged. "*Correct it?* I don't understand."

Sloan frowned. "Shouldn't we set the record straight?"

"Hell no," Wendy Chow responded. "Not yet anyway." The

White House Chief of Staff had been on the job for less than a month. But her tough "I don't suffer fools gladly" persona had already made itself felt.

"Correct me if I'm wrong, Reggie," Chow continued. "But we never pointed the finger at the Confederacy . . . We said that an investigation was under way. I think we should leave it at that for a few weeks. Then we can issue a report."

Sloan knew that he should force his staff to tell the truth. He also knew that there was a need to cement public support for the war. And, if the public believed that the Confederates were behind the assassination attempt, that would help. He let the matter ride. The meeting droned on.

MURFREESBORO, TENNESSEE

Second Lieutenant Thomas Lyle was something of a surprise. Rather than the fuzz-faced kid Mac had expected, Lyle was a hard-edged veteran who'd spent six years in the army prior to graduating from OCS. Mac, Lyle, and Haskell were geared up and standing next to Stryker one-two as the light continued to fade. "Okay," Mac said. "Any last-minute questions?"

"Yes," Lyle said with a straight face. "Can I have my mommy?"

Mac laughed, and Haskell stared. "Too late for that," Mac replied. "Let's haul ass." With Mac in one-one, Lyle in one-two, and Haskell in one-three—every vehicle would have a leader even if the others were lost.

Once the officers were inside their respective vehicles, the ramps came up, and the mission began. Mac didn't like being cooped up in a steel box, especially one that stank of sweat and hydraulic fluid. So she made her way forward to the point where she could stand on a filthy seat and stick her head up through an air-guard hatch. The Stryker was in motion by then—and the ride was smooth when compared to other military vehicles.

After rolling through the inner perimeter, the Strykers had to pass through a buffer zone prior to exiting the base via a heavily guarded gate. It wasn't dark yet, and Mac waved at a sentry. He waved back.

The truck's commander was a noncom named Lamm . . . And Mac heard the usual high-pitched whine as he put his foot on the accelerator. The house where General Revell's lover lived was out in the country. The plan was to swing wide, go off road, and use the cover of darkness to reach the objective without engaging the enemy.

Would someone notice the vehicles? Yes, of course they would. But given all the military activity in the area, Mac didn't think the locals would report the Strykers. Even if they did, what could the caller say? "Something drove through my pasture." Maybe the rebs would respond, but it didn't seem likely.

Lamm could see the manually loaded route on his nav system and didn't require directions from Mac. That left her free to eyeball the surrounding countryside. It had a greenish glow thanks to her night-vision gear, and there wasn't much to see other than the widely separated lights belonging to people who were ignoring the blackout. And that was fine with Mac.

The next twenty minutes were spent pursuing a zigzag course that took the Strykers to within a mile of the constantly shifting front line. Then, confident that friendly forces could see their identification friend or foe (IFF) signals, Lamm sent BULLY BOY through a fence and into a field.

Mac was forced to hang on with both hands as the truck bucked over a rock and headed downslope to what was supposed to be a shallow stream. And if it wasn't? They'd be screwed. But the rebs wouldn't expect Union vehicles to use the streambed as a road.

The stream was shallow but thick with water-smoothed rocks, and Mac was thrown every which way as all eight wheels fought for a purchase. When Mac looked back over her shoulder, she took comfort from the fact that two sets of taped headlights were following along behind. So far, so good.

As Mac turned forward, she saw a head-high obstruction coming straight at her, and heard Lamm yell, "Duck!" Mac realized that the vic (vehicle) was going to pass under a bridge as she dropped into the cargo compartment. That was when she felt the Stryker jerk, heard a muffled bang, and realized how lucky she'd been. Fortunately, the soldier who'd been standing in the rear hatch had heard the warning as well. He grinned and gave her a thumbs-up.

Mac returned the gesture before going topside again. The light machine gun mounted forward of the air-guard hatch was still there, but the .50 cal and the remote weapons station had been sheared off, along with one of two whip-style antennas.

The vic rocked from side to side as it powered its way through a rock garden. The transmission dropped into a lower gear as Lamm drove up a sloping bank and into the adjoining field. Mac had seen drone footage of their route and didn't remember seeing a bridge. Shit! They were lost. "Lamm . . . That bridge shouldn't have been there. We took a wrong turn somewhere. Tell the others that we're going to pull up and kill the lights."

Mac ducked down into the cargo bay, where four amped-up Green Berets stared at her. "No problem," she assured them. "I'm checking our twenty . . . We'll be off and running in a minute or two."

The rebs had taken control of the country's nav sats early on and were encrypting all of the signals. That meant Mac couldn't rely on GPS to find her location. But she had a fistful of maps collected from the battalion's Intel officer the day before, and one of them was titled HISTORICAL LANDMARKS, RUTHERFORD COUNTY, TENNESSEE. It was the sort of cartoony map often found in motels but might help her to get oriented. And sure enough . . . As Mac scanned the map, she spotted the bridge that, according to the caption, had been the site of a skirmish during the first civil war.

By comparing the historical map to a road map, Mac managed to figure things out. After going off road, Lamm had turned south into the *first* streambed he'd come to rather than waiting for the second one and entering that. But if they turned east, and crossed the streambed they'd left, the task force could get back on track.

Mac took the maps forward to share with Lamm. His face fell once he realized the mistake. "I'm sorry, ma'am. I screwed up."

Mac knew Lamm, and knew there was no need to chew him out. He would take care of that himself. "No prob," she lied. "Shit happens. Warn the others. Let's roll."

Mac directed a reassuring smile to the green beanies before returning to her perch topside. She was acutely aware of the fact that one-one had been stripped of its most potent weapon, leaving it with two pintle-mounted M249 light machine guns for self-defense. And that was one more reason to avoid a shoot-out if she could.

BULLY BOY waddled over broken ground, dived into the streambed, and threw gravel as it powered up the opposite bank. Wires snapped as the Stryker broke through a fence and kept going. The terrain was fairly level until they entered the *next* stream, and Lamm took a right.

Mac was forced to hang on as the vic wobbled over another streambed filled with water-smoothed rocks. The other Strykers were close behind. After a quarter mile or so, Lamm turned and angled upwards before arriving on a flat spot next to a country road. That led to a stand of trees about half a mile from their objective. "Get off the highway and position the truck for a quick getaway," Mac instructed.

Then, using her tactical radio, she gave the other truck commanders similar orders. The ramps went down the moment the vics were parked. That was Lieutenant Lyle's opportunity to run a last-minute check on his troops. Then he came to see Mac. She was standing next to one-one's hatch. A bar of light leaked sideways to illuminate the left side of her face. "I don't expect a lot of resistance," Lyle told her. "Revell won't have much of an escort, assuming he's there. How could he? Without everyone finding out what he's been up to? So things should go smoothly.

"But," Lyle continued, "if the poop hits the fan, and I tell you to haul ass, then do it. I'm aware of your reputation, Captain. And that includes the Silver Star. But if I say 'go,' it's your duty to save as many people as you can. Do you read me?"

Mac was a captain, and Lyle was a lieutenant. So he couldn't give her orders. But Mac understood. "I read you, Thomas."

"It's Tom. Only my mother calls me Thomas."

Mac grinned. "Roger that, Thomas."

Lyle chuckled, whispered something into his mike, and disappeared. At that point, all Mac had was six crew people to defend the vics. But what was, was. The waiting began.

Now that the engines were off, Mac could hear the distant rumble of artillery as North and South fought a war not that much different from World War II. Was her sister Victoria out there somewhere? Killing Union soldiers? And what about their father, General Bo Macintyre? The man who, both wittingly and unwittingly, had done so much to shape his daughters. Was he doing battle with his peers? The men and women with whom he had gone to West Point.

And then there was President Sloan. After fighting their way north from Mississippi together, they'd been forced to go their separate ways. He was an interesting man . . . A leader who would put his life on the line—even if he was something of a Boy Scout. *But what's wrong with Boy Scouts?* Mac asked herself. The question went unanswered, as an engine was heard and a pair of headlights appeared. Mac held her breath as the pickup rolled past and vanished around a curve. How long had it been? Fifteen minutes since Lyle's team vanished into the night?

Mac glanced at her watch. Only five minutes had passed, and it would be at least half an hour before the operators reached the house. Time seemed to slow.

Mac made the rounds, issued unnecessary orders, and generally made a pest of herself. It was either that or go stark raving mad.

Finally, after what seemed like a lifetime, Mac heard Lyle's voice on the radio. She could hear him pant in between bursts of words. "Charlie-Six. We're two out—no casualties—don't shoot us. Over."

Mac felt a tremendous sense of relief as she acknowledged the transmission. The team was safe! Nothing else mattered. Mac ordered the truck commanders to start their engines and drop their ramps. Lyle appeared out of the darkness seconds later. He was followed by two operators, with the general sandwiched between them.

The scene had a greenish hue, but Mac could see the duct tape that covered Revell's mouth and how big his eyes were. "We caught him with his pants down," Lyle announced.

"Load him onto one-two," Mac ordered. "What about his bodyguards?"

"Dead," Lyle replied flatly. "We had to smoke his mistress, too. She tried to shoot Corporal Fredrick with a pearl-handled .38."

Mac wondered what the woman's husband would think, put the thought aside, and was there to welcome the rest of the operators as they appeared out of the darkness. A noncom finished the count. "All present and accounted for, sir!"

Lyle nodded. "Load 'em. Let's haul ass."

The three-vehicle column was under way three minutes later. Given the possibility that the Strykers had been spotted earlier, and a trap set for them, Mac had ordered Lamm to use a different route for the return trip.

The route was calculated to take the vics through a suburb where very little combat had taken place on the theory that there wouldn't be a lot of patrols in that area. Mac was standing in the air-guard hatch, and by tracking the unit's progress on a map, she could ensure that Lamm was making the correct turns.

Everything went well at first. Thanks to her night-vision device, Mac could tell that they had left farm country for the burbs. Minimansions were visible on both sides of the two-lane road—most of which sat on at least an acre of land.

Lamm had to steer around shell craters as they passed through a small town. Some of the downtown area had been destroyed by a fire. Once they were clear of the business district, the Strykers entered the more densely populated area that lay beyond. Tract houses stood shoulder to shoulder, and the gated neighborhoods had fanciful names.

Mac figured they were about five miles out at the point where she spotted the roadblock. It was a casual affair that consisted of two Humvees and a squad of soldiers. A regular thing, then . . . Not the sort of heavily armed force the rebs would send to intercept the Union Strykers. She keyed her mike. "This is Bravo-Six . . .

Blow through the roadblock and keep going. Two and three will engage the Humvees. Over."

BULLY BOY came up on the roadblock seconds later. Mac fired the light machine gun mounted in front of her and saw sparks fly as her bullets glanced off a Humvee. That was when the one-one clipped the front of a Humvee and pushed it to the left.

The Confederates were quick to respond. A fusillade of bullets chased one-three, even as the Stryker's gunner turned the remote-weapons station to the rear and fired the vic's 40mm automatic grenade launcher. Explosions marched down the street.

The enemy soldiers weren't easily deterred, however. The first Humvee was drivable and took off in hot pursuit. The driver veered right and left in an effort to avoid the exploding grenades even as his gunner fired the .50 that was mounted up top. The second Humvee was close behind but couldn't fire without hitting the lead vehicle.

Mac swore and keyed her mike. The most important thing was to get Revell into Union-held territory, where the spooks could interrogate him. "This is Bravo-Six . . . One-two will pass one-one, and proceed to base. One-one and one-three will turn and engage. Execute. Over."

Mac heard Lyle object, told him to shut up, and felt a sense of relief as one-two passed BULLY BOY and accelerated away. Lyle might be a second louie—but the truck commander reported to Mac.

Once two was clear, Mac ordered Lamm and one-three's TC to part company at the next intersection, turn, and confront the on-coming Humvees. Both drivers managed to execute the maneuver perfectly. BULLY BOY was largely toothless without the .50 . . . But the vic had two LMGs. And the angle was such that both could fire.

One-one was beginning to take rounds from a Confederate .50, when Second Lieutenant Marvin Haskell stood on top of one-three.

He was holding an AT4 launcher on his right shoulder, and the range was short. The rocket flew straight and true. A flash of light marked the hit. The Humvee bucked and blew up. Mac felt the shock wave.

Maybe Haskell saw that . . . And maybe he didn't, as a stream of bullets swept across the top of one-three and dumped him into the street.

Every weapon that one-one and one-three could bring to bear was focused on the remaining Humvee at that point, and it shook as a hail of grenades and bullets struck it. Something gave, a gout of flame shot straight up, and the vehicle came to a sudden stop. Two rebs jumped out, but one of them was on fire.

"Let them go," Mac ordered. She could see that one-three's ramp was down and knew why. Mac watched as dimly seen figures carried something up and into the cargo compartment. The first platoon wasn't about to leave their CO behind even if he was the most serious son of a bitch in the army.

It was wrong in a way, since even the slightest delay could prove costly. But there was a rule: "Leave no man behind." And Mac believed in it. So she waited for one-three's ramp to come up before giving the order. "This is Six. One-one will take point. Let's haul ass. Over."

The final leg of the trip went smoothly, thanks to the platoon of Union tanks that surged into enemy territory at the last minute, thereby opening a hole through which the first Stryker could pass. But things were beginning to heat up by the time Mac and the rest of her command passed through fifteen minutes later. And the tanks were happy to pull back the moment they could.

One-two's return to base was somewhat anticlimactic to hear Lyle tell about it. A delegation of spooks was waiting to hustle General Revell onto a helo, which took off a few minutes later. All without so much as a "thank-you." Neither one of them was sur-prised. Both had been in the army too long for that.

After chatting with Lyle for a few minutes, Mac excused herself and made her way across the tarmac to the motor pool. The first platoon was gathered around a burn barrel. Lamm shouted, "Ten-hut!"

Mac said, "As you were," and could feel the sadness in the air. A sergeant offered her a stool—and a private gave her a cup of coffee. It was laced with rum. Drinking on duty was forbidden, but the troops knew that Mac would understand. They had gath-ered to say good-bye to Haskell . . . And a drink was in order.

Stories were told about the lieutenant, about the fact that he never laughed at jokes and could quote lengthy passages from army maintenance manuals. And there were other anecdotes, too. Like how he helped Private Kai cram for a test, the day his pet rat got loose in one-four, and his fear of hypodermic needles.

And as Mac listened, she realized how little she'd known about the young man who, when push came to shove, was a badass hero. Could she capture that? For the letter she would write to his par-ents? She'd try.

It was noon by the time Mac made it back to her quarters, only to find that a note was taped to the door. "Major Granger wants to see you."

Mac sighed, turned around, and went outside. Shafts of sunlight angled down through broken clouds to turn the slush into water. Mac stomped her boots on the porch outside the command shack prior to going in. Woods was on duty and nodded. "It's good to have you back, Captain . . . Dr. Havers is with the major now. It won't be long."

The prediction was borne out when the medical officer stormed out of the shack three minutes later. *Why?* Because Havers liked to put in requests for impossible things, that's why . . . Like a full-on MRI unit for his dispensary. Mac knew because the doctor had to submit the requests to her first. She got up and went in.

After returning Mac's salute, Granger made a face. "That son of a bitch is crazy. Have a seat."

Mac sat down. "Sir, yes, sir. You wanted to see me?"

"Yes. First, congratulations on a job well done. The Intel people are thrilled! I'm sorry about Haskell."

"I am, too," Mac said simply. "You heard what he did?"

"Yes," Granger answered. "That was very brave. If you want to write a rec, I'll sign it. Maybe we can get him a Bronze Star."

"I'd be happy to," Mac said.

"Good. That brings us to item two. Some bastard at HQ cut a set of orders for you."

"*Orders?* What kind of orders?"

"It's a temporary assignment to a counterinsurgency battalion in Wyoming. It seems they have a warlord problem out there, and this outfit is supposed to cap him."

"But why *me?*"

Granger shrugged. "Because you were a mercenary? And a mercenary isn't all that different from a warlord? Or because your last name starts with M? How the hell would I know?"

Granger was pissed, and Mac knew why. The army was borrowing his XO but had no intention of giving him a replacement. A platoon leader would be named to run Bravo Company while she was gone. But neither one of them was ready to play XO. And that meant more work for Granger. "Who's the CO?" Mac inquired.

"His name is Wes Crowley," Granger replied. "We were in the same class at West Point. He graduated 998 out of 1,011 cadets."

Mac's eyebrows rose. "And he's in command of a battalion?"

Granger made a face. "Yes, he is . . . With the temporary rank of lieutenant colonel. He'd been sidelined prior to the meteor strike. But now, what with the war, they're giving him another chance.

"That said," Granger continued, "don't get the wrong idea. In spite of the fact that Wes wasn't the best student at West Point—he's got a talent for war. Something he demonstrated more than once in Afghanistan."

"Sir," Mac said, "I'm going to resign my commission and open a café. I will put that in writing and submit it later today."

Granger laughed. "Don't waste your time, Captain. You're going to Wyoming. Give Crazy Crowley my best."

ST. PAUL, MINNESOTA

The train was Doyle Besom's idea—and Sloan had been resistant at first. Why ride a train if you could fly? Even if Air Force One was grounded frequently due to poor weather.

But Besom was a clever son of a bitch, and knew Sloan was an amateur historian. So once the press secretary reminded him of the way in which President Lincoln used train trips to build public support, Sloan became more interested. And now, after dozens of well-publicized stops, he had a new appreciation for an old method of politicking.

Sloan felt the train slow as it pulled into Union Depot Station. As Sloan looked out the window, he saw a large crowd waiting for him. That was in stark contrast to the thinly attended events held on his behalf months before.

Sloan was scanning his stump speech, looking for places where he could make mention of Minneapolis–St. Paul, when his Chief of Staff entered the compartment. She was dressed in a blue business suit, and her black hair was cut pageboy style, with bangs that hung down to her eyebrows. "Excuse me, Mr. President, but Secretary Henderson is here . . . He'd like to speak with you."

Sloan frowned. "George is *here*? That's a surprise. Of course. Send him in."

Chow opened the door, waited for Henderson to enter, and withdrew. Sloan stood and extended his hand. "Good afternoon, George . . . What's up?"

"Nothing good," Henderson replied, as they shook hands.

Sloan sighed. "Okay, have a seat. Lay it on me."

Henderson sank into a well-padded chair. "It's about Canada, Mr. President."

"*Canada?* What about it?"

"Canada invaded the United States just before dawn this morning. Or, more specifically, Canadian troops invaded the state of Maine."

Sloan laughed. "Get serious."

"I *am* serious," Henderson replied. "General Jones will brief you soon. He's on his way . . . But I wanted to make sure you received news of the incursion *before* you gave your speech. So the American people can hear it from you."

"Thank you, but *Maine*? Just Maine?"

"Yes, sir."

"But *why*?" Sloan demanded. "Don't the Canadians have enough maple syrup?"

Henderson offered a weak smile. "I don't know for sure, Mr. President. They haven't said. But two possibilities come to mind. First, it could be a land grab, pure and simple. The current government is both conservative and nationalistic."

"Okay," Sloan said. "And the second possibility is?"

"The second possibility stems from the first," Henderson replied. "According to a report from the CIA, Confederate diplomats were spotted in Ottawa recently. And the libertarian principles espoused by CEO Lemaire's government are quite similar to those put forward by Canada's newly elected prime minister."

Sloan knew the "libertarian principles" that Henderson referred to would transform landed citizens into "shareowners" who would "own" a portion of the country. Corporations, which were people according to Lemaire, could buy shares and vote them. All in the name of "free markets." "So you're saying that the two governments are in cahoots?" Sloan demanded. "Anything's possible, I guess . . . But why attack Maine?"

"General Jones has a theory about that," Henderson replied. "He thinks it's a way to suck resources away from General Hern—making it easier for the Confederates to hold the line south of Murfreesboro."

Sloan considered that. The second theory made sense. If he ignored the attack on Maine, it would seem as if he'd written the state off, thereby alienating the entire country. Yet by sending troops to Maine, he'd weaken General Hern's forces, and that's what the Confederates *wanted* him to do. If true, it was a brilliant stroke on their part . . . And one he was completely unprepared for.

What about the rest of the almost four-thousand-mile-long border with Canada? All of it was undefended. The Canucks could launch a *dozen* mini-invasions if they wanted to . . . And Sloan would have to respond to each one.

The crowd on the platform was waving signs and chanting his name. What would he tell them? How would they react? Why was he so stupid? Someone should have been thinking about Canada . . . And that someone was him.

CHAPTER 2

||||||||||||||||||||||||||||||||||

Of all those in the army close to the commander none is more intimate than the secret agent; of all rewards none more liberal than those given to secret agents; of all matters none is more confidential than those relating to secret operations.

—SUN TZU

FORT HOOD, TEXAS

The air should have been eighty-five degrees instead of sixty-five. But that's how things were now that less sunlight reached the surface of the planet. Still, the cooler air would make for a comfortable run. Not a long one, just 3.15 miles around an oval-shaped course located just off Sadowski Road.

The run was a daily ritual . . . something Victoria Macintyre did each morning before taking a shower and reporting to work at Fort Hood's Special Forces Command.

As Victoria ran, she heard the rhythmic slap, slap, slap of feet coming up from behind her and pulled over to let the fast mover by. Except that he *didn't* pass, and when she turned to look, Victoria saw that General Bo Macintyre was running next to her. Her father had a high forehead, arched eyebrows, and intense eyes. His typical "I don't give a shit" grin was firmly in place. "I knew I could find you here . . . You're way too predictable. That could get you killed."

"Would that bother you?"

"Of course it would," he answered. "Good officers are hard to find."

And that, Victoria knew, was as mushy as any conversation with her father was going to get. That was fine with her. They knew what they knew, and there was no need to discuss it constantly. Would Robin agree? No, she liked the gushy stuff.

Bo began to pull ahead, just as he always did, trying to finish first. Victoria knew that her sister Robin would allow him to beat her, and Bo would resent it. He wanted to win fair and square or not at all. So Victoria increased her pace, blew past him, and left her father in the dust. She was sitting on a bench when he finished the run. He plopped down beside her. "I'm getting old."

Victoria nodded. "And cantankerous."

"I've always been cantankerous."

"True . . . I can't argue with that."

Bo smiled. "I have orders for you." Victoria reported to a colonel, who reported to Bo and was careful to stay out of the way.

"Okay, what's up?"

"There's a warlord in Wyoming. His name is Robert Howard. He was a Green Beret before the meteor strikes. Then he went over the hill—and took two of his buddies with him. Now he calls himself the warlord of warlords, and he controls a large chunk of north-central Wyoming. More than that," Bo added, "Howard claims to be the reincarnated spirit of Subutai."

Victoria frowned. "Genghis Khan's chief strategist."

"Exactly," Bo said approvingly. "As Subutai, Howard claims to be the spiritual nexus around whom other members of Khan's horde are supposed to organize prior to fighting a war for world dominance. That's when the Khan will return to rule them. It's total bullshit, needless to say, but an idiot is born every minute."

Victoria eyed him. "Okay, and we care because?"

"We care because Howard is, and could continue to be, a destabilizing force. For example, Howard sent suicide bombers to kill Sloan a week ago and damned near succeeded."

Victoria nodded. "According to the Intel summary, Sloan killed two people himself."

"The man has balls," Bo admitted. "And he's a bigger problem than Lemaire thought he'd be."

"Okay, I get it," Victoria replied. "Howard is a good thing. For the moment at least."

"Correct," her father confirmed. "So the general staff wants you to go up there, give Howard a present, and make nice. The more resources he sucks away from General Hern's army, the better. Hern is a grinder . . . Once he takes a yard of ground, he tends to hold it . . . And we need a way to weaken him."

"Kind of like the Canadian attack on Maine."

"Exactly like the Canadian attack on Maine."

"I'll get on it."

"Written orders are waiting in your office."

"Thanks."

"There's one other thing, Victoria . . . Something you need to know. The Union wasn't paying much attention to Howard, but they are now, and that includes assembling a battalion to go after him."

Victoria shrugged. "That's predictable."

"Yes, it is," her father replied. "But there's something more. We have an agent in that battalion . . . And, according to him, your sister has orders to join the unit."

Victoria knew that Robin was fighting for the Union and that they had been within miles of each other in Murfreesboro. She frowned. "Why are you telling me this?"

"Because even though Robin was too lazy to attend the academy, and went to OCS, she's had more than her share of success as a cavalry officer. Robin was the one they sent to rescue Sloan from the fuck-up in Richton . . . And she pulled it off. She's dangerous, Victoria . . . Don't underestimate her."

Victoria felt a swirl of conflicting emotions. This was the first time she'd heard her father express approval of her sister since the day Robin graduated from high school, and it didn't sit well. She was Bo's favorite and wanted it to stay that way. "Don't worry, sir," Victoria said, as she switched to being a major again. "If I run into Robin, I will take her very seriously indeed."

CASPER, WYOMING

The Osprey V-22 banked as it passed over Casper, Wyoming. The aircraft didn't have windows, but the rear hatch was open, which allowed Mac to catch glimpses of the ground. What had been a small city to begin with was even smaller after the cholera epidemic had decimated the population two months earlier.

The pain and misery associated with that wasn't visible from the air, however . . . And as the VTOL continued to make a wide, sweeping turn—Mac had the impression of orderly streets, bare-limbed trees, and occasional patches of dirty snow. Then she got a glimpse of what must be Fort Carney. The makeshift military base was adjacent to a fire-ravaged housing development south of town. An array of antennas marked the center of the fort and were located next to what looked like a mound of dirt but probably marked the location of an underground command center.

That was surrounded by a ring of prefab buildings, some of which were vehicle shelters. A spiderweb-like network of roads and trenches led out to the vehicle-mounted surface-to-air missile launchers that would protect the base from unmanned drones, low-flying fixed-wing aircraft, and helicopters. And all of it was protected by a forty-foot-long wall of shipping containers.

They were made of steel, and the tops of the rectangular boxes had been removed so that they could be filled with tons of dirt. Mac knew that such containers were approximately eight feet wide. That meant the wall could withstand just about anything fired directly at it. And with machine-gun emplacements on top of the barrier and mortar pits behind it, Fort Carney would be a tough nut to crack. "Check your seat belts," a voice said over the intercom, "we're thirty from dirt."

The engines tilted up, and what had been a plane became a helicopter. The Osprey landed hard, and the rotors were responsible for a momentary dust storm. Mac was content to let the engines spool down before releasing the harness and getting to her feet. "Don't worry about your bags, ma'am," the crew chief told her. "We'll send them over to the BOQ."

Mac thanked him, took her M4 carbine, and made her way down the ramp. A lieutenant was waiting to greet her. He was wearing a black Stetson like those worn by cavalrymen in the 1800s. It was covered with a fine patina of dust and decorated with crossed sabers and a gold cord. Being a cavalry officer, Mac knew that such hats weren't authorized. But some unit commanders would tolerate them for the sake of morale, and it appeared that Lieutenant Colonel Crowley was one of them.

The lieutenant came to attention and saluted. "Good morning, ma'am. Lieutenant Bobby Perkins at your service . . . I'm one of your platoon leaders and the acting company commander. Welcome to Fort Carney."

Mac returned the salute. "Thank you, Lieutenant . . . My name is Robin Macintyre. But I suppose you knew that. Where do I report?"

"The colonel would like to meet with you, ma'am . . . Please follow me."

The officers fell into step as they left the landing pad and made their way toward the mound located in the middle of the compound. Had Perkins been hoping for a bump to captain? And the slot as Bravo Company's CO? If so, Mac couldn't see any sign of it on his face. "I see our personnel are wearing Stetsons," Mac observed, as a private crossed their path. "Is this a special day?"

"No, ma'am," Perkins replied. "We wear them every day."

That was strange but in keeping with what Granger had told her about Lieutenant Colonel Crowley. And there was something else as well. "Tell me about your shoulder patch," Mac said. "The one with Uncle Sam on it."

Perkins glanced at her. "The battalion consists of people like me. All of us are from the South, but we oppose the New Order and came north to fight for our country. That's why we were authorized to wear the patch. The government doesn't trust us, though. So they dropped us into a single battalion and sent it here."

Perkins's voice had been flat up until then. But some bitterness was starting to come through. "Wyoming is a long way from the New Mason-Dixon Line," he added. "So if we run, they'll have plenty of time in which to track us down."

When Mac stopped, Perkins had to do likewise. Their eyes met. "Is that why they sent for me? Because they don't trust *you*?"

Perkins looked away. "I'm sorry, ma'am . . . I was out of line. Please accept my apologies."

"Answer the question, Lieutenant."

Perkins looked at her. His eyes were green. "Yes, ma'am. As things stand now, none of the Southern volunteers are allowed to command a company. Even if they had that level of responsibility prior to the meteor strikes."

"I see," Mac replied. "Thanks for the briefing."

"Bravo Company, which is to say *your* company, is ready for anything, Captain. You can depend on us."

"I will," Mac promised him. "What kind of vehicles do we have?"

"Strykers, ma'am. Three for each platoon. Plus a couple of Humvees, a fueler, and a wrecker."

Mac nodded. "Good. After I meet with the colonel, I'd like to make the rounds. Nothing formal . . . Just a 'Hi, there.'"

"Yes, ma'am. I'll be ready."

A sergeant saluted the officers as they neared the mound, and they responded in kind. As they got closer, Mac was surprised to see that two soldiers were guarding the entrance. "You'll need to show ID," Perkins said as he produced a card.

"Why? We're inside the wall."

"Suicide bombers," Perkins replied. "Crazy people who believe that Robert Howard is the reincarnated spirit of Genghis Khan's XO. And, since they believe in reincarnation, they aren't afraid to die. One of them managed to roll under a six-by-six, cling to the frame, and infiltrate the base a couple of weeks ago. She was two hundred feet from the command post when her vest exploded prematurely."

"Okay, then," Mac said as she proffered her card. "Suicide bombers, check."

Once inside, Perkins led Mac down a ramp into the spacious room below. The lighting was dim, live drone feeds could be seen on flat-panel displays, and the atmosphere conveyed a sense of hushed efficiency.

Perkins led Mac around the circular "war pit" to a side room. It was separated from the pit by a curtain that consisted of long leather strips. A wooden block was attached to the wall under a plaque that read, LIEUTENANT COLONEL WESLEY CROWLEY.

Perkins rapped his knuckles on the block, and Mac heard a voice say, "Enter."

Perkins stepped inside first, came to attention, and announced himself. Then it was Mac's turn. "Captain Robin Macintyre, reporting for duty, *sir*."

Crowley was seated behind a wood table. His neck-length blond hair was way out of compliance with regs and parted in the middle. And, while the army didn't allow mustaches or goatees, Crowley had one of each.

And the eccentricities didn't stop there. Rather than camos, Crowley was dressed in a buckskin shirt with chest fringe and colorful beadwork. The overall look reminded Mac of General Custer. Was that intentional? And if so, *why*? Especially given the way Custer's career came to an end. *Two* pearl-handled Colt .45 semiauto pistols were revealed when Crowley stood. "Welcome to Fort Carney, Captain . . . We're lucky to have an officer like you . . . If you'll excuse us, Lieutenant, the captain and I have some things to discuss."

Perkins came to attention, saluted, and did an about-face. The leather strips made a swishing sound as he left.

"Please," Crowley said, "have a seat. So you were serving under my classmate, Major Frank Granger. Is he still a brown-nosing, by-the-book asshat?"

Mac couldn't remember hearing a superior officer refer to a peer that way before and wasn't sure how to respond. Was Crowley joking? Or was he serious? There was no way to be sure. "Major Granger is my CO, sir . . . And he sends his regards."

Crowley chuckled. "Well played, Macintyre . . . Well played. Enough happy horseshit. Let's get down to brass tacks. The powers that be gave me this command for three reasons: To get rid of me, to get rid of me, and to get rid of me.

"But I'm going to surprise the spineless bastards by tracking Sergeant Robert Howard down, removing his balls, and hanging them over my door."

"Sir, yes, sir."

"And that," Crowley continued, "will be in spite of the Confederate traitors they sent me. Rebs! Can you believe it? Fighting for the North. But not you, Captain . . . You're from Idaho. I checked."

Mac didn't know what to say, except, "Sir, yes, sir."

"Sleep with a gun," Crowley advised. "That's what I do. Who knows? The whole lot of them might go over the hill. But not before we nail Howard! I'll give you two days to settle in. Then we're going to launch Operation Hydra."

"Hydra, sir?"

"Yes. Howard refers to himself as the warlord of warlords. And it's true. No less than five lesser warlords have sworn allegiance to him. His logo is a serpent with six heads. I plan to sever them one by one. Perkins has the operational stuff. Study it and be ready to roll."

Mac knew a dismissal when she heard one and stood. "Is there anything else, sir?"

"Yes. My other company commanders are a bit green . . . So I'm going to name you as XO. Perkins will bring you up to speed."

Serving as second-in-command to a nutcase was the last thing

Mac wanted to do. But there was only one answer she could give, and that was, "Yes, sir. I'll do my best." The meeting was over.

FORT KNOX, KENTUCKY

Rather than helicopter into the American base, Canada's ambassador was forced to land in Louisville, where a limo was waiting to pick him up. Because in the wake of Canada's attack on Maine, the two countries were theoretically at war . . . even if none had been declared. And Fort Knox's commanding officer wasn't about to let hostile aircraft enter his airspace.

So with a police escort ahead of and behind his car, the ambassador was forced to endure a long ride. And the route had been chosen with care. It took him onto a freeway that was half-clogged with military traffic before taking him to Fort Knox, where even *more* military might was on display.

Finally, the ambassador was delivered to the front of an enormous tent. Sloan no longer lived there. But the tent had become a symbol of his presidency, and he continued to use it for ceremonial purposes. Secretary of State Henderson was waiting out front to greet the ambassador and escort him inside.

First, the two men had to pass through the gauntlet of reporters that Besom had allowed to witness the arrival. They peppered the diplomats with questions. "Mr. Secretary! Is the United States going to surrender to Canada?"

"Mr. Ambassador! Is it true that Canada has entered into an alliance with the Confederacy?"

"Mr. Secretary! Is the United States planning to invade Canada?"

Henderson waved to them before following Ambassador McGowan into the tent's chilly interior. An aide led them back to

Sloan's office. The fact that it was equipped with campaign-style furniture and was reminiscent of a Civil War general's field quarters was no accident. There were some modern amenities as well, including electric lights and the bank of flat-panel TVs mounted on a roll-around rack.

Sloan had met McGowan before, but as Secretary of Energy and under more pleasant circumstances. Now, as they shook hands, the mood was anything but cordial. "Mr. President."

"Mr. Ambassador . . . Please have a seat. Would you care for some refreshments?"

A space heater was purring in a corner, but McGowan could still see his breath. "Yes, a cup of tea would be nice."

"Good," Sloan replied. "One will be along shortly. So, let's speak frankly . . . Your government sent soldiers into our sovereign territory, where they killed a number of our troops and civilians. I'm prepared to accept an immediate apology and your promise to withdraw your forces by noon tomorrow."

McGowan opened his mouth to speak but closed it as the tea arrived. Once both men had been served, the conversation resumed. "I will convey your offer to my government," McGowan said stiffly. "But it's my duty to inform you that an apology and withdrawal are extremely unlikely. Some of our leading legal scholars have called the Webster-Ashburton Treaty's legality into question and, until that matter is resolved, the troops must remain."

Henderson cleared his throat. "The treaty that Ambassador McGowan refers to brought the Pork and Beans War of 1838 to an end. No shots were fired."

"As I said," McGowan said, "it is our wish to renegotiate what was, and is, a lopsided treaty. The territory presently occupied by our troops is rightfully a part of Canada. We suggest a cooling-off period of sixty days with discussions to follow. Or, if you prefer, the United States can simply cede the area in question to Canada."

It was all grade-A horseshit. The Canadians were trying to aid the Confederacy by opening negotiations that would drag on and on. In the meantime, Sloan would have to park a regiment of troops in Maine to prevent any further incursions and placate thousands of irate voters.

Sloan sighed and took a sip of coffee. "Okay, Mr. Ambassador . . . Have it your way. Please direct your attention to the television monitors. If you examine the programming closely, you'll find that all of the feeds are coming in from Canada. And, all of them are coming to us via satellites launched by *other* countries. That's because you have no space program to speak of. It's been a thrifty policy but one that's going to cost you since we're about to destroy the satellite that carries the Canadian Broadcasting Corporation. Secretary Henderson? Give the order."

Henderson was seated next to McGowan. He spoke into a cell phone. "This is Secretary Henderson. Kill it."

The Canadian Broadcasting Corporation channel snapped to black. "That's impossible," McGowan said contemptuously. "You're trying to trick me."

"Nope," Sloan replied. "CBC is off the air . . . The SRC network will go down an hour from now—and the CTV network will go dark an hour after that. Though the Confederates took control of our country's GPS satellites early on, they didn't get everything, and that includes the killer satellites that were developed to wage war on China and Russia.

"So, unless you apologize and withdraw, we will not only kill all of the satellites that you rely on, we'll cut your transatlantic and transpacific telephone cables, too."

McGowan's cell phone was in his coat pocket. It began to chime. "Uh-oh," Sloan said. "I think someone in Ottawa is watching CBC."

McGowan looked up at the CBC monitor. It wasn't black anymore. A shot of a wind-whipped American flag filled the screen. And when Sloan aimed his remote at the TV, and pressed the MUTE button, the sound came on. McGowan's face turned a deathly shade of white as the strains of "America the Beautiful" were heard. "Secretary Henderson will see you out," Sloan said. "Don't let the door hit you in the ass."

CASPER, WYOMING

The steel gates rumbled as they parted to let Alpha Company leave Fort Carney. A Humvee led the way, with the Stars and Stripes flying and Lieutenant Colonel Crowley riding shotgun. The name BETTY SUE had been stenciled onto both sides of the vehicle. But most of the enlisted soldiers called it the "BM," or bullet magnet, because any fool could tell that it was a staff car. And nine times out of ten, the person assigned to drive it had done something to get on the sergeant major's shit list. Nine Strykers followed. Each carried a squad of infantry.

Mac and her company departed next. Bravo Company was almost identical to Alpha Company although Mac preferred to ride in a Stryker rather than a Humvee.

That left the men and women of Charlie Company and Crowley's headquarters company to hold the fort, and that was important. Because if the fort were undermanned, Howard might very well attack.

The plan called for Crowley to take Alpha Company west, then north, to the tiny town of Arminto. It had originally been home to a handful of people. Then a band of convicts led by a brute named

Cory Burns broke out of the state pen in Rawlins. They were in the process of laying waste to the surrounding area when a combined force of Shoshone and Arapahos drove them out. The gang arrived in Arminto shortly thereafter, with a convoy of tractor-trailer rigs, a wild assortment of RVs, and a dozen rat rods.

In less than a week, Arminto was transformed from ghost town to a miniature sin city, complete with a whorehouse, a busy saloon, and a store where their loot could be purchased at bargain prices. Sometimes by the very people from whom it had been stolen.

Of course, that was small-time to a man like Howard, who sent a message to Burns. It was written on a piece of paper that had been nailed to a man's forehead. "This could be you. Join the horde or die. Yours truly, Robert Howard."

Burns hurried to accept the invitation and had been paying a 10 percent "tithe" to Howard ever since. And that's why Crowley was going to level Arminto.

In the meantime, Mac was being sent north and east to show the flag and keep Howard off balance, which was fine with Mac. The trip would give her a chance to get the lay of the land and assess what her company was capable of. Mac felt the wind buffet her face as she led them onto 87 eastbound. She was standing in the Stryker's forward air-guard hatch with her feet planted on the bench seat below. Her jacket was zipped, and she was wearing three layers of clothing. Unfortunately, the cold air still managed to find its way in and make her shiver.

The land on both sides of the highway was flat and arid, which made it perfect for cavalry. That gave Mac an idea . . . Rather than wait for the 59 north turnoff and follow the highway north as planned, she threw Perkins a curve. "This is Bravo-Six. Bravo-Five is going to take us to the town of Wright by traveling cross-country. One-one will fall back, and three-one will take point. Over."

If Perkins was surprised or concerned about his ability to follow Mac's orders, there was no trace of it in his voice. "This is Five. Roger that . . . Moving up. Over."

So far so good, Mac thought to herself, as one-one pulled out of the column and let the rest of the trucks pass. Her impressions had been positive so far. The Southerners had been regular army or reservists prior to the war and were technically proficient. They were also polite and almost unfailingly cheerful.

But those characteristics weren't enough to conceal the dissatisfaction that was eroding the unit's morale. In spite of all they had sacrificed to fight for the North, the Union Army didn't trust them. That rankled.

With three-one in the lead and one-one in the nine slot, Perkins led the company off the north side of the highway. Mac listened approvingly as her XO ordered their UAV pilot to launch the company's RQ-11 Raven. The drone was equipped with color cameras and an infrared night-vision camera. Under prewar conditions, the tiny aircraft could use GPS waypoint navigation. But the rebs controlled the GPS system, so Staff Sergeant Maureen "Mo" Henry would have to "fly" the Raven while bouncing around in a Humvee.

Still, thanks to the UAV, Perkins would be able to eyeball what lay ahead. Because even though the terrain was mostly flat—there were plenty of dips, riverbeds, and gullies in which the enemy could be hiding. What followed was an often jarring ride as the trucks waddled over boulders, lurched up out of ravines, and sprayed loose gravel at the vehicles behind them. Mac felt sorry for the soldiers down in the cargo bay and hoped they were strapped in.

It was interesting to watch Perkins solve problems. His first decision was to increase the intervals that separated the vics so each Stryker had more room in which to maneuver. But as the space between the trucks increased, the column started to lose cohesion.

That raised the possibility that attackers could cut the company in two.

Perkins solved that problem by creating *two* columns traveling side by side. That meant they could still support each other *and* laager up if that became necessary. Mac approved. Perkins knew his shit. A female voice came through her headset. "Bravo-Twelve to Bravo-Five. I see a flat area up ahead. It looks like an airstrip. Over."

Mac consulted her map and couldn't see any indication of an airfield. She spoke into her mike. "This is Six . . . Let's pull up. Keep your heads on a swivel. Over."

Mac heard a series of double clicks as she dropped down into the cargo bay. The air was thick with the stench of vomit. "Private Ray barfed into his brain bucket," Sergeant Fisk explained. "Can we drop the ramp and air the bay out?"

"Absolutely," Mac responded. "But let's stay ready to roll."

Fisk nodded. "Yes, ma'am."

Mac turned to look at the forward-mounted drone monitor. The Raven was circling an area so flat, and so clear of obstructions, that it didn't look natural. In fact, as Mac looked more closely, she saw the mounds of debris that bordered both sides of the runway. "This is Six," she said. "I'm taking Bravo-One-One and his squad forward to take a look. Five will assume command. This would be a good time for a bio break. Over."

As Mac turned toward the ramp, she heard Perkins issue an order that half of the trucks were to be manned at all times. Her confidence in him continued to grow.

Fisk and his squad were waiting outside the vehicle. "The flat is about a mile away, Sergeant. I'll take the point. Let's move."

Mac chose to jog and, since she wasn't wearing a pack, it felt good. When Mac glanced over her shoulder, she saw that the rest of the squad was behind her, with Fisk in the ten slot. That meant both halves of the squad would have leadership if it was cut in two.

The route took them across some hardpan, down into a snowy riverbed, and up a gravelly slope. As they neared the top, the terrain began to flatten out. That was when Mac raised a hand, and the squad came to a halt. "I don't know who created this," she told the soldiers. "Or why they did so. So don't leave any more tracks than you have to. Fort up while I take a look."

Fisk didn't like that, judging from the expression on his face. He wanted to send the entire squad. But that couldn't be helped. The flat area didn't *look* right . . . And if the bad guys were up to something, then why let them know that people were onto them?

Mac sat on a rock in order to remove her boots. Then she went forward without them. The ground was cold, too cold for socks, and there were lots of little rocks.

But as Mac looked back, she could see that the strategy was working. There were no footprints. Not so in the middle of the flat area. Mac could see that a plane had landed during a thaw and left tracks that were frozen in place. But *why?* The makeshift landing strip wasn't adjacent to a ranch, much less a town, so what was its purpose?

But, Mac thought, *maybe that's the point. Maybe somebody put it out in the boonies, so it wouldn't attract attention.* Mac looked up, and because she knew it was there, could see the drone. "Six to Bravo-Twelve. Can you see a trail, or a road that leads away from the airstrip?"

"That's affirmative," Henry replied. "A dirt track leads to the northwest."

Mac thought about what that could mean. If the trail continued in that direction, it might connect with a highway. And the highway could take passengers or cargoes north to the area controlled by

Howard. Of course, it could take them south, too. The secret strip was interesting either way. She turned and made her way back. Her feet were getting numb, and she hurried to pull her boots on. "Sergeant Henry."

UAV pilot Mo Henry was standing nearby. She had red hair, green eyes, and freckles. "Ma'am?"

"Did you bring some trail cams with you? The ones we can leave behind?"

Henry nodded. "Yes, ma'am. Two of them."

"Find a place to hide them. Let's see who uses this strip . . . Sergeant Fisk, assign someone to give Henry a hand."

The motion-activated cameras were similar to those used by hunters and scientists to snap pictures of elusive animals, except that they could upload data to a drone, and that's why the UAV pilot was in charge of them.

After backtracking, the company resumed its trip to Wright, Wyoming. It was located on the edge of what Howard considered to be his fiefdom. And that's why the town had been attacked on numerous occasions. But the people who lived there were tough—and had been able to keep "Howard's Horde" at bay thus far.

As the Strykers continued cross-country, Mac took the opportunity to put each platoon leader and each platoon sergeant in command for a while, so that all of them could gain more experience. That resulted in a couple of screwups, but nothing serious. And rather than jump in, Mac made it a point to let people extract themselves from whatever trouble they were in.

The plan was to stay the night in Wright and return to Fort Carney the next day. But as the light started to fade, and Mac saw columns of smoke in the distance, she felt something cold trickle into her bloodstream. She was about to contact Henry when the UAV pilot spoke. "Bravo-Twelve to Six . . . The Raven is over

Wright, and at least a dozen buildings are on fire. It looks like the town was overrun. Over."

Mac knew she shouldn't feel guilty but did. Had she pushed the company north, rather than going sideways, maybe things would have been different. "Can you see troops? Are they in control?"

"No," Henry replied. "The smoke makes it hard to see, but it looks like they pulled out. Over."

"This is Six," Mac said. "One-one will take point. Stay sharp . . . We might be rolling into a trap. Over."

There was no trap. That was evident when Bravo Company arrived on the outskirts of Wright twenty minutes later. An effort had been made to protect the center of the city by using the one thing the locals had plenty of, and that was rock. Countless tons of the stuff had been used to create the eight-foot-high barrier that circled the town. The only thing that could break through was a huge bulldozer. And in order to do so, the operator would have to cross a kill zone under fire from marksmen concealed behind the rocks. So how had the horde been able to succeed?

Mac dropped to the ground, ordered Perkins to secure the area, and led a squad of soldiers up to the rock wall. A blast-scorched truck had been left there. A ramp had been attached to the rear end of the vehicle. One end touched the ground, and the other was aimed at the compound beyond. *Why?*

Mac was thinking about that as she scrambled up over a pile of boulders to the top of the wall. The sun was about to set, but fires lit the city.

As Mac led the squad down onto the ground, a man emerged from the smoke-drifted gloom. His hair was white, his eyes stared out of caves, and a bloody arm hung useless at his side. "Now you come," he said, as if correcting a child. "Late . . . *Too* late."

"I'm sorry," Mac replied. "We didn't know. What happened?"

"We pulled back inside the wall when the horde came. But they were ready for that. They had trucks with ramps attached to them. Once the trucks were in position, motorcycle riders raced up the ramps and jumped over the wall! Each bike carried a rider . . . And each rider had a machine pistol. They rode every which way, killing and killing. Oh, we nailed some of them," the man said grimly. "We sure as hell did . . . But not nearly enough. So they captured the town. And that's when the *real* horror began."

Mac felt a sense of foreboding. "What do you mean?"

"They herded everyone together, sorted them out, and shot every male they could find. Little boys included."

"But *why*?" Mac wanted to know.

"To eliminate any possibility of revenge," the man said, as tears ran down his cheeks. "I ran and hid in the church steeple . . . So I saw it happen. After dividing the females into two groups, young and old, they . . . they . . ." The man couldn't bring himself to say it, but there was no need to. Mac knew that the older women had been executed.

Mac had never been exposed to an atrocity on such a scale. But she could imagine it—and fought to maintain her composure. "And the younger ones?"

"They were taken away," the man said, "to be sold and used. They have my granddaughter, Sissy," the man added. "I should have killed her . . . I thought about it, and I pointed the rifle, but I couldn't pull the trigger. Find them, Captain . . . Find them and kill them."

Mac was trying to formulate some sort of response when the man moved. "He has a gun!" Sergeant Gray shouted, but her warning came too late.

Mac was just starting to react when the gore-covered pistol came up under the man's chin. His eyes were locked with hers as he pulled the trigger. Mac heard a bang and saw the light vanish from the man's eyes. Then, as all strength left his knees, he crumpled to the ground.

It happened so quickly that the soldiers were caught flat-footed. Sergeant Gray was the first to speak. "The poor bastard . . . May he rest in peace."

There isn't going to be any peace, Mac thought to herself. *Not until we find Robert Howard and kill him. And we need to do it quickly . . . For the women. For Sissy.* There was a harsh quality to her voice. "Sergeant Gray."

"Ma'am?"

"There has to be a gate. Find it. I'll send for the second platoon's ESV. We have lots of bodies to bury."

"Ma'am, yes, ma'am."

As it turned out, there were *two* gates. Both blocked by sliding steel doors, and both open. After entering through the one that faced west, the company's Stryker M1132 Engineer Squad Vehicle or ESV went to work. It had a bulldozer blade mounted up front, and even though it had been designed to clear mines, the vic could be used to scoop out a mass grave. And when a soldier from the third platoon showed up driving a CAT, the task went that much faster.

Meanwhile, Mac put a squad to work photographing bodies, identifying them when that was possible, and "taking scalps." A process that involved removing a small section of scalp from unidentified bodies that could be subjected to DNA testing later on. It was a grisly, heartbreaking business, and Mac told Perkins to rotate the "collection" teams every half hour.

Finally, as the sky began to lighten in the east, the job was done. During the hours of darkness, 253 bodies had been laid out side by side and covered over.

As far as the soldiers could make out, none of the dead had been members of the horde. That in spite of the fact that Howard's "warriors" had suffered casualties. How could that be?

Mac knew the answer, or believed she did. Howard had been a Green Beret. That meant he was familiar with the injunction, "Leave no man behind." Obviously, it was an injunction that had been imposed on the horde. It was more than a gang . . . It was an army.

They had no chaplain. But, according to Perkins, Corporal Forbes was the next best thing since he'd been studying to be a priest when the seminary he was going to kicked him out. And as the sun speared the town with rays of golden sunshine, Forbes removed his Stetson. He had a deep and resonant voice.

> *In your hands, O Lord,*
> *we humbly entrust our brothers and sisters.*
> *In this life, you embraced them with your tender love;*
> *deliver them now from every evil*
> *and bid them eternal rest.*
>
> *The old order has passed away:*
> *welcome them into paradise,*
> *where there will be no sorrow, no weeping or pain,*
> *but fullness of peace and joy*
> *with your Son and the Holy Spirit*
> *forever and ever.*
> *Amen.*

The company was exhausted. But by taking Highway 387 to I-25, they could reach the fort in a matter of hours. And that beat the hell out of staying in the burned-out town.

Besides . . . the faster they returned to Casper, the faster the battalion could go after Howard, rescue the women and girls from Wright, and stop the slaughter. Or so it seemed to Mac.

It was always dangerous to travel down a highway because that's where the threat of IEDs and ambushes was highest. This, plus the fact that Mac's soldiers were tired, was a recipe for disaster. So Mac spent the return trip on the radio pestering her troops with reminders, alerts, and friendly insults.

Fortunately, nothing happened. And as the company approached Fort Carney, Mac saw something new next to the main gate. It was a gore-drenched pole with a head on it. Warlord Cory Burns? Yes. It appeared that Colonel Crowley was back. And his attack on Arminto had been successful.

Would the general staff approve of a colonel who took heads? And put them on display? Hell no. But Mac knew that Crowley didn't care. He was sending a message to Robert Howard. And the message was, "Fuck you, asshole. You're next."

Good, Mac thought to herself. *Crazy Crowley is coming off a victory. That should put him in the mood to rescue those prisoners.* She was wrong.

CHAPTER 3

||||||||||||||||||||||||||||||||||

Freedom is hammered out on the anvil of discussion,
dissent, and debate.

—HUBERT H. HUMPHREY

CLEVELAND, OHIO

In spite of all the tasks associated with reconstruction, and his
responsibilities as commander in chief, Sloan had to spend a great
deal of time on politics. An activity that could be divided into two
piles: the give-and-take of getting things done—and the need to
raise money. Sloan preferred the first over the second.

But what choice did he have? His term, which was to say his
predecessor's term, was going to end in a year. So he could either
run or hand the presidency over to *whom*? That was the problem.
The Patriot Party's back bench was rather thin. Of course, the
people seated on that bench would disagree.

But the decision had been made, and Sloan was butt deep in a
campaign to become president. An *elected* president . . . And it was
hard work. He heard applause as a stagehand waved him forward.
Sloan entered the auditorium from stage left, and the Whig Party's

candidate emerged from stage right. Her name was Senator Marsha Pickett—and Sloan heard a number of rebel yells as she waved to the crowd. All ten thousand seats were filled, and Sloan knew that millions of people were watching their TV sets or listening via radio. Unfortunately, millions more didn't have telephone service, never mind cable television or the Internet. And that was just one of the many problems that one of them would face.

Two podiums were located at the center of the stage. And as Sloan walked over to them, he knew that Pickett was a formidable opponent. She had a modelish face and high cheekbones. Her clothes weren't so expensive as to make her appear wealthy, which she was, nor were they frumpy. So to the extent that a portion of the electorate would cast their votes for anyone with good looks, Pickett would do well. Better than he would? Yes, definitely.

But Pickett was more than a runner-up for Miss Oklahoma. She was a Harvard-trained lawyer, a world-class skier, and the mother of two adorable children. All of which were accomplishments that Sloan couldn't match. Pickett's perfect teeth were very much on display as they met and shook hands. "Mr. President."

"Senator Pickett."

A second passed. Her perfectly plucked eyebrows rose incrementally. "Can I have my hand back?"

Sloan felt himself flush as he let go. What the hell was wrong with him? Was her mike on? Had the comment gone out over the air? He was struggling to think of a rejoinder when the moderator took over. He was a much-respected journalist with a reputation for fairness. "Good evening, ladies and gentlemen . . . My name is Lester Hollings, and I will serve as your moderator. As the participants take their places, let's review the rules. Each candidate will have five minutes to introduce themselves, with President Sloan going first.

"That will be followed by ten questions, all of which were sent in by members of the public and selected by a panel of six people split equally between the two parties. For those of you here in the auditorium, please don't applaud until the end of the debate, and remember . . . the place for demonstrations is outside. Now, without further ado, it's my pleasure to introduce the President of the United States, Samuel T. Sloan! Mr. President?"

The cameras were on him, and Sloan knew better than to waste any of his precious airtime sucking up to the citizens of Cleveland. He went straight to what he thought of as "the pitch," the centerpiece of which was a proposal to spend four trillion dollars on his America Rising Initiative. A program that would not only serve to rebuild the nation's infrastructure, but put millions of people to work and jump-start the economy.

"But make no mistake," Sloan added after the summary. "The America Rising Initiative will benefit the *entire* country, including the South. Because once we defeat the people who stole our oil reserves and imposed an oligarchy on the South, we will welcome our brothers and sisters back . . . just as our forefathers did after the first civil war."

"Yes!" a man shouted, as he stood. "God bless President Sloan!"

"There will be no demonstrations," Hollings said sternly. "Escort that man out. Senator Pickett? Please proceed."

Sloan's proposal was anything but secret. He'd been saying the same things over and over for weeks. So Pickett's people had been able to prepare a point-by-point response.

"Good evening," Pickett said. "It's a pleasure to be here even if the man standing next to me favors an imperial presidency and a weak Congress. Is Mr. Sloan our chief executive? Or has he declared himself king?"

There was fire in Pickett's eyes as she scanned the audience. "Were any of us allowed to vote for or against the so-called 'war of national reunification'? No. According to Mr. Sloan, and his Attorney General, the Insurrection Act of 1807 gives him all the authority he needs to turn family against family and state against state.

"So without any sort of vote by the House or Senate, Mr. Sloan launched an airborne assault on Richton, Mississippi, where we lost a battalion of Army Rangers. I want to change that. I want to give *you* a voice in what happens next. If I'm elected, I will ask Congress to change the Constitution so as to make sure that the people who work hard and pay taxes will make the decisions! And once the changes I propose are in place, voters will shift the balance of power from Emperor Sloan to the men and women of the United States Congress. Then, if Congress wants to spend four trillion dollars and fight a war with the South, we will do so. My job, which is to say the president's job, will be to implement what your elected representatives choose to do.

"Yes," Pickett added, as she raised a hand, "I know this would represent a change. And that Emperor Sloan doesn't want to change. But new situations demand new solutions! And I stand ready to welcome the future rather than attempt to block it. Thank you!"

Pickett's statement was so practiced that only one second remained on the clock when the last word left her mouth. The questions were tough, but predictable. "Will you raise taxes?"

Sloan answered, "Yes, I would. Upper-income taxpayers will reap huge benefits from the America Rising Initiative, so it makes sense for them to pay more."

Pickett replied by saying, "No. By reducing the size of government, I will *lower* taxes."

And so it went. Finally, when all of the questions had been answered, it was time for Sloan to deliver his three-minute summary. His eyes scanned the room. "Let's take a moment to consider what will happen to this country if Senator Pickett wins. Rather than rebuild the country, and seek to unify it, she wants to change our time-honored Constitution. To do that, she would need commanding majorities in both Houses of Congress . . . And that's unlikely to happen.

"But we're talking about a fantasy world, right? So let's suppose that newly elected President Pickett has the votes she needs. Months would pass while members of both Houses debate the exact wording of each proposed change. Then, supposing Congress can reach an agreement, at least three-fourths of the state legislatures would have to approve it.

"Ladies and gentlemen . . . It took 202 years to ratify a commonsense amendment that keeps congressional salary increases from being implemented until after the *next* crop of representatives comes into office." That comment produced widespread laughter.

"Now," Sloan said, "ask yourself a simple question . . . Who would benefit from such a delay? *You?* Or the oligarchs who run the New Confederacy and need more time in which to consolidate their power? The answer is obvious. Thank you."

The possibility that the New Whigs might feel an affinity for the New Order had been voiced before. But the direct, unapologetic attack from Sloan was sufficient to elicit gasps of surprise from some members of the audience. And that gave Sloan a sense of satisfaction. It was a strong close . . . And Pickett's response turned out to be little more than a list of lame denials. So when Sloan left the stage, he was in a good mood. Press Secretary Doyle Besom was waiting. "That was an outstanding summary, Mr. President . . . You dropped the hammer on her."

Sloan frowned. "I hear the words . . . But they don't match the expression on your face."

Besom shrugged. "Pickett's mike was on. So the entire country heard what she said, and that's what people are talking about. Half the reporters left *before* your closing statement in order to scoop the competition, and you can bet the headline writers are having a field day. 'The president hands Pickett a win.' 'Senator Pickett gives the president a hand.' That sort of thing. I'm sorry, Mr. President . . . Politics sucks."

Sloan sighed, and his spirits fell. "You got that right . . . Let's get out of here." Meanwhile, south of the New Mason-Dixon Line, people continued to die.

CASPER, WYOMING

After showing her ID to the guards, Mac was allowed to enter the battalion's underground command center. Crowley had summoned her, and Mac was eager to meet with him even though she was extremely tired. Chances were that he'd read her report . . . And, if they moved quickly enough, they'd be able to find the women who had been captured in the town of Wright.

When Mac arrived at Crowley's door, it was to find that the curtain was parted and a lieutenant was seated in one of two guest chairs. Crowley waved her in. "Good morning, Macintyre . . . Have you met Lieutenant Casey? No? Well, it's high time that you did. Casey is our public affairs officer, and an important member of the team. It doesn't matter how many battles we win if no one knows about them! Right, Lieutenant?"

"That's right, sir," Casey said as he stood. "It's a pleasure to meet you, ma'am."

Casey was tall, slim, and projected a sense of old-world dignity. Mac liked his Southern drawl. *Too bad you're a lieutenant,* she thought to herself. *Just my luck.* "And it's a pleasure to meet you," Mac said, as they shook hands.

"Casey and I were discussing the battle at Arminto, and how to best publicize it," Crowley said.

"Yes," Casey agreed, as he sat down. "My techs are busy editing battle footage into a sixty-second clip. That's the most any TV network will run . . . And it can be used on the Internet as well."

"Who clears that sort of material?" Mac inquired. "Someone at Fort Knox?"

Crowley chuckled. "Under normal circumstances, yes. But the regular process can be cumbersome. So when we find ourselves with a really important story to tell, we submit it to the army and the media at the same time."

Mac raised an eyebrow. "What happens then?"

"The shit hits the fan," Crowley said with a smile. "And I get a nasty note from General Gowdy telling me that Intel, PSYOPS, and the REMFs at regimental HQ need to review stories *before* they go out. But what's she going to do? Send me to Wyoming?" Crowley laughed, and Casey smiled.

Mac wasn't entirely surprised, given her commanding officer's rep for self-promotion and eccentric behavior. But Mac knew that sort of thing could come around to bite him one day, and she planned to stay clear of the impact zone. "So the story's going out?"

"It certainly is," Crowley replied. "The American people need some good news, and we're going to provide it! Speaking of which . . . I read your report. What a shame. I wanted to put a forward operating base in Wright, but the mayor and city council objected."

"Why?"

"They were afraid that an FOB would constitute a 'provocation,'" Crowley replied. "Meaning they thought Howard would attack it. I told them he'd attack anyway, but they refused to listen." Crowley shrugged. "I wish they had chosen differently."

Mac nodded. "Yes, sir. We can't do anything about that . . . Not now. But we *can* go after the people who were taken prisoner."

"Yes," Crowley agreed. "And we will. But first things first. Alpha Company lost six soldiers in Arminto. They need a couple of days to regroup. And your company just returned from a long patrol. But I promise to give the matter some thought."

Mac was disappointed. Time was critical. How long would it take for Howard to sell the women? It might be a matter of days. But there was nothing she could do. All she could say was, "Thank you, sir."

Subsequent to the meeting with Crowley, Mac spent two hours on the sort of administrative matters that all executive officers have to cope with before returning to the company area where *her* XO had been equally busy. They were sitting in the shed that constituted Bravo Company's HQ, sipping sludge-like coffee. "So, Lieutenant," Mac said, once Perkins had delivered his report. "You raised some extremely important issues."

Perkins looked surprised. "I did?"

"Yes, you did. And I think we should convene a command conference to address them. It will include the other platoon leaders, as well as their platoon sergeants who, as all of us know, actually run the company.

"However," Mac added, "a conference of such importance should be held in the right environment. An establishment that has good food and the kind of liquid refreshment that's likely to enhance the brainstorming process. Would you know of such an establishment?"

Perkins's expression brightened. "Yes, I would . . . Dolly's Place would fit the bill."

"Excellent. Please pass the word. We will assemble here at 1800 hours."

Mac spent the rest of the day in meetings with the battalion's medical officer, the engineer in charge of the fort's septic system, and Company Sergeant Hank Boulineau. There was only *one* army insofar as Boulineau was concerned. And that was the one he'd joined fifteen years earlier. Just as there was only one way to do things, and that was by the book.

That's why Boulineau was upset with the lack of military discipline exhibited by certain members of the company and wanted to clamp down. "We may be at war, ma'am," Boulineau said. "But that ain't no excuse for slackness."

Mac had to tread carefully. Boulineau was the company's senior noncom and a critical link between her and the enlisted people. And he was correct in many respects. Just that morning, she'd run into a private wearing a buckskin vest and ordered him to remove it. And whose fault was that? Crowley's, because he set the example. And Boulineau resented that.

"I read you, Top," Mac said. "And I agree . . . Things are beginning to slip. So pass the word. Except for Stetsons, which were specifically authorized by the CO, I expect everyone to wear army-standard uniforms at all times. As for the haircuts, and the matter of military courtesy, let's bring our platoon leaders in on that discussion. We're going to hold a command conference in town this evening, and you're invited . . . I'll make sure those items get covered. Meet us in front of the command shack at 1800."

Boulineau stood. "Thank you, ma'am . . . I'll be there."

The salute was textbook perfect. Mac gave one in return and watched him leave. *And that,* she thought to herself, *is a man who will make a good sergeant major.*

The group gathered on time. In addition to Lieutenants Perkins, Gilstrap, and Huff, Platoon Sergeants Gray, Tinley, and Nunez were there. And when Boulineau arrived, that made a party of eight. Civvies weren't authorized, so all of them were in uniform. They weren't armed. Not visibly, anyway. But Mac was carrying a baby Glock under her right arm and suspected that the others were "strapped" as well.

Once outside the main gate, Mac led them over to the taxi line, where she hired two vehicles. Dolly's was what Mac expected it to be. Concrete barriers had been put in place to prevent car bombings, and a squad of heavily armed "cowboys" were on guard out front.

The interior was large, noisy, and decorated country style. And that included a huge Confederate flag since most of Wyoming's population were Confederate sympathizers, never mind the fact that the Union Army was protecting them from the warlords.

The barstools were made out of old tractor seats, glassy-eyed animal trophies stared down on the dance floor from high above, and the log-style tables were shiny with varnish. The girl who led them to a booth was dressed in a white-and-red-checkered shirt, tight shorts, and cowboy boots. Mac waited for the predictable commentary, but there wasn't any. The men were on their best behavior. "Okay," she said, once they were seated. "Have whatever you want. Dinner's on me."

"And we'll buy the drinks," Perkins said as he gestured to the other platoon leaders.

"Thank you, Lord," Tinley said. "My prayers were answered!"

That produced some laughs, and once their drinks arrived, the meeting got under way. Mac took the opportunity to bring up a variety of issues, including those Boulineau had voiced earlier in the day. And she was pleased to see that her platoon leaders were taking the discussion seriously. The nature of the conversation changed when the food came—and the soldiers began to tell stories. Gray was especially good at it and soon had everyone in stitches.

Mac excused herself after finishing her steak and went looking for the ladies' room. It was on the second level, just off the gallery that surrounded three sides of the open room below.

The lighting was dim, and two-person tables lined the outside railing. A familiar figure was seated at one of them. Crowley was dressed in full Crowley regalia—and seated across from a pretty blonde. His wife? Probably. Crowley said something, and the woman giggled. Neither of them took notice of Mac as she passed by.

As Mac returned to the table, Tinley was finishing a story about the time he and his girlfriend went skinny-dipping in a hotel's hot tub, locked themselves out of their room, and had been forced to visit the front desk to get another key card. That generated sympathetic laughter and more stories in the same vein.

It wasn't until they were about to leave that Mac mentioned Crowley. "This place is hopping," she said. "The CO's here, too . . . He's upstairs, with his wife."

The announcement was met with an awkward silence. None of the other soldiers were willing to meet her gaze. "What's wrong?" Mac demanded. "Did I step in something?"

"Was the woman a blonde?" Perkins inquired.

"Yes," Mac replied. "She was."

"That's Captain Lightfoot's wife," Huff told her. "Everyone knows except for the captain."

"Who happens to be out on patrol," Gray added. "The poor bastard."

"It's a regular thing," Boulineau said. "And it ain't good for morale."

Mac tried to keep it light. "Okay . . . I'll file that under things I wish I didn't know. As for morale, that takes us back to what we were discussing earlier. We can't control the CO, but we can keep everything else tight, and we will."

"Roger that," Boulineau said.

"Yes, ma'am," Perkins added.

"Got it," Gilstrap agreed.

That was the best Mac could do for the moment. But she was pissed. Rather than go after Howard and try to rescue the female prisoners, Crowley was spending the night with another man's wife. And not just *any* man . . . But one of his subordinates. Should she take it up the chain of command? Probably. But what would happen then? An investigation would begin, Crowley would be relieved of duty pending the outcome, and the brass would download a colonel to take his place. In the meantime, Robert Howard would sell his prisoners. The cold night air was like a slap in the face, and the darkness took her in.

NORTHEAST OF CASPER, WYOMING

The Cessna JT-A produced a mind-numbing drone as it winged its way north. It was flying low, no more than three hundred feet off the ground, in order to stay off enemy radar. That was necessary but scary since visibility was iffy, and left the single-engine plane with no margin for error. Victoria turned to the pilot. "How much longer?"

The man was sixtysomething. What hair he had was pulled back into a gray ponytail. "It's like I told you ten minutes ago," he said. "We're almost there."

Victoria opened her mouth to put the man in his place, thought better of it, and forced herself to remain silent. The minutes crawled by. And then, just when it seemed as if the flight would go on forever, the plane began to turn.

Victoria looked down. What she saw was anything but promising. The airstrip consisted of a patch of flat ground surrounded by rocks. "We're going to land on *that*?" she demanded.

"Hell no," the old man replied. "We're gonna land at Kennedy, take the shuttle to the terminal, and have a latte."

Victoria thought she heard him say, "Dumb shit," under his breath as he brought the plane into alignment with the runway and pushed the yoke forward. Two red highway flares marked the end of the strip. They lost altitude quickly, hit hard, and came to a stop a few yards short of the flares. Victoria had been holding her breath. She let it out. "Welcome to Wyoming," the pilot said. "And thanks for keeping your breakfast down."

"Glad I could help," Victoria said as she pushed the door open. It was cold, but she was dressed for it. A small pack was stashed behind her seat, and the man made no effort to help her with it.

"Forty-eight hours," he said. "That's when I'll come for you . . . If I fail to show, it will be due to bad weather or because I'm on a binge. Wait twelve hours. Then, if I'm still MIA, start walking. Got it?"

Victoria put her right arm through a pack strap. "Got it."

"Good. Close the fucking door . . . It's getting cold in here."

Victoria closed the door and stepped back. The engine roared as the plane turned to face the other way. Then, after opening the throttle all the way, the pilot released the brakes. The Cessna took off like a jackrabbit and cleared the pile of rocks at the other end of the runway with ten feet to spare.

That was when Victoria heard a crunching sound—and turned to find a man wearing a tasseled stocking cap and sheepskin coat approaching her. A rifle was slung over his left shoulder. He stopped six feet away. His skin was brown, and there was a wispy goatee on his chin. "Where did they bury the great Khan?"

"In an unmarked grave."

"Where does he live?"

"In our hearts."

The man bowed. "My parents named me Thomas Styles. But my warrior name is Jebe, which means 'the Arrow.'"

"You killed Kuchlug."

Snow fell like a veil. The man bowed again. "The Confederacy chose its messenger with great care. Can you ride?"

"Yes."

"All will be well then. Follow me."

Two men and four horses were waiting just off the airstrip. Jebe's companions wore balaclava-style white-on-black skull masks. To look scary? Or to stay warm? Both, most likely, and Victoria wished she had one. The army-issue knit cap left her face unprotected.

Victoria's horse was a big brute named Montana. Victoria could feel the stares as she placed her left boot in the stirrup and swung her right leg out and over the horse's hindquarters. Victoria felt Montana stir uneasily as she landed on the Western-style saddle. She stroked his neck, and two streams of vapor appeared when he snorted. Victoria had learned to ride during summer vacations in Idaho, and Jebe nodded as if satisfied with her performance.

Jebe and his horse led the way, followed by Victoria and the two skull faces. The trail wound around a snowcapped rock formation, down into a ravine, and up the other side. The landscape was turning white, and that forced Victoria to don her sunglasses.

The first hour was enjoyable in a weird, otherworldly sort of way. But by the time they were fifteen minutes into the second hour of riding, Victoria's knees had started to ache. Had it been that way when she was sixteen? No, she didn't think so.

Thirty long, painful minutes passed before they followed a switchbacking trail down the side of a hill to the point where two trucks and a large horse trailer were waiting. Jebe aimed a remote at the blue pickup, and Victoria saw the lights flash. "Throw your pack in the cab," Jebe told her. "I'll take care of Montana."

Jebe led the horses over to the horse trailer, tied them up, and returned to the pickup. "We aren't likely to be stopped," Jebe said as he slipped behind the wheel. "But should that occur, we're ranchers headed up to Kaycee for supplies. Are you armed?"

"With a handgun, yes."

"Good. If the poop hits the fan, shoot everyone on your side of the truck. And don't hesitate to use the sawed-off if you need to."

Victoria followed Jebe's glance to the shotgun clamped above the windshield. "Got it."

The truck was in motion by then. It bounced through a series of potholes. "We're going to take back roads west to I-25," Jebe told her. "We'll follow it north to Buffalo. High Fort is a half hour beyond that."

"High Fort?"

"Yes. That's the name Subutai gave to the Huntington Lodge after he captured it," Jebe replied. "It was the site of a gold mine before that."

Captured? That was one word for it . . . Although Victoria was willing to bet that the people who owned the lodge would call the theft something else.

The next thirty minutes were spent winding their way through a maze of snow-covered backcountry roads. They turned onto a two-lane highway that provided access to I-25 ten minutes later. There was some traffic, but less and less as they traveled north. Because of the horde? That made sense. Some people would *have* to enter the horde's territory and pay Howard's road tax. But anyone who could avoid doing so would.

Interestingly enough, there were no signs of military activity. "I thought the Union had a battalion of troops stationed here," Victoria said. "Where are they?"

"They spend most of their time at Fort Carney," Jebe replied. "Although they did attack one of our strongholds two days ago. And believe me . . . They're going to pay for that."

There was no mistaking the anger in Jebe's voice. Victoria was reminded of what her father had told her. Robin was stationed at Fort Carney. Had she taken part in the attack? And how would she fare when Howard took his revenge?

It was something Victoria should care about. Then why didn't she? Was there something wrong with her? Possibly. Or maybe there was something *right* with her. "Each of us makes choices—and each of us has to live with the consequences." That's what Bo Macintyre liked to say. And it applied to Robin, along with everyone else.

The horde had established a checkpoint and toll booth adjacent to the small town of Kaycee. It was a flimsy affair that consisted of a motor home, lanes that were defined by traffic cones, and six well-armed rat rods. "Anyone can blow through it," Jebe admitted, as they entered the VIP lane. "But the rat rods will chase them down if they do . . . And the rat riders don't take prisoners."

When a man wearing a pullover skull mask appeared in the window, Jebe raised his right hand palm out. Skull face bowed deeply and waved Jebe through. Victoria was curious. "Did you show him some sort of ID?"

"Yes," Jebe replied, as he held his right hand up for her to look at. An intricate tracery of tattoos covered his palm. Could it be copied? Yes, of course. But Victoria's ID card could be duplicated as well.

"Each tattoo shares common elements with all the rest," Jebe explained. "Yet each is unique. Like pieces in a vast puzzle."

Victoria was beginning to take the horde more seriously by then. She'd been expecting to deal with a wacky bandit cult. But Jebe was more than a thug. Was he the exception? Or should she take all of them seriously? Victoria would know soon. And the knowledge would go into her report.

Victoria didn't see much traffic during the forty-minute trip to Buffalo. And that wasn't surprising given the things she did see. At one point, they passed an off-ramp where three bird-pecked corpses were dangling from a light standard. When asked why the people had been executed, Jebe shrugged. "There are laws," he said. "And they were lawbreakers."

Victoria was pretty sure Jebe didn't have the foggiest idea why the people had been executed. Nor did he care. And that was the flip side of the man behind the wheel. Though seemingly profound at times, he wasn't very analytical.

If the horde continued to rule with an iron hand, the locals would find ways to resist, one of which would be to collaborate with Union forces. So while Howard was likely to rule for a while— he would have trouble holding on to what he'd conquered. As a result, his value to the Confederacy was limited.

They had to pause at a checkpoint just outside Buffalo but not for long. Once Jebe presented his palm, a guard bowed and waved him through. Mountains were visible to the west. And, based on what she'd heard earlier, Victoria assumed that they were home to the High Fort.

That theory proved to be correct when Jebe left the freeway for a two-lane highway that led into the Bighorn National Forest. Even though there was no reason for her to believe that she would need to find her way out of the forest alone, Victoria did her best to memorize the route just in case. The road turned, began to climb, and passed a snow-clad gun emplacement. Three skull-faced bandits stood like statues as the truck passed them. Victoria noticed that one of them was armed with a spear.

A series of switchbacks took them up past a well-sited Bradley to what Jebe said was the final checkpoint. It consisted of what looked like a new metal gate mounted on wheels. "We have to walk the rest of the way," Jebe said, as the pickup came to a halt. "The guards will take your pistol—and return it when you leave."

The process went the way Jebe said it would except for one thing. The guard assigned to search Victoria was male—and took full advantage of the opportunity to feel her up. Fortunately, Jebe was there to intervene. "Stop it! She's Subutai's guest, you fool . . . He'll take your head."

The man immediately released her, bowed, and backed away. "I'm sorry," Jebe said, as they climbed a set of switchbacking stairs. "Subutai doesn't get a lot of female visitors."

"I can see why," Victoria said, as they arrived on what had been a lawn. The mansion loomed above them. It had turrets, steeply sloping roofs, and at least half a dozen chimneys. A well-protected porch fronted the building. Everything about the lodge shouted elegance, even if the place had fallen on hard times. But something bothered her. "Union forces could destroy this place with a single plane . . . or a couple of drones. Why don't they?"

"We keep prisoners here," Jebe answered. "Some are sold, but new ones arrive. The Union Army knows that."

The strategy made sense so long as the Union brass had a certain mind-set. But Victoria knew that if her father were running the Union Army, he'd bomb the shit out of the place and blame faulty intelligence for the civilian deaths.

They walked past a crudely constructed AA emplacement, past a pile of trash, and through an impromptu graveyard. "The men buried here have lived many lives and been buried in many places," Jebe said. "They'll be waiting when my turn comes."

Was Jebe crazy? Hell, yes. And that's what Robin and her battalion would have to face if they wanted to defeat the horde. An army of crazy people. *Good luck with that,* Victoria thought to herself.

Victoria followed Jebe up a flight of snow-dusted stairs into an enormous foyer. It was crowded with people. Some were seated on chairs, some were standing, and one man was asleep on the muddy floor. The air was so cold that Victoria could see her breath. "They're waiting to see Subutai," Jebe explained. "Some have been here for days. But don't worry . . . He will see you soon." And with that, he left.

"Soon," turned out to be half an hour. And as Victoria listened to the chatter around her, she got the impression of a thinly stretched government run by a paranoid micromanager. Not a recipe for success. Something more for her report.

Victoria could feel jealous eyes on her back, as Jebe returned and led her away. After climbing a flight of stairs, they had to pass between heavily armed guards before entering what had been a ballroom. Groups of men stood here and there . . . There was no way to tell if they were guards or part of Subutai's retinue. The only women to be seen were servants, who kept their eyes down as they brought food and drink.

Victoria felt a momentary wash of heat as they passed a large fireplace. Then the air cooled as they followed a red carpet up to a velvet rope, where Jebe bowed deeply. "Greetings, great one . . . This is the New Confederacy's emissary, Major Jeri Ferris."

Rather than use her own name, Victoria had chosen to establish a cover which, if Howard had the means to check, ran quite deep.

He was sitting on a throne-like chair made out of antlers. Had the piece of furniture been built for him? Or did it come with the lodge? The latter, Victoria supposed . . . Although the look was very much in keeping with the man Howard had chosen to be.

The warlord of warlords was wearing a softly rounded Afghan pakoz hat rather than the Mongol equivalent. Victoria knew because she'd spent a year battling the Taliban. Was the hat a mistake? Or a preference? The latter seemed more likely since she'd read his file and knew that he had served in Afghanistan, too. The rest of Howard's outfit consisted of a sheepskin jacket, Levi's, and cowboy boots. Howard was clearly Caucasian, but his wide-set eyes and high cheekbones gave him a Slavic appearance. A wispy mustache decorated his upper lip.

A pair of Rottweilers lay sprawled next to the warlord's elaborate chair. One of them growled, and Howard patted its head. "Welcome to the High Fort, Major Macintyre . . . I hope you had a pleasant trip."

The extent of Victoria's surprise must have been visible on her face because Howard laughed. "That's right, Major . . . I have sources of information inside the Confederacy."

Victoria's mind was racing. Howard had been a Green Beret only months earlier . . . So he knew special ops people in *both* armies. More than that, he had bled with them. So if some were on his payroll, that would make sense. What did that mean to her mission?

Howard nodded as if able to read her mind. "Never fear, Major . . . I don't blame you for using a cover. I would if I were in your position. And one more thing . . . The fact that General Macintyre was willing to send his daughter means a lot to me. But it raises questions, too . . . What *are* you, Major? A warrior? Or Daddy's girl?"

Victoria could feel the man's hostility. At officers? At *female* officers? Is that why he referred to her rank so often? "I fought in Afghanistan," Victoria answered. "Just as you did."

There was no warmth in Howard's smile. "You read my file? Good on you. Well, there were a shitload of rear-echelon mother-fuckers who went to Afghanistan and never fired a shot. How 'bout *you*, missy? Did you kill anyone up close and personal? Or were you staring at a screen?"

Victoria didn't like the way the conversation was going. Was there some sort of purpose behind the grilling? Or was Howard mind fucking her for the fun of it? "My activities in Afghanistan are classified," Victoria told him. "As are many of yours."

Howard reached inside his jacket and dragged a shiny revolver out into the light. Victoria felt a stab of fear. He was going to shoot her! And there was nothing she could do about it. "Maybe you worked for the dark side, and maybe you're full of shit," Howard said. "Let's find out. Guards! Grab that girl!"

Howard's left index finger was pointed at a girl with mousy-brown hair. She had glasses and was dressed in one of the sack-style dresses that all of the female servants were required to wear. She uttered a shriek of fear and tried to run. Two men grabbed the teen and held her arms. She was sobbing by then—and a puddle of urine appeared between her feet.

Howard's eyes were on Victoria. "If you're the woman you say you are, then you know this is a Colt Python and that it holds six rounds."

As if to illustrate that fact, Howard flipped the cylinder open—and dumped six shiny .357 cartridges onto the table next to him. He chose one of the bullets and held it up to the light as if inspecting it for flaws. Then he inserted the cartridge into an empty chamber, flipped the cylinder closed, and ran it along the outside surface of his left arm. Victoria heard a series of clicks.

"Here," Howard said as he offered the weapon butt first. "If you want an alliance with the horde, then aim the pistol at the girl and squeeze the trigger. Maybe the bullet will rotate in under the hammer, and maybe it won't. But either way, I will take you seriously from that point forward. Or you can run back to Daddy. You choose."

Victoria wanted to laugh. Howard thought he was talking to Robin! Or someone like Robin . . . And that was a mistake.

A dog growled as she unhooked the velvet rope, stepped forward, and accepted the Colt. She could have killed the warlord of warlords then, and his bodyguards knew it. At least six weapons were pointed at her.

Victoria smiled, pointed the barrel of the handgun up at the ceiling, and turned to the teenager. The men who stood to each side of her looked worried. What if the woman with the Colt missed? But orders were orders, and they had no choice. "Pull her arms straight out," Victoria instructed.

The girl struggled, but the men were too strong for her. Victoria held the revolver in a two-handed grip, took aim, and waited for Howard to stop her. He didn't. She pulled the hammer back to full cock and squeezed the trigger. The hammer fell, and the Colt bucked in her hands. The big slug hit the teen with such force that it passed through her chest and hit the wall beyond. The guards let go of the body, and it slumped to the floor.

"Well, well," Howard said, as Victoria handed the pistol to Jebe. "You are for real. Let's have lunch . . . There's a great deal to talk about."

CHAPTER 4

||||||||||||||||||||||||||||||||||||

I do not believe in using women in combat, because
females are too fierce.

—MARGARET MEAD

CASPER, WYOMING

The so-called com cave was a side room just off Fort Carney's
underground command center. Flat-panel screens covered two of
the four walls—and cables ran like snakes between the timbers
that helped to support the ceiling. The cave was where the battalion's UAV pilots spent their time when not in the field, and Mo
Henry was no exception. She got up from her chair when Mac
entered. "Good morning, Sergeant . . . What's up?"

"There's something I want you to see, ma'am. Remember the
motion-activated cameras we left on the airstrip? We scored some
footage."

Mac looked at the screen that fronted Henry's chair. There was
nothing to see at first. Just a field of white and some dark, snow-
crusted rocks beyond. Then a small plane entered the frame,

touched down, and blew snow every which way as the pilot stood on the brakes. "All right," Mac said. "This should be interesting."

Unfortunately, there was very little to be learned as the plane stopped and turned. Four people entered the picture. All of them were mounted on horses. One dropped to the ground. He or she was wearing a pack. But that's as much as Mac could determine as the person was enveloped by the cloud of snow associated with the plane's prop wash.

The man or woman climbed up into the cabin, and the Cessna took off two minutes later. That left Mac with more questions than answers. Someone had a secret airstrip. But *who*? And *why*? She sighed. "Thanks, Henry. Let's pull those cameras the next time a patrol goes in that direction."

From there, Mac returned to the surface, where the sky was clear, but the air was cold. A short walk took her over to the battalion command shack. The premission briefing was scheduled for 0800, and the conference room was crammed with people, including a civilian scout named Wilbur Stratton. Charlie Company's CO was present, too. Captain Lightfoot had a round, almost cherubic face—and was known for his sense of humor.

There was a stir, and a platoon leader shouted, "Atten-hut!" as Crowley entered the room. Crowley was dressed in full Western regalia, and his high-heeled boots made a clumping sound as he made his way to the head of the table. "At ease. Please sit down," Crowley said as he looked around. "All of you know why you're here . . . But some may wonder about the late start. There is, I assure you, a method to our madness."

Having already snapped a couple of photos, Lieutenant Casey stepped forward to rip a blank sheet of paper off a large map and throw it aside. Crowley used his swagger stick as a pointer. "The idea is to trick Howard into believing that everything is normal.

At 1000 hours, Bravo Company will depart and drive north through Arminto. In the meantime, Charlie Company will go east, turn just shy of the airport, and head north from there. The companies will converge at the old Hole-in-the-Wall Hideout just before nightfall.

"The Wild Bunch used to hang out there back in the late 1800s," Crowley added, as his eyes roamed the room. "But a warlord named Ron Goody is using the place now. He's in the kidnapping business, so be careful . . . There's a good chance that noncombatants will be present when we grease Goody. That will open the way for an all-out assault on Howard's mountain fortress. Are there any questions?"

Stratton raised a hand. He was wearing a beat-up Stetson and a grungy parka. "Yes, Wilbur," Crowley said. "What's on your mind?"

Stratton had a raspy voice and a no-nonsense manner. "I think you're making a big mistake, Colonel . . . I was up that way two days ago—and Howard's people were all over the place. I'd keep those companies together if I were you."

"Well, you *aren't* me," Crowley replied. There was a smile on his face, but that wasn't likely to fool Stratton, or anyone else for that matter.

"We sent a drone up there this morning," Crowley said. "And the enemy's there . . . But not in the numbers you suggest. Plus, the element of surprise should give us a significant advantage."

"There ain't gonna be no surprise," Stratton insisted. "Howard has spies *everywhere*. That includes inside this fort. So when you head out, he'll be waiting."

It was starting to feel uncomfortable in the conference room. Crowley frowned. "That's an interesting assertion, Wilbur . . . But it isn't true. We surprised Cory Burns at Arminto."

"You got *lucky* in Arminto," Stratton replied.

"You're entitled to your opinion," Crowley said stiffly. "But I'm in command, and the plan will remain as is."

Stratton stood. Beady eyes scanned the room. "Maybe some of you will survive," Stratton said. "I hope so. Personally, I plan to go home and do some chores." And with that, he left.

"Civilians," Crowley said, as the door closed. "I suggest that you ignore Stratton. Maybe he saw enemy activity, and maybe he was two sheets to the wind. The drone flew over the Hole-in-the-Wall a few hours ago. And, by the time we attack, our force will have reunited. Now, does anyone else have a question? No? Let's get ready. Dismissed."

If Mac had been in command, she wouldn't have been so quick to dismiss Stratton's concerns, especially where the element of surprise was concerned. Crowley was correct about the drone video, though . . . She'd seen it. And so long as the companies came back together prior to the attack, they should be able to carry the day.

So Mac put her misgivings aside and made last-minute preparations for the mission. To his credit, Crowley insisted on leading from the front. So Mac assigned the call sign one-one to his Humvee. As second-in-command, she was going to ride in the *last* vehicle, which was Stryker three-four, better known to its two-person crew as BIGFOOT. Crowley's call sign was Viper-Eight—and Mac was Bravo-Six.

Both companies left the fort on schedule and went their separate ways shortly thereafter. The previously blue sky had clouded over by then, and the sun was a yellow smear beyond the blanket of gray.

Mac couldn't see the BULLET MAGNET at the front end of the column but could listen in as Crowley offered all sorts of observations to people who didn't need them. That in spite of the fact that the unit was supposed to maintain radio silence. Yes, the transmissions were scrambled . . . But by monitoring the volume of radio traffic, the bad guys could tell that something was going on. And that wasn't good. Mac sighed. Stratton thought Crowley had been lucky. Maybe that luck would hold.

The column turned north shortly after that and rolled through Arminto twenty minutes later. Alpha Company had leveled the place. The saloon was little more than a pile of charred wood, shot-up rat rods littered the area, and the brand-new graveyard was thick with crudely made crosses. As **BIGFOOT** rolled through town, Mac saw only *one* resident, and that was a painfully thin dog. It skittered away, tail between its legs, looking back over a shoulder.

With the exception of some low-lying hills and the gullies that separated them, most of the surrounding terrain was flat. That was good since there were very few places for the horde to hide. But, even though Mac was standing in the Stryker's forward air-guard hatch, she couldn't see what lay ahead of the column. What did the road look like? Were there lots of tire tracks? Tracks made *before* the column rolled through? If so, that might indicate that the horde was on the move.

About fifteen minutes north of Arminto, the column was forced to pass through a narrow passageway between two hills. Mac caught glimpses of it from her position at the tail end of the convoy. Then, as the ground began to rise on both sides of her, Mac heard Crowley say, "Put the hammer down. Let's get through this as quickly as we can."

That was when an explosion tossed the **BULLET MAGNET** up into the air. Mac didn't wait to witness the Humvee's fate. She was shouting into her mike. "This is Bravo-Six actual! Back up! Back up! Back up!"

BIGFOOT's truck commander was a corporal named Niki Chin.

She brought the vic to a momentary stop, shifted into reverse, and stomped on the accelerator. Mac was thrown forward as huge wheels spun, and the Stryker backed out of the trap.

But, as BIGFOOT cleared the passageway, *more* charges went off. These explosives were located high on the hillsides, where they weren't likely to be detected. Avalanches of dirt and rock struck the rearmost Stryker from both sides and nearly buried it. That blocked the road. Bravo Company couldn't move forward—and it couldn't back out. It was trapped.

Mac knew what would happen next. Howard's warriors would appear on the skyline and fire down on the vehicles below. "This is Six actual," she shouted. "Remain in your vehicles! Gunners will fire upslope! Let the bastards have it. Over."

The words were hardly out of Mac's mouth when hundreds of bandits appeared on top of both hills and opened fire. Stratton's words came back to haunt her: *Maybe some of you will survive.*

Compared to earlier generations of wheeled vehicles, the Strykers had a lot of advantages, not the least of which was thicker armor, and their remotely controlled weapons stations enabled gunners to fire without exposing themselves. Their .50 caliber slugs raked the skyline, 40mm grenades exploded along both slopes, and the horde was forced to take cover. They continued to fire, however . . . And Mac suspected that fighting positions had been dug along the top of both ridges. Was that Howard's doing? Probably.

Three of Mac's Strykers were armed with 105mm guns that, if they could be brought to bear, could do serious damage to the bandits. But Mac knew the cannons couldn't elevate high enough to hit the ridges. Still another indication that someone knew what they were doing.

All of that and more raced through Mac's mind as she spoke over the intercom. "Take us to the right, Chin . . . And drive up onto that ridge. Hooper . . . Commence firing the moment that you have targets. Sergeant Ivey . . . Get ready to deploy your squad. We're going to attack their left flank."

The CAT engine roared as the Stryker lurched off road, and the vic's eight-wheel drive propelled it upslope. A light machine gun was mounted in front of Mac. She ran a check on it as Lieutenant Perkins directed fire. "Higher, two-two . . . There you go. Nice job!

"Swing right one-three . . . Get those bastards!

"Eyes west, three-one! They have a rocket launcher!"

Mac knew Perkins must be up top, just as she was, in order to see so much of his surroundings. And she was about to order him to get down when a bandit spotted **BIGFOOT** and opened fire. Bullets pinged the vic's armor and Mac heard them snap around her. She fired the machine gun, saw geysers of snow shoot up just short of the man, and made the necessary adjustment. A long burst cut him off at the waist. Blood stained the snow.

The truck's grenade launcher began to chug as Hooper spotted targets and opened fire. Bright yellow-orange explosions marched upslope, consumed a machine-gun crew, and kept going. Chin fought for control as **BIGFOOT** lost traction, found it, and sent the vic lurching forward. "Find a place to stop and drop the ramp," Mac told her. "Use the vic for cover, Sergeant Ivey . . . And grease some of those bastards for me."

"Yes, ma'am," came the reply, as **BIGFOOT** came to a halt. Rather than turn, and watch the squad deploy, Mac kept her eyes to the front. "Bravo-Six to Bravo Company . . . Switch your fire to the west. I repeat, switch all of your fire to the *west*. Three-four is on top of the east ridge. Over."

Mac heard a chorus of clicks as **BIGFOOT** topped the ridge, and the slaughter began. Howard, or the person responsible for laying the ambush, had failed to anticipate the possibility that a Stryker would make its way up onto the ridge. And that was a serious mistake.

Suddenly, one of the metal beasts was in among the bandits. And the crew was out for revenge. Chin rolled over a fighting position, crushing those within. Some of the ambushers fled. Grenades followed them, caught up, and cut most of them down. A few turned to fight. Mac fired the machine gun. They fell like tenpins.

Then, as suddenly as it had begun, the fight was over. Mac dropped to the ground and looked around. Sergeant Ivey and his squad were walking the ridgeline, checking to make sure that none of the bandits were playing dead, and collecting whatever intel they could.

Mac made her way past an abandoned mortar pit and up to the spot where she had a clear view of the other ridge. At some point in the battle, Perkins had released the soldiers from the Strykers and sent them up the western slope. That in spite of her order for the troops to remain in their vehicles. Mac made a mental note to thank him. The uphill assault hadn't been easy, though . . . Mac could see bodies on the hillside. The rest, those who made it to the top, were clearing the area.

Mac felt her heart sink as she looked down onto the road. It appeared that three of Bravo Company's twelve Strykers had taken repeated hits from mortars and been destroyed. Two of the trucks were on fire, and the third lay on its side. Each vic carried a total of eleven soldiers. So as many as thirty-three people could be dead in addition to the bodies that lay on the slope. Mac felt an almost overwhelming sense of sorrow and had to fight back the tears.

Had she been wrong to keep them buttoned up inside their vehicles? Would more people have survived if she'd let them loose right away? *That's bullshit,* the inner voice told her. *You made the correct call.*

Mac was still thinking about that when Crowley appeared next to her. There was a cut on his forehead and some blood on his buckskin jacket. He was otherwise unhurt. "Hello, Macintyre . . . I'm glad to see that you're okay."

It occurred to Mac that Crowley hadn't crossed her mind until then. Why was that? "You too, sir . . . I saw your Humvee take to the air. Did your driver make it?"

"No," Crowley said, as he looked down at the carnage. "She's dead."

Another one. Sisley? No, Sampson. A volunteer from Louisiana. Mac swallowed the lump in her throat. "I'm sorry."

Crowley's eyes slid past hers to a point off in the distance. "I just got off the horn with Captain Lightfoot. I told him to abort the mission and return to the fort."

"That makes sense, sir."

People were moving in among the Strykers by then. Two-three had backed into two-two early on, and a sergeant was inspecting the damage. It would take a while to clear the traffic jam.

"I'm going to take your Stryker and head back," Crowley said. "Salvage what you can." And with that, he turned away.

There had been no expression of grief—and no admission of responsibility. What would Crowley do back at the fort? Work with Casey to weasel-word an after-action report? Yes, Mac decided. But there wouldn't be any press release. Not on that dark day. Mac sighed, made her way downslope, and went to work.

BOSTON, MASSACHUSETTS

Sloan was in a bad mood. There were three reasons for that. First, General Hern's forces were still stalled just south of Columbia,

Tennessee, where the Confederacy's 3rd Tank Regiment was putting up a stiff fight. And the same was true to the east and west as well.

Second, the handshake thing was *still* in the news, and Senator Pickett was beginning to creep up in the polls.

And third, Sloan was scheduled to meet with a reporter from the *World News*. Not just *any* reporter . . . but Beth Morgan. The woman he'd been living with until two months prior to the May Day disaster. Besom's advice was to, "Be nice. Maybe she'll go easy on you. Lord knows, we could use some positive press."

And maybe pigs will fly, Sloan thought to himself. *This is Beth's chance to get even.*

But Sloan couldn't choose whom *World News* sent, and he couldn't afford to ignore such an influential newspaper, especially since print media were enjoying a postdisaster resurgence. That meant Sloan had to sit for the interview whether he wanted to or not.

Sloan knew Beth a lot better than most interviewees did, including her passion for organization. It was Beth's firm belief that e-mails should be returned within twelve hours, thank-you cards were a must, and "good" people were always on time.

So when 3:57 rolled around, and Sloan was still on a call with IRS Commissioner Ralston, he broke it off. "Sorry, Marsha, but I'm supposed to sit down for an interview at four . . . And this particular reporter has been critical of me in the past. If I'm two seconds late, you'll read about how arrogant I am on page one of the *World News*." Ralston laughed, and they agreed to talk later.

Sloan's hotel suite included a separate bedroom, and he left it for the sitting room at exactly 4:00 P.M. As he entered, Sloan saw that Beth was checking her watch. Beth had blue eyes, permanently arched brows, and kissable lips. *Whoa!* the voice cautioned. *It didn't work out. Remember?* Beth stood and extended her hand. "Right on time . . . That's a surprise."

Sloan shook her hand but was careful to let go quickly. "It's good to see you, Beth . . . How are you? And when did you join *World News*?"

"I'm fine," Beth replied. "I was covering a story in Minneapolis when the meteors struck. The *Washington Post* was destroyed along with the rest of D.C. So I applied for a slot at *World News*, and here I am."

"I'm sorry about the *Post*," Sloan said sincerely. "I know how it feels to lose coworkers. We were lucky you and I. Please, have a seat."

Once they were seated, Beth placed a recorder on the table that separated them. "I'd like to record our interview."

Sloan nodded. "Go right ahead."

The questions were what Sloan expected them to be. "Why was it taking Hern so long to push the Confederate Army south?" "What was Sloan doing to push his America Rising proposal through Congress?" And, "When was he going to nominate a vice president?"

It took about thirty minutes for Sloan to provide variations on his stock answers. The essence of which was that the Confederates were tough, the Whigs were determined to block reconstruction, and he was in the process of choosing a nominee.

Beth smiled knowingly. His tendency to procrastinate had been one of the things that caused friction between them. "Sure you are," she said. "Once you make that decision, please have Besom call me first."

And with that she leaned forward to turn the recorder off. "Thanks, Sam . . . Now, if you've got a couple of minutes, I'd like to tell you about another story that I'm working on. Under normal circumstances, I couldn't. But since this could represent a matter of national security, my editor thinks that we should share."

Sloan was intrigued. "Okay, what's up?"

"Before I get into it I want a verbal agreement," Beth said. "*If the story pans out, you'll let me break it.*"

Sloan shrugged. "Sure, that sounds fair. So, like I said, what's up?"

"I'm working on an in-depth piece on Senator Pickett," Beth replied. "Where she's from, how that shaped her views, and her life in Iowa after she got married. And that's where things get interesting. When Pickett ran for the Senate in Iowa, she received financial support from the American Eagle PAC, and it was receiving 60 percent of its funding from the Huxton Oil Company."

Sloan knew that Huxton Oil was owned by Fred Huxton, who had been instrumental in creating the New Confederacy and was a member of the government's board of directors. But although the connection was interesting, there was nothing illegal about receiving predisaster support from the PAC, so where was Beth headed? "That makes sense, given her politics," Sloan allowed. "But it doesn't qualify as front-page news."

"No," Beth agreed, "it doesn't. But there's more . . . According to a person I interviewed in Iowa, a man who used to be on Pickett's staff, the senator is still receiving cash payments from Huxton. They arrive once a month by courier."

Sloan stared at her. "You must be kidding."

"No," Beth replied. "I'm serious. But here's the problem . . . All I have is the allegation. And that won't cut it. We need proof."

Sloan could see where things were headed. *World News* lacked the resources to carry out a full-scale investigation—and wanted the government to do it for them. Was that ethical? Yes, no, maybe. If Picket was taking money from the insurgents in return for votes in the Senate, that was a crime. And the Whig candidate would go down in flames.

But what about *his* involvement? Using government resources to submarine a political opponent would look bad to some people even if it was legally appropriate. "I can't get involved in this," Sloan told her. "What I *can* do is ask the Attorney General to take your call. Then, if he decides that an investigation is appropriate, the wheels will start to turn. But if he says no, then it's game over."

Beth nodded. "I will call him tomorrow."

Sloan glanced at his watch. It was nearly five. "So how about some dinner? I can't take you out . . . not without a motorcade and an army of Secret Service agents. But we could eat here." *Are you crazy?* the voice demanded. *You dumped her! Because she's OCD, bossy, and extremely transactional.* But it was too late. The icy blue eyes seemed to soften a bit. "That would be nice, Sam. But no sex. Not while I'm working on a story that could benefit you."

"Of course not," Sam replied. And that was when he remembered something important. The last time he'd had sex had been with *her.* And it had been quite enjoyable. That was one area where they had always been sympatico.

A smile tugged at the corners of Beth's mouth. "Good. So what's on the menu?"

CASPER, WYOMING

A cold wind was blowing down from the north. The flag snapped in the breeze, hardware rattled, and halyards slapped against the aluminum pole as the funeral service continued. Mac was standing behind Colonel Crowley and in front of the battalion. Two days had passed since the ambush. During that time, the wreckage had been removed from what had become known as "the squeeze," and thirty-nine bodies had been returned to Fort Carney.

Prior to the May Day disaster, the dead would have been

processed and sent home for burial. That was no longer possible because of civil unrest, the war, and the country's crumbling infrastructure. So a military graveyard had been commissioned half a mile south of the fort. And, with assistance from a local funeral home, the dead soldiers were being laid to rest. Each casket was draped with an American flag. And, because the soldiers were from the South, the symbolism took on additional significance.

Tears ran down Mac's cheeks, and she made no attempt to wipe them away, as each casket was lowered into the ground. The rifle party fired a three-shot volley for each soldier lost. And as the bugler played "Taps," the sweet-sad sound of it nearly broke her heart.

Once the battalion was dismissed, Mac half expected Crowley to turn and address his troops. He didn't. A Humvee was waiting. Crowley made his way over, got in, and was whisked away. So Mac led the members of Alpha and Bravo Companies back to the fort, where Charlie Company was on duty. Once they arrived, Mac made her way to the company's command shack—and was pouring herself a mug of coffee when Perkins arrived. He had Company Sergeant Boulineau in tow. "Have you got a minute, Captain?"

"Sure," Mac replied. "What's up?"

"It's Kline, ma'am. And Porter. They went AWOL last night."

Kline was the gunner in two-three, and Porter was a mechanic. Neither had been trouble before so far as Mac knew. "Did we catch them?"

"Yes, ma'am," Boulineau answered grimly. "The MPs found them on 220 trying to hitchhike south. They're being held in the stockade."

Mac took a sip of coffee. It was cold. "Good. Do we know why they ran?"

Perkins was visibly uncomfortable. "Kline and Porter are of the opinion that the CO doesn't care about the troops—and that's why so many people were killed in the squeeze."

Mac was in a difficult position. The deserters were right— Crowley *didn't* care about them. But she was the battalion's XO, and Bravo Company's CO. As such, she couldn't side with Kline and Porter no matter how correct they might be. "Colonel Crowley led the way," Mac reminded them. "An IED went off under his Humvee and sent it flying through the air."

"That's true," Perkins allowed. "But he left the scene of the ambush before all of the wounded had been treated, much less evacuated. That left a bad taste in the mouths of some."

"Okay," Mac said. "You know the drill . . . Charge them with desertion. I'll sign the paperwork."

Neither man moved. Mac eyed them. *"Well?"*

Perkins cleared his throat. "Permission to speak freely, ma'am?"

"Shoot."

"We think Kline and Porter are part of a larger problem."

"That's right," Boulineau agreed. "There are rumblings. Things that worry me."

"Such as?"

"Such as a large number of people pulling out . . . and making a run for the New Mason-Dixon Line."

Mac was reminded of what Crowley had said to her. *"Who knows? The whole lot of them might go over the hill."*

"Are you referring to Bravo Company?" Mac wanted to know. "Or the entire battalion?"

"All of them," Perkins replied. "Most, anyway."

Mac sighed. "First, thanks for the heads-up. Second, let's do what we can to make sure that doesn't happen."

Perkins looked skeptical. "No offense, ma'am . . . But how will we do that?"

A plan was starting to form in Mac's mind. "Let's begin with a proposal to reorganize the battalion. By redistributing our personnel, we can create three companies of equal size . . . And that makes sense since it could be quite a while before reinforcements arrive. Then, assuming the CO approves of the plan, we'll start an aggressive training cycle."

Perkins eyes grew wider. "A reorganization would be like shuffling a deck of cards. It would break up cliques, redistribute opinion leaders, and buy us time."

Mac smiled. "Yes. *If* it works. What do you think, Sergeant?"

Boulineau nodded. "You're a fucking genius, ma'am. No disrespect intended."

"And none taken," Mac assured him. "Let's bring Captain Lightfoot and Captain Withers in on our plan. Then we'll go to work."

The proposal to reorganize the battalion came together quickly—and Mac was ready to submit a draft the following morning. But, before she could request a meeting with Crowley, he sent for her. She took the plan along.

When Mac arrived the colonel, Lieutenant Casey, and the other company commanders were crammed into Crowley's office. He was standing with his back to the earthen wall. "Good morning," he said, as Mac entered. "Let's begin." His eyes roamed the faces in front of him.

"We got our asses handed to us a few days ago. But, rather than sit here and lick our wounds, I'm going to take most of the battalion up north and put Howard down like the mad dog he is. In a perfect world, we would call on the air force to destroy his so-called fort . . . But Howard has a lot of prisoners there . . . So we've got to do it the hard way."

Crowley paused. "Right about now, you're asking yourselves *how* we're going to do it. I'm not ready to disclose that yet. Based on what happened in the so-called squeeze, we know that our plans were compromised in advance, and I'm not about to let that happen again."

Mac was amazed. Stratton had warned Crowley about spies, the colonel had ignored the scout's warning, and more than thirty soldiers had been killed. Yet here he was . . . talking about the need for security as if it were a new issue!

"Suffice it to say," Crowley continued, "that I'm consulting with a *new* scout. And I expect to finalize a strategy within the next forty-eight hours. In the meantime, I want you to prepare your units for battle without tipping them off to what's about to take place. And that shouldn't be too difficult since we're expected to maintain a high state of readiness at all times. Okay . . . That's it for now. Dismissed."

Mac waited for the others to leave. "Can I have a couple of minutes, sir?"

Crowley waved her toward a chair. "Of course . . . I'm sorry about leaving you out of the loop . . . But I'm sure you understand."

Mac thought Crowley had veered from sharing too much to sharing too little. But what was, was. "Yes, sir. The other company commanders and I came up with a plan to rebalance the battalion . . . And I'd like to share it with you."

"That's a good idea," Crowley replied. "Especially in light of what we're about to do. I'll read it and get back to you later today."

As Mac left, she could tell that Crowley didn't have the foggiest idea of how bad morale was, his role in making it that way, or the fact that the "rebalancing" was part of a plan to prevent a mutiny. But he'd been receptive, and that was good.

Mac went back to the command shack and all of the administrative work that waited there. A runner brought Crowley's response two hours later. There was some markup, but not much. And the words, "Approved with changes," were scrawled above his signature.

That was good news. But now it was necessary to contact her peers, hold meetings to let the troops know what was coming, and enter the necessary changes into a dozen different databases. Those efforts consumed what remained of the day.

By the time Mac hit the sack, she was exhausted and immediately fell into a deep sleep. And she was still out when the car bomb detonated at 0512 hours. The blast was so powerful that it shook the ground, rattled the room's single window, and woke her.

Mac sat up in bed. What the? Had she been dreaming? Hell, no. The emergency Klaxon had started to bleat—and she could hear machine-gun fire. The fort was under attack!

Mac rolled off the cot, hurried to pull a pair of pants on, and grabbed her boots. Once the laces were tied, Mac stuck her head up through the hole in her tac vest and felt the familiar weight settle onto her shoulders. The carbine was leaning next to the door, and she grabbed it on the way out.

It was like stepping into hell. A cloud of black smoke was billowing up from the main gate. And as Mac looked in that direction, she saw that men with skull masks were flooding into the fort. Not without opposition, however . . . The soldiers on top of the walls were firing down on the invaders as people on the ground tried to push them back. Mac fumbled her radio on. "This is Bravo-Six actual . . . Be careful up on the wall! There are friendlies in the compound, too! Over."

Shit! Shit! Shit! Where was Crowley? Was he in command? Or was everything up to her? The question went unanswered as three Black Hawk helicopters swept over the fort. Reinforcements! And just in time, too . . . Then the door gunners opened fire! Bullets chased a private, caught up, and took him down.

Mac's mind raced. What the hell was going on? Were the helo pilots confused? Did they think that the enemy was in control of Fort Carney? No, that wasn't likely. Then it hit her . . . The Confederates! They were helping the horde!

Mac's radio-telephone operator was a fuzz-faced kid named Worsky. His place was with her, and to his everlasting credit, he appeared at her side. "Holy shit, ma'am . . . What the hell is going on?"

Mac threw him to the ground as gouts of slush marched across the ground and passed within inches of them. "Get on the horn!" Mac shouted. "Tell fire control that those helos belong to the Confederacy . . . and to shoot them down!"

Worsky was still talking as the Black Hawks hovered, and bandits jumped to the ground. Once they were clear, the helicopters began to rise. Their mission was complete—and the pilots were eager to haul ass. But the fort's surface-to-air missile launchers had swiveled around by then. Two helos exploded in quick succession. The third managed to clear the wall, and was a mile away, when a missile caught up with it. The result was a flash of light, a boom, and a shower of flaming debris.

The bandits split up. Some ran toward the vehicle sheds, but six made a dash for the underground command post. Two guards were stationed out front. They fired but were cut down. Mac was up on one knee by then. She raised her carbine and triggered a three-round burst. The bullets hit the last bandit between the shoulder blades. He threw his arms out, took a nosedive, and slid through the slush. "Warn the people in the command post," Mac said, as she fired again. "Tell them to lock the door!"

But before Worsky could obey, Lieutenant Casey made his way up the ramp and onto the surface. He was armed with a light machine gun, which he fired John Wayne style. The bandits seemed to dance like puppets and collapsed in a heap. "Good morning, ma'am," the PA officer said as he passed Mac. "They need help on the gate . . . I thought I'd lend a hand." Then he was gone.

Mac still hadn't heard anything from Crowley. Maybe he'd been hit. But, whatever the reason, her place was in the CP unless the CO showed up to relieve her.

Mac ordered Worsky to stand guard outside, went down the ramp, and entered the underground com cave. She could hear garbled radio traffic and lots of it. A tech sergeant named Tully was in charge and hurried over. There was a look of relief on her face. "Thank God . . . We could use some help, ma'am."

"Give me a sitrep," Mac said, as her eyes flitted from screen to screen. "But keep it short."

"They blew the main gate," the noncom answered. "It's secure now, but at least a hundred bandits got inside." Mac went to work. It soon became apparent that without any centralized control, the battle had devolved to the company and platoon levels, as small contingents of troops battled to keep the invaders away from the com towers, the Strykers, and the ammo dump.

Bit by bit, Mac worked to reintegrate the battalion. And by 0623 hours, Fort Carney was secure again. But how had things gone so wrong? And where was Crowley?

Mac ordered Captain Lightfoot to take temporary command as she sought answers to both questions. She pulled Tully aside. "Okay . . . Give it to me straight . . . What happened? Give me the longer version this time."

Tully looked scared, and that was understandable. Was Mac going to blame *her* for the debacle? "At about 0500, a Humvee flying the stars and bars rolled up on the outer perimeter," Tully said. "The guards attempted to wave it down, but the driver kept going. That's when Corporal Inthy called in and asked me what to do."

Tully swallowed nervously and looked down at her boots. "I wasn't sure. So I was going to escalate the decision when the Humvee ran over a guard stationed on the *inner* perimeter. Our people opened fire. But the Humvee's armor held, the driver made it through the concrete obstacles, and slammed into the door. Then it blew up. The door gave way. That's when three truckloads of bandits rolled in. They charged the gate."

Mac wrapped her arm around the other woman's narrow shoulders. "Write it down before you go off duty . . . while it's still fresh in your mind. And one more thing . . . You kept things going. I won't forget that. Now, what about the helicopters?"

Tully's eyes came up, and she looked more confident. "That was different . . . They had the right recognition signals."

"*What?*"

"Yes, ma'am. The lead pilot called in from fifty miles out, said that General Garrett was aboard, and requested permission to land. We asked for today's recognition code and received it. Fire control was notified, along with all of the AA batteries."

Mac took it in. Crowley had been careful this time. Even she didn't know what the plan of attack was. Yet Howard knew . . . And the Confederacy knew. "Write that down, too," Mac instructed. "It will go into the after-action report. And let's stay vigilant. Who knows? Those bastards could launch a follow-up attack."

Mac turned and made her way back to Crowley's office. She didn't know what to expect. Was the man drunk? Cowering under his desk? She'd be tempted to shoot him if he was.

But Crowley *wasn't* cowering under his desk. He was dead. And that was glaringly obvious the moment Mac entered. The colonel was sitting in his chair, head back, staring at her. Except that instead of two eyes he had *three* . . . The one in the middle was rimmed with blue and leaking blood. It ran down onto the bridge of his nose and into his mustache.

Mac swore under her breath as she went over to look for the pistol. But there wasn't any pistol. Crazy Crowley had been murdered! By one of the Southerners he feared so much? By Captain Lightfoot? No, that didn't seem likely, given all that was going on. Plus there were guards out front. Or had been until the bandits killed them.

Then it came to her. *Lieutenant Casey!* He was from the South, he'd been there, and Crowley trusted him. But the bastard was a spy . . . An enemy agent who'd been ordered to shoot the fort's CO at the height of the action, a moment when Tully and the rest of them were unlikely to notice the noise.

Mac wheeled, left the room, and returned to the com cave. "Sergeant Tully . . . get Captain Lightfoot on the horn. Tell him to find Lieutenant Casey and place him under arrest. Oh, and tell him that there's a very strong chance that Casey murdered the colonel. If so, he's dangerous."

Tully's eyes were huge. "Ma'am, yes, ma'am."

"And don't let anyone into the colonel's office," Mac added. "It's a crime scene." And with that, she left.

As Mac returned to the surface, she was greeted by the sight of two burning helicopters, people running to and fro, and a scattering of bodies. Most were bandits but not all . . . And that made her angry. *Very* angry. Someone was going to pay.

"There you are," Captain Lightfoot said, as he arrived. "You're serious? The colonel was murdered?"

"Yes," Mac replied. "And I think Casey did it."

"He's gone," Lightfoot told her. "He left in a Humvee. No one had any reason to stop him."

Did that amount to proof? No . . . But even if Casey wasn't a murderer, he was a deserter. "I'm assuming command," Mac said. "And I'm naming you as the acting XO. Have one of your platoon leaders contact the local police department and request assistance. Someone from the outside needs to conduct an investigation, and we don't have any CIC agents."

"Got it," Lightfoot replied. "And then?"

"And then we're going to find the new scout that Crowley told us about," Mac replied. "They had a plan. Was Casey in on it? If not, we're going to use it."

Lightfoot nodded. "That makes my fucking day . . . Let's do this thing."

CHAPTER 5

IIIIIIIIIIIIIIIIIIIIIIIIIIIIIIIIII

What goes around comes around.

—PROVERB

FORT HOOD, TEXAS

It was a nice day by postapocalyptic standards. That meant Victoria could leave her cold-weather gear in her condo. She was barely aware of the drive to work because her mind was on other things. Primary among them was the summons from the normally hands-off Colonel Oxley. According to Oxley's e-mail, he wanted to see her "regarding the Howard fiasco," and ". . . a new assignment."

Victoria had been reporting to Oxley for six months. On paper, at any rate. But in all truth, Victoria's orders came from Oxley's CO, which was to say her father. Now it seemed as though Oxley was going to get in her face. Something had changed. But *what*?

Victoria was approaching the gate by that time. She braked, waited for the line to jerk ahead, and had her ID at the ready when her turn came. An MP eyed it and took a step back. The salute was textbook perfect. Victoria returned it and drove into the fort. The III Corps headquarters building consisted of two squares and a central triangle.

Victoria parked behind the complex and made her way across the parking lot. After entering the building, Victoria had to show ID again before continuing on her way.

Oxley's office was three doors down the hall from her father's. Victoria glanced at her watch, confirmed that she had enough time for a side trip, and took a right instead of a left.

A well-worn carpet led her to a door that should have borne her father's name, rank, and title. The plaque was missing, and the door was locked. Mystery solved. Her father had been promoted, reassigned, or both. And because Bo's movements were classified, he hadn't been free to tell her.

So, Victoria thought to herself, as she did an about-face. *It looks like I'll have to take Oxley seriously.* She made her way to Oxley's office, went inside, and paused at the reception desk. "Major Macintyre to see Colonel Oxley."

The civilian clerk was a middle-aged man with a comb-over and a snippy manner. "The colonel is busy. Sit down. He'll see you when he's ready."

Victoria chose one of six empty chairs. Most of the New Confederacy continued to enjoy Internet service, and she was checking her e-mail when the clerk called her name. The door to Oxley's office was open. Victoria stepped inside and came to attention. "Major Macintyre, sir . . . Reporting as ordered."

Oxley was fortysomething and runner thin. His uniform looked as if it had been sprayed on. "At ease, Major . . . Have a seat."

"Thank you, sir."

"So," Oxley said, as he made a steeple with his fingers. "I read your report regarding the attack on Fort Carney. The fact that we had an agent on Colonel Crowley's staff led to a successful ambush. That part of the affair was well done."

Oxley smiled thinly. "Unfortunately, the rest of it was a full-on shit show. In response to Robert Howard's request, and *your* recommendation, we took part in the attack on Fort Carney. *Three* Black Hawk helicopters were lost along with their crews even though the pilots had the correct recognition signals. That's eighteen million predisaster dollars, Major . . . Never mind the lives lost. Howard doesn't care . . . But *I* do."

Oxley's comments had been carefully worded. At no point had he accused General Macintyre's daughter of being incompetent, but the implication was there. And Victoria was seething with anger. She'd been able to watch the attack via a drone circling above. And it *was* a shit show. Something she was forthright about in her report.

So what was the rehash about? Oxley wanted to throw his weight around and get back at the Macintyre family for the manner in which he'd been sidelined. Victoria was reminded of the old saying: *What goes around comes around.*

But Victoria had been forced to deal with pissy COs before and wasn't about to provide Oxley with a reason to write her up. "Yes, sir," Victoria said. "I understand."

"Good," Oxley said, as if an important understanding had been reached. "I'm glad we're on the same page. And there's no point in crying over spilled milk, is there?"

"No, sir."

"That's the spirit," Oxley said. "As I mentioned in my e-mail, we have a new assignment for you."

"What about Howard, sir?"

"Don't worry," Oxley replied. "We'll take care of him . . . But he won't be on the receiving end of any more helicopters."

The dig hurt, but Victoria kept her face blank. "Yes, sir. And the assignment?"

Oxley was enjoying himself. He leaned back in his chair. "You've been busy . . . So it's possible that you missed the news stories regarding the so-called Resistance. They've been killing our troops, blowing things up, and spreading antigovernment propaganda. They claim to be fighting for what they call 'a full restoration of the United States government,' but they're terrorists, pure and simple.

"So the decision was made to create a military counterterrorism team, and the folks in Houston chose *you* to lead the team." It wasn't clear whether Oxley approved of the choice, but Victoria suspected that he didn't.

"Everything you need to know is on this thumb drive," Oxley told her as he pushed a USB drive across the surface of his desk. "The material on it is classified, so take good care of it."

"Thank you," Victoria said, as she accepted the device. "Whom will I report to?"

Oxley produced a shit-eating grin. "That would be *me*, Major . . . I think we'll make an excellent team. Don't you agree?"

Victoria *didn't* agree, but nodded anyway. "Yes, sir."

"Good. Study the information on the drive and let me know if you have any questions."

Victoria knew a dismissal when she heard one and stood. "Yes, sir." She saluted, Oxley threw one in return, and Victoria left. What was the old saying? "If you can't take a joke, don't join the army?" It was true.

NEAR CASPER, WYOMING

The Flying H Ranch was located in the Rattlesnake Hills region west of Casper. And as the van bounced along a dirt road, Mac wondered why anyone would choose to live in such a desolate place.

Most of the terrain was rocky and cut by ravines. What grass there was stood in frozen tufts and seemed unlikely to support more than a few dozen cattle.

But that's where Sarah Huntington, the great-granddaughter of Fergus Huntington, had chosen to live. And she was the scout that Crowley had been working with prior to his death. So if Mac wanted to learn about Crowley's secret plan of attack, Huntington was the person to see.

That's why Mac and a small group of soldiers had chosen to travel in a civilian van. Assuming that Howard's spies weren't aware of Huntington, and her relationship with Crowley, Mac didn't want to tip them off.

Perkins swore as the van topped a rise, took to the air, and landed hard. Perkins was riding in back with Mac's RTO and two soldiers. "Damn it, Johnson . . . What's wrong with you? Slow down."

"Sorry, sir," Johnson said. But Mac was sitting next to the driver and noticed that he didn't *look* sorry. She smiled. Even though officers were in charge, and NCOs ran the army, privates could make life miserable for their superiors when they chose to.

Johnson braked as the road rounded the side of a hill—and passed a weather-faded sign. It was succinct if nothing else. TRESS-PASSERS WILL BE SHOT.

The road ran straight as an arrow after that, and Mac could see a cluster of trees ahead. They framed a yellow double-wide and a scattering of shabby outbuildings. Huntington's home? Yes. It was quite a comedown for the family that once owned a gold mine, lived in Huntington Lodge, and owned vast tracts of land.

How Huntington wound up on Crowley's radar wasn't clear . . . But, while trolling through Crowley's laptop, Mac came across her name under CONTACTS, and the note that went with it: "New scout/ Operation Payback." But it was password protected. And that meant Mac would have to talk with Huntington if she wanted to learn about Operation Payback.

The van came to a stop. The old four-by-four pickup parked in front of the house suggested that Huntington was home. If so, she was in no hurry to come out and welcome uninvited guests. Mac didn't blame her. Not with the horde roaming the land. "Stay in the van," Mac instructed as she opened the door.

It was cold outside—and Mac could see her breath. There were boot prints in the snow . . . Plus a lot of paw prints. Mac felt the hairs on the back of her neck rise. She was being watched. That's how it felt. And as she looked around, Mac saw them. Dogs . . . At least a dozen of them. Some of the mutts were sitting with tongues lolling out of their mouths. Others were crouched, as if prepared to attack, and one lay on its side as if waiting for her to scratch his tummy. Vapor misted the air around its snout.

Mac's carbine was in the van—but her pistol was holstered on her vest. Could she draw and fire in time? No. Her heart was beating like a trip-hammer. "Ms. Huntington?" Mac shouted. "My name's Macintyre . . . *Captain* Macintyre. Colonel Crowley was murdered. I found your name on his computer. I'd like to talk to you about Robert Howard."

Seconds passed. Mac heard a noise and turned to see a person roll out from under the pickup truck. She stood and took a moment to brush snow and ice off her clothes. One by one, the dogs gathered around her. One of them growled. "Are you Sarah Huntington?" Mac inquired.

"Yes," the woman answered. Huntington appeared to be in her fifties because of her sun-ravaged skin, but she could have been younger. Her hair hung down in braids, and she was wearing a duster. "Say your piece."

Mac saw that Huntington was holding a long-barreled revolver down along the outside surface of her right thigh. It was pointed at the ground but could come up in a hurry. "You were working with Colonel Crowley to finalize a plan called Operation Payback. Maybe that plan has been compromised. If not, I'd like to use it. Howard is a murderer, a thief, and a slaver. Plus he took prisoners in the town of Wright . . . *Female* prisoners. We might be able to save them."

Huntington's hand moved, and the pistol seemed to jump into the cross-draw holster on her belt. "Show me some ID."

Mac produced her card, gave it over, and watched Huntington scan it. "Okay," the scout said. "Your soldiers can leave the van . . . The dogs won't hurt them."

Mac turned to the van and gave a thumbs-up. Doors opened, and her troops got out. Then, on an order from Perkins, they deployed with their backs to the vehicle.

Mac turned back to Huntington. "Did you know that Crowley had been murdered?"

Huntington nodded. "Yes, I did."

"The police told you?"

"No."

"Then how did you find out?"

"Follow me," Huntington said, and walked away. Mac followed her to one of the sheds out behind the house. Smoke dribbled out of a metal stovepipe.

"This is my smokehouse," Huntington announced as she opened the door, and Mac followed her inside. Big chunks of meat hung from hooks. Mac was about to ask, "Why did you bring me here?" when Huntington pointed to a carcass. "*That's* how I knew Crowley was dead."

The light was dim, and the air was thick with drifting smoke, so it took a moment for Mac to recognize Lieutenant Casey. He was nude and hanging head down. Large chunks of flesh had been

ripped from his body. "The bastard is heavy," Huntington com-
mented. "But a buck weighs even more. That's where the chain
hoist comes in." It was said matter-of-factly, one woman to another.

Mac was aghast. "What happened to him?"

"He came for me," Huntington said. "And the dogs tore him
up. I called them off, but it was too late by then. He bled out."

"But why store the body in *here*?" Mac inquired.

"Where else would I put it?" Huntington countered. "I couldn't
go to the police, not without alerting Howard to my involvement,
and the ground is frozen. I'll bury him in the spring."

They left the smokehouse. Huntington's story made sense. Not
that Mac cared. Huntington could use Casey for dog food as far
as she was concerned. "Did Casey know about Operation Payback?"

"No," Huntington said. "He didn't."

"Good. What *is* the plan? And could it work?"

It took Huntington three or four minutes to explain. Once she
was finished, Mac couldn't help but smile. "I like it. Are you still
willing to sign on?"

Their eyes met. "Howard is like a cancer that needs to be cut
out," Huntington answered. "Plus, if we free those prisoners, then
so much the better. And there's one more thing."

"Which is?"

"That bastard is camped in my granddaddy's lodge. That pisses
me off."

SPRING HILL, TENNESSEE

President Sloan was in Fort Knox, Kentucky, working on a speech.
That's what the press had been told. It wasn't true, however. After
weeks of grinding warfare, the Union Army had been able to advance

a few miles. Reporters were calling it "the Battle of Spring Hill." That was the sort of victory that Sloan had been hungering for. And rather than simply read the reports and watch battle footage, he had decided to visit the battlefield.

No one liked the idea, especially the Secret Service, which was understandably worried about putting the president down so close to the front lines. But Sloan was insistent. So under the cover of darkness, he'd been flown to Murfreesboro, given a uniform to wear, and helicoptered out to the battlefield. General Hern had been notified, but no one else knew. And rather than lay on extra security, which might alert the rebs, Secret Service Director Jenkins was keeping everything low-key.

That's why no one other than Hern, his adjutant, and a squad of special ops troops were on hand to welcome "Major" Sloan when he landed. Once he was clear of the LZ, Sloan saw occasional flashes along the horizon—and heard a series of thumps as artillery rounds detonated. The Battle of Spring Hill might be over, but the war wasn't.

The still-rising sun was hidden by a thick layer of clouds as the two men shook hands. Hern was a big man. Not fat, just big. The general didn't have a neck so far as Sloan could discern, which made it appear as if his head were perched on his shoulders.

And jutting out over a pugnacious jaw was the unlit cigar that Hern was so famous for. When a reporter asked him about the stogie, Hern replied, "I'm going to light that son of a bitch when we enter Houston," and Sloan hoped that day would come soon. "Good morning, Mr. President," Hern said. "Thanks for coming."

Hern didn't want him there, and Sloan knew that. It was a nice thing to say, however . . . And Sloan smiled. "Thank you, General . . . And congratulations."

"I'll pass that on to the troops," Hern promised. "They fought well."

Sloan nodded. "How bad is the butcher's bill?"

"We don't have a final count yet," Hern answered. "But according to the preliminary figures, we lost 6,241 soldiers. Another 11,748 were wounded. Some won't make it."

The numbers were high. Higher than Sloan thought they'd be. What had the Duke of Wellington said? "Compared to a battle lost, the greatest misery is a battle won." Or something like that. "And the rebs? They were Americans, too."

"Some were," Hern conceded. "But something new has come to light. The Confederates are using Mexican mercenaries as cannon fodder. That's one of the reasons why we won . . . Our forces attacked the section of the line that the mercs were in charge of. They fought bravely, but most were poorly trained."

Mercenaries . . . Bought and paid for with revenue from America's oil reserves! Sloan had been forced to rely on mercs during the early days of the war. But that practice had been discontinued shortly after the debacle in Richton, Mississippi. He felt sorry for *all* of the dead soldiers, regardless of which side they'd been fighting for. "Show me. I want to see."

They got in a Humvee, followed by other Humvees, and drove away. The route took them down a country road and past a burned-out minimart.

As they drove along, Sloan saw an artillery piece that was pointed at the sky, a row of body bags awaiting pick up, and the arrows that pathfinders had spray painted onto walls. All of the images were tiles in a ghastly mosaic Sloan would never forget.

The Humvee left the road at that point, bounced through a drainage ditch, and entered a field. It looked as though an artillery shell had landed among a herd of cows. Their mangled bodies lay in concentric circles liked the petals of an obscene flower.

Tires fought for purchase as the driver directed the vehicle uphill.

They passed a group of rebel prisoners before arriving on the top of the hill. "This is as far forward as we can go," Hern said. "But the view is pretty good."

Once outside, Sloan saw that the view *was* pretty good. Or pretty bad . . . depending on how one chose to look at it. Hern gave Sloan a pair of binoculars. As he brought them up to his eyes, Sloan saw a clump of shattered trees, some hastily dug earthworks, and a clutch of fire-blackened vehicles. Way off in the distance, a soldier could be seen. He was carrying a buddy on his back as he trudged south. *Victory,* Sloan thought to himself. *This is what victory looks like.* He gave the binoculars back. "Thank you, General. It isn't pretty . . . But I'm glad I came."

CASPER, WYOMING

It was just past 0700, and Mac was standing atop Fort Carney's defensive wall, looking north toward the city of Buffalo and what Robert Howard called "the High Fort." A chilly breeze stung her cheeks—and ruffled her hair. Mac responded by ramming her hands even deeper into her pockets. She was in a bind.

After reporting Crowley's death, word had come down that a new commanding officer would arrive at Fort Carney in seven days. Meanwhile, assuming that Howard's prisoners hadn't already been auctioned off, that could happen at any time. Never mind whatever cruelties they were forced to endure in the meantime.

There was something else to consider as well. What if the new CO refused to act on the Crowley-Huntington plan? And that was more likely than not. Even the most aggressive officer would want to get acquainted with their new command before launching an attack on the warlord of warlords.

Plus, since the battalion had lost almost fifty people during the last week, the new CO might very well wait for reinforcements before heading north. All of which argued in favor of launching the attack *immediately*, before anyone could tell her not to.

On the other hand, Mac knew that folks up the chain of command expected her to sit tight even if they hadn't issued specific orders to that effect. So if she went after Howard on her own, and things went wrong, they'd hang her out to dry. What to do?

Mac remembered the guilt-ridden man she'd spoken to in the town of Wright. The man who had committed suicide in front of her. What was his granddaughter's name? Sissy? Yes. Was Sissy worth risking her career for? Yes. And time was short.

It took the rest of the day and some of the night to get organized. Mac couldn't justify taking more than one company after the attack on the fort. And, since Charlie Company was in the best shape, she chose it for the task. Bravo Company's platoon leaders were pissed . . . But that couldn't be helped.

So at 0200, a fueler, plus fourteen Strykers and 108 soldiers left Fort Carney on a mission that was almost guaranteed to produce a stunning victory or a terrible defeat. As the convoy drove west on Highway 20, doubts plagued Mac's mind as they passed through Natrona, Shoshoni, and veered north to Thermopolis. From there it was a short trip to Worland and Highway 16 east.

By the time 0445 rolled around, Mac knew they were deep inside horde-occupied territory. The fact that they'd been able to travel that far without being forced to fight was thanks to good luck, the early hour, and complete secrecy. Only Mac and Lightfoot knew where the convoy was headed—although the troops could guess by then.

Mac felt an emptiness in her gut as they cleared Worland and continued east. The first part of the mission was over—but the most dangerous section lay ahead. Mac had chosen to ride in the lead vehicle. It was an ESV Stryker with a dozer blade mounted up front. She ducked down into the cargo area below. The air was warm and heavy with the smell of hydraulic fluid. Her RTO sat up straight. "Send *this* message on *this* frequency," Mac told him.

Worsky accepted the piece of paper, made the necessary adjustment to his radio, and spoke into his mike. "Starlight to Star Bright . . . We cleared Worland. Over."

The reply consisted of two clicks. That meant Huntington had received the scrambled message, understood it, and was waiting. Mac felt a sense of relief. Thank God. The whole plan would have gone up in smoke had the civilian scout been intercepted or killed.

Fifteen minutes later, Mac was standing in the hatch, struggling to stay warm, when the vehicle rounded a curve. Lights appeared in the distance, and Mac knew they were approaching the town of Ten Sleep. Huntington claimed that Ten Sleep had been a favorite with tourists prior to the May Day disaster. Now it was home to fifty or sixty bandits who were stationed there to protect Howard's southwestern flank and collect taxes from travelers.

The outlaws were a threat in and of themselves, of course . . . But the greater danger lay in the possibility that they would tip Howard off to the convoy's presence.

Even though the sun hadn't cleared the horizon, there was enough light to see by as Mac raised her binoculars. Barricades to channel vehicles through a checkpoint had been put in place. "This is Bravo-Six," Mac said. "One-one and one-two will pull over to the side of the road. One-three and one-four will engage the position ahead. Hit them *hard*, people . . . And take that antenna out immediately. Execute."

Mac was thrown sideways as the ESV swerved to the right and stopped. One-two turned left and pulled over. That cleared the way for one-three and one-four to advance side by side. One-three, AKA **OL' SLAB SIDES**, was equipped with a 105mm cannon. Mac heard a loud boom and saw a bright flash as a shell hit the checkpoint. "Good morning, assholes," the Stryker's driver said. "Eat lead!"

"That will be enough of that," Captain Lightfoot said from his position at the tail end of the convoy. "Cut the crap. Over." Mac grinned and knew that everyone else in the convoy was grinning, too.

One-four was armed with a 40mm grenade launcher, and it chugged away as the vic called **LUCKY LOU** closed in on the concrete barriers. A steady stream of grenades swept left to right across the enemy checkpoint. The overlapping explosions threw bodies into the air.

SLAB SIDES jerked to a halt, its gunner sent another round downrange, and Mac saw a flash as it hit the thirty-foot-tall com mast. That was followed by a loud bang. The top half of the antenna crashed onto the top of the thirty-foot trailer parked beside the highway. An office perhaps? Or a ready room? Mac hoped so. She keyed her mike. "Nice shooting, one-three . . . All right, get some troops in there and mop up. Over."

Two squads left their Strykers and made their way forward. Mac heard firing and a series of bangs as more grenades went off. A lieutenant named Swanson was in charge—and she called in five minutes later. "This is Charlie-Two . . . The area has been secured. Twelve bandits are down—and about ten got away. One of my soldiers was wounded, but the doc says he'll make it. Over."

Mac swore. Some bad guys were on the loose and, if they had the right kind of radio, were talking to Howard. And even if they couldn't, the survivors would send a messenger to the High Fort in order to warn him. But that was to be expected. The race was on. "Roger that, Charlie-Two. Well done. Pull back and mount up. We're out of here. Over."

Mac ducked down into the cargo compartment. "Worsky . . . Send this message on the same frequency as the last one."

Worsky accepted the slip of paper and read the words aloud. "Starlight to Star Bright . . . We're leaving Ten Sleep. Over."

Mac listened for the clicks, heard them, and felt the ESV jerk ahead. She went forward to speak with the driver. "Watch for a flashlight on the left. It will blink three times. Stop when you see it—but warn the rest of the column first."

The truck commander was named Castel. He kept his eyes on the road. "Yes, ma'am."

Mac went up top. The sun was higher but hadn't cleared the mountains. Five minutes dragged by as Mac waited. Then she saw it! A blink followed by two more. Huntington was waiting at the point where a dirt road met the highway.

Castel put out a call to the other TCs and braked. As the ESV came to a stop, Huntington climbed up onto the vic. She was carrying a scope-mounted rifle and a light pack. "Good morning, Captain. You're right on time."

"So far so good," Mac said. "Hang on."

Then, to Castel, "Hit the gas and turn left. Let's get off the highway."

"Bravo-Six actual to Charlie-Six . . . We need to clear the highway without being seen. If you see a vehicle, destroy it."

It was a cold-blooded order, and one that might cause completely innocent people to die. But Mac had 107 other lives to preserve, prisoners to free, and a scumbag to kill. Did that make it okay? No, it didn't. And Mac knew that if Lightfoot was forced to obey her order, it would haunt her forever.

Seconds turned into five incredibly long minutes punctuated by a burp of static. "This is Charlie-Six. The last vehicle cleared the highway. No vehicles passed in either direction. Over."

Mac felt a tremendous sense of relief. "This is Bravo-Six. Roger that . . . Once your vehicle is hidden, send a squad back to clear our tracks. Over."

Mac knew Lightfoot would understand. It was just a matter of time before Howard learned about the attack in Ten Sleep. But if he didn't know where the column was, he'd have to send people to find it. That meant a large contingent of bandits would be ordered to block Highway 16 west of Buffalo—and that would reduce the number of men available to defend the High Fort. "This is Bravo-Six actual . . . All units will stop. Bring the fueler forward. TCs will top off their tanks. Over."

The column came to a halt, and it wasn't long before the tank truck pulled up level with one-one. Once the lead ESV was fueled, it pulled forward so that one-two could take its place, and so on until all of the Strykers had full tanks. And that was important because it would be disastrous if any one of them ran out of gas during the final phase of the attack. In the meantime, each squad had a short bio break. The entire process consumed thirty precious minutes but was absolutely necessary.

Finally, assured that the company's tracks had been obliterated a full fifty feet back from the highway, Mac told Castel to get under way. The ESV jerked ahead, forcing Huntington to hang on or fall off. The scout had been invited to ride down below, but she wanted to see, and Mac couldn't blame her.

Before long, the dirt road narrowed to one lane, and the company entered the Bighorn National Forest. An alpine meadow lay to the left, with a lightly treed slope on the right and craggy mountains in the distance.

Eventually, they came to a Y in the road. Huntington was crouched next to Mac. "Stay to the right!" she shouted, and pointed. Mac relayed the message to Castel. And that's how the next hour was spent. The scout would point the way, and the column would follow along.

Most of the roads weren't maintained. So there were times when the Strykers had to power through creeks, circle around washouts, and crash through thickets of saplings to proceed. They passed an old log cabin at one point—and a rusty pickup half a mile later. But there was no traffic. And for that, Mac was grateful.

That didn't mean they were safe from observation, however. Howard was no fool . . . The ex–Green Beret would have lookouts up high somewhere. Mac's train of thought was interrupted as the ESV topped a rise, and Huntington raised a fist. "Stop here."

Mac gave the order, and the Stryker came to a stop. Huntington dropped to the ground, walked a few yards, and pointed at the ground. "Here it is! Just like I told you it would be!"

Mac felt a rising sense of excitement as she lowered herself to the ground and went to join the scout. And sure enough . . . There they were. Two rusty rails! "The main line used to run south from Buffalo, around the mountains, and up to Sheridan," Huntington explained. "But the trains stopped running when my great-grandfather's gold mine played out. And eventually they built Highway 16 over part of the line. We need to follow the old right-of-way for two miles . . . That's where we'll run into the spur that leads to the mine."

"And the mine is located *under* the lodge," Mac added.

"That's correct," Huntington agreed. "When the mine closed, my great-grandfather went into the cattle business, did well, and built his home over the mine. So all we have to do is follow the track in and *boom*! We win."

Mac knew it wouldn't be so simple but smiled anyway. "Okay, let's get going."

Once the women were aboard, Castel lowered the ESV's dozer

blade and angled it to the right. One-two's driver angled his blade the other way. And with the rest of the column tagging along behind, they turned onto the track.

Mac had done her homework and knew that the Strykers could straddle the narrow-gauge tracks with room to spare. And by mowing the brush down, the lead vehicles could clear the way for the vics following behind them.

The ESV shook, and gear rattled as the Stryker bumped over a long succession of railroad ties. But that was the price to be paid if they were going to close in on Howard. The spur was right where Huntington said it would be, and the company turned east. Now they were west of the High Fort and aimed directly at it. "Two miles," Huntington announced. "Then we'll enter the tunnel."

That was the moment when three F-111 fighter-bombers appeared from the south and began to circle. Mac saw them, as did a dozen other people, all of whom tried to report at the same time. "This is Bravo-Six actual," Mac said. "I see them. Worsky . . . Get on the horn. Contact the zoomies. Tell them to hold off . . . There are hostages on the ground. Over."

"Roger that," the RTO replied from inside the ESV.

Mac's mind was racing. She hadn't requested the fighters . . . So who sent them? Some REMF at Fort Knox? In retribution for the attack on Fort Carney? Probably.

If so, that was on her since rather than request permission for a raid on the ground, and have her request denied, Mac had chosen to proceed on her own. Shit! What if prisoners died? It would be *her* fault!

"This is Bravo-Ten," Worsky said. "The F-111s belong to the rebs! Some guy told me to fuck myself."

Mac swore as the lead plane completed a wide turn and dived. "Step on it Castel! We need to reach the tunnel and fast!"

The ESV was already making pretty good time given the conditions, but the TC put his foot down. Mac's teeth rattled as the big tires bumped across ancient railroad ties. "Bravo-Six to all units . . . Pick up the pace! Stand by to repel aircraft. Fire at will."

The order to fire was largely meaningless since the only AA capability the Strykers had were the light machine guns mounted on the top of each vic. Mac turned hers toward an incoming plane as rockets flared off its wings and cannon shells ripped through a stand of trees to the north. Mac saw a flash of light out of the corner of her eye and turned to see a Stryker explode. "Keep going!" Lightfoot yelled from his position at the tail end of the column. "Push the wreckage out of the way!"

Mac looked up, fully expecting to see another F-111 coming straight in. But, rather than attack Charlie Company the way she expected them to, the other jets were focused on a target in the distance. She heard a thud, followed by a boom, and saw smoke billow up into the sky. Were the planes dropping bombs on the High Fort? Yes! But *why*?

Then it came to her . . . Maybe someone from Ten Sleep had been able to alert Howard. Or, given his alliance with the Confederacy, maybe the column had been spotted from orbit!

The exact mechanism didn't matter. What mattered was that unlike the Union and Fort Carney, Howard didn't give a shit about the High Fort, or the prisoners located there . . . He was a nomad . . . Or a renegade playing the part of a nomad. And, rather than surrender his headquarters to the Union, he preferred to destroy the old building. *And* the Strykers. A victory even the Khan would admire. "There it is!" Huntington exclaimed. *"The tunnel!"*

Mac turned, saw that the entrance was guarded by a pair of rotting doors, and told Castel to break through them. Then she grabbed Huntington's arm and pulled the scout toward the hatch.

They tumbled into the cargo compartment as the bulldozer blade struck wood. The impact threw Mac into Worsky, and they wound up in a tangle of arms and legs as the Stryker broke through. Once Mac was on her feet, she turned to the hatch. "Don't go up there," Huntington warned. "There's less than a foot of clearance."

"We lost the remote-weapons station," Castel added, as the ESV bounced over a chunk of wood. Mac winced. So much for her planning. If the ESV's primary weapon was gone, others would be lost, too.

Worsky had recovered by then, and Mac took his mike. "Bravo-Six to Charlie-Six. Give me a sitrep. Over."

There was a pause followed by the sound of an unfamiliar voice. "Vic three-four didn't make it Bravo-Six . . . They took a direct hit. The rest of the column entered the tunnel."

Mac felt the ESV come to a sudden stop as she struggled to assimilate the news. At least ten people were dead, including Captain Lightfoot, who'd been riding drag. It took an act of will to keep her voice steady. "Roger that, over. Charlie-Three will use a squad to secure the entrance to the tunnel. All other units will prepare to deploy . . . Over."

After returning the mike to Worsky, Mac went forward to speak with Castel. But there was no need. She could see the cave-in on the screen in front of him. "Drop the ramp . . . I'm going out."

Mac heard the whine of hydraulics as she made her way toward the rear of the vehicle. Was there enough room to get past the cave-in? If so, she could take the entire company through the gap. If not, they'd have to exit through the west entrance. That would take them back the way they'd come—and it would take forever to find a way up over the ridge.

Mac made her way down the ramp, with Worsky and Huntington right behind her. As soon as she cleared the ESV, Mac turned east. There was very little room between the Stryker and the wall. That meant the officer had to turn sideways in order to get through.

Once Mac arrived at the front end of the vic, things opened up. She was wearing her helmet and night-vision gear but had no need of it yet. The cave-in was easy to see thanks to the glare from the Stryker's headlights. Mac eyed the pile of dirt, rock, and broken timbers, looking for a passageway. She didn't see one at first. But up top, and off to the right, she saw what looked like a hole.

After climbing up the pile of debris, Mac confirmed that yes, there was a way through, and allowed herself to slide back down. Worsky was waiting at the bottom of the slope. "Get on the horn . . . Tell Charlie-Three to remain where he is. Tell the rest of the company to shed everything except their combat gear and follow me."

Worsky was relaying her instructions as Mac and Huntington scrambled up the slope and wiggled through the hole and into the darkness beyond. The tunnel assumed a greenish hue as Mac turned the night-vision gear on—and Huntington was using a penlight to find her way. The rusty tracks led them east. Water dripped from the ceiling, and Mac was forced to splash through a series of puddles.

It wasn't long before Mac spotted blobs of light up ahead. As she got closer, Mac realized that they were holes in the wooden doors that protected the east end of the tunnel. They were a problem, but a relatively minor one. Her people could blow them open if necessary.

The larger issue was Howard . . . Where was he? Miles away? Laughing as the rebs bombed her? Maybe. But Mac didn't think so. She stopped as soldiers ran forward to deal with the doors. Huntington was standing next to her. "Tell me about the lodge, Sarah . . . Does it have a basement?"

"No," the scout answered. "But the doors open onto an old trestle that leads to the mine. And it's located under the lodge."

"Is it possible to enter the mine from the lodge?"

"Yes. Immediately after the lodge was converted into a hotel, the owners installed a spiral staircase in one of the air shafts. The staff took guests down for tours."

That's where he is, Mac thought to herself. *Waiting for the bombing to stop. Then he plans to come out and ride away.*

Maybe her theory was accurate, and maybe it wasn't. It didn't matter. Because if the warlord of warlords was gone, then the battle was over. But if the bastard was there, waiting for her, then it was important to be prepared. A sergeant yelled, "Get back!" and the women obeyed.

Then a private shouted, *"Fire in the hole!"* and pressed a button. That produced a flash of light, a loud boom, and a cloud of dust. As a hole appeared, the horde opened fire from the opposite side of the canyon. The hail of machine-gun bullets sent everyone scuttling for cover. *He's there all right,* Mac concluded. *That's why the mine is so well defended.*

From her position against the left wall, Mac could look up and see smoke billowing up from what remained of the High Fort. But that was irrelevant. *Focus,* Mac told herself, and shifted her gaze to the trestle. She turned to find Worsky standing there. "Put out a call for every AT4 we have. Get 'em up here."

While the RTO took care of that, Mac spoke over her radio. "Bravo-Six to Charlie-One . . . We're going to put rockets into the entrance. Then we're going across. Get ready. Over."

Lieutenant Kevin Tyler, AKA Charlie-One, was a platoon leader. His delivery was matter-of-fact. "This is One. Roger that. Over."

Mac grinned. She'd been a platoon leader and knew how Tyler felt. Scared, excited, and sick to his stomach. None of which could be allowed to show.

Bullets raked the entrance to the tunnel as three soldiers arrived.

Each was carrying *two* single-use AT4s. "Take cover!" Mac shouted. "And put your rockets into the tunnel on the far side of the canyon."

One of the men took up a position behind a rusty ore car, another knelt next to a pile of timbers, and the third chose to stand just inside the mouth of the tunnel. All three of them fired. Two of the rockets sailed into the hole and exploded. The force of the explosions blew smoke and dust out over the ravine.

The third rocket was high. It hit a spot over the entrance to the mine and detonated. That produced a small avalanche of rock and dirt. The curtain of debris continued to fall as volley two went home. Mac was already running by the time the explosions were heard. "Follow me!" she yelled, and hoped that someone would.

The heavy machine guns had fallen silent. But some of the bandits were not only alive but firing assault weapons, as Mac made her way forward. It would have been nice to fire back. But the two-foot gaps between the railroad ties meant that it was necessary to look down or risk a fall.

Bullets buzzed like angry bees, tore chunks out of the wooden bridge, and took some of the soldiers down. Mac heard a scream but couldn't look back. Fortunately, Charlie Company's snipers were hard at work smoking targets from the west side of the canyon. And that gave the soldiers on the trestle a chance to make it.

Mac tripped, fell onto a tie, and lost her carbine. And that's where she was when a rocket hit the bridge behind her, blowing a hole in it, as an F-111 screamed overhead. Mac looked back over her shoulder. At least a third of the company had been cut off!

A bullet snapped past Worsky's head as he reached down to give her a hand. The fuzz-faced kid was a hard-assed soldier now. "Stop lying down on the job. We aren't there yet."

Mac couldn't help but laugh even if it sounded hysterical. Mac crossed the rest of the trestle with two dozen troops. The entrance to the mine yawned in front of her, and there was a quick flurry of shots as Union soldiers flooded the tunnel.

Now they were in the area that had been targeted earlier. Bodies, and parts of bodies were strewn all about, and the soil was wet with blood. Mac accidentally stepped on a hand and heard a groan. The bandit's guts were hanging out. She shouted for a medic and knelt beside him. "Howard . . . Where is Howard?"

His eyes blinked rapidly. "I'm going to die again," the bandit said. "My brothers are waiting."

"That's nice," Mac said heartlessly. "Where's Howard? The Khan wants to speak with him."

The man squinted up at her. "The strong room . . . Where the gold was kept."

A medic arrived as Mac stood. Lieutenant Tyler was waiting a few feet away. "Let's find the strong room," Mac said. "And be careful."

Tyler sent soldiers deeper into the mine, and Mac followed, with Huntington at her side. A spiral staircase appeared on the right, and the strong room was just beyond. It was labeled STRONG ROOM for the benefit of hotel guests—and protected by a rust-pitted iron door. Mac turned to Tyler. "Blow it."

It took the better part of five minutes to get people positioned and set the charge. It went off with a bang, the door sagged open, and smoke eddied. At least a dozen weapons were pointed at the person who emerged. She was a thin slip of a girl. Robert Howard was there, too . . . With an arm wrapped around her chest and a pistol to her head. He said, "Back off," and pulled the revolver's hammer back to full cock. "And I mean *now*."

Mac's eyes were on the girl, or more specifically on the girl's face. She saw determination there . . . And that's as far as the thought went before the hostage allowed herself to sag. That exposed part of Howard's head. Mac was reaching for her pistol when Huntington's six-shooter left its holster. The .45 produced a loud boom, and a chunk of Howard's head flew off. The warlord's eyes went blank, his body swayed, and he collapsed.

The girl turned to look. She nodded and turned back again. "Thanks."

"You're welcome," Huntington said, as the Colt slid into its holster. "Some things need killing. He was one of them."

Mac's hand was on her pistol. She allowed it to fall. The warlord of warlords was dead . . . But what about his prisoners? "The people from the town of Wright," Mac said. "Did they survive? And if so, where are they?"

"*I'm* from Wright," the girl answered. "And yes, most of us survived. Come . . . I'll show you."

As they made their way deeper into the mine, the girl explained that the prisoners had been brought down into the mine when the planes arrived. And sure enough, there they were, all penned up behind a chain-link fence. They cheered when they saw the girl, and Tyler sent soldiers forward to free them. "I'm looking for a girl named Sissy," Mac told them. "Is she here?"

"I'm Sissy," a girl in a ragged dress said shyly. She looked to be seven or eight and was standing next to a young woman.

"I met your grandfather," Mac said, "just before he died. 'Tell Sissy I love her.' That's what he said. And I promised I would."

That was a lie, of course . . . But some lies are better than the truth. Tears ran down Sissy's face as Mac turned away. The cost had been high. But a battle had been fought—and a battle had been won.

CHAPTER 6

||||||||||||||||||||||||||||||||||

Politics have no relation to morals.

—NICCOLÒ MACHIAVELLI

FORT KNOX, KENTUCKY

Sloan was lying on his back, staring at the wedge of light that was leaking out through the bathroom door. And, even though she shouldn't be, Beth Morgan was sleeping next to him. They weren't going to have sex. Not while she was working on the Pickett story. That's what she'd told him, and that's what he had agreed to. Yet there they were . . . And Sloan knew that the decision to renew his relationship with Beth was a horrible mistake. Not just because of the ethical problems involved, but because Beth was *still* OCD and *still* a pain in the ass.

But what to do? The reporter was working on a story that, if true, would destroy Senator Pickett's candidacy. What would happen if he dumped her? Would Beth seek revenge? Of course she would. What was the saying? *Hell hath no fury like a woman scorned.*

Sloan cursed his own weakness. *You shouldn't have gone to bed with her, and she shouldn't have gone to bed with you.* Both statements were true . . . And both were meaningless. What was, was.

Hang in there, Sloan told himself. *The FBI investigation is nearly complete. If the proof is there, Beth will break the story, and the public will learn that the Confederacy is feeding money to Pickett. Once the truth is out, you can back out of the relationship slowly, and everything will be fine.*

It felt good to have a plan, and Sloan fell asleep. When he awoke, it was to find that Beth was gone, a lipstick kiss was centered on his mirror, and his shirts had been reorganized. And not just tidied up but hung according to type and color. Sloan knew that was just the beginning. If Beth were allowed to, she would apply the same degree of precision to every aspect of his life. He sighed.

After a shave and a shower, Sloan got dressed and left his underground quarters for the brightly lit executive dining room down the hall. It had all the charm of a military prison. But his breakfast was waiting, along with the news summary that Wendy Chow's staff prepared each day. The first item grabbed his attention. The subhead read: WARLORD OF WARLORDS KILLED IN RAID.

Sloan was painfully aware of the fact that Robert Howard had sent assassins to kill him and had come close to getting the job done. He was also aware of the fact that some of the Whigs claimed the assassination attempt was an indication of how unpopular he was. A thinly veiled call for him to resign.

Sloan sipped his coffee and began to read. He hadn't gotten far when a familiar name popped up. Captain Robin Macintyre! The officer who led a convoy of Strykers deep into rebel-held territory in order to rescue him. He could still see the amused smile on her face. And something else, too. Interest? Maybe. But no more than that. It would take a lot to impress a woman like Mac. More than a title.

Sloan read on. It seemed that Macintyre's CO had been murdered by a rebel spy. Rather than sit around and wait for a new commanding officer to arrive, she went looking for Robert Howard, found him, and released thirty-two hostages. All while the Confederate Air Force dropped bombs on her. Where the hell had the Union's interceptors been? Sloan made a note to look into that.

Robert Howard's death was, according to the reporter who had written the story, more than a victory. It was a sign that the administration's efforts to restore order in the wake of the May Day disaster were working. That put a smile on Sloan's face.

Sloan placed a call to Chief of Staff Chow, told her what he wanted to do, and hung up the phone. His breakfast was good.

CASPER, WYOMING

Mac was exhausted and for good reason. Two days had been spent chasing the surviving members of Robert Howard's horde. Many were captured, some were killed, and a few got away. But even if a dozen bandits were still on the loose, the people of northern Wyoming were free from Howard's tyranny.

But nature abhors a vacuum. And if Mac wasn't careful, some other warlord would move in to take Howard's place. So before she could return to Fort Carney, she had to establish a forward operating base just outside of Buffalo and bring Alpha Company up to man it. That took two days.

Then it was time to return to Casper. And there, much to her surprise, was Crowley's replacement. Colonel Marcus Owen was young for his rank and raring to go. He wanted to review every roster, eyeball the supplies he was being asked to sign for, and personally verify the money in petty cash. All of which was appropriate, and all of which required assistance from Mac.

Once those chores had been taken care of, Owen turned his attention to the troops. Mac was relieved to discover that he didn't share Crowley's suspicions where the Southerners were concerned—and wanted to make sure that those who deserved recognition would get it.

That meant Mac had to write up recommendations for a dozen medals and, in the case of those who had been killed, letters of condolence that would go to their loved ones. One such letter would be sent to Mrs. Lightfoot, who'd run off with a man from town and hadn't been seen since.

All of those activities took time. So now, a full week after her return, Mac still felt tired. The duty runner found her drinking black coffee in Bravo Company's command shack. Owen's style was a lot more laid-back then his predecessor's had been. "I have news for you," the note said. "Drop by when you can."

Mac thanked the runner and let him go. What sort of news did Owen have? Good news? As in, "Reinforcements are on the way." Or *bad* news? As in, "No replacement Strykers are available." There was only one way to find out.

After emptying her cup, Mac made her way across the compound to the underground command center. Two sentries were on duty and, even though they knew the XO, were still required to check her ID.

Once that was accomplished, Mac walked down the ramp, took a left, and made her way to what had been Crowley's office. The rawhide curtain had been replaced by a wood door. It was ajar. Mac knocked and heard Owen say, "Come in."

She was about to come to attention when Owen waved the formality off. His head was shaved, his skin was brown, and he had perfect teeth. They were on full display when he smiled. "Take a load off, Robin . . . Thanks for all the hard work. Just for the record, I tried to keep you, but the brass said no."

It took a moment for the words to sink in. The assignment had been temporary. A way to plug an organizational hole. And now, in the wake of Howard's death, Colonel Granger wanted her back. "I see," Mac said. "Thanks for the vote of confidence."

Owen shrugged. "A lot of good it did. But that's to be expected. You're a hero now, and all over the news. That's the other thing . . . You have orders to swing by Fort Knox on your way to Murfreesboro. The president wants to thank you."

"The president?" Mac remembered the man with mud on his face and the pain in his eyes. The attempt to establish an airhead in Richton had been a mistake. *Sloan's* mistake. But he'd been there, fighting shoulder to shoulder with the Rangers, many of whom died for him. And for their country. She would never forget that.

"Yes," Owen said. "The president. And the press will have a field day. You pulled Sloan's ass out of Richton, then you smoked the warlord who was trying to kill him. I'm no reporter, but that sounds like one helluva good story to me."

Mac had zero media-relations experience, and knew it would be easy to say the wrong thing. "I would prefer to join my battalion, sir. That's where I can make a difference."

Owen laughed. "Nice try, Robin . . . But if the commander in chief wants to see you, then guess what? He's going to see you.

"Oh, and there's one more thing . . . You're scheduled to meet with a *New York Times* reporter at 1100. I'd send our PA officer with you, but we're still waiting for a replacement. One who doesn't work for the enemy."

Mac left Owen's office with a new set of orders and a feeling of dread. But the interview with reporter Molly Thomas wasn't as bad as Mac feared. Most of the journalist's questions were of the sort that could be answered by anyone who knew the facts. But, toward the end of the interview, Thomas dropped a bomb on her. "So, Captain . . . You're a combat veteran. How is the war going?"

Mac chose her words with care. "I'm a junior officer . . . So I don't have enough information to answer your question. But I *can* tell you this . . . Most of the men and women of this battalion are from the South, and they fought bravely. They're the ones who deserve credit for bringing Howard's reign of terror to an end."

Thomas winked, as if to say, "Well played." Then she turned to the subject she'd clearly been waiting to bring up. "I assume you know that your sister and your father are fighting for the New Confederacy."

"Yes," Mac replied stiffly. "That's what I've been told."

Thomas nodded. "Are you aware that, according to a story in the *Dallas Morning News*, your father has been named Chairman of the Confederacy's Joint Chiefs of Staff?"

That came as a shock. Her father, the man Mac most wanted to please, was in charge of the military machine she was sworn to fight. "No," she replied. "I didn't know that."

The follow-up question was teed up and ready to go. "Do you have a message for your father?"

At least twenty seconds ticked by as Mac considered various answers. Finally, having rejected all the rest, she spoke. "My father taught me to fight for what I believe in. That's what I'm doing."

Later, while Mac was waiting for her train, she saw the story online. The comment about her father was featured as a boxed pull quote, inside the larger article. The headline was: A FAMILY AT WAR.

It ran front page left, just below the fold. Would her father see it? *Yes,* Mac thought. *He will.*

Airliners couldn't fly without fighter escorts, and there was a shortage of them. The net effect was a huge demand for train travel. Unfortunately, the country's long-neglected railroads weren't ready for the increase in traffic, and the system was struggling to cope. The result was a lot of scheduling problems, delays, and derailments.

So as Mac boarded the train that would take her to Kansas City, and on to Louisville, it was standing room only for civilians. And the two cars that had been set aside for military personnel were almost full. Mac made her way to the second one, where she found a seat among a group of engineers. Someone said, "Atten-hut!" but Mac waved the soldiers back into their seats. A sergeant was nice enough to heave her bags up onto the overhead rack.

As the soldiers returned to playing cards, Mac curled up in a corner. Here was a chance to get some much-needed shut-eye, and in spite of all the noise, Mac was asleep before the train cleared the station.

But rather than the dreamless nothing she'd been hoping for, Mac found herself back in combat. She and her troops were pinned down, a wounded soldier kept calling for his mother, and Huntington's intestines were piled in her lap. "Stuff 'em back in," the scout ordered. "And zip me up. I have work to do."

In the meantime, Worsky was battling to get her attention. "It's Bravo-Two, ma'am . . . He says his platoon is surrounded, and they're running out of ammo. What should they do?"

Mac felt a touch and awoke with a jerk. As her eyes opened, she saw that the corporal sitting across from her was settling into his seat. "Are you all right, ma'am? You were making noises."

Mac looked around. The engineers were gone. She glanced at

her watch. It was 1322. Mac had slept through the first stop. She forced a smile. "Sorry, Corporal . . . I had pizza for dinner last night. It didn't agree with me."

The soldier nodded, as if that explained everything, and went back to playing a game on his laptop. Mac could hear shouting and the rattle of machine-gun fire. The corporal was playing a combat game! How could he? Why *would* he? She looked down at her hands. They were shaking. *You're cracking up,* the voice said.

"Bullshit," Mac replied. "I'm tired, that's all."

Right, and you're cracking up, the voice responded.

The train swayed as it rounded a curve, and Mac put her hands in her pockets. How much combat was too much? The question went unanswered as the train rattled over a bridge and roared past a barn. The landscape became a blur after that . . . Mac closed her eyes. There weren't any dreams this time, and when she awoke, the train was in Kansas City.

A conductor helped get her bags down, but Mac was on her own after that. Because she couldn't carry both pieces of luggage, Mac wore one like a pack while dragging the other behind her. It produced a series of thumps as it tumbled down the stairs and fell into the entryway. From there, Mac managed to kick the duffel bag onto the platform as a man in civilian clothes stood and watched.

Then Mac had to wait two hours for a connection that was scheduled to depart an hour and a half earlier. Once it arrived, and loading began, an air force pilot stepped in to help with the bags. His name was Charlie something . . . He was a C-17 Globemaster pilot and quite attractive.

But Mac saw him slip his wedding ring off shortly after they boarded the train and kept her guard up after that. Slimeball or not, it was interesting to hear Charlie's take on the air war. "Their pilots are as good as ours," Charlie observed. "And that makes sense. We were part of the same air force six months ago. So both sides are even where the human dimension is concerned.

"But here's why we're going to win . . . Northrup Grumman produces a lot of military aircraft up north, and so does Boeing. That leaves Lockheed to manufacture planes in the South. The so-what being that the Union has the upper hand where industrial production is concerned."

It was a convincing argument, and Mac hoped that Charlie's analysis was correct. But her father was a very resourceful officer. Would he use the proceeds from the country's oil reserves to buy planes from abroad? Hell yes he would, depending on what was available.

Much to Mac's surprise, a soldier was waiting for her on the platform in Louisville. He was holding a card with her name on it—and hurried forward when she waved at him. He loaded her belongings onto an ancient luggage cart. One of the wheels produced a persistent rattling sound as he led her through the crowded station and out into a poorly lit street. "Sorry, ma'am . . . The car's parked a block away. That's as close as I could get."

Mac told him not to worry about it and was amazed to discover the vehicle in question was a staff car and not a Humvee. Was that intentional on someone's part? Or a matter of happenstance?

Whatever the reason, it felt good to settle into the backseat and let Specialist Lee do the driving. Traffic was heavy, which meant that the trip to Fort Knox took more than an hour. Soldier that she was, Mac noticed that there were lots of military vehicles on the roads. More than the last time she'd been there.

Mac had to show her ID at the gate. From there it was a short trip to Bachelor Officers' Quarters, where a room was reserved for her. A message was waiting: "Please join Colonel Roy Caskins in his office at 0830 tomorrow." The message was signed by a master sergeant Mac didn't know. She'd heard of Caskins, however . . . He was the 8th Armored Cavalry Regiment's commanding officer, which made him Granger's CO.

Suddenly it was imperative to come up with a clean uniform. No small task since Mac hadn't had time for anything more than some hand washing in many weeks. So immediately after she arrived in her room, Mac took a load of laundry down the hall to the shared utility room. It took more than an hour to cycle things through.

The dreams were waiting for Mac when she hit the sack. And when she awoke, it was to hear herself whimpering. It took the better part of an hour to get back to sleep.

Mac got up early, dressed with care, and went to the chow hall for breakfast. She ate a generous serving of bacon and eggs before following a map to Regimental Headquarters. A flight of wooden stairs took her up to the second floor and a spartan waiting room. What decorations there were consisted of photos. *Cavalry* photos . . . Which meant the walls were covered with pictures of tanks, Bradleys, and Strykers.

After presenting herself to the staff sergeant behind the reception desk, Mac was told to take a seat. Half a dozen other officers were waiting to see the colonel or one of his staff officers.

Mac knew very little about Caskins other than the fact that his nickname was "Casket Caskins," because of a well-publicized incident in which the remains of two soldiers had been mishandled by a subcontractor. And, after learning of the slight, Caskins punched the civilian in the face. Charges were brought and subsequently dismissed. But, in spite of the fact that his fellow officers were sympathetic, very few of them thought that Caskins would make general.

The sergeant called her name. And, before Mac could do more than stand up, Caskins was there. He had a bald spot, stood no more than five feet, eight inches tall, and radiated energy. His magnetism seemed to fill the room as he came forward to shake her hand.

"Captain Macintyre!" Caskins proclaimed loudly. "Look at her!" Caskins demanded, as his bright blue eyes probed the room. "This is what an ass-kicking cavalry officer looks like! Come on, Macintyre, let's have some coffee." Mac could feel curious eyes on her back as she entered the colonel's office.

Caskins closed the door behind himself and circled a nearly bare desk. "You did one helluva job in Wyoming," Caskins said, as he sat down. "I hate to say it, but the spy did us a favor . . . Crowley was one crazy son of a bitch! Thank God you were there to pick up the pieces. But you're back now, and maybe that will get Granger off my ass!"

It seemed as if the coffee was a ritual because it arrived without being requested and was placed between them. The corporal who brought the tray vanished as if by magic. Caskins stood to pour. "Describe the battle to me . . . I read the after-action report, but there's nothing like hearing the unabridged version."

So Mac took him through it as concisely as she could. "And that's when Howard appeared," she said finally. "He had a girl as his hostage. She allowed herself to sag, and that gave my scout a chance to shoot Howard in the head."

"With a Colt .45," Caskins said, "I love it. A story well told, Captain . . . And honest, too! You have no idea how much bullshit comes my way. That said, let's talk about the things you could have done better."

What followed was a review of the iffy decisions Mac had made. Those included going after Howard before her new CO arrived, placing too much reliance on luck, and failing to anticipate the possibility that enemy aircraft would attack. "*Three* Confederate helicopters took part in the attack on Fort Carney," Caskins pointed out. "What did Captain Macintyre learn from that? Zip."

Mac knew he was right, and some evidence of how she felt must have been visible on her face. Caskins smiled. "Sorry, I know how it feels . . . But you're a promising officer. That's why I took the time to poop on your parade.

"Now . . . Let's talk about tonight's get-together. I like the president. Not only does he respect the military—he's willing to fight alongside us. Your objective is to get through the evening without embarrassing yourself or the army. And that may be difficult given all the press coverage you've had. Do you read me?"

"Sir, yes, sir."

"Good. Have a good time. I'll see you down South before long. Give Granger my best."

Mac stood, delivered a salute, and got one in return. It wasn't until she was outside and walking toward the BOQ that Mac had time to appreciate the skill with which Casket Caskins had taken her apart and put her back together again. She smiled. Lessons had been learned.

MELLOW VALLEY, ALABAMA

It was a sunny day in Mellow Valley, Alabama. The high school band was playing "Dixie" as the terrorists were hauled into town. There were three of them, all wearing black hoods and sitting in

the back of a shiny pickup truck. Mr. Berkowitz was a business-
man, Mrs. Berkowitz taught yoga, and their daughter, Ella, was a
sad creature best known for being thirty pounds overweight.

Victoria didn't think people should be executed for owning a
jewelry store, having a couple of American flags stored in their
attic, or being Jewish. But the local chapter of the Right is Right
coalition had the necessary permit, and as Colonel Oxley put it,
"Everyday citizens can be useful in fighting Yankee imperialism."
That in spite of the fact that he'd been born in Connecticut.

But, since the proceeding was legal, all Victoria and her team
could do was watch as the Berkowitz family was forced off the
pickup and marched to the intersection where three truck-cranes
were waiting. A noose dangled from each. Ella was sobbing.

Victoria turned her back on the scene. Because the executions
were wrong? *No,* Victoria told herself. *Because there could be
agitators in the crowd. Folks who might cause trouble.*

About a hundred people gathered around. Victoria figured that
was a big crowd by Mellow Valley standards. There was an introduction followed by a smattering of applause as a local minister
launched into a minisermon about "King" Sloan's hatred of everything Southern. And that was when Victoria heard the roar of un-
muffled engines. The sound sent a jolt of adrenaline into her
bloodstream. The mike was attached to her vest. "Heads up! Vehicles
inbound. Take cover!"

The resistance fighters were riding in all manner of rat rods—
and the crowd scattered as they converged on the intersection.
Some of the locals were armed and fired pistols at the invaders.
That was a mistake. Machine-gun fire cut them down. "Kill the
drivers!" Victoria shouted. "Stop them!"

Victoria's team consisted of four special operatives, three of whom had worked with her before. All were excellent shots. So it was only a matter of seconds before the woman behind the wheel of an old flatbed truck was killed. Her vehicle veered off course and flattened a stop sign before crashing through the front of the local café.

The invaders wasted no time retaliating, and that forced Victoria's team to take cover. Meanwhile, a rat rod swooped in to rescue the Berkowitz family and spirit them away. A blizzard of paper fluttered out of the last vehicle to depart.

Victoria emerged from behind a bullet-riddled sedan. Five bodies lay sprawled in the street. Some were shooters, and some had been standing next to the shooters. She went out to retrieve a flyer.

RESTORE AMERICA, the headline said. That was followed by a list of reasons why the New Confederacy was illegal and people should oppose it. Victoria heard a buzzing sound and brought her carbine up to see a civilian drone hovering in front of her. It had four engines, a rounded fuselage, and was equipped with a belly cam. The light gray paint would make the aircraft difficult to see against the sky.

Now Victoria realized that the drone had been there all along, hanging over the town square, feeding video to *who*? One of the people she was supposed to catch, that's who. Someone who would put the footage up on the Internet for propaganda purposes.

The voice was distorted but understandable nevertheless. "My name is Nathan Hale. A terrorist who calls himself *El Carnicero*, or the Butcher, has been assassinating your soldiers while claiming membership in the Union Underground. If you'd like to catch him, we're willing to help. Send an e-mail to nathanhale@unionunder ground.org. We'll talk."

Victoria gave serious consideration to blowing the drone out of the sky but thought better of it. Maybe the Underground could help—and maybe it couldn't. But *El Carnicero* was at the top of her hit list, and a lead would be welcome. Or, maybe she'd find Nathan Hale and smoke him instead. Victoria allowed the drone to fly away. It shrank to the size of a dot and disappeared.

FORT KNOX, KENTUCKY

Most of the world's developed countries had been hit hard on May Day, while the citizens of many so-called third-world nations barely noticed because they were leading hard lives *before* the shit hit the fan. But now, having dealt with the immediate crises, industrialized countries were beginning to direct some of their attention outward again. More than that, they *had* to because so many things had changed, not the least of which was the situation in North America. A place where *two* governments claimed to control what had been the United States.

What were the Koreans and Brazilians to do? Should they back the Union, which, according to the laws extant on May Day, was the more legitimate government? Or would it be better to support the New Confederacy? Because of its "we can do business with you" mind-set.

As a result of this uncertainty, it was necessary for Sloan's administration to woo traditional allies like France, Germany, and Great Britain in hopes of maintaining previous military alliances, trade agreements, and legal structures. That's why Sloan, along with members of his cabinet, was about to spend the evening shooting the shit with all manner of diplomats, including some who had been seen in Houston.

But in spite of Sloan's dislike of receptions, and all that they entailed, there was one thing to look forward to . . . And that was the opportunity to spend a moment with Captain Robin Macintyre. Or "Mac," as her troops referred to her. Sloan knew that the prospect of that would help him wade through the endless rounds of toasts, the mind-numbing bullshit, and the posturing that would be served with dinner.

So Sloan kept an eye out for Mac throughout the meeting. The first sighting took place while he was standing on a riser, giving a short speech about the importance of old friendships and new opportunities.

Mac was toward the back of the crowd with some military types. She was dressed in a blue uniform and far prettier than the women wearing expensive dresses. Or so it seemed to him. That was when Sloan lost his place, coughed to cover the moment of confusion, and launched into the close. "So, ladies and gentlemen, thank you for coming tonight. Please enjoy the appetizers but save some room for Chef Franco's main course."

There was polite applause and a quintet began to play as Sloan stepped down. Secret Service agents shadowed the president as Secretary of State Henderson appeared with the Italian ambassador at his side. The Italians were trying to play the Union off against the New Confederacy in a blatant attempt to extract money from both. But what the ambassador didn't seem to understand was that Sloan didn't have any money to give. Not with a war to fight and a country to rebuild.

Sloan couldn't say that, however, so he took the first opportunity that came along to redirect the conversation to the subject of soccer, and Italy's upcoming game with Germany. That set the ambassador off . . . And all Sloan had to do was nod occasionally as the ambassador expounded on how horrible the Germans were.

Beth materialized out of the crowd. Her hair was just so, diamonds sparkled on her ears, and the blue dress looked as though it was sewed on. *She*, not to mention *he*, had been the subject of published rumors. The latest of which was that she'd been removed from the political beat due to her relationship with Sloan. And her presence at his side would add fuel to the fire. But what to do? He was trapped.

Sloan was about to introduce Beth to the ambassador when they exchanged air kisses and began to chatter in rapid Italian. Damn it . . . She was perfect for him! Good at everything except making him happy.

After what seemed like an eternity, the reception came to an end, and the dignitaries were herded into the dining room. Eight people were seated at each circular table. Beth was on Sloan's left, and the other diners included the Russian ambassador, her husband, South Korea's Consulate General, his wife, and a well-known comedian with her wife. The hope was that the pair from Hollywood could keep the conversation light. And the plan worked for the most part. That despite intel reports that Russia and Canada had designs on Alaska.

After an hour-and-a-half dinner came to an end, people began to leave, and Sloan parted company with Beth. "I've got a meeting . . . It could take as much as an hour."

"I'll wait," Beth told him, and what could he say? Don't bother? No, that wouldn't do.

Secret Service agents escorted Sloan upstairs to a small meeting room. They were about to enter when Sloan told them to wait outside. "No offense guys . . . But you're intimidating. Maybe it's the shades." Both men chuckled but left the glasses on.

Sloan opened the door and stepped inside. Mac was looking out through a window. Snow was falling through the wash of light beyond the glass. She turned, and there was the same softly rounded face he'd seen on that terrible night in Richton, Mississippi. Her eyes were what? Intelligent? Cool? Curious? All of those things and more. He went forward to shake hands. "We meet again, Captain. Thank you for coming."

Mac smiled. "No offense, Mr. President . . . But I did my best to get out of it."

Sloan laughed. "No problem. Hell, I'd get out of it myself if I could. But I'm glad they forced you to come. The country owes you a debt of gratitude, and so do I. What you accomplished in Wyoming was nothing short of miraculous. Please, have a seat."

The conversation area consisted of two chairs, a coffee table, and a couch. Mac sat on one end with Sloan at the other. "Tell me everything," Sloan said. "Starting with the day after we parted company."

She told the story military style—so it came across as a report. But Sloan didn't care. He wanted to hear the sound of her voice— and to watch the expressions on her face. "So that's it," Mac said finally. "And here I am."

"Yes," Sloan replied, "here you are. I wasn't lying . . . You deserve our thanks. But I have a confession to make."

Sloan saw Mac's eyebrows rise. "Which is?"

"My motives aren't entirely professional. You made quite an impression on me. So much so that I think of you frequently. And, due to the nature of my job, I haven't had the freedom to contact you. And that explains this kind of creepy moment."

Mac laughed. He liked the sound of it, but not what followed. "Thank you, I think. And, if you lose the next election, give me a call."

"So you *would*? See me that is?"

Mac smiled. "Yes. But what about Ms. Morgan? How does she fit in? I read an article about the two of you earlier today."

Sloan was struggling to formulate an answer when there was a knock on the door. He went to open it, and there was Beth. She was wearing her coat and carrying his over one arm. "The car is out front," she said. "I'll be out here when you're ready."

Then, having turned to Mac, she nodded. "The uniform becomes you, Captain . . . Congratulations on your victory." Then she was gone.

Mac stood. Her face was professionally blank. "Can I be excused, sir?"

Sloan swallowed. "Yes, of course."

Mac walked past him and out the door. The reception was over.

FORT HOOD, TEXAS

Victoria was in a covert-action suite within the Internet Warfare section of the fort's military-intelligence complex. Her video conference with Union Underground leader Nathan Hale was about to begin. The meeting had been arranged through a series of e-mails, and was scheduled to last thirty minutes.

Like any mission, this one had priorities, the most important of which was to learn whatever she could about the terrorist known as *El Carnicero*, or the Butcher. But Victoria hoped to capture Hale as well and thereby score a deuce. That's why specialists were waiting to trace the incoming call.

Victoria was seated on a white Tulip chair in a pool of light. A roll-around TV monitor was positioned in front of her, and the rest of the studio was dark. The tech sergeant who was in charge of tracing the call could communicate with her via an earbud. His name was Orson, and his voice was unnaturally loud. "Stand by. The call's coming in."

Video appeared on the screen, swirled, and locked up. And there was a much younger Victoria. She was dressed in a high school cheerleader outfit and smiling for the camera. Had the shot been lifted from her yearbook? Yes, it had.

The first photo was followed by a well-produced slideshow that included pictures of her as a cadet at West Point, running a marathon, and being promoted to major. All of which were intended to send a message: "We have resources, we know who you are, and we can find you."

Victoria's respect for the Underground went up a notch as the final picture dissolved into a shot of a man wearing a latex mask. The likeness was that of Morton Lemaire, President of the New Confederacy. A joke then. "Good morning," the man said. "I'm Nathan Hale."

"And I'm Victoria Macintyre." Her identity was something she would normally protect, but there was no point in doing so now. Hale knew who she was even though *his* identity remained a secret. Union Underground one, Victoria zero.

"Yes, you are," Hale replied. "Plus you are General Macintyre's oldest daughter and Captain Robin Macintyre's sister. Did you know that forces under your sister's command located and killed Robert Howard? He was an ally, wasn't he?"

Victoria *didn't* know. The New Confederacy's censors didn't have the means to prevent determined citizens from getting outside information. But they could prevent it from appearing in local newscasts. Victoria felt a twinge of regret about the girl. The one that she'd been forced to kill in order to prove herself. "Yes," Victoria lied. "My sister is on a roll. I suggest that we put the posturing aside and get to work."

Orson broke in. "They're using onion routing to route the feed from computer to computer. Our Internet service provider will use timing analysis to determine where the call originated. So stall."

Hale was oblivious to the fact that Orson was speaking, so their words overlapped. "Absolutely," Hale said. "As I indicated earlier . . . the Butcher is *not*, I repeat not, a member of our organization."

"Then what *is* he?"

"He's a serial killer," Hale replied. "If the North and South weren't at war, he would kill people anyway. He enjoys it."

The experts Victoria had spoken with agreed with that analysis. But she was playing for time. "Okay, but how do you explain the fact that all of his victims are Confederate soldiers?"

"It's like I said," Hale replied. "He's a psycho who is using the Underground as an excuse for what he does."

"*Or*," Victoria said, "he's an Underground operator who went rogue. And, because you have been unable to find him, you turned to us." It was a stall . . . a way to keep the conversation going but one that produced some unexpected results.

Hale shrugged. "There's some truth to that. But what I said is true. He's crazy."

Victoria felt the same sense of satisfaction she felt after winning a tennis match. "Thanks for your honesty . . . But I still don't get it. So long as he kills *our* people, rather than yours, why get in the way?"

"We have him!" Orson exclaimed. "And the bastard is only a few miles away . . . A special ops team is in the air. They'll land in a minute or two."

"The Butcher is unpredictable," Hale told her. "Who knows what he'll do next?"

Victoria felt the excitement that preceded a kill. "Like target *you*?" she demanded.

There was a sudden commotion on the screen as what might have been a body passed in front of Hale. Then the image grew smaller as the camera zoomed out to reveal a monitor and the empty room around it. That was when Victoria understood the truth . . . The transmission was originating from a place other than the spot she was looking at. Hale laughed. "Seriously? You think we're *that* stupid?" The video snapped to black.

CHAPTER 7

||||||||||||||||||||||||||||||||||

No man left behind.

—US ARMED SERVICES

NEAR READYVILLE, TENNESSEE

The trip from Fort Knox, Kentucky, to the base in Tennessee involved hitching rides on half a dozen southbound army trucks and took the better part of three days. So Mac was both relieved and tired when her latest ride dropped her off in front of battalion headquarters. Rather than the old warehouse complex, where the outfit had been quartered in Murfreesboro, the battalion was operating out of a rock quarry near the town of Readyville.

A number of soldiers were out and about, but none of them looked familiar. Mac felt like a stranger until she heard a familiar voice and turned. Sergeant Lamm had been in command of BULLY BOY on the night they snatched General Revell. There was a smile on his face. "Good morning, ma'am, and welcome back. Here, let me help with that bag."

As Lamm escorted Mac past the helipad and over to one of the sandbagged tents, she had the perfect opportunity to quiz him. According to Lamm, the battalion was spending most of its time on recon and special ops missions. As for the war, Lamm was anything but optimistic. "We keep grinding away," he said. "But the rebs continue to hold the line. This thing could go on for years."

Once they reached the tent, Mac thanked him and dropped her gear next to an empty cot before heading over to the Conex container where headquarters were located. The steel box was furnished with com gear, folding chairs, and a huge coffeepot. Major Granger was seated at a makeshift desk and rose to greet her. "You were supposed to arrive yesterday . . . When you failed to show, we ate the cake. Sorry about that."

Mac laughed. "The story of my life. Colonel Caskins sends his best."

"He's a good man," Granger observed. "The kind you can count on. Come on, I'll give you the tour."

Mac knew the tour was an excuse to get out of the Conex and away from all the ears inside it. "We're fine," Granger told her, as they strolled past the makeshift maintenance shed. "Or as fine as a shorthanded Stryker battalion can be. But the big picture isn't so good. The rebs have been using Mexican mercenaries to do a lot of fighting for them. Not only does that increase the number of people they can put in the field, it lowers their casualty rate and gives voters the impression that they're winning."

Mac frowned. "So the mercenaries are that good?"

"They're better than we thought they'd be," Granger confessed. "And there are a lot of them. A division, according to current estimates."

Mac took it in. A division. That could mean as many as twenty thousand soldiers. It was a sobering thought, and one that caused

Mac to think of her father. Was he responsible for the use of mercenaries? Or had the policy been foisted on him? Not that it mattered.

"Captain Colby has been serving as the interim XO," Granger
continued. "But I want you to step in. Colby's good . . . but not
good enough to lead a battalion should that become necessary."

Though well acquainted with all of the extra work that went
with the XO slot, Mac couldn't help but enjoy the implied compli-
ment. "Yes, sir."

"So get ready to jump in tomorrow," Granger told her, as they
circled back to the Conex. "Congratulations on killing that warlord, by the way . . . Too bad about Crowley."

"Yeah," she lied. "Too bad about Crowley."

Mac spent the next two days shadowing Colby, meeting new
people, and assessing the battalion's readiness. She also spent a
significant amount of time with her own company, which was short
two vehicles and five people. One of whom was a mechanic. A
situation not likely to be resolved anytime soon.

Maybe it was the return to normal duty, or maybe it was the
passage of time, but after two days with the battalion, Mac felt
less jittery. And when she held her hands out in front of her, the
tremors were nearly invisible. Not perfect . . . but better.

On her fourth day back, Mac elected to lead a two-vehicle patrol down along the north bank of the Stones River. The tributary
had been the scene of fierce fighting over the last few weeks as
troops from both the North and the South surged back and forth
across it. Now, having momentarily exhausted themselves, both
sides had settled into an uneasy stalemate.

That situation wouldn't last much longer. But things were quiet
as the **GERONIMO** and **LUCY** rolled along the highway that paralleled
the river.

Mac was up top, in **GERONIMO**'s front air-guard hatch, where she could see the surrounding countryside. Holes in the omnipresent cloud cover allowed shafts of early-morning sun to splash the forest on the far side of the waterway and promised a rain-free morning. The kind of morning cavalry officers loved because it's easier to maneuver on dry ground.

Mac didn't expect to fight, however . . . The purpose of the patrol was to show the flag to the rebs camped on the south side of the river and get reacquainted with her troops. Not to mention the fact that it felt good to escape the Conex, and the administrative crap that went with being XO.

Meanwhile, off to the south, Mac could see contrails—and hear the sounds of aerial combat. It served as a reminder that while her world was peaceful at the moment, other people weren't so lucky. The detritus of past battles lay everywhere. And as the GERONIMO rolled past, Mac saw partially submerged tank traps out in the water, a section of pontoon bridge that was grounded on a sandbar, and all manner of defensive earthworks along both sides of the river. Union troops waved, and she waved back.

Around noon, Mac ordered the drivers to pull over so that the Stryker crews could eat and take a bio break. She was sitting atop GERONIMO, spooning some diced fruit into her mouth, when Riley stuck her head up through the rear hatch. The RTO was new to the company and generally referred to as "the Owl" because of the army-issue glasses she wore. "We have orders, ma'am . . . An A-10 went down ten miles south of here . . . The pilot is alive and in hiding. The major wants us to go get him."

Mac's mind began to race. Ten miles into enemy-held territory! That was a long way to go. "What about air cover?" she demanded.

"We'll have it," Riley assured her. "The zoomies take care of their own."

Mac knew that was true. The enemy would have a hard time

capturing the pilot with a couple of hogs circling above him or her. She tossed the fruit cup away and keyed her mike. "This is Six . . . The break is over. Button up and prepare for action. One of our pilots bailed out ten miles south of here, and he needs a ride. Over."

Ramps came up, hatches closed, and gunners checked their weapons. The GERONIMO was armed with a .50 caliber machine gun, and LUCY was equipped with a 40mm grenade launcher. Both were excellent weapons for the task at hand.

The Strykers weren't carrying any troops, however . . . So Mac's total force consisted of herself, Riley, the truck commanders, their gunners, and a couple of ride-along privates who were there for training purposes. They could man a couple of M249s, though . . . And that would provide more firepower.

Riley continued to relay information to Mac and the TCs as the two-vic unit pulled onto the road. "There's a ford a mile east of here," she told them. "And, according to HQ, a squad of rebs is on the south bank. Over."

"You heard her," Mac said, as she fastened her chin strap. "*Lucy* will take the lead. Start firing as you enter the river. Over."

"Roger that," LUCY's gunner said. "Over."

Mac checked her machine gun as the LUCY passed. There was a tight feeling in her gut. She was scared and what else? Excited. Mac looked down at her hands. Were they shaking? It was impossible to tell because the GERONIMO was in motion.

The LUCY took a hard right, ran down the riverbank into the water, and began to fire. Grenades arched high into the air and fell on the bunker beyond. Mac could see laundry strung up between the trees—and knew the rebs had been caught flat-footed. She felt sorry for the unsuspecting grunts as a grenade landed next to their ammo dump and set it off.

Dirt, wood, and body parts were still raining down as LUCY

lurched up out of the water—and waddled through the smoking ruins. "Way to go," Mac said. "Put your foot in it. Over."

Wheels spun, locked up, and the **GERONIMO**'s tires threw mud as it followed the first vic up between shattered trees onto the level ground beyond. A voice crackled in her ear. "Short Bird to Bravo-Six . . . Do you read me? Over."

"Five by five," Mac replied. "Over."

"My wingman and I are approaching you from the north," Short Bird told her. "We're going to mow the grass. Over."

Mac started to answer, but her words were drowned out by the roar of jet engines as a plane passed overhead. The A-10's 30mm cannon produced an ominous growl as Short Bird fired on a target that Mac couldn't see.

In the meantime, Riley was feeding info to the truck commanders. "The brass put a drone up," she explained. "They're going to provide routing information. Take a left onto the highway, and the first right you come to. Over."

Mac saw the **LUCY** turn, and was thrown sideways as the **GERONIMO** followed suit. Regimental command was throwing everything they had at the rescue attempt, and that was good. But the rebs weren't likely to sit on their hands. A Yankee A-10 pilot would be one helluva prize, not to mention a propaganda coup, when his picture appeared on the front of the *Dallas Morning News*. "Watch out!" **LUCY**'s TC hollered. "Roadblock ahead!"

Mac swore. A quick-thinking Confederate had parked a six-by-six across the highway in an attempt to block it. But there was room on the right, and **LUCY**'s TC was quick to make use of it. Small-arms fire began to rattle against **GERONIMO**'s armor, and Mac could see that three soldiers were sprawled under the six-by-six, shooting at her. She sprayed them with 5.56 caliber rounds, and the firing stopped.

After clearing the front end of the six-by-six, **LUCY** raced ahead, with the second vic in hot pursuit. And when the lead Stryker turned right, **GERONIMO** followed. The unpaved road ran straight as an arrow—and Mac could see smoke boiling up from a clutch of Bradleys up ahead. Short Bird's work? Hell yes, and the air force pilot was still at it.

The Warthog was so low that Mac could count the fittings on the plane's belly as it flashed overhead. Rockets leapt off the plane's wings, and orange-red explosions marked a target hidden in among the trees a thousand yards beyond the Bradleys. "You're looking good, Bravo-Six," the pilot assured her. "Sleeping Beauty is five miles ahead and taking a nap. Over."

Mac couldn't help but grin. "Roger that, Short Bird. We'll wake him with a kiss. Over."

"He'll like that," the pilot replied. "Especially since he doesn't get very many kisses. We're going around. Over. Hold one . . . Uh-oh . . . Two F-15s at twelve o'clock! Gotta go . . ." The transmission ended as the A-10 started to climb, and the reb fighter fell like a hawk as it dived on its prey.

Mac wanted to watch but couldn't. Her air cover had been pulled away, she was ass deep in enemy territory, and a pilot called Sleeping Beauty was waiting up ahead. "Riley," Mac said. "Get Sleeping Beauty on the horn . . . Tell him to keep his head down and watch for us. Over."

Mac heard two clicks and knew the RTO was on it. They were up on the Bradleys by then. The tracks were on fire, and Mac could feel the heat as **GERONIMO** rolled past. Two bodies lay sprawled nearby. Death from above . . . Had Short Bird put eyes on any of the people he'd killed? It didn't seem likely. Not when traveling at more than 400 mph.

The trees Short Bird had fired at were coming up fast. *Why?*

What had the pilot seen there? The answer arrived in the form of a 105mm cannon shell. It screamed past and exploded behind her. A tank! A fucking Abrams, which, having pushed out into the open, was preparing to fire again. "Take evasive action!" Mac shouted. "Fire smoke . . . And don't run into each other."

LUCY cut left and GERONIMO angled to the right as another 105 round ripped through the space where they'd been. LUCY's gunner was firing smoke grenades. So it was only a matter of seconds before a gray fog enveloped the scene. Mac couldn't see but took some comfort from the fact that the tank commander couldn't see either, as the GERONIMO bucked over an obstacle and nearly threw her out of the hatch.

As the Strykers emerged from the cloud of smoke, they entered a cow pasture. Most of the animals were dead, but one stood munching away. The .50 began to chug, as GERONIMO's gunner yelled, "Target's left!"

When Mac turned to look, she saw the soldiers. They were spread out in a skirmish line. Some raised their weapons. *They're searching for our pilot,* Mac thought to herself, as she brought the LMG to bear. *Where is the son of a bitch anyway?*

Bullets buzzed past her, pinged the hull, and left bright smears where they hit. Mac pulled the trigger and saw half a dozen soldiers go down. Some had been hit, and the rest were diving for cover. A distant part of her brain took note of the fact that they were wearing strange uniforms. Mexican mercenaries? Yes, that made sense.

Then the thought was gone as LUCY waddled up out of a gully, and GERONIMO followed. "Sleeping Beauty is directly in front of us," Riley announced. "Don't shoot him."

It was a levelheaded order, and Mac was impressed. The Owl had a good head on her and would make an excellent corporal, assuming she lived long enough to sew the stripe on. Mac turned forward in time to see a man wearing a flight suit rise up out of a filthy pond! He waded toward them with a pistol in hand.

Mac was about to issue an order when she saw that **LUCY**'s ramp was falling. In the meantime, **GERONIMO**'s commander turned to place his vic between **LUCY** and the Mexican troops. That's when the .50 began to send heavy slugs downrange. Geysers of brown soil leapt into the air as the heavy machine gun traversed from left to right. "We have him!" **LUCY**'s TC exclaimed. "Over."

"Well done," Mac said. "Let's haul ass. *Geronimo* will take point. We're going out the way we came in, so watch for the tank. Over."

Surviving members of the infantry fired on the Strykers as they left but to no effect. Mac's eyes were focused on the trees where the tank had been. Was the monster still there? A shell exploded next to the **GERONIMO**, went off, and flipped the vic over onto its left side.

Mac was thrown clear and hit hard. She was lying on the ground, trying to breathe, when Riley came into view. The RTO's black-rimmed glasses were firmly in place, but the right lens was cracked. "Are you okay? The *Lucy*'s waiting for us."

Mac accepted Riley's hand, let the other woman help her up, and heard the tank fire. The armor-piercing shell had scored a direct hit on **GERONIMO** and blown the Stryker to smithereens. She couldn't see them. So it seemed safe to assume that Ramirez, Stephano, and private what's-his-name were dead.

"Come on," Riley said, and took Mac's arm. As they ran, Mac knew the tank was aiming at the Stryker. And when the Abrams fired, **LUCY** would cease to exist. Then something streaked down out of the sky, hit the tank, and exploded! A secondary blast blew the turret straight up . . . It seemed to pause in midair before crashing down.

Mac was still trying to understand the sequence of events as she followed Riley up the ramp and into **LUCY**'s cargo compartment. As she fell into a seat, Mac saw that the pilot was seated across from her with his back to the hull. He was sopping wet, but he was pretty. So pretty that he could be called beautiful. As for the "sleeping" part of his call sign, there had to be a story to explain that. Falling asleep in a class? Something like that. The pilot spoke as **LUCY** pulled forward. "I'm sorry."

Mac was about to say, "Sorry for what?" Then she remembered Ramirez, Stephano, and the nameless private. She could see his face . . . A kid trying to look tough. The pilot didn't know any of them, needless to say. But he knew that people had died to rescue him. And he was sorry. Mac forced a smile as **LUCY** lurched over some unseen obstacle. "Shit happens, Lieutenant. It wasn't your fault. Remember that."

He nodded. "Yes, ma'am." But Mac could see the pain in Sleeping Beauty's eyes and knew that some vestige of it would live there forever. "I think Short Bird killed the tank," she said, in an attempt to change the subject.

"No, ma'am," Riley said from the seat next to her. "The Hellfire missile was fired by a Predator drone. It's circling overhead."

I'm going to survive, Mac thought to herself. *Again.* She looked down at her hands. They were steady. *Why?* Mac closed her eyes and let her helmet touch the hull. Three people had died in order to save a comrade. It didn't make sense. Not mathematically. Yet, it did. And Mac felt proud.

FORT KNOX, KENTUCKY

The lighting was dim and the mood in the subterranean situation room was dark. People spoke to each other in hushed tones, as if in church. And no wonder. Live video was streaming in from Missouri, and all of it was grim. It appeared as if multiple tornados had ripped through Kansas City, leveling everything in their path. Malls, schools, homes . . . Everything.

And, according to preliminary estimates, more than five thousand people had been killed. But not by Mother Nature. No, this destruction had been wrought by man. Specifically, three B-2 Spirit stealth bombers based out of Lackland, Texas. Somehow, in spite of all the technology that was supposed to spot them, the planes had been able to cross into Union territory undetected.

Up until that point, neither side had intentionally bombed population centers. And that was something Sloan took pride in. The people who lived south of the New Mason-Dixon Line might be rebels, but they'd been Americans once and would be again one day. How could he bring the country back together if he bombed their homes?

President Lemaire had drawn the same line until now. Why the change? The answer was obvious. In spite of the stalemate on the battlefield, the North was winning. *How* wasn't clear. Maybe perceptions had begun to change now that Southerners had lived under the oligarchs for a while. Perhaps government polling reflected that.

There was also the possibility that the resistance movement was gaining traction, or that Northern psyops efforts were succeeding, or who knows what else? Whatever the reason, the decision had been made to escalate. What to do? Sloan and his advisors would have to decide.

Secretary of Defense Frank Garrison was in the room along with Chairman of the Joint Chiefs General Herman Jones, National Intelligence Director Martha Kip, National Security Advisor Toby Hall, and half a dozen others. They were seated around a long oval table—and all of them were staring at Sloan. That was when Sloan realized that he'd been silent for an uncomfortably long period of time. He cleared his throat. "Yes, well, you've seen the damage assessments. I'm sure you have suggestions about how to deal with this horrific act. Let's start with General Jones."

Jones had a buzz cut so short his black hair was barely visible against his brown skin. He had bright brown eyes and a square chin. "I'd like to tackle the second issue first," Jones said. "Efforts are under way to figure out how the rebs managed to suppress our detection systems. That's the first step.

"We will also increase the number of E-3 airborne early-warning and control missions. And, if you approve, we'll move some surface-to-air batteries down from the Canadian border. Finally, we're going to borrow twelve fighters from the navy in order to increase the number of interceptors available to deal with incursions."

"I like it," Sloan replied. "All except for moving the surface-to-air batteries. I don't trust the folks who are leading Canada right now. Let's leave the missiles where they are." Jones nodded and made a note on the pad in front of him.

"Now," Jones said, as he looked up, "let's talk about offense. As it says in Leviticus, 'an eye for an eye.' Just say the word, and we'll level the city of Dallas."

The recommendation, or something like it, was what Sloan had expected to hear from Jones. And there was no way in hell that he was going to agree to it. But experience had taught him that it was best to let everyone have a say before saying no. And maybe, if he got lucky, someone else would take issue with the idea.

Sloan thanked Jones and continued to call on people until each person had spoken. All of them offered good suggestions, but only one of them took exception to Jones's plan, and that was Secretary of Homeland Security Roger Alcock. He was from Colorado—and favored cowboy hats, bolo ties, and Western boots.

"With all due respect, General," Alcock began, "I think your plan is a bit shortsighted. Let's say we succeed, and we level Dallas. Or some other city. How will the rebs respond? They'll destroy Philly or some other soft target. We will retaliate, and so on, until the entire country is a field of rubble. There has to be a better way."

Sloan took the opportunity to jump in. "I agree. But we can't sit back and take it either. The general's right about that. So while I oppose carpet bombing Dallas, or any other Confederate city for that matter, I don't object to hitting strategic targets. And I have some in mind. As you know, Texas had something approaching energy independence prior to the war. What you may not be aware of is that in spite of a well-earned reputation for pumping oil, the Lone Star State was the nation's *fourth* largest coal producer when the meteors struck.

"But here's the rub . . . The stuff they mine in Texas is a low-grade form of coal called lignite. It's found in deposits that sweep from the northeastern edge of the state down south. And guess who owns eleven of the twenty-four mines in the state? The answer is Coruscant Southwest, the largest electric utility in the state. The same company that enables Lemaire to provide his constituents with cheap electricity even as it pollutes their air.

"But that's not all," Sloan added, as his eyes roamed the faces around him. "Coruscant's CEO sits on the Confederacy's Board of Directors . . . So, if we strike a blow against the company, we strike a blow against him."

"I don't know," Jones said doubtfully. "I guess we could drop some bunker-busters on top of the mines. That would shut them down for a while . . . But deep targets are difficult."

"I have some good news for you," Sloan replied. "Most of the coal mines in Texas are located in rural areas. That limits the possibility of collateral damage, and they're on the surface. Destroy the draglines used to harvest the lignite, and the operators will be out of business. What do you think?"

All eyes were on Jones. He smiled. "Holy shit, Mr. President . . . No offense, but I'm not used to getting targeting guidance from civilians! But I like it. We'll put those mines out of business by this time tomorrow."

There was more. And an hour's worth of discussion followed. Sloan should have felt better as he left, but he didn't. Another problem loomed. How to best part company with Beth Morgan? Especially now that the FBI investigation inspired by Beth's journalism was over, Senator Pickett had been arrested, and Sloan was about to benefit.

But the need to part company with Beth had been clear to Sloan ever since the evening when he'd met with Robin Macintyre. He was unhappy already. But seeing Mac, and talking to her, had given him the impetus to do what he'd been putting off. *Tonight,* Sloan thought to himself. *I'll do it tonight.* The prospect filled him with dread.

It was a full day. There were all the usual briefings to attend in the morning, a related press conference to survive at one, and a signing ceremony at three. The Whigs had done everything in their power to oppose the America Rising Reconstruction Bill but hadn't been able to stop it, and that was something to feel good about.

But Sloan's spirits were dampened by the knowledge of what was to come. And when he left his office to join Beth in his private quarters, it was with a heavy heart. *Buck up,* he told himself. *Don't drag it out.*

That plan went out the window as he opened the door and

entered the dimly lit sitting room. A linen-covered table sat at the center of it. Candles flickered, silverware gleamed, and soothing music filled the air. "Happy birthday," Beth said, as she came forward to give him a kiss. "And congratulations regarding the reconstruction bill. It's a historic piece of legislation."

Sloan felt the usual spark as her lips pressed against his and her perfume embraced him. All sorts of emotions battled each other for supremacy. It felt good to have someone remember his birthday—and praise his achievement. But, sweet though the moment might be, the relationship was doomed. "Thank you, Beth . . . How thoughtful! I really appreciate it."

"You'll appreciate it even more when your steak arrives," Beth replied. "But let's have a drink first."

A small bar stood against one wall, and Sloan went over to make drinks. A rum and Coke for her . . . and a gin and tonic for him. Both doubles.

They sat next to each other on the couch, arms touching. Beth was all wound up about some politics at work, and Sloan forced himself to listen as she chattered away. Eventually, when they were on their second drinks, he took the plunge. "Beth, we need to talk."

Beth's eyes narrowed slightly. "Really? About what?"

"About us."

Sloan saw her smile tighten. "Uh-oh . . . I don't like the sound of this. Are you about to dump me? *Again?*"

Sloan tried to come up with a way to soften it and failed. "I'm sorry, Beth. You're a wonderful person. But a very different person from me."

Her eyes were like bottomless black pools. "Does this have something to do with Captain Macintyre?"

Sloan felt flustered. "Yes, I mean no. The captain and I don't have a relationship if that's what you mean."

There was a hard edge to her voice. "But you'd like to have one."

"Yes, I suppose I would," Sloan admitted. "But that misses the point. It's like I said earlier. You and I are very different people. And that would be a problem even if I didn't know Captain Macintyre."

Beth placed her glass on the coffee table and stood. There were no tears in her eyes. Just an implacable anger. "I'm not a toy, Sam. Something to be used, reused, and discarded. Everything has a price—and you will pay."

With that, Beth turned, snatched her coat off the back of a chair, and left. Someone else might have slammed the door. Beth didn't.

Sloan sighed. He'd known it would be bad but not *that* bad. There was a discreet knock on the side door. Sloan frowned. "Come in."

Sloan heard a soft thump as a stainless-steel trolley pushed the door open. It was followed by a waiter dressed in white. "Good evening, Mr. President. Steaks for two . . . May I serve?"

Sloan felt his stomach rumble. "Tell me something, Louie . . . Do you like steak?"

The waiter was sixtysomething, gray, and extremely dignified. "Yes, sir . . . I do."

"Good. Please serve. Then, if you'd be so kind, please join me for dinner. It's my birthday."

Louie was in no way perturbed. "It would be my pleasure, sir. And happy birthday."

NEAR READYVILLE, TENNESSEE

Three days had passed since the rescue mission—and the battalion had been ordered to move again. It was an arduous process, especially for the XO, who was expected to handle most of the logistics.

So Mac was in a meeting with the battalion's supply officer and her staff when the private came looking for her. He was a gangly kid who had graduated from high school six months earlier. "I'm sorry to bother you, ma'am. But Major Granger wants to see you right away."

"Right away as in *now*?"

"Yes, ma'am."

Mac eyed the faces around her. "Sorry, but I've got to go. Remember what I said. Don't trust anybody. Count *everything* before you load it."

Lieutenant Simmons nodded. "Don't worry, Captain. We're on it."

"Good," Mac said, as she stood. "I'll check with you later."

There was activity all around as Mac crossed the compound. Tents were coming down, boxes of gear were being stacked for loading, and a line led into the first-aid station. Vaccinations had to be renewed on a regular basis, and Mac knew her name was on the list. When would she find the time?

As Mac entered the Conex container, she saw that it was nearly empty—and knew the techs were working out of the battalion's com truck. Two people were present. Granger and a staff sergeant who looked strange in his class-A blue uniform and mirror-bright street shoes. That was when Mac saw the military police insignia. Shit. One of her people was in trouble. Granger looked grim. "Have a seat Captain," he said. "This is Sergeant Wilkins."

Mac sat on a folding chair. "Good morning, Sergeant . . . Did one of our soldiers screw up?"

Wilkins's eyes were like black buttons, it appeared as if his nose had been broken at some point, and his mouth was little more than a horizontal slash. "None of your soldiers are in trouble, ma'am. Not that I'm aware of anyway. I'm here to arrest *you*."

It came as a complete shock. Mac could hardly believe her ears. "*Me?* What for?"

"You have been charged with disobeying a direct order from a superior officer," Wilkins replied.

Mac wasn't in trouble with Granger. She knew that. Who then? Crowley? No, even though she disagreed with the colonel regarding all sorts of things, Mac had obeyed his orders. Besides, Crowley was dead. She looked at Wilkins. "Who is my accuser?"

"Major Jeremy Fitch, United States Air Force," Wilkins answered.

Fitch, Fitch, Fitch . . . Who the hell was Fitch? Oh, shit . . . Now she remembered. The incident had occurred months earlier as Mac and her soldiers were making the long, arduous journey from Washington State to Arizona. Along the way, they'd stopped outside Mountain Home, Idaho, in hopes of finding weapons, ammo, and supplies in the National Guard armory.

The sheet of plywood propped up in the middle of the road had been visible from half a block away. The words GOV. PROP. DO NOT ENTER had been written on the wood with white paint.

Mac remembered seeing the ruins of a building on the right. It looked like the structure had been leveled by the Chinese missile that had destroyed nearby Mountain Home Air Force Base. "I see movement at two o'clock," Brown had announced as he brought the .50 around.

Mac looked in time to see a man emerge from the hut located adjacent to the remains of the building. He was dressed in combat gear and carrying a light machine gun. After ordering a sniper to target the man, Mac had gone forward to speak with him.

Mac remembered how the ice crystals glittered in the sunlight as she jumped down off the truck—and made her way over to where the man was standing. He was a major, or some guy pretending to be a major. "I'm Lieutenant Macintyre, United States Army. And you are?"

"Major Fitch, United States Air Force."

The way Mac remembered it, Fitch had deep-set eyes and a gaunt appearance. And, when Mac asked Fitch what he was doing, the answer had been clear. "I'm guarding what remains of a building."

During the following exchange, Fitch had asserted his authority over Mac, and she had refused to accept it. *Why?* Because she and her troops were cut off from their battalion, the country was in the shitter, and she had no way to accurately assess the man in front of her. Was he a die-hard hero? Or some sort of mental case? Who else would hole up next to a National Guard armory and guard it all by himself?

So she'd refused to obey Fitch's orders, and now, after what seemed like a lifetime, that decision had come back to haunt her. Would her story get her off? Hell, no. The people Wilkins worked for didn't care what her perceptions of Fitch were. The only thing they cared about was the answer to a simple question: Did you, or did you not, disobey a direct order? Mac felt a sudden emptiness at the pit of her stomach. "What happens next?"

"Pack your gear," Wilkins instructed. "*All* of it. We're going to Fort Knox. That's where the court-martial will be held. It's going to take a while."

Mac swallowed. "Court-martial?"

"Yes, ma'am."

Granger cleared his throat. "I'm sorry, Robin . . . But there's nothing I can do. You are hereby relieved of duty pending the outcome of the trial."

Mac stood. She felt light-headed. "Are you going to cuff me?"

Wilkins eyed her. "Do I need to?"

"No."

"Then I won't."

"Thank you."

Mac left the Conex with Wilkins in tow. Dark clouds were moving in from the north, and the air felt chilly. Suddenly, in less than half an hour, Mac's world had been turned upside down. The future was bleak.

CHAPTER 8

||||||||||||||||||||||||||||||||||||

Give Peace A Chance

—JOHN LENNON

JACKSON, MISSISSIPPI

The Metrocenter Mall was filled with Saturday-morning shoppers. And why not? The war was a barely felt presence in the city of Jackson. Because of all the military spending, everybody who wanted a job had one—plus the air inside was cleaner than the stuff outside. And because the mall was the closest thing to neutral territory available, Victoria and resistance fighter Nathan Hale had agreed to meet at the mall.

Their first meeting, which had taken place electronically, had been an unmitigated disaster for Victoria. Instead of gathering more information about the anti-Confederate assassin called the Butcher *and* capturing Hale, she had come away with nothing.

Now, after apologizing to Hale via e-mail and days of groveling, he'd agreed to meet with her again. And in person. Rather than try to grab Hale, Victoria had decided to play it straight. The first priority was to obtain intel regarding the Butcher. Then, once *El Carnicero* was neutralized, she would find a way to smoke Hale.

Meanwhile, just in case Hale was planning to double-cross *her*, Sergeant Cora Tarvin and Private Roy Post were providing security. Victoria scanned her surroundings but couldn't spot the operatives. And that was good. Because if she couldn't see them, Hale's people couldn't either.

The Fountain Restaurant had indoor and outdoor seating. By prior agreement, the meeting was to take place outside, where the noise generated by the small fountain would make it difficult for other diners to listen in.

As Victoria neared the restaurant, she saw that roughly half of the outside tables were taken. Hale was nowhere to be seen, but that wasn't surprising since she was five minutes early. Victoria went inside, requested a table near the fountain, and followed a girl out to a linen-covered table. After taking a seat, she began to eye the pretentious menu. It was heavy and loaded with items that would make her heavy, too. "May I join you?"

Victoria looked up to see that the fashionably dressed woman who'd been seated a few feet away was standing next to her table. She was about to say "No," and realized her mistake. "Mrs. Hale, I presume?"

Hale laughed and took the other chair. Now Victoria could see through the makeup even though it was quite convincing. Hale smiled. "That's right, honey . . . This isn't the first time I've dressed as a woman. And one girl to another, I love your cropped jacket! It's just enough to kick the outfit up a notch *and* hide a shoulder holster."

Victoria couldn't help but smile. "Thanks. You look pretty good yourself." And it was true. He'd been wearing a mask the last time she'd seen him. Now he was wearing a wig, pink lip gloss, and

enough foundation to hide his beard. The disguise, plus some carefully chosen clothing, created a convincing picture. Was Tarvin
snapping photos of him with a long lens? She'd better be.

After a waiter arrived, and their orders were placed, the ma-
neuvering began. During the first meeting, Victoria had guessed,
correctly as it turned out, that *El Carnicero* had been a member
of the Union Underground before going rogue. Now the resistance
fighters wanted him dead. So much so that they were willing to
conspire with the Confederacy to get the job done.

But there was a limit on how cooperative Hale could be without
revealing the sort of information that would help Victoria attack
his organization. That's what Hale claimed. But by the time lunch
had been served, Victoria was beginning to get suspicious. Nothing
had been accomplished up to that point—and Hale was too relaxed
for someone with a lot at stake. *Why?*

Victoria was about to bail out when Hale opened his purse and
removed a sheet of paper. He pushed it across the table. "There
you go," he said. "Now you have the Butcher's *real* name, his last-
known address, and a personality profile."

The paper was folded into thirds. And when Victoria opened
it, she saw that the page was blank! What the? Victoria looked up
and was reaching for her pistol, when Hale shot her in the stomach.
He was holding the Taser low, under the tabletop, where it couldn't
be seen.

Victoria felt the dart-like electrodes penetrate her clothing. That
sensation was followed by something similar to a bee sting—and
an electronic shock so strong that she lost control of her muscula-
ture. She jerked, slumped to one side of the chair, and was hanging
there as Hale stood. "Bye, hon," he said. "Sorry to eat and run."
Then he was gone.

Victoria's body had been immobilized, and although her brain was foggy, it remained functional. She'd been suckered. *Again*. What was Hale trying to accomplish? Then it came to her. The resistance fighter knew that Victoria would have backup, and he hoped to draw them out so his operators could kill them. Then, as Victoria struggled to stand, they would nail her as well. And bingo . . . Not only would Hale have eliminated one of the Confederacy's hunter-killer teams, but General Bo Macintyre's daughter would be dead! A psychological as well as a physical blow.

All of that and more flashed through Victoria's mind as she heard a gunshot! Post! Or Tarvin! One of them had seen Victoria slump over and rushed to the rescue. And that was the sniper's signal to fire.

"No!" What was supposed to be a shout emerged as a croak. Victoria battled to stand, failed, and heard a *second* report. People were screaming by then—and a good Samaritan appeared at her side. "Can you breathe?" he wanted to know. "I called 911."

As he leaned in to hear her reply, a bullet hit him in the head. The bang was like an afterthought. Victoria felt something warm splatter her face as the man collapsed on top of her. The chair went over, and both of them hit the floor.

Victoria's muscles were starting to respond by that time and she struggled to roll free. Once on her knees, she stood. Only then did Victoria realize how stupid the move was. A follow-up shot would put her down for good! None came.

Victoria used a napkin to wipe some of the blood off her face as she staggered out into the mall. People were running every which way as police flooded the area. Someone called for a medic as Victoria knelt next to Tarvin's body. They hadn't been friends. Both of them knew better than to let that happen. But they'd been in some tight spots together, and Victoria would miss the noncom.

"Don't worry," Victoria told the body, as an EMT arrived. "I'll find the bastard. And he's going to die."

FORT KNOX, KENTUCKY

As Mac made her way across the sprawling base, she felt depressed. The previous night had been spent tossing and turning. Why had she been stupid enough to refuse a direct order?

Because you had every reason to believe that the country was in the shitter, her inner voice replied. *And it would be, except for Sloan.* The statement was true but brought very little comfort. Mac consulted the slip of paper in her hand, confirmed that she was standing in front of the correct building, and climbed a short flight of stairs. A door opened into a sparsely furnished reception area. Mac made her way over to a fortresslike desk. A bright-eyed corporal looked up from what she was doing. "Good morning, ma'am . . . How can I help you?"

"I'm Captain Macintyre, and I'm here to see Judge Advocate Sanders."

The corporal consulted a screen. "Yes, ma'am. Please have a seat. I'll let him know you're here."

Mac found a place to sit. About a dozen people were seated around her. Did they know about the charges that had been lodged against her? No, that was absurd. What would her father think? Mac could imagine the disappointment in his eyes. The same disappointment she'd seen many times before. A major appeared and made his way over. "Captain Macintyre? I'm Judge Advocate Sanders."

Mac stood. Sanders had thinning flyaway hair, a slight stoop, and was dressed in a uniform that appeared to be a size too big. They shook hands. "Please follow me," Sanders said, and led the way.

Mac followed him through a maze of cubicles and corridors to a windowless room. "Please have a seat," Sanders said, as he circled a cluttered desk. "Or should I say *the* seat, since there's only one. They called me back to active duty two months ago and, as you can imagine, the regulars have the good offices." It was said without rancor. As if such indignities were to be expected.

Mac forced a smile. "Yes, sir."

"Let's dispense with the formalities," Sanders said, as he sat down. "Please call me George, and I'll call you Robin. Now, allow me to bring you up to speed on the process. You've been charged with disobeying a direct order and threatening the life of a superior officer. Those are serious allegations, needless to say, so a general court-martial will be convened.

"The trial will involve a military judge, a prosecutor, and a defense counsel. By the way," Sanders added, "you have the right to choose a defense counsel other than me should you desire to. And no, I won't be offended."

Mac felt a terrible emptiness where the pit of her stomach should have been. "I won't need a defense attorney. I plan to plead guilty."

Sanders frowned at her. "*What?* Are you crazy?"

"No," Mac said miserably. "I'm guilty. Not only that, there were witnesses, plenty of them. So that's that."

"Maybe," Sanders allowed, as he picked up some papers. "And maybe not. It's true that Privates Wessel and Dooly gave statements that support the charges. But your driver, Corporal Garcia, said he couldn't hear the interchange between you and Major Fitch. That in spite of the fact that he was outside the Stryker and standing a few feet away!

"Then there's Dr. Hoskins. He said that Major Fitch appeared to be suffering from PTSD, and Private Hadley indicated that Fitch was threatening you with a machine gun. All of which can be used to attack Fitch's credibility. Or lack thereof."

The fact that Garcia, Hoskins, and Hadley had been there for her was heartening. "I'm glad to hear it," Mac said. "But be honest with me. What are my chances?"

Sanders frowned. "Of going scot-free?"

"Yes."

"I'd put the odds at five to one against it."

Mac swallowed. "Okay, so why fight it?"

"Which would you prefer?" Sanders inquired. "Twenty years? Or two? A short sentence. That's worth fighting for. I know things look dark . . . But you have an extraordinary record, and believe me, the court will take that into account. But only if we tell them the story. So what do you say? Do we fold? Or fight?"

Two years in prison. *If* she was lucky. Mac felt sick to her stomach. "Okay, George, we'll fight."

The smile made Sanders look younger. "Good. I'll push for a speedy arraignment. Be sure to follow all of the rules and stay out of trouble during the interim."

The next two weeks were difficult. Mac had to check in four times a day. But, other than occasional meetings with Sanders, she had no other duties. So rather than sit around and think dark thoughts, Mac put in two hours at the gym every morning. Then it was time to shower, eat breakfast, and do chores.

Once lunch was over, Mac had all afternoon in which to read. *The Art of War* by Sun Tzu was a favorite, and histories, including the four-volume *A History of the English-Speaking Peoples* by Winston Churchill.

And Mac had time for lighter fare as well . . . including both online and print publications. That's how she came across a story concerning Sloan's love life. "The love affair between the President of the United States and *World News* reporter Beth Morgan is over." That's how the article began. And, farther down, there was an equally interesting sentence. "According to people in the know, the president broke off the relationship, and Ms. Morgan is anything but pleased."

Mac remembered the room, what Sam had said to her, and her reply. What part, if any, had the conversation played in ending his relationship with Morgan? And what would the president think of her now? Nothing good.

The arraignment was a good deal less dramatic than Mac had imagined. The charges were read, her rights were made clear, and a trial date was set. Rather than stall for time, Sanders was pushing for a speedy trial. "I don't want to be morbid," he said. "But what if Dr. Hoskins gets killed? As a physician, and someone who is clearly on your side, his testimony is very important to us."

Mac understood the logic of that, even if it was a bit cold-blooded, and wanted to get the whole process over with. The sooner she was convicted, the sooner she could serve her time, and the sooner she'd be released. To do *what*? Mac didn't know. *But,* she thought to herself, *I'll have plenty of time to think about that.*

ABOARD THE VIRGINIA-CLASS ATTACK SUBMARINE *JOHN WARNER*

The President of the United States had never been aboard a nuclear attack submarine before. And he didn't like it. Because, in spite of the fact that the boat was more spacious than its predecessors, the close quarters made Sloan feel claustrophobic. It was a sensation he was determined to conceal.

Sloan was standing in the control room next to Captain Raw-lings. Each time the officer gave an order, Sloan could monitor changes on the screens located in front of the pilot and copilot. Only three people were required to steer, rather than the five or six that was standard in the Ohio-class subs. "We're pausing just below the surface," Rawlings said, "so we can take a look around."

The rest went unsaid. Had the Confederates kept their word? If so, there wouldn't be any vessels in the area other than the Ohio-class submarine *Alabama*. And it, according to Rawlings, was under the command of an old friend. A classmate from Annapolis who had chosen to fight for the Confederacy instead of the Union. "*He's* trustworthy," Rawlings had said. "But the people he reports to? Not so much."

And that's typical of this war, Sloan thought to himself. *Friend against friend, brother against brother. God help us.*

Like all Virginia-class subs, the *John Warner* was equipped with photonics masts rather than the hull-penetrating periscopes of yesteryear. As Sloan looked at the screen in front of him, he saw that the Caribbean sun was an orange smear in the dusty sky. At the water level, and directly ahead, a tropical island was visible. And not just *any* island . . . but an eighty-acre Balinese-style retreat that belonged to a British billionaire.

How the island had been secured for the meeting wasn't clear because Sloan hadn't been involved in the negotiations. But the *why* was obvious. The billionaire, not to mention the UK generally, would benefit in a multitude of ways if peace broke out. "There are no enemy aircraft in the area," a disembodied voice said.

"We have an AWACS in the air," Rawlings explained. "And they'll warn us if rebel aircraft come this way. So far so good."

After completing a careful 360-degree scan of its surroundings, the sub started to creep forward. "We have company," a sonar operator announced. "The signature is consistent with that of an Ohio-class sub."

"We have radio contact," another voice put in. "They have the recognition code."

"Okay," Captain Rawlings said. "Take her up."

It took the better part of an hour for both subs to send teams ashore, confirm that it was deserted, and radio in. Once the all clear was received, Sloan was instructed to climb up through the submarine's conning-tower-like "sail" to the bridge, and make his way from there to the deck, where a life jacket awaited him. Then it was time to enter a RIB boat for the trip ashore. Six heavily armed SEALs grinned at him as he sat down. "Welcome aboard, sir," one of them said. "We'll have you there in no time."

The twin engines roared, and the bow slapped the waves, as the low-lying island grew steadily larger. Off to the left, another in-flatable was making the same journey, only it was equipped with a whip-style antenna. A Confederate flag fluttered in the breeze, and spray flew as the boat powered ahead.

What was Lemaire thinking? Sloan wondered. Could a deal be done? Sloan wanted to believe that it could. But Secretary of Defense Frank Garrison was doubtful, as was Secretary of State George Henderson. They were of the opinion that the Confederate president was simply going through the motions to appease the small clique of "accomodationists" who were members of his board.

The Confederate inflatable arrived first, and Lemaire's security team was already gathered on the pier as the Union boat pulled in next to the floating dock. After getting rid of his life jacket, Sloan followed a ramp up to the point where Morton Lemaire stood waiting for him. They'd met before the war, down in Houston, where Lemaire and his cronies offered Sloan a job as puppet president. And when Sloan refused, Lemaire called him ". . . one stupid son of a bitch."

But Sloan could detect no signs of animosity as Lemaire came forward to shake hands. The Confederate president had gray hair and a keen mind. So friends and enemies alike referred to him as "the silver fox." His long, oval-shaped face would have been perfect had it not been for a mouth that was a little too small. "We meet again," Lemaire said. "No hard feelings, I hope."

"None," Sloan said while managing to keep a straight face. "I enjoyed my stay in the swamp."

Lemaire chuckled. "Shall we take a stroll?" the Southerner inquired. "Or find a place to sit down?"

"Let's walk," Sloan replied. "I'd like to stretch my legs." The politicians followed a meticulously kept path up through lush greenery toward the buildings beyond. "So," Lemaire began, "we're here because we have a common interest in making peace."

"True," Sloan agreed. "But not at any price."

"Of course," Lemaire responded. "That's understood."

So far so good, Sloan thought to himself. "Do you have something specific in mind?" Sloan inquired. "Or do you see this meeting as an opportunity to explore the possibilities?"

"I have a plan I'd like to put forth," Lemaire replied. "Or the general outlines of one. If you and I can agree on general principles, our staff people can collaborate on the details."

Sloan was surprised by the reasonable tone. Especially in light of their last meeting. "That sounds good," Sloan said. "What do you have in mind?"

"The first step would be to declare a cease-fire," Lemaire answered.

"Okay," Sloan replied. "That makes sense. The sooner the killing stops, the better."

"Exactly," Lemaire said. "The second step would be to announce peace talks. Our diplomats would work together to determine how the talks would be structured and when they would start."

They stopped in the shade provided by the palm trees. Leaves rustled as a bird hopped across the path. "The devil would be in the details," Sloan observed.

"I'm glad we agree," Lemaire said. "I've been here before, you know . . . As a guest. It's an amazing place." They were standing twenty feet from the pool and the three-story Balinese-style house beyond.

So that's why the island was chosen, Sloan thought to himself. *Lemaire has a relationship with the owner.* "I assume you could see the sun back then," Sloan put in.

"Yes," Lemaire replied. "And feel it. I miss the warmth . . . But enough of that. Where was I? Ah, yes. Peace talks. The moment talks begin, representatives from both sides will want to define how much territory will be held by each entity. I suggest that we adopt the New Mason-Dixon Line as the official border between North and South."

Sloan felt a sudden surge of anger and battled to control it. "No way," he responded. "As things stand now, Union forces control everything north of Spring Hill, Tennessee. If we pull back to the New Mason-Dixon Line, we will cede a large chunk of territory to you . . . And, should talks fail, we would have to spend thousands of lives to take it back."

"I get that, Sam," Lemaire replied. "But we need to set the table. There's a whole lot of folks down my way who would oppose any sort of deal. But there are moderates, too . . . And if we can show them a genuine act of conciliation by the Union, that'll go a long way toward securing the support I need. And if you genuinely believe in peace, then I think you'll be better off betting on success instead of failure."

Lemaire was one helluva salesman. So good that Sloan was tempted. But a lot of good men and women had died to take the ground south of the line. And to give it back would be a betrayal of them and their families. Sloan looked into Lemaire's eyes. "I was with you right up to the territorial giveback. But, as you Southerners like to say, 'that dog won't hunt.'"

Lemaire frowned. "I'm sorry to hear that, Sam. *Real* sorry. But if we agree to peace talks now, with Union troops in Tennessee, it will look like we're losing."

"You *are* losing," Sloan said emphatically. "Not big-time, not so far, but bit by bit. And that's why the accomodationists on your board want to cut a deal. They can see where this is going. So why not draw the line where it is? And get what you can? It's bound to be better than the other possibility . . . which is an unconditional surrender."

Lemaire's features seemed to harden. His voice was tight. "I said you were a stupid son of a bitch when we met in Houston, and nothing has changed. Memorize this moment, Sam . . . And play it back to yourself when Confederate forces roll into Fort Knox."

Sloan was about to reply when Lemaire turned his back and walked away. Peace would have to wait.

FORT KNOX, KENTUCKY

Mac felt as if she were having an out-of-body experience as she followed Sanders into the room where her court-martial would be held. It was large, but a good deal more spartan than the courtrooms that she'd seen on TV.

As Mac walked down the center aisle, she saw that the spectator seats were full and knew why. WAR HERO FACES COURT-MARTIAL.

That was the headline over a story penned by Beth Morgan two days earlier. Farther down, in paragraph five, mention had been made of what Morgan described as "the special relationship between Captain Macintyre and President Sloan."

There was no relationship other than the fact that Mac had been in command of the column that rescued Sloan's ill-fated force from Richton, Mississippi. But Morgan's story seemed to hint at something else—and her peers had been quick to seize on it. As a result, a routine disciplinary process, which would normally be of no interest to anyone outside the army, had become a cause célèbre. And as Mac passed the reporter, Morgan smiled broadly. The meaning was clear: "I can't have him, but neither will you."

A table for use by the defense attorney and the accused was located to the left of the central passageway—while the prosecutor and her assistant were on the right. The judge's chair was located on a riser directly in front of the other participants, with the witness stand to the left, and the five-member "forum" on the right. Thanks to Sanders's efforts, two members of the jury were female, three had seen combat, and all of them were officers.

As Mac sat down, she knew that everyone in the room was staring at her, and she felt an overwhelming sense of shame. Like most military personnel, Mac placed a high value on organizational integrity. So to sit there accused of disobedience, knowing that she was guilty, was the most humiliating moment of her life. All she could do was hide her trembling hands under the table and stare straight ahead.

Ten seemingly interminable minutes passed before the judge, a colonel named Elmore Apitz, entered the room. Everyone stood as Apitz took his seat, and the court-martial began. Mac experienced a sense of disassociation as the attorneys for both sides made their opening statements. Their words merged into a meaningless drone.

Everyone, Mac included, knew what the verdict was going to be. The only question was the nature of the punishment. Would the officers of the forum give her a slap on the wrist? Or would they drop a bomb on her? All Mac could do was wait to find out.

Once the opening statements were over, the prosecutor made her case. And for the first time since meeting him in Idaho, Mac had a chance to see Major Fitch. The uniform fit him like a glove, rows of ribbons decorated his chest, and he was every inch an air force officer.

But Fitch looked even more gaunt now—and his eyes were like chips of obsidian. When questioned, he spoke like a regretful teacher referencing an errant child. "Captain Macintyre's intentions may have been good," he allowed. "But military discipline is the backbone of the armed forces and requires that we obey those placed over us. Captain Macintyre put her desires before the needs of the country. It's as simple as that."

But no, it *wasn't* as simple as that. Not according to Sanders, who put Dr. Hoskins on the stand. It was good to see the navy officer again, and his presence gave Mac reason to hope.

"So, Doctor," Sanders said, once Hoskins had been sworn in, "you were present when Captain Macintyre and Major Fitch met. Is that correct?"

"Yes," Hoskins replied. "It is."

"And you could see both parties? And hear what was said?"

"Yes, I could."

"Please describe Major Fitch's manner."

"The major was suspicious and aggressive," Hoskins replied.

"Objection," the prosecutor interjected. "The doctor had no way to know what was going on inside the major's head. Appearances can be, and often are, deceiving."

"All of us are aware that nonverbal communication can be very effective," Sanders countered. "The doctor is a trained observer who is reporting on the way Major Fitch presented himself and could reasonably be perceived by Captain Macintyre."

"You may proceed," Judge Apitz said.

Sanders turned to Hoskins. "What else did you observe, Doctor? Was the major armed? And if so, with what?"

"He was," Hoskins confirmed. "The major was carrying a light machine gun. It was pointed at the sky, but could have been dropped into firing position very quickly. That, combined with his caustic manner, caused me to believe that he was hostile."

And so it went. The prosecutor put Fitch back on the stand to explain why he had reason to be suspicious of Mac's unit, and *any* unit that happened along, given the overall circumstances.

Sanders introduced evidence that Fitch had been suffering from PTSD at the time. And the prosecutor countered with an expert who maintained that the diagnosis didn't matter unless the major had been found unfit for duty prior to the encounter in Idaho.

Mac sat immobile throughout. She'd never been so helpless, and a supreme effort was required just to keep her head up. And even though she'd been in at least a dozen battles, and always found the courage to keep going, a feeling of hopelessness rose to consume her.

Hours dragged by. Summary statements were made, the case was given to the forum, and they left the room to deliberate. Everyone else was dismissed but given orders to remain on call in case the jurors came back with a verdict. "They won't reach a decision today," Sanders predicted. "We gave them a lot to think about."

Mac hoped that was true. And, in keeping with the attorney's prediction, the forum was still deliberating when 1700 rolled around and Mac was allowed to return to the BOQ. A gaggle of reporters and photographers was waiting outside. "Captain Macintyre! When did you last speak with the president? And what did he say?"

"How 'bout it, Captain . . ." a woman shouted. "*Are* you having an affair with the president?"

"Is it true that you're pregnant?" a man demanded. "And if so, who's the father?"

Mac pushed her way through the crowd and hurried away. The press would have been able to follow her if she'd been off base. But not on Fort Knox, where the reporters' movements were restricted. That meant Mac could turn a corner and escape.

Mac walked and kept walking. She'd been holding the tears back all day. Now, as they rolled down her cheeks, she wiped them away. A sergeant saluted, and she responded. It was, Mac knew, one of the last such courtesies she would receive. More than that, it was her last night of freedom. How did other people handle that? Did they get drunk with friends? Did they eat their favorite foods? Or did they curl up in the fetal position and sob? Mac hoped to avoid the third option. *Be tough,* she told herself. *Woman up.*

There were a number of places to eat on base, and Mac chose the largest and most crowded chow hall, hoping to go unnoticed. And the strategy was successful as far as she could tell. Because if people were talking about her, they were hiding it well.

Mac didn't have much of an appetite, though . . . And at least half of the chicken salad remained on the plate when she turned her tray in.

It was dark outside, and a heavy sleet was falling as she made her way to the BOQ. Once in her room, Mac found that a message was waiting. For the first time since returning to Fort Knox, she was to report to base's security center in person.

Mac smiled grimly. Of course . . . The evening before the verdict.

The night when she might decide to run. The next hour was spent trudging over to security, checking in, and walking back. It was about 1930 by the time she put her coat away, turned the TV on, and began to pack. The instructions from Sanders were explicit. "If a verdict comes in tomorrow, and if you're found guilty, the MPs will take you to the stockade. At that point, they will dispatch someone to get your belongings. So make sure that everything is packed and ready to go."

Mac was in the process of removing her underwear from the dresser when she heard the anchorwoman say her name. Mac turned just in time to see footage of herself as she broke through the press and fled. "Captain Robin Macintyre, who some claim is having an affair with the president, refused to take questions this afternoon as her case went to a military jury. The captain is accused of disobeying a direct order. Jury deliberations will resume tomorrow." The TV snapped to black as Mac pressed the power button.

Mac slid into bed half an hour later, but sleep wouldn't come. Would her father see the news reports? Would Victoria gloat? And what about Sloan? Did he know?

When the dreams arrived, they were tangled things, slippery with night sweat and filled with dread. And when the alarm went off, Mac experienced a sense of relief. More than that, she felt a lightness of spirit. As if something had changed. Did that flow from acceptance? Perhaps. But regardless of the reason, she felt better. Not happy, but better. And that would have to do.

Mac got up, showered, and dressed with care. What was it that the Green Berets liked to say? "No matter what happens, look cool." Yeah, that would be her motto for the day. Mac eyed the image in the mirror and threw her shoulders back. *You look good,* she told herself. *Work it.*

Once Mac was ready, she performed an idiot check on the room, said good-bye to her belongings, and left. The sleet had stopped by that time, and there were occasional breaks in the clouds. Mac even caught a glimpse of the sun on the way and chose to interpret that as a positive omen.

A gaggle of reporters was waiting for her, and Mac could see them from a distance. But rather than attempt to avoid them, she walked up to the group and paused. Then, as they started to barrage her with questions, Mac said, "Quiet!" And the authority with which she said it had the desired effect. "All right," Mac told them . . . "Here you go. I am *not* having an affair with the President of the United States. I have *not* spoken to him regarding my court-martial. And I am *not* pregnant. That will be all. Thank you." And with that, she walked up the steps and entered the building. More reporters were stationed inside, but she ignored them.

As Mac entered the courtroom, it seemed as if all her senses were maxed out. She could see, hear, and feel everything with the same intensity she had experienced while in combat.

Sanders was waiting for her, and Mac saw what might have been relief in his eyes. Had he been afraid that she'd run? Probably.

Judge Apitz arrived on time, everyone stood, and the proceeding got under way. "We have a verdict," Apitz announced, as he looked at a sheet of paper. "The defendant will rise."

Mac felt sick to her stomach but managed to keep her face blank as she stood. *No matter what happens, look cool.* "It is the forum's finding that Captain Robin Macintyre is guilty of both charges," Apitz said, as his eyes came up to meet Mac's. "A jury of your peers has found you guilty of violating Articles 90 and 92 of the Uniform Code of Military Justice. You could serve twenty years for those offenses. However, in light of your otherwise spotless record, and your well-documented acts of valor, I'm going to give you a sentence of four years to be served at Fort Leavenworth in Kansas.

Your attorney can file motions on your behalf and appeal the findings of this court should he find grounds to do so. This court is adjourned."

Mac felt her heart sink. *Four years!* Sanders had been hoping for two. "I'm sorry," Sanders said. "Hang in there. I'll be in touch."

A female MP stepped forward to take Mac into custody. "I won't cuff you here," she said kindly. "Not in front of the cameras."

Mac said, "Thank you." And, as she was led away, Mac saw Morgan standing against the wall. The reporter had a smirk on her face. She winked and turned away.

CHAPTER 9

||||||||||||||||||||||||||||||||||||

One of the many lessons that one learns in prison is, that
things are what they are and will be what they will be.

—OSCAR WILDE

NEAR SPRINGFIELD, MISSOURI

Rain tapped on the van's roof as Victoria and two members of her
team sat and waited. What was it? Day three? Yeah, day three.
And the man who called himself Nathan Hale had yet to show.
But he will show, Victoria assured herself. *He's a busy man. But
he'll come by. It's just a matter of time.*

After being outsmarted, and very nearly killed inside the Metrocenter Mall, Victoria felt a wide range of emotions including
sorrow, shame, and embarrassment. And her commanding officer's
scathing critique of the operation added to her misery. Because,
even though she didn't like or respect Colonel Oxley, she'd been
raised to respect authority figures, so his opinion mattered.

The strength of some emotions had started to fade, but one
burned bright. And that was an intense anger directed toward

Nathan Hale. The anger could have been corrosive. But for Victoria, it was like the oxygen a fire requires in order to burn.

Every day was a workday. Not just for Victoria, but for her team, including the soldiers brought in to replace Post and Tarvin. Thanks to the photos Tarvin had taken during the minutes prior to her death, investigators had something to work with. Hale was disguised as a woman. But, by subjecting the images to computer analysis, Victoria's techs had been able to render an image that they believed to be a good match to Hale's actual appearance.

So far, so good. But what was Hale's actual identity? Victoria had a theory about that. Rather than the home-grown resistance fighter he claimed to be, Victoria thought Hale was a member of the Union's military-intelligence apparatus. An army officer? Quite possibly.

The next step was to use facial-recognition software to compare the new image with prewar photos of the country's military officers. All of which were available thanks to a predisaster Department of Defense database that both sides had copies of.

It took the computer two minutes and forty-two seconds to produce seven possibles, each graded according to the degree of match. It was tempting to focus on the top three at the expense of the others, but Victoria demanded that the team be more systematic than that.

The evaluation consumed three days. According to articles from northern publications, three of the possibles had been killed in action. That didn't mean they were actually dead, however, since the Union's Intel people could have planted the articles in hopes that the Confederacy would believe them.

Still, odds were that the reports were accurate. And, since one of the men was being held in a Confederate POW camp and another was African-American, only two candidates remained. One was a captain named Gregory Salazar. The other was a major named Thomas Toby. Both had dark hair, green eyes, and even features. But Victoria had a hunch that Salazar and Hale were one and the same.

That was a subjective judgment, to say the least, and one she didn't share. Rather than do so, Victoria ordered the team to look for factors that would help to narrow the choice. And after days of hard work, they found it. Two years earlier, while attending staff college, Salazar had written a paper titled: "The Role of Military Intelligence During a Civil Insurrection."

According to the scenario that Salazar and his classmates had been ordered to address, a loosely linked alliance of right-wing hate groups, religious fanatics, and gun nuts had taken control of Texas and Oklahoma, producing a conflict similar to the one that was under way. And the tactics that Salazar put forward bore a strong resemblance to those that Hale was using. That included the creation of a unit designed to target teams like hers!

Once the focus was on Salazar, the effort to find him began. It turned out that Salazar had been raised in Wichita. And some of his relatives, including his sister, were placed under surveillance. Would Salazar visit her? All they could do was wait and see. But, when the break finally came, it was more a matter of luck than skill.

There had been a burglary two doors down from what proved to be a Union safe house. And as the police went door to door looking for witnesses, they asked neighbors to provide footage from their security cameras, footage that was dumped into a police database and scanned with facial-recognition software. The computer contained wants and warrants on thousands of people, including one Gregory Salazar. Military intelligence was notified of the "hit," and that led Victoria's team to the safe house.

"Heads up," Sergeant Fray said. "We have a possible." Fray was an experienced operative and Tarvin's replacement. He was sitting behind the steering wheel staring out through the rain-smeared glass.

Victoria leaned forward. "What have you got?"

"A car circled the block twice," Fray answered. "And now it's back."

Victoria felt her pulse quicken. That's how a pro would play it. Even though Salazar might feel reasonably safe, he'd be wary. So, rather than pull into the driveway right away, he would circle the block, looking for anything out of the ordinary. And Victoria felt confident that there was nothing about the van that would trigger his suspicions. Victoria opened her mike as the car slowed. "Cooper? Do you read me? Over."

"Five by five."

"He's about to pull in. Get ready."

"Roger that. Over."

Cooper and two other operatives had been living in the house for five days, waiting for this moment. Victoria watched the garage door open as the car *backed* in. A small detail but one that was consistent with her hypothesis. Who, other than a pro, would *back* in? Thereby making ready to depart in a hurry.

The headlights went off as the door closed. Victoria held her breath as light appeared in the windows. The interior of the house was lousy with security cameras. Cameras that Salazar could check prior to visiting the house. What the Union operators didn't realize was that their outgoing feed had been hijacked and replaced with a loop.

Victoria heard a burb of static, followed by Cooper's voice. "We have him."

Victoria felt a flood of relief. "Search him for weapons, suicide paraphernalia, and trackers. And look *everywhere*."

Cooper sounded hurt. "Of course. We're on it."

Victoria turned to Fray. "Keep a sharp lookout. If you see any-thing even remotely suspicious, let me know. I'm going in."

Corporal Hamad opened the front door for her. According to the official records, the house belonged to a woman named Deb-orah Lee, although Victoria figured that the safe house was actually the property of the Union government.

The interior was decorated fifties style, with sixties lamps and brightly colored plastic chairs. Salazar had been stripped and taped into one of them. He sat with his legs spread. It was a psycholog-ical ploy for the most part, a way to make him feel vulnerable, but it had practical value as well since there was the possibility that something was hidden in Salazar's groin. A tech was running her fingers over the surface of his skin, searching for subdural implants.

"Victoria," Salazar said conversationally. "This *is* a surprise. Please excuse me if I don't get up."

Salazar was frightened. Victoria could see it in his eyes. She was about to reply when the tech beat her to it. "Hmm . . . What's this? An implant, if I'm not mistaken. It's high up on the inside surface of his left thigh."

"Cut it out," Victoria ordered. "Let's see what we have."

Salazar winced, and blood dripped onto the white rug as the tech made the necessary incision. "Here we go," the tech said, as she applied pressure to both sides of the cut.

Victoria watched with interest as a bloody blob popped out and knew that it was either a suicide capsule or a distress beacon. The kind Salazar could activate by squeezing it. But Salazar hadn't had an opportunity to do so, which meant he was on his own. "Good work," she said. "Keep looking. There could be a backup."

The search continued for another five minutes but with no success. "Patch him up," Victoria ordered, "and get him dressed. We're leaving."

It took half an hour to transfer Salazar to a Confederate safe house. Three days of interrogation followed. Who did he work for? Who did he work with? And what operations were currently under way? On and on it went but with only limited success. First, because Salazar was one tough cookie. Second, because he answered most of their questions with lies . . . And third, because the Union Underground was highly compartmentalized. Odds were that Salazar didn't *know* who he was working for, and the only operations Salazar had knowledge of were his own.

Still, there were bits and pieces that, when combined with other intelligence, might add up to something. Now, as the van drove out into the countryside, Salazar was passed out in his seat. Or was he? It didn't matter. The shackles on his wrists and ankles would prevent a surprise attack.

The van cleared the suburbs, passed between green fields, and crossed a bridge. A graveled road led up onto the summit of a hill topped with a cell-phone tower and a scattering of beer cans. A well-known spot, then, a place where the locals could party.

The persistent cloud cover prevented the air from being warm—but it was a pleasant day by postimpact standards. Cooper got out of the van first. He was wearing a black hood and armed with a suppressed assault rifle. The agent brought the weapon up and fired a burst at the cell tower's security camera. Maybe the phone company would notify the police, and maybe they wouldn't. Victoria didn't care. They'd be gone by the time someone arrived to investigate.

Victoria got out of the van and made her way over to the east side of the hill. A farmhouse was visible below, and a party was under way. Two dozen adults and four children could be seen. They looked like ants viewed from above.

Victoria sensed movement and turned to find that Salazar had arrived. His face was bruised, one eye was swollen shut, and his upper lip was swollen. Torture doesn't work. That's what the experts claimed, but Victoria wasn't so sure. So the beatings had been part of the overall mix, along with sleep deprivation and loud music.

Salazar's head was hanging low, so Victoria forced it up. "Look downhill, turd blossom . . . Do you recognize the house?"

"It's my sister's house," Salazar said thickly.

"Very good," Victoria said. "And the people? Who are they?"

Salazar frowned, winced, and swallowed. "My family."

"That's right . . . We tapped your sister's phone. Today is your niece's birthday."

A look of horror appeared on Salazar's face. "You wouldn't."

"Oh, but I would. You killed my family . . . My *military* family. So I'm going to kill yours. Fair is fair. Look up into the sky. See the drone? It's armed with a Hellfire missile."

"No, please," Salazar said desperately. "Don't do it!"

"Too late," Victoria said, as the missile struck. A loud boom was heard as the house was transformed into a ball of yellow-orange fire. Pieces of debris soared high into the air, a car performed a backflip, and black smoke billowed up to stain the sky.

Salazar attacked her then . . . or tried to. But Cooper was ready and kicked the agent behind a knee. Salazar fell into a sobbing heap.

Victoria felt better. *Much* better. Her honor had been restored. She smiled. "Load him into the van. Maybe the people in Houston can sweat some more information out of him. Oh, and call 911 . . . Tell them that a house went boom."

THE MIDWEST JOINT REGIONAL CORRECTION FACILITY
FORT LEAVENWORTH, KANSAS

Mac's feet were on her bunk, her hands were on the cement floor, and she was doing push-ups. She counted them out. "Twenty-eight, twenty-nine, thirty." A full set. The first of what would be six sets by the end of the day. To stay in shape? No. To get in *better* shape. Why? To make progress. To control something if only by a little. Because the JRCF's jailers dictated everything else, including what Mac ate, when she showered, and with whom she could mix, which was to say no one. Mac had been told that social privileges would come later, *after* the induction process was over.

She stood. Her cell consisted of eighty square feet, thirty-five of which were classified as "usable." The rest was occupied by the bunk, a desk/seat combo, and storage space. There was a window, too, with a magnificent view of a parking lot. Mac sighed. Three weeks down and 205 left to go.

Mac knew she shouldn't dwell on the length of her sentence. So to avoid that, she spent a lot of mental time elsewhere. And reading books was a good way to accomplish that. Not just as a means to escape, but as a way to exert control over what would and would not be allowed to enter her head.

Sit-ups came next. Six hundred a day, and Mac was busy working her way through the first set when the guards came for her. There were two MPs, and both had their game faces on. "Get up," the tall one ordered. "You're going for a stroll."

Mac got up off the floor. "Where to?"

"The multi," the short MP answered. "Multi" being shorthand for the prison's multipurpose building.

"What for?"

"Who the hell knows?" the taller of the two replied. "Maybe they need a hero to mop the floor."

That produced a guffaw from the short soldier. "That's a good one, Hawkins, you're funny."

Mac had heard such comments before and was careful to maintain a straight face. Pushback, no matter how minor, could trigger a hundred subtle forms of revenge. "You know the drill," Shorty added. "Let's get on with it."

Mac backed up to the bars, stuck her hands through the waist-high hole, and waited for the cuffs to go on. Once she heard the telltale click, Mac took two steps forward. A clanking sound was heard as the door slid open. "Okay," the tall MP said. "Turn around and step out."

With an MP on either side of her, Mac was escorted outside for the short walk to the multi. It housed food service, medical/dental, and the prison's administrative offices. Mac figured she had been summoned for inoculations or something. But that theory went out the window as the MPs led her into the administrative area of the building. Her attorney was still fighting to get her sentence reduced. Or so he claimed. Had something gone wrong? Were they going to tell her that? Mac felt the first stirrings of fear.

They hadn't gone far when Mac was handed off to a couple of men in civilian clothes. Criminal investigators? That was her best guess. They led Mac to a door marked COMMANDER. Holy shit! She was going in front of the *man* . . . or the woman, as the case might be. And that was a bad thing.

One of the agents opened the door for her, and the other one told Mac to enter. No words were spoken as they hustled her through an empty waiting room and past a middle-aged receptionist. The door to the office was open, and the room was empty.

"Have a seat," one of the agents said. "You might have to wait for a while."

The comment proved to be prophetic. Fifteen interminable minutes passed as Mac sat and waited for *what*? There was no way to know. But eventually she heard the sound of voices, followed by a commotion out in the hall, and movement behind her. "Remove her cuffs," a female voice ordered. "And wait outside."

Mac felt the handcuffs come off and turned to see that a lieutenant colonel was standing a few feet away. The woman nodded. "I'm Commander Omada . . . It was nice to meet you." And with that, she was gone.

Mac was still trying to make sense of the comment when President Samuel Sloan entered the office. He grinned. "Hi, Mac . . . It's good to see you."

Mac was both dumbfounded and embarrassed by the prison outfit. She came to her feet. "What are you doing here?"

"I wanted to deliver the news myself," Sloan told her. "I pardoned you."

Mac couldn't believe her ears. "You *what*?"

"I pardoned you effective 0800 this morning, *and* I promoted you to major."

"*No,*" Mac said. "You can't! You shouldn't. Don't you understand? People will believe that the gossip is true! The scandal will bring you down."

Sloan smiled. "You look pretty when you're worried. Of course, you look pretty the rest of the time, too."

"It's not a joke," Mac said emphatically. "The country needs you."

"And they need *you*," Sloan countered. "Putting one of our most promising officers in the slammer for refusing an order from a man with severe PTSD was just plain stupid. And that's what I'll tell the press. A version of it, anyway. More than that, I'm going to announce the creation of a new cavalry battalion called Mac's Marauders! It will consist of military prisoners chosen by you. There will be a tremendous ruckus at first . . . But after the dust settles, people will love it! You'll have to deliver, though, or it could bring me down."

Mac's head was spinning. "But what about the rumors?"

Sloan's expression hardened. "I will challenge the press to produce a single photo, or a credible individual, who witnessed any sort of romantic activity between us—and tell them to shut the hell up until they do. Unfortunately, that means I won't be able to take you to dinner, ply you with alcohol, and seduce you as quickly as I had hoped to."

Mac smiled in spite of herself. "That's how it was going to play out?"

"Of course," Sloan replied. "I'm irresistible."

Mac laughed. "We'll see about that . . . *After* you leave office."

Sloan's eyes were locked with hers. "You promise?"

"I promise."

Sloan forced a smile. "Good. That's settled then. A supply sergeant has a full set of uniforms waiting for you. Put one on and get ready . . . You and General Brady will join me at the press conference."

Sloan left after that, and Mac was led to a nearby office, where a supply sergeant was waiting for her. She was fortysomething and sporting a buzz cut. "Good morning, ma'am. Please remove what you're wearing—and put your camos on. Let's see how you look."

Mac did as she was told. She'd lost a couple of pounds while in prison, but the camos fit well. So well that she knew they'd been tailored. Someone wanted her to look sharp. Sloan? Or one of his handlers? None of whom were likely to support the president's initiative.

Mac could imagine the kind of objections they'd have. Why buy trouble? Don't you have enough of it already? And the obvious answer was yes, he sure as hell did.

A full-length mirror had been brought in . . . And when Mac stood in front of it, a major looked back at her. Could she be dreaming? Was Sloan really risking his presidency to free her from prison? Yes. And that was both good and bad. Good because she would be back on active duty and bad because now she owed him. *But how awful can that be?* her inner voice wanted to know. *It isn't as though you dislike him.*

"It's time to put this on," the sergeant said, as she gave Mac a black beret. Mac saw that an emblem bearing a silver skull and crossed lightning bolts was pinned to the front of it. The design was unique insofar as Mac knew, and clearly had been created to make her unit stand out. Mac put the beret on her head and tilted it to the right. *Own it,* she told herself. *Don't let him down.*

The press weren't sure what to expect when they were bused onto the base and herded into position. A platform had been set up with the JRCF in the background. Rumors flew, the most popular of which had to do with a North-South prisoner exchange.

The cynics in the crowd said no and pointed to the fact that none of the Confederate POWs were being held at Fort Leavenworth. So the discussion was still going on when General Teddy Brock stepped up onto the stage. President Sloan arrived next, followed by a female army officer. That was when a correspondent recognized Mac. "Look!" he said. "That's Captain Macintyre! The officer who was court-martialed!"

"You mean *Major* Macintyre," Brock said sternly. "Please hold your questions. I promise that they will be answered after the president makes an important announcement. Mr. President?"

Sloan stepped forward. "Thank you, General, and good morning. As you know, the United States of America *was*, and will be once again, the land of second chances. A place where a long list of famous names made mistakes and, by dint of hard work, were allowed to climb back up. President Clinton comes to mind. And it's in that spirit that I announce the new Military Reintegration Program.

"The purpose of this initiative is to remove nonviolent offenders from our military prisons and put them back on the battlefield. A new cavalry battalion has been created for that purpose. It will consist of three companies of soldiers under the command of Major Robin Macintyre who, as one of you correctly pointed out, was court-martialed for disobeying a direct order. There's no question that she was guilty, but it's important to remember that when *Lieutenant* Macintyre disobeyed that order, the chain of command was in tatters—and it was difficult for a junior officer to know from whom to take orders.

"In light of that fact, as well as her well-documented acts of valor, I granted Captain Macintyre a full pardon as of 0800 this morning—and promoted her to major two minutes later. She, along with officers selected by her, will choose the individuals permitted to join the new battalion. All of those appointments will be reviewed and approved by General Brock.

"Furthermore, a zero-tolerance policy will be in effect. That means that a single infraction of the Uniform Code of Military Justice will be sufficient to send a soldier back to prison where they will have to complete their original sentence.

"But," Sloan added, "those soldiers who serve twenty-four months without disciplinary problems will receive full pardons. Now, I suspect you have some questions."

The press *did* have questions. The first of which had to do with the rumored love affair between Sloan and Macintyre. Sloan tackled the subject head-on. "I admire Major Macintyre for her many acts of bravery in service to our country, and more than that, will be eternally grateful for the lives she saved during our retreat from Richton, Mississippi. And that includes my own.

"But that's the full extent of our relationship, and I challenge you to produce a single photo or credible witness who says otherwise. The major will report through Colonel Lassiter to General Brock without any involvement by me. This story is about redemption, ladies and gentlemen . . . And the opportunity to return trained soldiers to the battlefield."

"Is the Union Army in such desperate straits that it needs to recruit soldiers from prisons?" a television correspondent demanded. "Are the rebs winning?"

"No," Brock put in. "The rebs aren't winning. But the Military Reintegration Program represents an opportunity to put even more trained troops into the field *and* lighten the load on our prison system."

There was more, much more. And even though the questions became increasingly repetitive, Sloan addressed each and every one of them until the newspeople became visibly weary of hearing the same answers over and over again.

So one of the reporters turned his attention to Macintyre, and the whole thing started over. Did she have a personal relationship with Sloan? When did she learn about the pardon? How did she feel about it? What was prison life like? And had she been in touch with her father, General Bo Macintyre?

Mac did the best she could to imitate Sloan's slow, methodical style with the same result. Eventually, having run out of questions, the press became less contentious. That was when Brock stepped forward to bring the conference to a close. "A final note, ladies and gentlemen. The new battalion will be called Mac's Marauders, and those who join will fight under the motto: *Optima pessima*. The best of the worst. That will be all."

Sloan left the moment the press conference was over. There were no waves, no good-bye, and no opportunity to thank him. Mac knew that to be a good thing because a picture of them talking to each other might be used to suggest some sort of clandestine relationship. She regretted the suddenness of the parting, however—and was looking forward to seeing him again someday.

The events that followed took place with neck-snapping speed. Mac and two bags of newly issued gear were loaded aboard a Black Hawk for the short flight to the field where the reserve element of General Brock's division was quartered. Once on the ground, Brock accompanied Mac to brigade headquarters, where she was introduced to her new CO.

Colonel Marvin Lassiter was a lot of things—including a veteran of the war in Afghanistan, an avid runner, and a well-known hardass. He had a hawk-like nose and a mouth that rarely smiled. And when they shook hands, Mac felt as if his laser-blue eyes could see right through her. "Have a seat, Major, and welcome to the 31st."

Mac sat on the chair next to Brock's. "Thank you, sir."

Rather than circle his desk, Lassiter chose to perch on one corner of it. "I'm not one for small talk, or for beating around the bush," he told her. "So I'll give it to you straight. When General Brock told me what the president was going to do, and that your so-called Reintegration Battalion was going to be part of the 31st, I gave serious consideration to resigning."

"Except that he *can't* resign," Brock put in, "not unless I sign off . . . Which I won't."

Lassiter made a face. "That means I have to put up with you and your battalion of losers. But understand this . . . I am *not* Major Fitch. If you refuse one of my orders, I will shoot you in the face, make up a story to explain it, and grab a good night's sleep."

"I didn't hear that," Brock said.

"Of course you didn't," Lassiter agreed. "Because I never said it. So, Major Macintyre . . . do we understand each other?"

"Sir, yes, sir."

"Good. Now here's how this is going to work. Under no circumstances will you or your pet criminals mix with the fine men and women of the 31st except during a battle. Your convicts will be quartered on a civilian airstrip called Peavey Field. It's located adjacent to the division, but separated from it by an eight-foot-high fence. And to ensure that your jackoffs behave themselves, I'm going to place one of my officers on your staff. The so-what is that I'll get a report every time you pass gas. Do you read me?"

Mac swallowed. "Five by five, sir."

"I'm glad to hear it," Lassiter said. "Now get your ass out there and go to work! You have thirty days to build a battalion. Not a second more."

Mac knew a dismissal when she heard one. She stood, came to attention, and popped a salute. Lassiter gave one in return. "And Macintyre . . ."

"Sir?"

"You did a good job up in Wyoming. Dismissed."

The parting comment left Mac with a sense of hope. Maybe, just maybe, she could win Lassiter over. Not with bullshit . . . But by creating the best battalion in his brigade.

Mac exited the building to discover that a captain was waiting for her . . . A skull-and-lightning pin was affixed to his beret. He came to attention and rendered a salute. "Good morning, Major . . . Captain Roy Quick reporting for duty."

Quick had dark skin, a round face, and a boyish demeanor. Mac returned the salute. "Reporting for duty as *what*?"

"I'm your XO, ma'am."

Mac remembered what Lassiter had said. "Are you the spy?"

Quick grinned. "Yes, ma'am . . . The colonel told me to keep a close eye on you."

"And you intend to do that?"

"Yes, ma'am."

"Fair enough . . . Tell him the truth, and we'll get along just fine. So, Roy . . . The colonel mentioned a base. Have you been there?"

"I have," Quick replied. "It isn't fancy, but it'll do. Here's the problem, though . . . Someone in the chain of command has been sending supplies there. And we don't have anyone to receive, inventory, and track them."

"So we need some supply people."

"Yes, ma'am."

"Okay . . . I'll go shopping for people in the morning. In the meantime, I'd like to see what the battalion is entitled to. Do you have a table of organization?"

Quick did. And a Humvee as well. They chatted as he drove them out through the main gate, and along a fence, to Peavey Field. It seemed that Quick had seen action in the Middle East, as well as the opening battles of the Second Civil War. That was good news from Mac's point of view, and a sure sign that, while Lassiter didn't approve of the reintegration concept, he wasn't trying to sabotage it by assigning a second-rate XO to her battalion.

A pair of MPs were guarding the gate to Peavey Field. They knew Quick and hurried to let the officers in. The situation inside the wire was what Mac expected it to be. With the exception of a wingless Cessna, the rest of the civilian planes had been removed, leaving two rows of hangars behind. "I figure we can park two Strykers under each roof," Quick said. "That will make it more difficult for the rebs to count them from above—and the wrench turners will be able to get in out of the weather."

Mac was impressed by her XO's interest in strategic matters and the well-being of the battalion's troops. "That's a good idea, Roy. What about barracks? Are there any buildings that could serve?"

Quick shook his head as the Humvee came to a stop in front of a small building. The sun-faded sign read: TERMINAL. "No, ma'am," Quick replied. "But I took the liberty of requisitioning two modular tent systems from the division. I figured we could set them up on the east side of the runway with porta potties along the fence."

"You the man," Mac said approvingly. She gestured toward the terminal building. "And what about that?"

"Battalion HQ," Quick replied. "Assuming you approve. Plus the three Conex loads of the supplies that I mentioned earlier."

Mac got out to take a look around. Quick was correct. The empty terminal would function as her headquarters, and the supplies were a pressing problem. What if someone came in and stole them? She'd be in deep shit, that's what. She had to "recruit" some troops and do it fast.

Mac spent the night in the division's BOQ, and hoped that doing so wouldn't violate Lassiter's prohibition against mixing with "the fine men and women of the 31st." There was so much to think about that she had difficulty getting to sleep at first. But once fatigue overcame her, it was like falling off the edge of a cliff. Mac awoke rested and eager to get going.

A hurried breakfast was followed by a short helo ride to Fort

Leavenworth. Something she wouldn't have been able to arrange without assistance from Quick. Mac wished she could bring him along. But with thirty, no, twenty-nine days left to work with—someone had to stay behind and manage the paperwork that went with commissioning a new battalion.

The flight went smoothly, and it felt strange to land near the building where she'd been imprisoned the day before. She recognized some of the soldiers on the gate and could tell that they recognized her. A corporal grinned as Mac flashed her new ID card. "Welcome back, ma'am . . . And congratulations."

Once inside, Mac went straight to the multi, where she was given access to all of the prisoner records. There were about five hundred in all, which represented about a third of the military's prisoner population. Not that many, really . . . A fact that critics could use against Sloan if they chose to, and maybe they would.

It would have been nice to visit all of the army's detention facilities, but there wasn't enough time, so Mac would have to settle for what she could source locally. Later, once the outfit was up and running, she could look farther afield.

After reviewing the records, Mac saw that only twelve 03-level officers were being held in the prison, and of those, two had been convicted of violent crimes, making them ineligible for the program. Mac was camped in a spartan conference room, where she spent the next hour studying the ten remaining candidates. Her goal was to identify people who had combat experience and been convicted of crimes that weren't representative of their past performance.

Once that process was over, the "candidates" were brought in one at a time and invited to sit across from Mac, while an MP stood guard. Having been a prisoner herself, Mac wasn't surprised to learn that they knew all about the Military Reintegration Program and her role in it. News like that was bound to travel quickly in the JRCF's closed universe. And some, like Captain Patrick Rowley, were eager to join. "I'm your man," he assured her. "You were a mercenary before the war, right? What a great gig."

Mac frowned. "As I understand it, you and two of your soldiers put on Confederate uniforms and robbed a bank."

"Yeah," Rowley admitted. "No one was hurt, and we got away clean . . . But Solby got drunk and spilled his guts."

"You know my battalion will be part of the regular army, right? And not a criminal gang."

"Sure," Rowley said with a wink. "I know that."

Mac turned to look at the guard. "Take this man back to his cell and show the next candidate in."

"Wait!" Rowley said, as he was led away. "That was a joke! I'm your man!"

The next prisoner was a supply officer, Amy Wu. She had short black hair and severe bangs. Mac could see a wariness in Wu's almond-shaped eyes. "So," Mac began, "you're doing time for stealing government property."

"No," Wu said flatly. "I'm in prison for stealing *rebel* property."

"What *had* been rebel property," Mac countered. "Until it was captured and became Union property."

Wu's prison-issue clothes were too large for her tiny frame. Her shirt barely moved when she shrugged. "Technically, yes."

"And you did it because?"

"I did it for the money," Wu said defiantly.

Mac frowned. "I'm looking for a supply officer . . . More than that, a person who can run my headquarters company. You're qualified, on paper at least, but what about the fuck-you attitude? Is that who you are? Or is that prison bravado?"

Mac saw something change in the other woman's eyes. She looked down at her lap. "I made a mistake, Major. I regret it. I'd like a second chance."

"If I choose you, and you steal so much as a pencil, you'll be back here the next day. You understand that?"

Wu looked up. "Yes, ma'am."

"Okay . . . I'll think about it. Next."

The next officer was a drug trafficker who had been selling speed to his troops and using it himself. He was sober now and swore that he would stay that way. But Mac had doubts. It was difficult for the man to make eye contact, and he had a tendency to mumble. She wasn't impressed.

The pusher was followed by an officer who, after discovering that his CO was having an affair with a subordinate's husband, took the opportunity to blackmail her. He was handsome, smooth, and subtly flirtatious. None of which would be useful on a battlefield. He had led a platoon of Strykers however, and *that* was relevant. Mac placed him on the maybe list.

The next candidate was Captain Avery Howell who, according to his file, was a decorated company commander *and* inveterate gambler. A habit that was his undoing when he borrowed money from a mob boss, lost it playing poker, and was ordered to make good on his debt by stealing a tank. He'd been caught in the act and sentenced to eight years. He had an honest straightforward manner, however—and Mac liked him from the start. But could he part with his addiction? She asked him that.

"I think I can," Howell answered. "I want to . . . And the busier I am, the better it will be."

"No problem there," Mac assured him. "If I choose you, you'll work your ass off."

Mac took a lunch break at that point and discovered that the food served in the staff cafeteria was just as bad as what they fed her in the prison! Then it was time to return to the conference room.

The next four candidates were unacceptable. The first was thirty pounds overweight, the second wanted to know if she could go on leave prior to joining the battalion, the third wanted to wait until the results of his appeal came in. As for the fourth . . . she claimed to be the Virgin Mary . . . and was clearly looking for some sort of medical discharge.

That left Captain Irwin Overman. He had a buzz cut and a pair of fierce eyes that stared out from bony caves. According to Overman's file, he was serving a six-year sentence for desertion. Not in the face of the enemy, but after 60 percent of his company had been killed in a single battle, leaving him untouched. After three days on the run, Overman turned himself in.

"*Why?*" Mac wanted to know. "Why run, and come back? I've read the reports. The high casualty rate wasn't your fault. Your outfit was in the wrong place at the wrong time."

Overman shrugged. "That's what the shrinks tell me."

"And the voices? What do *they* tell you?"

Overman looked surprised. "How do you know about the voices? I never told anyone."

"I hear voices of my own," Mac said.

"Then you know what they say. They want to know why they're dead and you're alive."

"I know," Mac said. "But what is, *is*. The fact is that you survived . . . And you can save other troops by providing them with good leadership. I need officers who won't run from the enemy but won't waste lives either. How about it? The rebs killed your soldiers. Would you like to get even?"

"You're trying to manipulate me."

"Yes, I am . . . For a cause. A *good* cause."

The eyes stared at her. Thirty long seconds passed. He nodded. "If you want me, I'm in."

"I want you," Mac acknowledged, and she made the decision on the spot. "Welcome to Mac's Marauders."

CHAPTER 10

IIIIIIIIIIIIIIIIIIIIIIIIIIIIIIIIIIIIIIII

Take me to the brig. I want to see the "real Marines."

—MAJOR GENERAL "CHESTY" PULLER, USMC

PORT ST. JOE, FLORIDA

The two-story house sat atop stilts and was located well back from the glittering water. Victoria was wearing a black two-piece and gloried in the feel of the sun on her skin. Such moments were rare now that the postimpact haze obscured so much of the sky. Victoria heard movement and turned to look as her father stepped onto the deck. He offered her an ice-cold beer. "Here . . . This will wet your whistle."

General Bo Macintyre was in good shape for a man in his early sixties. But his skin was a bit looser than it had been a few years earlier, and he had an incipient paunch, both of which frightened Victoria. What would she do when he died? Her life was organized around the never-ending task of earning his approval. She knew that wasn't healthy yet couldn't stop.

They talked about fishing for a while, then golf, then the war. "How are we doing?" Victoria wanted to know.

Bo took a sip of beer and stared at the sea. "That depends on how you choose to measure it. We're holding the bastards off, but that won't lead to victory. To accomplish that, we've got to push them back across the New Mason-Dixon Line, destroy their in-dustrial base, and sap their will to fight."

Victoria stared at him. "Can we do those things?"

Bo's eyes were invisible behind his sunglasses. "We can . . . But we've got to be willing to use *all* of the weapons at our disposal."

Victoria took a moment to consider that. "Do you mean nukes?"

"Yes. The present situation reminds me of what they called mutually assured destruction, or MAD, during the Cold War. Both side had nukes, and both sides were afraid to use them."

Victoria frowned. "So, what are you saying? That we *should* use nukes?"

Bo turned to look at her. Victoria could see reflections of herself in his glasses. "You tell me, Victoria . . . Let's say you're facing a grizzly, and you're carrying a .22 and a .338 Weatherby. Which rifle would you choose?"

"The .338," Victoria replied. "But that's a false analogy. In this case, the griz has a . 338, too."

"True," her father replied. "But a series of well-targeted pre-emptive strikes would solve that problem."

"And destroy a lot of what we're fighting for."

"Victory always comes at a cost," Bo replied. "And I think we should pay that price before the Union can grow any stronger. Or," he continued, "we should make peace. But Lemaire took a run at that, and Sloan refused to listen. What happens next is up to the politicos in Houston."

The fact that Lemaire had attempted to negotiate with Sloan was news to Victoria. And it served to put her father's comments in a different light. If Sloan wasn't willing to negotiate, then he, and the idiots who backed him, deserved what came their way. And that included nukes. "I'm sorry to hear that," Victoria said.

"You *didn't* hear it," Bo said, as his gaze returned to the water. "Any of it."

"No, of course not."

Bo's secretary appeared at that point. Victoria knew her as Mrs. Walters, even though her husband had been dead for many years, and her first name was Kathy. She had carefully arranged blond hair, a nice figure, and made the summery outfit look good.

Victoria had been aware of the love affair for a long time and approved of it. Her mother was dead after all—and there was no reason why her father shouldn't have some companionship. But this was the first time that the twosome had been so open about their relationship. Kathy was carrying a glass of iced tea, which she placed on a side table prior to sitting down under an umbrella. Bo removed his glasses and produced a rare smile. "There you are . . . and just in time, too. We were talking shop."

"Shame on you," Kathy replied. "You came here to escape that."

"And to be with the two of you," Bo replied gallantly. "Which reminds me," Bo said, as he turned to look at Victoria. "Kathy and I have some news to share . . . We're going to get married."

Victoria felt a surge of jealousy and hurried to suppress it. "That's wonderful," she said. "I'm so happy for you! Have you chosen a date?"

"Not yet," Kathy replied. "Your father's calendar is pretty full at the moment, but you'll be the first to know when we nail it down."

"I don't think Robin will be able to attend," Victoria said. It was meant to be a joke but didn't come across that way.

Bo scowled. "I guess you haven't heard . . . Your sister was charged with disobeying a direct order, found guilty, and sentenced to four years in Leavenworth."

Victoria felt a sense of triumph. The contest was over! "I'm sorry, Daddy," she said sweetly. "But not surprised. Would you like another beer?"

PEAVEY FIELD, KANSAS

Dark gray clouds had massed in the north and were preparing to roll south. The temperature was starting to drop, causing Mac to shove her hands into her pockets. Fifteen days had passed since President Sloan had signed her pardon, and Mac was standing in the airport's two-man control tower, looking out across the airstrip. The battalion's troops were lined up for PT, and Sergeant Major Price was putting them through their paces. The noncom wasn't using a bullhorn—but Mac could hear him anyway.

Price had been serving six months for "borrowing" a Bradley while intoxicated and doing doughnuts in a city park prior to joining the Marauders. He'd been chosen by Quick, who had served with Price in the past and swore by him. Was Price's crusty persona for real? Or part of an elaborate act? It didn't matter. The noncom's hard-ass manner was perfect for a battalion comprised of ex-criminals.

Later, once PT was over, Price would form the troops into companies and march them up and down the runway like ROTC kids on parade. Not to train them . . . All of the battalion's soldiers had been through basic. No, the purpose of the exercise was to forge them into a team. A process Quick likened to "herding cats."

But while Price worked to turn prisoners back into soldiers,

Mac had to find the means to house, feed, and arm them. The latter was especially difficult since supplies of every sort were in high demand. Fortunately, Mac had a secret weapon in the person of Captain Amy Wu, who had already proven herself to have the combined skills of a street hustler, a beady-eyed accountant, and a thief. Not the outright thievery that had landed her in prison, but the sort of borderline shenanigans that were often a bit sketchy.

The recent delivery of three wrecked Strykers served as a case in point. The vics were sitting in the division's junkyard, where they were slated for shipment to a reconditioning center in Michigan, when Wu came across them. It wasn't clear how the transaction had gone down. But somehow the vehicles were reclassified as "available for reassignment" and trucked to Mac's Marauders. Within a matter of days, Wu's mechanics had been able to create *two* fighting machines by using parts from the third. And that was nothing short of a miracle.

But not everything had gone so smoothly. Because the battalion's soldiers weren't allowed to mix with the 31st, they couldn't use the brigade's chow hall. That meant they were living on a steady diet of MREs. It was a problem that was starting to take a toll on the unit's morale.

Such were Mac's thoughts when she heard movement and turned to see Quick poke his head up through the hatch. "Good news, boss . . . They found Private Arley! He was at his mother's house, eating cookies."

Arley had gone AWOL three hours after being released from prison. Mac said, "Good . . . At least he didn't rob a gas station or something. Put him in front of the troops, remind them why desertion constitutes a serious crime, and send his ass back to the slammer."

"Yes, ma'am."

"I'm supposed to attend a meeting at brigade HQ. Keep an eye on Wu, and everyone else for that matter."

Quick grinned. "Will do." Then he was gone.

Rather than keep a private from spending time with Sergeant Major Price, Mac chose to drive herself. An MP saluted as she left the base. The presence of so many soldiers was a boon to the civilians who did business out of the colorfully painted trucks that were parked along the fence. There were barbers, tailors, and food vendors.

Mac passed them and took a left. There was a line to get into the base. After a short wait, she entered the checkpoint. A sharp-looking MP threw a salute, checked her ID, and waved her through. Mac was early for the meeting, and there was a reason for that.

The 31st was camped on the campus of what had been a technical school. After asking a pedestrian for directions, Mac found the two-story building with the HEADQUARTERS COMPANY sign out front and went inside. A corporal looked up from her computer. "Yes, ma'am? What can I do for you?"

"I'd like to speak with Major Kroll."

"Do you have an appointment?"

"No, I don't."

"Which command are you part of?"

"I'm the commanding officer of the 2nd battalion, AKA Mac's Marauders."

Mac saw the corporal's eyes widen. Everyone knew, or thought they knew, what the Marauders were. Which was to say a battalion of fire-breathing ax murderers. The soldier behind the desk was no exception. "I'll let Major Kroll know that you're here. Please have a seat."

Mac didn't want to sit, so she continued to stand, and was staring out of a window when she heard a polite cough. Mac turned

to find that Kroll was waiting for her. She had a steely-eyed demeanor and the blocky body of an amateur weight lifter. "I'm
Major Kroll . . . You wanted to see me?"

"Yes," Mac replied. "Thank you."

"Let's take this to my office," Kroll said. "We'll be more comfortable there."

Mac followed Kroll into a box furnished with three chairs, a
messy worktable, and twin computer screens. "So," Kroll said,
once they were seated. "What can I do for you?"

"My battalion is quartered at Peavey Field," Mac began. "And,
according to verbal orders from Colonel Lassiter, my soldiers aren't
allowed to enter this area. That means they can't use the chow hall.
Yet, according to army regs, soldiers who are unable to access a
chow hall are entitled to a subsistence allowance of roughly $300
a month. So I'm here to request that they receive the money they're
entitled to."

Kroll's eyebrows met as she frowned. "Correct me if I'm wrong,
Major, but there aren't any food vendors at Peavey Field. That
means there's nothing to spend money on."

"That's true," Mac agreed. "But I have a solution for that. I
assume you're familiar with the civilian food trucks lined up the
road adjacent to the main gate. As soon as my soldiers begin to
receive their subsistence allowances, some of those vendors will
migrate to Peavey Field. Or the 31st could establish a field kitchen
at our location. That would be acceptable as well."

Kroll allowed her annoyance to show. "It would, would it? How
nice! Well, I can think of a *third* possibility . . . I could reclassify
your battalion as deployed, thereby making your personnel ineligible
for a subsistence allowance, and ship you another pallet of MREs."

"You *could* do that," Mac said tightly. "But if you did, I would
leak a story to the press about the way that my battalion is being

treated. What would the general think of *that*? Or the president, for that matter?"

There was anger in Kroll's eyes. "I don't like threats."

"And I don't like eating MREs three times a day."

A chilly silence followed. Kroll spoke first. "I will discuss the matter with Colonel Lassiter."

"Give him my best," Mac said as she stood. "And don't stall. That would really piss me off." Then she left.

Mac's body was trembling as she left the building. Had she overplayed her hand? Would Lassiter put her back in prison? Maybe . . . But how dare they! Her troops were entitled to food or the means to buy it—and what could be more basic than that?

Mac circled the block twice in an effort to calm down before getting back in the Humvee and driving to the headquarters building. It was a two-story affair topped with all manner of antennas and a Phalanx Close-In Weapon System.

Mac was expected inside and followed a staff sergeant into the auditorium where General Brock, Colonel Lassiter, and his direct reports were scheduled to meet. Most of her peers were polite but standoffish. The single exception was the lieutenant colonel in command of the brigade's cavalry squadron. His name was Connors, and he was built like a fireplug. "Welcome aboard, Macintyre," he said. "Don't mind our friends here, they'll come around after a while. I read the after-action report on the withdrawal from Richton, and you can join my outfit anytime!"

A lot of people were seated, but most of the front row was open. Connors led her down to the centermost seats. "Lead from the front. The legs will follow." Mac knew that "legs" was a not-altogether-complimentary term for the army's infantry units and couldn't help but laugh.

The meeting began right on time. As Colonel Lassiter took the stage, Mac wondered if Kroll had spoken to him yet. "Good morn-ing," Lassiter said. "And welcome to the command briefing for Operation Iron Shield. If that name sounds familiar, it's because of the Iron Dome mobile all-weather air-defense system deployed in Israel sometime ago."

Lassiter's eyes swept the room. "Not to belabor the obvious, but I can assure you that the rebs would love to use the *latest* ver-sion of Iron Dome, which Boeing was working on prior to the May Day impacts. Fortunately, we're the ones who will benefit from those efforts. And here, to talk about our role in Iron Shield, is Secretary of Defense Garrison."

There was a round of enthusiastic applause as Garrison entered the auditorium. And for good reason. Although Frank Garrison had been a gentleman farmer prior to the war, with no military experience, he'd proven himself to be a capable Secretary of De-fense. Garrison had wispy hair and wire-rimmed glasses. Energy seemed to crackle around him as he took center stage. True to his personal style, Garrison wasted no time getting to the point.

"Between 2000 and 2008, an estimated eight thousand projec-tiles rained down on Israeli population centers," Garrison said. "But, after the Iron Dome system went operational in March of 2011, roughly 90 percent of incoming missiles were intercepted. That was an amazing accomplishment and one we should seek to emulate.

"As I speak to you, cities like Springfield, Tulsa, and Nashville are being pounded by mortars and surface-to-surface missiles. Never mind the fact that two of those cities belonged to rebs un-til recently and are home to people who considered themselves to be Confederate citizens. That says a lot, doesn't it? These people don't care *whom* they kill . . . Here's what an Iron Dome battery looks like."

Mac looked up at a large screen as a series of images appeared. "The batteries are mobile, and each one of them incorporates a radar unit, missile-control unit, and several launchers," Garrison told them. "And since each battery is armed with twenty interceptors, it can protect about ninety square miles of territory! That means that a single unit could protect Louisville, Cleveland, or Baltimore."

Garrison pressed a button, and the screen went dark. "But that's the *old* system . . . And, if the rebs put enough missiles into the air all at once, they could overwhelm it. That's why Iron Shield will incorporate lasers that can converge on incoming targets and destroy them. But because weather conditions can interfere with laser technology, we'll have a backup capability that includes directed-energy weapons *and* conventional interceptors."

Mac could see the importance of not only protecting cities, but also what had been *reb* cities, as Sloan attempted to reunite the country. The scale of what he was trying to accomplish was enormous—and she hoped he'd be able to pull it off.

"So," Garrison said, "your job will be to protect the batteries from ground attacks, including commando raids. Our greatest moment of vulnerability is now, *before* the units deploy and come online. That suggests the need for considerable speed. We *must* put this system in place quickly. Are there any questions?"

The urgency in Garrison's voice triggered Mac's imagination. Rockets and artillery shells could be lethal and often were . . . But were they the only reason for concern? Or was there something more behind the sudden push? "Yes, sir," Mac said as she stood. "Is there any reason to believe that the rebs might throw short-range nukes at us?"

All eyes swiveled from Mac to Garrison. His face looked drawn. "Yes, ladies and gentlemen," he admitted. "That possibility exists.

Do we believe that such an attack is imminent? No . . . But there's no way to be sure. That's why it's important to act quickly. And not just along the line of conflict . . . but up and down the East Coast, too! I would remind you that the rebs have nuclear subs, and the capability to launch missiles from the Atlantic. That puts cities like Boston, Chicago, and Indianapolis inside the kill zone."

There was total silence in the room. Odds were that most of the officers had friends and/or family in one or more of the cities Garrison had mentioned. The Secretary of Defense took a seat as Colonel Lassiter returned to the stage. "Everything you heard is top secret, and for your ears only. Tasking orders will come your way by 1800 hours this evening. Dismissed. Major Macintyre will remain."

Mac felt a profound emptiness in the pit of her stomach as the other officers filed out. Once they were gone, and Garrison had departed, Lassiter stepped down off the platform. Mac stood. "So, Major . . . It didn't take you long, did it?" he inquired.

"Is this in regards to my conversation with Major Kroll, sir?"

"You know it is."

"Sir, yes, sir."

Lassiter stepped in close. Their faces were only a foot apart. Mac had to summon every bit of her willpower in order to stand fast. She could smell his aftershave. "Don't ever threaten one of my officers again," Lassiter growled.

Mac wanted to say something along the lines of, "I shouldn't have to," but knew that would be a big mistake. "I won't, sir."

Lassiter took a step back. "Good. As for the chow problem, that was *my* fault, not Kroll's. I should have anticipated the issue, and I failed to do so. That said, I still don't want to have *your* whack jobs running around *my* base. So from this point on, hot meals will be delivered to your battalion three times a day. Are you satisfied?"

It was an honest admission, as well as a good-faith solution to the problem. Mac's respect for Lassiter increased exponentially. "Yes, sir. Thank you."

"Good. By the way . . . you won't receive any orders this evening. There are two reasons for that. Your people are in a training cycle—and it looks like a special job might be coming your way. The kind of thing your unit should be perfect for. That's as much as I can say right now."

Mac came to attention. "We'll be ready sir."

Lassiter nodded. "Go back to Peavey Field and whip your outfit into shape. I'll let you know when more information becomes available. Dismissed."

FORT KNOX, KENTUCKY

Sloan was in a budget meeting when news arrived that a rebel tank column had pushed its way up from southeast New Mexico and captured the city of Albuquerque. The president learned of the loss when his Chief of Staff, Wendy Chow, arrived to pull him out into the hall. Secret Service agents tagged along as they walked to the underground situation room. Many of Sloan's National Security Council members were present—including the Chairman of the Joint Chiefs Herman Jones, the Director of National Intelligence Martha Kip, and National Security Advisor Toby Hall. "So what the hell happened?" Sloan inquired as he took his seat. He was pissed. "How could the Confederates assemble a tank brigade and move it north without being spotted?"

"We're looking into that," Jones said. "It's too early to say for sure. But the preliminary reports suggest that the rebs sent the tanks and their support vehicles into the Roswell area aboard trucks, hid them at separate locations, and assembled the unit at the last moment."

Sloan frowned. "Roswell as in *UFO* Roswell?"

"Yes, sir."

"Perfect. The press will love that. So, how long until we push them back out?"

"That depends," Jones said cautiously.

"On *what*?"

"On what we choose to do," Jones said equably. "Should we pull a brigade off the line in Oklahoma City or Little Rock? And send it west?"

"That would weaken the line," Sloan replied. "And create an opportunity for the rebs to break through."

"Precisely," Jones said. "And that might be what the Confederates are hoping for."

Sloan swore under his breath. "What would you recommend, then? We can't let them remain in Albuquerque."

"Actually, we could," Jones said. "Not forever . . . Just until the strategic situation shifts our way."

"You must be joking! The rebs take control of a Union city, and we allow them to stay! Try explaining that to an insurance agent in Cleveland . . . Never mind the people who live in Albuquerque."

Jones smiled tightly. "I don't have to. That's your job, Mr. President."

"You're a dickhead, Herman. You know that?"

"Yes, sir . . . So they tell me."

Sloan laughed. "Seriously . . . If we allow the rebs to stay in Albuquerque, what then? Could they break out? And take more territory?"

"I don't think so," Jones replied. "At this point, the rebs have stretched their supply chain as far as it can go without breaking. I believe that capturing Albuquerque was an inexpensive way to score a victory and make Southern voters feel good. And, if we're stupid enough to pull a brigade off the line, then so much the better."

Sloan was thinking. And as he did so, an uneasy silence settled over the room. "Okay," he said. "We'll let the rebs have Albuquerque for a while. But, while they're sitting there snacking on sopaipillas, we'll attack their supply line. They can defend it, or allow it to be cut. The choice will be up to them."

Martha Kip raised a well-plucked eyebrow. "If we don't plan to pull a brigade off the line, then what will we use to attack them?"

"We'll use our secret weapon," Sloan said mysteriously. "Notify the press . . . I'm going to Albuquerque, or as close as I can get. I need to show the country that I care. Oh, and find Major McKinney. I have a job for him."

PEAVEY FIELD, KANSAS

A four-engined transport was parked on the runway. But the rain was falling so hard that Mac could barely see the airplane as she stepped out of the headquarters building and prepared to make the mad dash across the tarmac to Shelter Five. Her poncho was equipped with a hood, which she pulled up over the black beret. Then she began to run.

The rain pattered on her poncho and water splashed away from her boots as Mac passed the C-130 and crossed the final stretch of pavement. Captain Roy Quick was there to welcome her as she entered the shelter. "I'm sorry to bring you out in the rain, boss," he said. "But we have a grade-A fuck-up on our hands, and I thought you'd like to see the problem firsthand."

Rain rattled on the metal roof as Mac threw the hood back and shook water off the poncho. Most of what had been a hangar was occupied by a Stryker M1126A2. The vic was equipped with slat armor, generally referred to as a birdcage, and was partially lit by a roll-around work light. "How come you never call me over to celebrate something that went well?" Mac inquired.

"Because nothing ever goes well," Quick replied with a grin.

"All right, what's the problem?"

"*That's* the problem," Quick said, as he pointed at the truck's slat armor. "According to the list of mission requirements issued yesterday, we're supposed to load two vics onto C-130s. And, since Strykers were designed with that possibility in mind, it should be easy. But, *with* slat armor on, each truck is two feet wider than a Herc's cargo bay. Fortunately, Sergeant Rico was smart enough to check."

Mac groaned. "Shit."

"Yeah, that's what I said. The so-what is that we've got to remove the cages from two vehicles."

"You'd better make that *three*," Mac replied. "In case one of the primaries develops engine trouble prior to takeoff."

"Roger that."

"How long will it take to remove the armor?"

"At least a day."

"We're supposed to be combat-ready on six hours' notice," Mac said. "What if we get a call twenty minutes from now?"

"Then we're screwed."

"Put *three* teams on it," Mac suggested. "One for each vic. And tell the wrench turners they have four hours to get the job done."

Quick made a face. "That means we'll have to *cut* the armor off. And that will make it difficult to put it back on later."

"Do it."

"Yes, ma'am."

"How about Alpha Company? Are they ready?"

"Overman is working them hard. They're running the perimeter."

"Okay . . . Stay on 'em. I have no idea what sort of fricking mission the brass have in mind, but whatever it is will have hair all over it. And some of our jailbirds have been sitting on their asses for years."

Quick produced one of his trademark grins. "Duly noted, boss. I'm on it."

Mac nodded. "I know you are, Roy . . . And thank God for that."

Mac returned to the little headquarters building where a long list of tasks awaited her attention. Wu and her staff had been busy. That meant there were requisitions to approve, personnel matters to attend to, and dozens of bulletins, memos, and briefing papers to read. And that's what she was doing when a sergeant yelled, "Atten-hut!"

Mac came to attention along with the rest of the headquarters staff as Colonel Lassiter and two companions entered the office. One was an aide and the other was a civilian in rumpled clothing. Lassiter wasn't wearing a poncho, so his beret was soaked, and his shoulders were wet. He paused to look around. "As you were."

Wu and her people went back to work, or pretended to, as Lassiter made his way over to Mac's desk. It consisted of a sheet of raw plywood resting on two sawhorses. She tossed him a salute, and he returned it. "Good afternoon, Major . . . I'm glad to see that you and your pirates are hard at work."

Mac was intensely aware of the fact that the people in the room could hear everything that was said and knew that some version of Lassiter's comments would make the rounds the moment he left. Rather than object to the pirate remark, she chose to ignore it. "Welcome to the 2nd, sir. Would you like a tour?"

"Yes, I would," Lassiter replied. Then he turned to the soldier seated to his right. She was busy entering data into a computer. "What's your responsibility, Corporal?"

Mac held her breath. What would Kobo say? She'd been in the slammer for faking records calculated to get her boyfriend a promotion. Kobo stood. "I'm a soldier, sir . . . My first job is to fight! But I'm a human-resources specialist, too—and responsible for the battalion's personnel records."

Mac suppressed a smile. Kobo was playing the colonel like a pro. Lassiter nodded. "Well said, soldier. As you were. All right, let's find out if the rest of the battalion is as sharp as Corporal Kobo is. Lead the way, Major."

Mac considered grabbing her poncho on the way out but feared that Lassiter would perceive that as a sign of weakness. So after putting her beret on, Mac led the other officers out into a steady drizzle. The tour took more than an hour. Lassiter spent most of his time talking to the troops. A process that was both nerve-wracking *and* instructive. Officers might try to bullshit him, but the enlisted folks had a tendency to tell the truth, and Lassiter was paying close attention. Mac filed the process away for future use.

The surprise inspection went well until Lassiter entered Shelter Five, where weary techs were busy using cutting torches to remove OLD BOY's slat armor. That was when the colonel demanded to know what the hell was going on.

The lighting was poor, so maybe Sergeant Hernandez didn't realize who he was talking to, although Mac believed he did. It had been a long day, and the noncom was pissed. "What does it look like we're doing? We're cutting the fucking slat armor off this fucking vic, so it will fit into a fucking C-130."

The comment was followed by an ominous silence as Lassiter absorbed the information. Then he laughed and slapped Hernandez on the back. "Well said, Sergeant. Carry on."

But there was a look of concern on Lassiter's face as he turned to Mac. He had to raise his voice in order to be heard over the background noise. "Will your Strykers be ready to load by 2100 hours?"

"Yes, sir."

"Good. Your mission is a go . . . Assemble your officers. I'll brief them."

It took fifteen minutes to clear the HQ building and bring all the battalion's officers in. Except that some of the platoon leaders weren't officers. They were senior noncoms. A compromise Mac had been forced to accept when it turned out that Leavenworth wasn't holding enough 01 and 02 officers to meet the battalion's needs. Just one of the many problems yet to be resolved.

"Okay," Lassiter said, once all of them were packed into the small room. "Here's the skinny . . . Your battalion has been chosen to carry out a top secret mission. Security is *extremely* important, and that's why this base is on lockdown. My MPs are on the gate and stationed at regular intervals around the perimeter. No one can enter, and no one can leave until the mission is over. Any questions about that? No? Good.

"Thanks to the information included in your pretasking orders, you already know that it will be necessary to transport a company of infantry and two combat-ready Strykers over a considerable distance. That will require *three* C-130s. From this point forward, the transports will be referred to as Yankee One, Two, and Three."

The battalion's officers and noncoms were scribbling notes, and Mac was no exception.

"Yankee One is already on the ground," Lassiter told them. "And Yankee Two and Three are slated to arrive at 2100 hours. Two will be carrying a nine-person special ops team. They will be split into two groups—one for each of the Strykers.

"Yankee One will depart first and land at Pyote Air Base near Odessa, Texas. The strip hasn't been used for a long time. And, based on an aerial reconnaissance carried out five days ago, we know that it's deserted. The runways and taxiways, hardstands and flight-line apron are usable but overgrown."

Mac took it in. *Texas!* Holy shit, right in the heart of Dixie! And she wasn't the only one to take note of the fact. Glances were exchanged, and someone said, "Oh, goody."

Lassiter nodded. "That's right, ladies and gentlemen . . . You are going to land inside enemy territory. Alpha Company will land and secure the base. Once that's accomplished, Yankee Two and Three will put down and off-load. Then the Strykers, with special ops personnel aboard, will haul ass for Odessa. The trip will take approximately forty-five minutes. The package will be asleep in the Tarlo Hotel when the operators enter and take him prisoner. Once he's in custody, the Strykers will take him to Pyote Airfield, where he will be loaded onto a C-21A Learjet for an all-expenses-paid trip up north.

"At that point, assuming the tactical situation allows, you will load the Strykers onto their respective planes. The moment they are wheels up, Alpha Company will board Yankee One for the return trip. The enemy won't be expecting us, and there aren't any military bases located nearby. So it's possible that you'll be able to go in and get out without a shot being fired. Do you have any questions?"

Captain Overman raised his hand. "Yes, sir. What about air cover?"

"That's a good question," Lassiter said. "The decision was made to bring the Hercs in low and slow in an effort to evade detection. And if we were to send fighters in high enough to protect the C-130s, they'll light up every radar screen in Texas. So some zoomies will be on standby with an estimated response time of fifteen minutes."

Mac suppressed a groan. Fifteen minutes would be an eternity in the midst of a firefight. And she'd been wearing a uniform too long to believe that the special ops people would be able to get in and out without firing a shot. But what was, was.

Once Mac's people had been dismissed, Lassiter and his companions made their way over to where she was standing. "What did you think?" Lassiter inquired. "Did I cover everything?"

"Yes, sir. I believe you did."

"Good. You may have noticed the civilian in our midst. This is Cory Olinger. Cory is a war correspondent for the *New York Times*, and he's going to accompany you on the mission."

Mac opened her mouth to speak but stopped when Lassiter raised a hand. "Don't waste your time, Major . . . The decision to bring Cory along was made at the very highest levels."

Mac wondered what "the very highest levels" meant. Had Sloan been involved? Was he trying to justify the Military Reintegration Program? He was rolling the dice if so, because the battalion would look bad if the mission went poorly.

But Lassiter expected the mission to go well. He'd said as much. So maybe the mission was a no-brainer that was calculated to make everybody look good. If so, the reporter would tell readers how good Mac's Marauders were. Olinger extended a pudgy hand. It was soft and damp. "It's a pleasure to meet you, Major . . . Maybe you could answer a question for me . . . Will they have barf bags on the plane? I tend to get airsick."

Mac looked at Lassiter, who rolled his eyes. "I have to get back to my office. Take care, Major . . . And make me proud." Then he was gone.

Olinger looked lost. "I'll check on the air bag thing," she assured him. "But I won't be able to spend much time with you during the next few hours. I have a lot to do."

"That's okay," Olinger said. "I'll tag along."

Mac's attention shifted to the multitude of details that could spell the difference between success and failure. What was it that President Carter had said when asked if he had regrets? "I wish I'd sent one more helicopter . . ." But he didn't, and the mission to rescue the hostages in Iran failed. Mac was determined to avoid that kind of mistake.

So she made her way from place to place, checking and rechecking. Were the soldiers in Overman's company carrying extra water? There wouldn't be any at the airfield in Texas, and what if they had to fight the following day? Each soldier could need eight or nine bottles of water. Then there was the question of ammo. Should the Strykers carry more than they usually did? Hell yes, they should.

And what if the so-called "package" was wounded? Or a special operator for that matter? Mac ordered Quick to identify the best medic in the battalion and assign him or her to the ops team. On and on it went until Yankee Two arrived. It was completely dark by that time, but the runway lights were on as the cargo plane touched down. Sheets of rainwater flew to the right and left as the C-130 came her way. Olinger was standing at Mac's side, holding a small recorder. "What's so special about that kind of plane?" he wanted to know.

"They have a range in excess of two thousand miles loaded,"

Mac replied, "and they can cruise at something like 360 mph. But their *real* claim to fame is that they can land on an unprepared field like the one in Pyote."

If Olinger said something, his words were lost in the roar as the C-130's pilots put all four engines into reverse, and the plane slowed dramatically. As soon as Yankee Two cleared the runway, Three came in for an equally noisy landing. It was still taxiing away when someone touched her arm. "Hey, Mac, we meet again."

Mac turned to find that Thomas Lyle was standing beside her. But now, rather than a butter bar, he was a first lieutenant. "Thomas! Are you running the special ops team?"

"Cory Olinger," the reporter interjected. "*New York Times*. Could I have your full name please?"

"No, you can't," Lyle replied. "Nor can you name any of the people on my team. Not unless you want to wind up in some deep shit. Tom will have to do."

"Tom?" Olinger inquired. "Not Thomas?"

"My mother is the only person who calls me Thomas," Lyle replied. "My mother and the major here."

"So the two of you have served together before?"

"That's classified," Mac said. "Turn the recorder off, Mr. Olinger. Or I'll have one of my men confiscate it."

Olinger looked hurt. "I'm just doing my job."

"So are we. Turn it off." Olinger obeyed.

Mac took Lyle aside. "So, Tom, what do you think?"

"The mission looks good on paper," Lyle replied cautiously.

Mac smiled. "So you're worried."

"Exactly."

"Me too." They laughed.

"I suggest we run this like the Revell snatch," Lyle said. "I'll handle the grab . . . The rest of it belongs to you."

"That works for me," Mac replied. "I'm giving you my best medic. Please make her feel welcome."

"We will," Lyle promised. "Are you coming with us?"

"Of course I am . . . Somebody has to keep an eye on you."

"Thanks, Mom. If anyone can get us in and out, you can."

"I'll do my best. Who's the target?"

"The Confederacy's Secretary of Energy. Some dude named Oliver Sanders. He's the one they put in charge of siphoning oil out of the petroleum reserves and selling it."

Sloan, Mac thought to herself. *This has Sloan written all over it. Does he know that I'll be part of the team that's going after Sanders? And if so, how does he feel about that?*

The question, like so many others, went unanswered. "Come on," Mac said. "We have work to do." The rain continued to fall.

CHAPTER 11

||||||||||||||||||||||||||||||||||||||||

Coyote is always out there waiting, and Coyote is always
hungry . . .

—NAVAJO PROVERB

NORTH OF TIJERAS, NEW MEXICO

The long, cold night was coming to a close, and the President of
the United States was sore. He'd been riding for the better part of
two days by then, and even though his parents had horses, he hadn't
ridden in years.

His mount was a huge but good-natured brute named Kenny.
He had only one fault, and that was to veer off the trail every once
in a while, in hopes of nibbling on whatever greenery was available.
Fortunately for Sloan, the horse didn't get many opportunities
because of New Mexico's semiarid countryside.

The presidential party consisted of six people, including a Navajo named Joe Akalii (Cowboy) who led the way, Major Sam
McKinney in the two slot, Sloan, and three Green Beret bodyguards, all of whom were suffering silently.

But even though the group was small, it could call on a lot of firepower. A Predator drone was circling high above, two A-10 Warthogs were flying lazy eights fifty miles north of their position, and a Black Hawk helicopter was parked on a mesa twenty miles away.

The purpose of the trip was to free Albuquerque from the Confederates. Sloan couldn't bring in troops to capture the city without weakening the line elsewhere. But what he *could* do was sponsor a resistance movement aimed at cutting the rebel supply line, which ran up from Texas and into Albuquerque.

He couldn't phone the request in, however. Not according to people who knew the area. No, if Sloan wanted to bring the Navajos on board, he'd have to show some nation-to-nation respect. And that meant a meeting with Chief Natonaba, a much-respected leader, who could cut a deal if he thought it was in the tribe's best interest.

But *would* he? According to Congressman Velasquez, who represented Albuquerque, Natonaba had a very Navajo-centric view of the world. "Don't promise anything you can't deliver," Velasquez had cautioned. "Natonaba has a long memory. He talks about the Scorched Earth Campaign of 1863 as if it took place yesterday."

After looking it up, Sloan discovered that 1863 was the year Kit Carson's troops forced Navajo captives to march 350 miles to Fort Sumner. Many of them died along the way.

Sloan's train of thought was interrupted as the horse in front of Kenny came to an abrupt halt causing his mount to do likewise. And when Sloan saw McKinney dismount, he was quick to do likewise. His butt was sore, and so were his knees. "Joe will take care of the horses," McKinney said. "We'll go forward on foot. Bring your rifle just in case."

Sloan was wearing a tac vest, *his* tac vest, meaning the one he'd worn in Richton. And he was carrying the same M4. He nodded as Joe went about the business of leading the horses in under a rocky outcropping, where they would be less visible from above.

Once the horses were secure, McKinney led the rest of the group forward. As the trail wound its way around the side of a hill, a sickly-looking yellow blob rose in the east. It was barely visible through a veil of particulate matter. But by the time the presidential party arrived on a flat area on the south side of the hill, there was enough light to see by.

A large water tank occupied the center of the site. Sloan could tell that the name TIJERAS had been painted on it even though the *E* and the *R* had been obliterated by a jagged hole. An artillery shell perhaps? Something like that.

Gravel crunched under their boots as the men advanced. When they were about fifty feet away from the tank, a man stepped out into the wan sunlight. He was wearing a flat-brimmed hat, a sheepskin coat, and a pair of ancient chaps. The M16 was barrel up and resting on his right shoulder. His eyes were focused on McKinney. "President Sloan, I presume?"

"Nope," McKinney replied. "That would be the gentleman behind me. Please place the assault weapon on the ground and take a step back. Are you carrying a pistol? If so, place that on the ground as well."

There was a twenty-second pause while the man considered the order. "Maybe you should do the same."

McKinney shrugged. "This isn't personal, sir. There are a lot of people who want to kill the president, and we don't know you."

Another five seconds passed before the man placed the M16 on the ground and took a step back. McKinney was about to follow up regarding the pistol when Sloan took three paces forward. Slowly, almost reverently, he laid the M4 next to the M16. Then he straightened. *"Yá'át'ééh."* (Good morning.)

The other man smiled. "*Yá'át'ééh*, Mr. President. You did your homework. I'm Chief Natonaba. Welcome to the Navajo Nation."

The challenge was there, since the Navajo Nation didn't qualify as a nation in the true sense, even though Natonaba wanted people to think of it that way. But Sloan chose to sidestep the issue for the moment. "Thank you, Chief Natonaba. I wish the circumstances of our meeting were different. We're in enemy-held territory."

"Yes," Natonaba agreed. "Yet you came to Tijeras. *Why?*"

"Come with me," Sloan said. "I'll show you."

Together they walked out to the point where they could look down onto the devastated town of Tijeras. I-40 cut through it like an ugly scar. Sloan had seen the community from above. But the aerial photographs had a clinical quality. These images were *real*. And the fire-blackened buildings, the shot-up vehicles, and the haphazard grave markers had the emotional weight that a picture couldn't convey.

Sloan felt a rising sense of sorrow knowing that 257 soldiers and civilians had died trying to keep the Confederate Army out of Albuquerque. Natonaba must have been experiencing similar emotions. "The Navajo Nation lost thirty-two warriors in the fight," he said tightly. "Together with the army, they held this pass for two days."

"That's a terrible loss, and I'm very sorry," Sloan said. "Unfortunately, I'm here to ask you and your people to make even greater sacrifices. My generals tell me that the Confederates are using two routes to funnel supplies into Albuquerque. One follows Highway 285 north through Vaughn, New Mexico, then west through Mountainair to I-25 north. And that takes them into the city.

"The other involves taking convoys north to I-40 before turning west and driving to Albuquerque. That means they have to pass through Tijeras."

"Yes," Natonaba agreed. "It always works the same way. They send attack helicopters through first. The gunships arrive during the hours of darkness. They attack anything with a heat signature, and that includes cattle. Once that's over mine-protected vehicles lead the convoy in. They are nearly impervious to mines and IEDS. Stryker vehicles follow, each carrying a squad of infantry. The supply trucks are behind them."

Sloan nodded. "That matches what I've been told. And that's why I came. I want you and your warriors to seal off both supply routes. We'll provide you with the military-grade weapons required to do so. In a month, two at the most, the rebs will be forced to withdraw."

Natonaba frowned. "Why don't you bring a brigade of troops in?"

"I don't have any to spare," Sloan told him. "If we pull a brigade off the line back East, the Confederates could break through."

"So you care more about the cities of Springfield and Clarkes-ville than you do about Albuquerque."

There it was . . . the sort of challenge that Sloan had been expecting. "No, that isn't true. We believe the attack on Albuquerque was a feint designed to boost morale in the South and pull troops away from the main line of battle. So we have three choices. We can do what the rebs *want* us to do, we can let Albuquerque remain under enemy control until the strategic situation improves, or we can cut their supply lines and take the city back in sixty days or so. Which course of action do you like the most?"

Sloan was playing hardball and could see the anger in Natonaba's eyes. "Hundreds, even thousands of my people could die," the chief objected.

"Yes," Sloan agreed. "Tens of thousands of Americans on *both* sides will die before the war is over. But remember . . . your people are Navajos, but they are Americans, too, with a heritage of valor.

More than three hundred code talkers received Congressional Silver Medals for saving thousands of lives during World War II."

Natonaba's expression softened. "You are a manipulative son of a bitch."

Sloan nodded. "That's part of the job. Will you fight?"

"We'll fight."

They shook hands.

IN THE AIR OVER NORTHERN TEXAS

Major Robin Macintyre was trying to look cool as the C-130 called Yankee Two flew low over Texas. Looking cool was important because it sent the right sort of message. "There she was," some private would say, "sitting there reading a magazine while we flew over enemy-held territory!"

And it was true. Mac *was* staring at a magazine even though the words were a blur, and her thoughts were elsewhere. She stole a look at her watch. It was 0036. Yankee One was supposed to land in ten minutes. What would Overman and his company encounter? A deserted airport? Or a whole shitload of trouble? Not knowing was driving her crazy.

Mac looked across the cargo bay to see that Lieutenant Lyle was asleep. Or was he? Were the closed eyes part of an act? She wouldn't put it past him.

As for *New York Times* correspondent Cory Olinger, *he* was hunched over an airsick bag, staring at the deck. The faint odor of vomit hung in the air. Mac wrinkled her nose. Still, the reporter was there, even if flying was difficult for him. And he deserved credit for that.

A crewperson appeared at Mac's side. Her flight suit was so

large it made her look like a kid. "Yankee One is on the ground," she announced. "And there is no resistance so far."

"That's good news," Mac said. "What's our ETA?"

"Fifteen minutes, ma'am."

Mac looked at Lyle. The Green Beret was awake now . . . Or maybe he had been all along. "It's time to load the team," Mac said.

Lyle nodded. "Yes, ma'am."

Three special operators were slated to travel aboard **CALIFORNIA GIRL**, in addition to Lyle, Mac, Olinger, and the Stryker's two-person crew. The other vic, a Stryker called **LUCKY LOU**, was riding on Yankee Three.

CALIFORNIA GIRL had been loaded ass in, so she could roll straight out the moment that the ramp was down. And as Mac entered the cargo compartment, it felt like walking into a coffin. She didn't like being cooped up inside a metal box even if it was safer there.

Once the special operators were strapped in, the bullshit began. They were teasing a member of the team about the size of his nose, and he was bragging about all of the many things he could do with it. But Mac knew it was an act . . . a way to conceal the fear they felt. The fear *she* felt . . . Fear of dying, yes. But the greatest fear was that she would fuck up, and in doing so, cost other people their lives.

"We're thirty seconds out," the copilot announced over the team's radio network. "Yankee One is off the runway, Alpha Company has deployed, and Yankee Three is fifteen minutes out. Have fun out there."

Mac waited for the thump as the plane's wheels made contact with the runway, followed by a series of bumps as the C-130 rolled through potholes and over pieces of debris. Engines roared as they went into reverse, and the passengers were thrown sideways.

As the transport jerked to a stop Mac knew that crew people

were hurrying to free the Stryker from its tie-downs. The moment that process was complete, Kona started the vic's engine and drove it down the ramp. There was a bump as the rear wheels came off. A Green Beret named Anders had agreed to serve as Mac's RTO. He was holding a handset to his ear. "Captain Overman is on the east side of the field," Anders said.

"Good," Mac replied. "Tell him we're on our way."

The trip across the field took no more than three minutes. After the truck came to a stop, Mac had to wait for the ramp to go down. It bounced under her boots. Overman was waiting to receive her. He produced a grimace, which Mac knew to be his version of a smile. "Good morning, Major . . . Here's your coffee." Mac watched Overman pour the steaming-hot liquid into a mug. "The cream and sugar is already in there," he added.

"I would promote you to colonel if I could," Mac said as she took a sip. "So things went well?"

"We own this dump," Overman replied confidently.

"How long can we hold it?"

"That depends on what the rebs throw at us," Overman said cautiously. "But, assuming we have air cover, we could hold the field for twelve hours. Then we'll run out of supplies."

Mac noticed that Olinger was standing a couple of feet away, recording the conversation. What had Lassiter told her? It would take the zoomies fifteen minutes to arrive on scene. That was a long time. And what if the rebel air force was waiting to intercept them? Would the brass send *more* planes? Or write the Marauders off? "Let's hope it doesn't come to that," Mac replied.

"Here comes Yankee Three," Lyle said. And sure enough . . . Mac could hear the C-130's engines. Flares had been placed along both sides of the strip, which meant that Three's pilots had it easy compared to their counterparts in planes One and Two.

It took the better part of fifteen minutes for the C-130 to land, and disgorge the **LUCKY LOU** before taxiing off the runway. "Okay," Mac said, as she met Overman's gaze. "Hold the fort . . . Assuming things go well, we'll return within two hours. But if the wheels come off, you are to pull out immediately. Do you read me?"

"Five by five."

"Good. Mr. Olinger will remain here . . . Please support his efforts to the extent your duties allow. Let's do this thing."

After returning to the **CALIFORNIA GIRL**, Mac made her way through the cargo bay and up into the forward air-guard hatch. Then it was time to don her brain bucket, complete with night-vision gear, and a pair of gloves. It was damned cold in the desert at night, and the windchill would make it worse. Maps had been downloaded onto the Strykers' nav systems, and the TCs had hard copies just in case. "This is Boomer Six," Mac said into her mike. "Let's haul ass."

Mac had to hang on as Corky Kona put her boot down. Then they were off. Roughly fifty miles separated the tiny town of Pyote from Odessa. And Mac hoped to make the trip in forty minutes. She looked back, saw the **LUCKY LOU**'s lights, and turned forward again. The lights weren't really necessary since both drivers had night-vision gear, but civilians would notice if they were off. Especially on the freeway.

Soldiers waved as the vics passed through the perimeter and onto the access road beyond. Kona turned left onto a paved road minutes later and followed that south toward the on-ramp to I-20 east. Once on the freeway, Mac saw that the land around them was mostly flat, and the road was mostly straight, both of which made it easy for the Strykers to hit their top speed of 60 mph.

There were other vehicles on the road, but not many, and none of the civilian drivers had reason to question the presence of military vehicles on I-20. Not with a war raging up north. It wasn't long before the Strykers passed the towns of Thortonville and Monahans. Things were going well so far, or so it seemed to Mac, until she heard Overman's voice on the radio. "Boomer Four to Six. Over."

"This is Six. Go. Over."

"According to Big Bird, *two* Confederate aircraft left Lackland Air Force Base and are headed this way. Over."

Mac felt a sinking sensation. Big Bird was the airborne early-warning and control aircraft flying lazy eights to the north. Thanks to the kind of gear the plane carried, the crew could monitor activity taking place within a 120,000-square-mile radius. "*Why? We came in low . . . Too low to detect. Or that's what they told us. Any theories? Over.*"

"They think the rebs spotted us from orbit. Over."

Mac knew that Confederate sympathizers had taken control of NASA's Mission Control Center in Houston, and the 20th Space Control Squadron at Elgin Air Force Base, just prior to secession. So maybe they had the capacity to monitor air traffic from space. Or had developed it during the last few months. Shit, shit, shit. The worst part was that Mac couldn't do anything about it except hurry and worry. "What's their ETA? Over."

"That depends . . . Transports would take an hour to get here, but fighters would arrive a lot faster. Over."

Mac considered that. Should she request air support? No, it was too early. What if the rebs *didn't* know about the landing? What if the airplanes in question were going somewhere else? The sudden arrival of some F-15s would tip them and draw an immediate response. "Okay, thanks. Dig in . . . And I mean deep! And tell the Zoomies that we may need them soon."

"I'm on it," Overman replied, which was a nice way of saying: "What the fuck do you think I'm doing?"

Mac laughed. "Sorry, Four . . . That was stupid. Keep me informed. Over."

Mac heard two clicks by way of a reply. They were passing through Penwell by then, which meant Odessa was coming up. Even though a partial blackout was in effect, a scattering of lights could be seen on both sides of the freeway. And, as the **CALIFORNIA GIRL** slowed, Kona took an off-ramp. Mac glanced over her shoulder to make sure that the **LUCKY LOU** was still there. It was.

Kona drove through Odessa's streets at a sedate 35 mph in order to avoid attracting attention. Mac left the hatch for the cargo bay below. She could tell that the green beanies were amped and ready to go. Mac looked at Lyle. "I assume you heard what Overman told me."

Lyle nodded. "Yeah . . . The rebs might be coming our way."

"Exactly. So don't linger in the hotel's bar."

It wasn't the funniest joke the operators had ever heard but garnered a laugh nonetheless. Lyle grinned. "No worries, Major. We'll be on our best behavior."

Mac felt the Stryker make a turn and heard Kona's voice. "We're pulling in . . . Stand by."

The **CALIFORNIA GIRL** came to a halt, and cold air flooded into the compartment as the ramp fell. And there, a couple of hundred feet away, was the dimly lit Tarlo Hotel. Lyle waited for his team to exit before tossing Mac a salute. Then he was gone.

Mac left the Stryker in time to see the operators who'd been aboard the **LUCKY LOU** fall in behind the others as all of them ran toward the hotel. It was six stories tall, and Mac had an unobstructed view of the walkways that fronted the rooms. She wished she could accompany the team . . . But that wasn't possible. All she could do was wait. Mac keyed her mike. "Boomer Six to Four . . . We're in position. Over."

"This is Four," Overman replied. "Roger that. *Six* planes are coming our way now . . . And, according to Big Bird, two are transports. The rest are fighters. ETA thirty minutes. Over."

Overman's tone was calm and clinical. Like a doctor delivering a potentially fatal diagnosis. And there he was . . . Preparing to fight overwhelming odds all over again, wondering how many of his people, *her* people—would die this time. Could Overman keep it together? Mac prayed that he would. "Roger that, Four. Are the zoomies on the way? Over."

"That's affirmative. Over."

"Good. I saw a flagpole there . . . Run an American flag up it, and hang on. This isn't over until it's over."

Mac heard two clicks followed by silence. She could see figures moving along the fourth-floor walkway. There was a flash, a bang, and some incomprehensible yelling. The snatch was in progress.

FORT KNOX, KENTUCKY

The situation room was almost full by the time Sloan arrived. Secretary of Defense Garrison was there, as was Chairman of the Joint Chiefs Jones, Director of National Intelligence Kip, National Security Advisor Hall, Chief of Staff Chow, and Press Secretary Besom. They came to their feet as the president entered, and he waved them back into their chairs. "Sorry I'm late . . . How's it going?"

All eyes turned to General Jones. "The Marauders arrived safely, sir . . . And the snatch is under way. But the rebs are responding."

Sloan frowned. "Responding to *what*? The landing? The raid on the hotel? Or both?"

"The landing," Jones replied. "The C-130s went in low, but we believe the enemy spotted them from orbit and ran a check. Once all of *their* planes were accounted for, they knew the transports belonged to us. Four Confederate fighters are inbound to Pyote Airfield, plus two larger planes, which are probably loaded with troops. ETA twenty-five minutes."

"So there's no way our people can get out of there without a fight."

"No, sir."

"Shit."

"Yes, sir."

"Do we have fighters on the way?"

"Yes, sir."

Sloan sat down. His eyes flitted from screen to screen but his thoughts were elsewhere. Mac was there . . . Where the shit was going to hit the fan. *Why?* Because of him, that's why. Because of orders he'd given. *And why did you give those orders?* Sloan demanded of himself. *Because you're a cold-blooded, calculating bastard. That's why.*

And it was true. Or mostly true. The decision to send Mac's Marauders rather than another outfit had been based on a number of factors, first and foremost of which was the fact that Mac had a proven ability to pull off missions that other people couldn't, regardless of how difficult the circumstances might be. That made her a logical choice.

Ah, the voice said, *but there was more to it than that . . . You hoped to prove that the Military Reintegration Program was more than a strategy to get Mac out of prison. And you wanted to prove that you weren't playing favorites even though you were playing favorites because you'd been led to believe that the mission would go off without a hitch.*

"Here's the latest," Jones said. "Our fighters are in contact with their fighters south of Odessa. Both sides are sending more planes." The Battle of Pyote Field had been joined.

ODESSA, TEXAS

"Here comes trouble." The voice belonged to the **LUCKY LOU**'s gunner, Private Nathan Bostick. Mac was crouched next to an enormous tire, with her M4 at the ready. It was the moment she'd been dreading. Someone was sure to call the cops after the special ops team blew the door open . . . And here they were. The police car entered the parking lot with lights flashing and screeched to a halt. When the driver's side door opened, a lone cop got out. Her pistol was drawn and tilted upward.

"Talk to her," Mac ordered. "But be ready to fire."

"This is a military security operation," Bostic announced over the **LUCKY LOU**'s loudspeaker. "Please holster your weapon and stand by. We'll let you know if we need assistance."

That was the approach the team had agreed on while planning the mission. None of the soldiers wanted to kill members of Odessa's police force. But would the policewoman buy Bostic's story? Mac allowed herself a sigh of relief as the pistol went into its holster. She went forward to stall. "Good morning, Officer . . . It looks like somebody screwed up! We have a deserter corralled in the hotel. Our people were supposed to notify your people."

The twentysomething cop was clearly angry. "Well, they didn't, not that I know of, and the chief is going to raise hell."

Mac nodded sympathetically. "Of course . . . I get that."

The conversation was interrupted as two members of the special ops team showed up holding their prisoner between them. The man had a hood over his head—and was nude except for a pair of wet boxers. Had he peed himself? That's the way it looked. Lyle nodded to Mac, and she turned to the police officer. "We have our man. Thanks for the assist."

"Wait!" the cop said, as Mac followed Lyle into **CALIFORNIA GIRL**'s bay. "I need to see your ID! I need to—"

The policewoman's words were cut off as the hatch closed. And once the soldiers were inside the Stryker, there was nothing the cop could do but call dispatch and complain as the vics left the parking lot. Mac didn't have to tell Kona to step on it. The TC was well aware of the need for speed. Tires screeched as the vic turned a corner and sped up the ramp onto I-20 west.

As Mac returned to her perch in the air-guard hatch, she heard a sonic boom and knew that planes were fighting overhead. She keyed her mike. "Boomer Six to Four . . . We have the package, and we're leaving Odessa . . . What's the situation there? Over."

"This is Four," Overman replied. "The zoomies are all over the sky . . . They've been able to keep the reb fighters off us so far. Over."

"What about the transports? Don't let the bastards land."

"Hold one," Overman replied, and Mac could hear the sound of firing in the background before he spoke again. "Sorry, it's kind of hectic here. The transports made no attempt to land. But it's raining Rangers right now . . . And some of the bastards landed *inside* the perimeter. Over."

Someone in the Confederate chain of command had been smart enough to send airborne troops! Mac cursed her own stupidity. That possibility hadn't occurred to her. Maybe it was because

Lassiter thought the mission would come off without a hitch . . . Whatever the reason, she should have anticipated the possibility and taken steps to deal with it. But what could she have done differently? That wasn't immediately apparent to Mac but would bear consideration later on. Assuming there was a later on. "Roger that," Mac said. "What about the C-21? Over."

The original plan had been for an Air Force C-21 Learjet to land and collect Secretary Sanders for a quick trip north. But now, with dogfights taking place in the sky above Pyote Field, an unarmed plane would be extremely vulnerable. So Overman's response didn't surprise her. "The C-21 was told to turn back," he told her. "We have orders to bring the package out on one of the Hercs. Over."

Mac could imagine the three C-130s sitting there, ready to take hits. One thing was glaringly obvious. Because it would take at least half an hour to load the Strykers, she'd have to leave them behind. "Got it," Mac said. "Get ready to load WIAs and KIAs, and pull our people back to defend the transports. Over."

"Roger that," Overman replied. "Over."

Mac clicked the mike key twice by way of a reply. She saw a flash of light in the western sky and heard what sounded like thunder. A fighter had been destroyed. But *whose?* All to capture the piece of shit in the blue boxer shorts. *I hope the bastard is worth it,* Mac thought to herself. But such considerations were above her pay grade.

The Strykers rolled past Penwell, Monahans, and Thortonville. And it wasn't long before the Pyote exit came up. Mac could hear the persistent rattle of automatic weapons by then, the occasional thump as a grenade detonated, and the roar of jet engines overhead. "Get ready," she told the team. "We'll have to fight our way in."

Then Mac put in a call to Overman. "This is Six . . . We're coming in. Warn the troops. Over." If Overman said something in reply, it was lost as a flash of light strobed the countryside, and a thunderous boom was heard. A C-130? *Yes!* At least one of the planes had been destroyed.

Mac was still in the process of absorbing that as the **CALIFORNIA GIRL** rolled up on an army Humvee. A *Confederate* Humvee. It was parked just outside Pyote Field and bristling with aerials. A command vehicle, then, which had arrived under a parachute, just like the rebel soldiers had. "Kill it," Mac ordered, and the vic's gunner opened fire.

The **CALIFORNIA GIRL** was armed with a 40mm grenade launcher, and the rebs didn't know that Union forces had armor on the ground. So instead of firing on the lead Stryker, the soldiers grouped next to the Humvee were staring at it, when the first round exploded. Bodies were torn asunder as successive grenades hit the vehicle itself and triggered a secondary explosion.

A pillar of orange-red flame shot up through the roof and sent sparks into the sky as the Strykers rolled past. Had the Confederate CO been killed? Mac hoped so. A disruption in the chain of command could slow the rebs down.

A vicious firefight was under way as the Strykers entered the field. Both sides of the engagement were firing machine guns, and since all of them had been members of the same army months earlier, they were using similar tactics. Every fifth round was a so-called "dim" tracer . . . Meaning tracer rounds that could be seen using night-vision gear but were less likely to reveal where they were coming from.

Streams of such tracers were crisscrossing the airfield as the rebels sought to overrun the C-130s, and the Union soldiers battled to keep them at bay. Mac heard the persistent ping, ping, ping sound of bullets striking **CALIFORNIA GIRL**'s armor and realized that the vic's lights were on! She ordered Kona to turn them off and keyed her mike. "Boomer Six to Boomer Four . . . It looks like the enemy is dug in along the west side of the field. Please confirm. Over."

"That's correct," Overman answered. "Over."

"How many Hercs do we have at this point?"

"Two," Overman replied.

"Roger that . . . Start loading now, and get both planes positioned for takeoff. We will suppress enemy fire until you call for us to come in. Over."

"Got it," Overman said. "Over."

"Boomer Six to Boomer Two-One and Two-Two . . . We're going to take a run down the west side of the field. Fire at will. Lieutenant Lyle . . . we need gunners in the rear hatches of both vics. Please order some volunteers to man those LMGs."

That got a chuckle, and Mac saw a Green Beret surface behind her as Kona began the run. The Stryker was armed with a 40mm grenade launcher, and it began to chug. Explosions marched down the edge of the airfield. The **LUCKY LOU** was equipped with a .50 caliber machine gun, and that was firing, too. Meanwhile, Mac and a couple of Green Berets used the pintle-mounted M-249s to keep the enemy pinned down.

But as Kona turned, and the **CALIFORNIA GIRL** began a run back to the south, a rocket fired from an AT4 hit the lead plane just forward of the starboard wing. There was a flash, followed by a dull thud, and a ball of flame. It floated up to pop like a balloon. Lives had been lost, the wreckage was blocking the runway, and only one plane remained.

FORT KNOX, KENTUCKY

The situation room was so quiet that Sloan could hear the blood pounding in his head. Slowly, but surely, the mission was coming apart. And for all he knew, Mac was dead. Meanwhile, he had to pretend he wasn't thinking about her and keep his cool for the benefit of those around him. "God damn it," Sloan said after Yankee One was hit. "Can they use Yankee Three?"

"Yes," Jones confirmed. "*After* it taxis out and around the wreckage."

"What about the package? Where is he?"

"He was inside one of the Strykers," Jones answered. "And both Strykers are intact so far as we know."

Sloan thought about that. Mac was with Secretary Sanders. So if he was okay, *she* might be okay. It was something to hope for. Then he realized how selfish that was and felt guilty. People were dead, and all of them were *his* responsibility, even those fighting for the South. The torture continued.

PYOTE FIELD, TEXAS

"We're ready," Overman told her, "and circling the wreckage. Come to Papa. Over."

Mac was proud of Overman and the way he'd been able to keep his company together in the face of unexpected resistance. "We're on the way," Mac assured him, as the Strykers sped across the airfield. Kona braked as the plane loomed ahead and the **CALIFORNIA GIRL** came to a stop. Mac ducked down into the cargo bay. "Everyone out! We're next to Yankee Three. Take the prisoner and get aboard."

Once the ramp was down, two Green Berets took hold of Sanders's arms and carried the official away. He was shorter than they were, which meant his feet never touched the ground. Mac waited for Kona and her gunner to get clear before throwing a thermite grenade into the bay. It was stupid to feel sentimental about a machine, but she did, and would feel better knowing the enemy wouldn't be able to use it.

Together with Lyle, Mac ran to the **LUCKY LOU**. Everyone was out of the vehicle by then, and Mac saw a flash as a second thermite grenade went off. She knew the resulting fire would find some of the Stryker's backup ammo. And when that happened, a secondary explosion would destroy the Stryker. "Follow me!" Mac shouted. "Let's get out of here!"

The C-130's rear ramp was bouncing just inches off the ground as the plane continued to pick up speed. Mac jogged next to it as she urged people forward. "Get the lead out, damn it . . . Is everyone here?"

"We are five people short of a full load," a green hat shouted from inside the plane.

Mac swore. Five soldiers. Dead? Maybe. That would be bad enough. "We leave no man behind." That was the motto. But did it make sense to sacrifice more lives, perhaps *all* of their lives, to retrieve dead bodies? No, not to Robin's way of thinking.

But what if one or more of the MIAs were alive? Lying in a ditch, watching the last plane take off? How would *that* feel? Mac knew how it would feel. But she also knew that fifty-plus lives were at stake. She looked at Lyle and knew that *he* knew. Here was the cost of command. "We're out of here," Mac said, as both she and Lyle made the jump. Hands reached out to pull them up as a soldier yelled, "Look out! Here comes a vehicle!"

The Humvee was behind them, and catching up quickly. It was

armed with a .50, which began to fire three-round bursts. "Throw your grenades!" Lyle shouted. "*All* of them!"

Half a dozen soldiers threw whatever they had left. That included a dozen fragmentation grenades, a canister of red smoke, and an illumination device. They bounced into the air and went off right in front of the Humvee. It swerved, hit a pothole, and flipped.

The Herc was airborne by then . . . And as the nose came up, Mac had to grab onto a metal support or be thrown back into the still-rising ramp. As the hatch closed, Mac took the opportunity to look around. That was when she realized that the plane was only *half* full! And that made sense. The rest of her troops had been on Yankee One.

Overman came back to greet her. A bloody bandage was wrapped around his head. "You made it. Thank God for that."

Mac's throat felt tight. It was difficult to speak. "How many? How many did we lose?"

Overman looked away. "Fifty-six, including the air crews."

That was something like half of the people who'd gone on the mission. Mac wanted to cry but *couldn't* because she was the CO. And COs have to suck it up. Mac struggled to swallow the lump in her throat. "And the wounded?"

"Just about everyone," Overman replied. "Nine of them are serious."

"Shit. And Olinger?"

"Follow me," Overman said, and led her forward.

And there, kneeling next to a wounded soldier, was *New York Times* correspondent Cory Olinger. His clothes were covered in blood, and he was helping a medic. "Olinger is okay for a fucking reporter," Overman said. And that, Mac knew, was high praise.

A pilot spoke over the intercom. "We're flying at thirty thousand feet with an F-15 Strike Eagle off each wingtip. Oh, and one more thing . . . General Jones sent you a message: 'Well done. Take the rest of the day off.'"

That produced laughter, and Mac managed a smile. Mac's Marauders. *Her* Marauders. A great deal had been lost . . . But something had been gained as well.

CHAPTER 12

||||||||||||||||||||||||||||||||||||||||||||

It would be our policy to use nuclear weapons wherever we felt it necessary to protect our forces and achieve our objectives.

–ROBERT MCNAMARA

HOUSTON, TEXAS

After carving a path of destruction across Mexico, what remained of Hurricane Gloria was about to strike Texas. And, as the black SUV wound its way through the streets of Houston, General Bo Macintyre caught occasional glimpses of the low-hanging clouds that were sweeping north from the Gulf. Drops of rain appeared on the windshield, only to be obliterated as the wipers squeaked back and forth. *I wish I could get rid of my problems that easily,* Bo thought to himself.

And there *were* problems . . . lots of them. Not the least of which was dealing with self-obsessed, weak-kneed, poll-driven politicians. But that's how he had to spend his day. So be it. He would use the opportunity to fight for more of everything. Because that's what he needed in order to win: *more* soldiers, *more* weapons, and *more* time. And if the past was a guide to the future, he would get at least some of what he wanted.

The Hotel Americas was shaped like a huge cube and boasted more than a thousand rooms. The building seemed to swallow the SUV as the vehicle followed a ramp down to the formal entryway below. A doorman hurried to open the door and, since Bo was dressed in civilian clothes, was unlikely to recognize the stern-looking general who appeared on TV at least once a week.

Other people did, however . . . including two of Bo's aides, who were dressed in mufti. They fell in behind Bo as a very solicitous assistant manager led the party to a private elevator. It took them to the fourth floor, where many of the hotel's meeting rooms were located.

Another assistant manager was waiting to greet Bo as he stepped out. And he was "thrilled" to have such a distinguished guest in the hotel.

Bo felt nothing but contempt for suck-ups and men of military age who weren't in uniform. So he didn't bother to acknowledge the manager's comments as he was shown into a medium-sized meeting room. And that was when Bo felt the first stirrings of concern. The tables were facing each other, and one was a good deal longer than the other. Five chairs were arranged behind it, while there was only one at the small table. *Why?* Had a mistake been made? Or was he about to be grilled?

There was some milling around, a good deal of glad-handing, and plenty of fake conviviality as a gaggle of civilians entered from an adjoining room. Had they been in a meeting? To discuss *him?* Bo sensed the answer was yes.

Finally, as the bullshit storm began to subside, staffers were asked to leave. And that included Bo's aides. He knew what that meant . . . The civilians were going to kick his ass but planned to do it privately, to prevent leaks.

After taking his seat, Bo found himself facing a panel that consisted of President Morton Lemaire, Secretary of Defense Harmon Gill, Secretary of the Army Orson Selock, National Security Advisor Mary Chaffin, and the Director of the Confederate Intelligence Agency Anthony Vale. Lemaire opened the meeting. "First, please allow me to thank you for coming, General Macintyre . . . We know how busy you are."

That was bullshit, of course, since Bo had no choice. But, like all generals, Bo was part politician. "You're welcome, Mr. President. And thank you for inviting me . . . I'd rather be here than working on the budget." That produced the predictable laugh.

"So," Lemaire began, "I'd like to congratulate you, your staff, and your soldiers on the capture of Albuquerque! It was the sort of lightning strike that General Patton would have approved of."

For some reason, Bo's superiors were obsessed with World War II generals, and rarely made mention of men like Harold G. Moore, Norman Schwarzkopf, and Stanley Allen McChrystal. Probably because they'd never heard of them. "Thank you, sir."

"And your people did a helluva job down in Brownsville," Gill added. "They kicked Cabrera's ass."

Victoria had been in charge of that mission, and Bo felt a momentary flush of pride. "Thank you, sir."

"Plus, I would be remiss if I failed to mention the commando raid on Norfolk," Lemaire added. "Three ships sunk. That's nothing to sneeze at."

They're warming me up, Bo thought to himself. "I hate to admit it, but the navy might have had something to do with that one," Bo replied. The joke produced a round of chuckles, but Bo knew that an avalanche of shit was coming his way.

"But," Gill said, "in spite of our considerable success, I would describe the present state of the war as a stalemate. Would you disagree with that assessment?"

Gill's father was a well-known conservative politician, and Gill had been the CEO of a large defense contractor prior to the war. The man was likeable in many ways, and a dyed-in-the wool Libertarian, which Bo perceived as a good thing. But what Gill *wasn't* was a soldier . . . And like so many civilians, Gill had a simplistic view of war.

Still, Gill was the boss, and Bo understood the need to choose his words with care. "I agree in the broadest sense, sir. Although the specifics are important. For example . . . we have the edge where orbital warfare is concerned, and they have the capacity to build more planes than we can."

"So noted," Gill said. "But rather than analyze the strengths and weaknesses of both sides, the purpose of this meeting is to find a way to *win*. And who better to consult than the Chairman of the Joint Chiefs? So tell us, General . . . Rather than keeping on keeping on, is there some way we could break the stalemate and put some points on the board *now*?"

Bo looked from face to face. "That depends," he temporized.

"On *what*?" Chaffin demanded.

"On what you're willing to do," Bo answered. "Are you willing to do the *hard* things? Will you authorize the air force to carpet bomb Chicago? Will you green-light the use of cluster bombs? And what about tactical nukes? If we nuke a hundred targets on Monday, we will be victorious by Friday."

Lemaire frowned. "But what good is a nuclear wasteland?"

"It wouldn't be good so far as our enemies are concerned," Bo replied. "But the use of tactical nuclear weapons could save the lives of our troops, the same way it did when our great-grandparents dropped a bomb on Hiroshima during World War II. A massive attack would destroy the Union's factories, break the enemy's will to fight, and put an end to Sloan's socialistic government."

"I don't know," Gill said doubtfully. "It would cost billions to rebuild."

Bo spoke as if to a child. "With all due respect, sir . . . Why would you rebuild? All you would need to do is prevent the rabble from streaming south. Kingdoms will rise and fall. Cults will rule . . . And die-hard socialists will attempt to re-create the existing freeocracy. But surveillance drones can be used to watch the sheep and target leaders as necessary. *That* is how we can win."

It wasn't the first time that such options had been discussed. But it was the first time they'd been put forward as part of an overall strategy. And Bo's unapologetic argument in favor of destroying half the country in order to save the rest of it left the civilians mute. A good ten seconds passed before Lemaire cleared his throat. "Thank you, General . . . I think I speak for everyone when I say that I appreciate your candor. I'm sure your comments will fuel some very interesting discussions during the days and weeks ahead.

"Now, there's another matter we need to address. Secretary Gill? I believe you have something you wish to share with the general?"

Gill stood and circled the table to place a newspaper in front of Bo. "It pains me to say this, General . . . especially in light of your selfless service to the Confederacy. But this sort of thing has to stop."

Bo looked down. A copy of the *New York Times* was lying in front of him. The headline read: A MISSION INTO HELL. And there, directly below it, was a photo of his younger daughter. Robin was a major now! Since when? She'd been court-martialed and sent to prison last he'd heard. "Go ahead," Gill said, having returned to his seat. "Read it. We'll wait."

The caption under the photo read: "Major Robin Macintyre,

commanding officer of Mac's Marauders, led a mission deep into enemy territory."

Bo could feel their eyes on him as he skimmed the article. He was, needless to say, familiar with the snatch. Finally, having finished the story, he looked up. "Kids these days . . . You never know what they'll do next."

Selock laughed. But he was the only one.

"I'm glad you can find humor in the situation," Lemaire said icily. "But we lost thirty-seven soldiers at Pyote Field, and their families are very upset. Nor can I ignore the fact that your daughter's troops were able to abduct a member of my cabinet."

Bo started to respond but was forced to stop when Lemaire raised a hand. "It would be one thing if the raid were an isolated incident. Many loyal Southerners have family members who are fighting for the North, and the reverse holds as well. But the raid is part of a pattern . . . Major Macintyre led the effort to rescue President Sloan from Richton, Mississippi. And it isn't unreasonable to suggest that Sloan would be dead had it not been for your daughter. And what then? There's a very good chance that the North would still be in chaos.

"Then Major Macintyre went after Robert Howard who, as you'll recall, was working with *us*. And now *this*."

Bo was angry. Angry at Robin . . . And angry at the assholes arrayed in front of him. "What am I supposed to *do*?" he demanded. "I don't have any influence over Robin. We're estranged . . . And we have been for years."

"I'll tell you what you can do," Secretary Gill replied thinly. "You can do one of the hard things that you like to talk about. Your daughter is an enemy combatant. Treat her as such."

Bo looked from face to face. All of them were willing to meet his gaze. They'd met, taken a vote, and sentenced Robin to death. And the assassin? That would be him, or someone chosen by him. But could he do it? The decision was easier than it should have been.

ARLINGTON NATIONAL CEMETERY
ARLINGTON, VIRGINIA

When the meteorite exploded over Washington, D.C., the National Cemetery across the river in Arlington was spared. Some called that a miracle, a sign of God's compassion. But Mac thought a truly compassionate God would have saved the living rather than the dead.

For whatever reason, Arlington had been spared except for damage to the trees, many of which were now branchless sticks or shattered stumps. But the graves? Some of the markers had been toppled. Fortunately, the remains were safe underground.

Mac had been there before to visit her ancestors' graves, the first of whom fought for the South and died at Gettysburg. The others had fallen in World War I and Korea. Macintyres had fought in World War II and Vietnam, too, yet come home safe, as her father had after fighting in Afghanistan. But Mac was there to bury half of Alpha Company.

Under normal circumstances, the services would have been spread out over days or weeks. But the public affairs people had gone to great lengths to group them together. *Why?* To better recognize the nation's loss? Or to create a made-for-TV spectacle that would remind people of the daring mission into enemy territory and make Sloan look good?

Or was that too cynical? Mac knew Sloan *had* to look good in order to get elected. And, all things considered, she wanted him to remain in office. *The fighting president.* That was the kind of president the nation needed.

The staff car slowed and came to a stop. A sharply dressed private opened the door and delivered a crisp salute as Mac got out. "Good morning, ma'am."

It *wasn't* a good morning, and Mac resisted the temptation to say so. "Good morning, Private. How long have you been here?"

"Since 0600, ma'am."

It was cloudy, cold, and well past 0900. "Thanks for getting things ready, Private . . . We appreciate it."

The soldier looked surprised. No one thanked him for anything. "You're welcome, ma'am. I'm sorry."

A snowflake twirled down between them. Mac nodded. "Me too. They were good soldiers." And with that, she walked away.

A lieutenant was waiting to lead her to the area where Mac's Marauders were to be laid to rest alongside the air force personnel who had died with them. Chairs had been set up . . . more than four hundred of them. A temporary speaker's platform was in place. And there, beyond the stage, the lines of open graves could be seen. They were on part of the 624 acres of land that had once belonged to Confederate General Robert E. Lee. It was an irony not lost on the reporters who were there to cover the event.

Overman showed Mac to her seat as streams of people filtered into the area. The officers acknowledged each other but didn't engage in chitchat. Neither was in the mood. What followed was a tried-and-true ceremony multiplied by fifty. Not fifty-six, because six soldiers were MIA and might be alive. Were they? It seemed unlikely. But what *if*?

Mac thought about that at least ten times a day. The army took pride in "leaving no man or woman behind." Yet she had . . . And the knowledge continued to eat at her. That in spite of what her soldiers told the debriefers. Mac remembered one in particular. The soldier's name was Cramer, but everyone called him Howdy, because that's how he greeted people. "The major arrived after loading was under way and fought to keep those bastards off our backs. There wasn't no way she could know where everyone was. As for taking off . . . Hell, we *had* to take off or die. And what good would that do?"

Investigating officers had agreed with Howdy, Mac had been cleared of what some family members called "dereliction of duty," and that was that. Except that it wasn't over because Mac couldn't stop thinking about it.

A train of caissons arrived. So many caissons that it had been difficult to find enough of them. The caskets were removed, placed in three carefully spaced rows, and covered with flags. *American* flags.

Then, as the officer in charge led his team off to one side, the Chief of Chaplains for the Union Army stepped forward. In keeping with the request for a nondenominational service, he had chosen the poem "Eulogy for a Veteran" by an unknown author. Puffs of lung-warmed air accompanied his words.

Eulogy for a Veteran

Do not stand at my grave and weep.
I am not there, I do not sleep.

I am a thousand winds that blow.
I am the diamond glints on snow.

I am the sunlight on ripened grain.
I am the gentle autumn rain.

When you awaken in the morning's hush,
I am the swift uplifting rush
of quiet birds in circled flight.
I am the soft stars that shine at night.

Do not stand at my grave and cry,
I am not there, I did not die.

The words were moving . . . And Mac allowed herself to cry as the chaplain backed away and the burial team took over once again. The audience was ordered to rise, and the volleys of carefully timed rifle fire began. Normally, a party of seven soldiers would fire three volleys. But in the case of *this* burial, there were so many salutes that *two* teams of riflemen were required so that each squad would have time to reload.

Gun smoke drifted through the air as the noise went on and on. Was that intentional? So the ceremony would look more impressive on television? Maybe. But Mac didn't give a shit. She wanted her soldiers to receive the honors due them.

Once the volleys were over, a bugler played "Taps," as the caskets were lowered into the ground. The mournful sound never failed to move Mac, and this time was no exception. Would someone play "Taps" for her someday? Of course they would. Every soldier has to die . . . The only question was when.

The snow fell more thickly as the spectators took their seats, and teams of soldiers folded each flag and delivered it to the next of kin. The ceremony came to a close after that, and General Herman Jones passed among the mourners, offering each a card, along with the nation's condolences.

Mac was there as well, and some of the family members came over to speak with her. Most were pleasant, but one woman wasn't. She was wearing a snow-dusted scarf over her long hair, her eyes were red from crying, and a handkerchief was clutched in her right fist. "How dare you come here!" the woman demanded. "Kevin was alive! I know he was! He came to me in a dream. 'The major left us to die.' That's what he said. May you rot in hell." And with that, she turned away.

Mac bit her lip and wondered if it was true. As the last of mourners left, Mac was still there, looking out over the graves, when a woman appeared beside her. She was wearing a white-knit cap and a thick coat. Another mother? Intent on damning her to hell? That's what Mac assumed as the woman spoke. "Major Mac-intyre?"

Mac braced herself. "Yes?"

"I have a message for you." The woman handed Mac an envelope. It was blank except for a presidential seal. Mac felt her heart beat a little faster. She opened it. And there, tucked inside, was a note card. Two words were scrawled on the heavy stock. "I'm sorry."

The note hadn't been signed, nor was that necessary. Mac felt a sense of warmth suffuse her body as she read the words again. Then, having placed the card back in its envelope, she turned to discover that the woman was gone. *"I am the diamond glint on snow."* The blanket of white lay over the cemetery like a shroud.

FORT HOOD, TEXAS

Warehouse 72 was a nondescript building located in an out-of-the-way part of Fort Hood. Victoria parked her car and went inside. The air was chilly and smelled of disinfectants. A civilian was seated behind the waist-high counter. She had short hair and too much eye shadow. "Hello . . . How can I help you?"

"My name's Macintyre . . . Kathy Ivers is expecting me."

The woman nodded. "Right . . . I'll page her."

Ivers arrived two minutes later. She was dressed in a white coat over green OR scrubs. Her white clogs made clacking sounds as she walked. "Major Macintyre? I'm Kathy . . . Everything is ready. Please follow me."

The facility was part of the Armed Forces Medical Examiner System, which was charged with carrying out autopsies on *all* soldiers killed in action, including those who fought for the North. The operation's main purpose was to gather detailed information regarding how each person had been killed in order to identify deficiencies in body armor and vehicle shielding.

But there were secondary benefits as well. Especially where the examination of enemy casualties was concerned. What about *their* body armor? Had improvements been made? And if so, should the Confederacy copy them?

Victoria was there for another reason, however. She wanted to look at the bodies of the people her sister had left behind when she fled Pyote Field. "Leave no man behind." That was the motto. But Robin had left *five* bodies behind rather than stay and fight for them. The bitch.

Ivers led Victoria back through a maze of corridors to the cold room, where the cadavers were laid out on stainless-steel tables. There were three men and two women. All were nude and, with the exception of an African-American male, looked exceedingly pale under the bright lights.

Victoria had seen dead bodies before. Lots of them. But always on the battlefield. And what she saw in front of her was unsettling.

Some of the soldiers were staring at the ceiling. Others lay with eyes closed. One woman had lost an arm in the fighting. It lay next to her . . . And there was a wedding ring on her hand.

A Y-shaped incision had been made under the soldier's breasts. It ran all the way down to her pubic bone. Widely spaced stitches had been used to close it. "The autopsies are complete," Ivers explained. "Their brains were taken elsewhere for examination, but their organs were replaced."

Victoria raised an eyebrow. "In the anatomically correct positions?"

"No, of course not," Ivers replied. "That would be a waste of time. We dump them into the chest cavity. The effects found on or near each body are displayed next to them. Is there anything else I can do for you?"

"No, thanks," Victoria replied.

"There are some coats hanging over there," the tech said. "Feel free to borrow one if you get cold." And with that she left.

Victoria eyed the bodies. They were a beginning point, a way to prepare for her latest assignment. "Kill your sister." Her father had given the order over drinks in a nice restaurant. And who better for the job? Victoria knew Robin the way only a sister could. And she hated Robin the way only a sister could. The psychiatrist Carl Gustav Jung had a theory about that . . . He called it the Electra complex, meaning a psychosexual competition between a girl and her mother for the affection of her father. Except that Victoria had been forced to compete with both her mother *and* her sister.

Victoria knew that some people, *most* people, would see that as a problem. Screw them. It was, to her mind, a logical extension of the Social Darwinism upon which conservative principles were based. It made sense that *she*, as the person most deserving of her father's affection, would have it. And the fact that Victoria knew what she was doing meant she was sane.

But orders to kill Robin were one thing . . . Getting the job done was another. There were plenty of potential obstacles. Robin wasn't likely to have bodyguards as such . . . Majors didn't rate that kind of protection. But she was in command of a battalion. And if even half of the press reports were true, Robin's jailbirds were in love with her. So an assassin would have to get past them in order to put the bitch down.

Then there was the woman herself. Somehow, some way, Victoria's once-reticent sister had transformed herself into a badass officer who was quite capable of defending herself.

So how to get close enough? Perhaps, by spending some time with the dead bodies, Victoria would find an answer. As Victoria circled the tables, she paused every now and then to examine a wallet, handle a piece of jewelry, or look at a photograph. One image caught her attention. The picture was that of a young man with a striking resemblance to one of the dead soldiers . . . a private named Linc Holby.

A brother perhaps? Yes. And the letter made mention of how happy their parents had been the day he was released from Leavenworth. Was that why Linc had kept the letter? And continued to carry it around? Of course it was.

As Victoria stood there, holding the letter, an idea occurred to her. What if someone pretending to be Linc Holby's brother turned up at Robin's base and asked to speak with her? Would Robin agree to a private meeting? Yes, she would! Robin was sure to feel guilty about leaving Linc behind. *Very* guilty. And that would provide the opening Victoria needed. She took all of Holby's effects, signed a receipt for them, and left.

NEAR FORT LEAVENWORTH, KANSAS

Traveling from Texas to Fort Leavenworth, Kansas, turned out to be a lot more difficult than Victoria had anticipated. Months earlier, she'd been able to ride her motorcycle north, using back roads and common sense. Now, security was tight, very tight, all along the heavily disputed border between North and South. So the team's first attempt to enter Union-held territory failed.

That forced them to request a plane. It flew them west across Mexico and out over the Pacific before turning north. After a long, nine-hour flight, the transport touched down in Canada. And, because the Canucks were on friendly terms with the Confederacy, the team was able to charter a second plane, which took them east to a rural airport north of Duluth, Minnesota.

From there, a hunting guide led them down through a myriad of trails to the point where a beat-up van was waiting. It was the property of a Southern sympathizer, and the Confederate flag sticker in the rear window attested to that fact. Victoria ordered Sergeant Ric Radic to scrape it off. His job was to provide security and handle communications.

Sergeant Jimmy Clay had been chosen to impersonate Holby's brother, lure Robin off base for a meeting, and kill her. Corporal Suzy Quan, better known as Suzy-Q, was an ex-beautician and makeup artist. Her task was to make Clay look like Holby to the extent that was possible. Who knew? Maybe Robin had met Linc's brother . . . If so, the likeness would be important.

From Minnesota, they followed a meandering path south through Iowa and into Kansas. So, by the time they arrived in Leavenworth, two weeks had passed since Victoria had viewed the bodies. Was Robin still there? Probably. Mac's Marauders had been badly mauled at Pyote Field, and Victoria figured it would take a while for her sister to get replacements and train them.

An apartment had been secured for the group, and the key was right where the Confederate agent had left it. The fully furnished crash pad was pretty funky, but that didn't matter. If all went well, the team would be gone within a matter of days.

After settling in, the next step was to learn as much as they could about what was going on inside the base. Were the Marauders there? And was Robin present?

Victoria figured that the best and least risky way to gather such intel was to visit the correct bar and make some new friends. With that strategy in mind, Victoria put on a skimpy outfit and, with Clay in tow, made her way to a military nightspot called the Bomb Shelter. It was, according to information online, "A favorite with off-duty army personnel." And, since the bar had 1,236 positive reviews, that appeared to be true.

So Victoria had every reason to expect the thump, thump, thump of bass as they arrived, a meaty bouncer on the door, and a packed room. But after making her way down a flight of concrete stairs, Victoria discovered that the door was unattended, the music wasn't that loud, and the nightclub was practically empty. "What's up with *this*?" Clay wanted to know. And Victoria wondered the same thing.

The décor consisted of army paraphernalia dating back to WWI. There were various types of helmets, sandbags around the empty stage, and a dramatically lit Huey in the middle of the room.

And that was just the beginning. Packs, entrenching tools, boots, and more were perched on beams or hanging from nails. And any wall space not taken up by regimental flags was covered with layers of photographs that had been taken all over the world.

Almost all of them featured one or more soldiers standing in front of a building, a vehicle, or a landmark.

Once the two of them were seated, a waitress arrived. Her outfit consisted of a tee shirt with GO ARMY on it, short shorts, and combat boots. A bejeweled utility belt with pouches completed the look. "Good evening . . . Would you like to order drinks?"

"Yes," Victoria replied. "But where *is* everyone?"

"You're from out of town?"

Victoria saw no reason to deny it. "Yes. We heard this was a hopping place."

The girl nodded. "It was until they split the brigade up into smaller groups and sent them off to who knows where. See that photo? The larger one? Those guys were regulars. Business sucks . . . especially when you're working for tips."

"Where did they go?" Clay inquired.

The waitress shrugged. "I asked, and they said it was secret. Are you ready to order? Or shall I give you a minute?"

"We're ready," Victoria assured her. Once the orders had been placed, and the waitress was walking away, Victoria turned her attention back to the montage. The photo with the three soldiers on it was not only larger than the rest but pinned on top of them as if it had been added recently. Victoria peered at the image in hopes of recognizing something in the background. An entire brigade had been subdivided and dispersed. *Why?* Army Intelligence would want to know.

"What is *that* thing?" Clay inquired, as he pointed to the vehicle immediately behind the soldiers. Victoria hadn't paid any attention to it until then. But now, on closer inspection, she realized that she didn't recognize it either. A missile launcher of some sort? Yes, but what kind?

The waitress arrived with drinks, and Victoria took the opportunity to ask more questions. "How about Mac's Marauders? Did they leave, too?"

"Oh, no," the girl answered. "They're still here. But they're in a training cycle, so we haven't seen them for a while."

If Victoria hadn't been a soldier herself, she might have been surprised by how much the girl knew. But that sort of savvy was typical of military bars. The soldiers would come in, shoot the shit, and unintentionally reveal all sorts of stuff. Never mind the warnings from officers like her.

Once the waitress turned away, Victoria took the group shot down and slipped it into her bag. Later, after they returned to the apartment, she would order Radic to scan it and send it off. Chances were that the people in Texas would know what kind of launcher it was.

After a couple of drinks and good food, the twosome returned to the apartment with boxed meals for Radic and Suzy-Q. They were inside enemy territory, so one of them would need to stand watch at all times. Victoria took the first two-hour stint and went to bed. She'd been asleep for less than an hour when Radic knocked on the door.

The apartment had only the bare minimum of furnishings and, while there were enough beds, there wasn't any bedding. So Victoria had to turn on a light and wiggle her way out of her sleep sack before she could answer the door. Quan had the neighboring twin bed and turned over to face the wall. "Yeah," Victoria said groggily. "What's up?"

"Some guy named Alpha-Four-Niner-Six wants to talk to you," Radic said as he offered the sat phone. Her father wanted to speak with her? That was a surprise, and Victoria felt a growing sense of apprehension as she took the phone. "This is Alpha-Four-Niner-Seven."

"There's been a change of plans," Bo Macintyre said flatly. "Get your team out of there by 0300. And when I say 'out of there,' I mean as far away as you can get . . . Oh, and one other thing . . . Your launcher is part of a new short-range antimissile screen that can blow our stuff out of the sky. We knew they were working on it but didn't realize the system was being deployed. Think about what that means." Victoria heard a click followed by static.

Victoria's mind was racing. A change in plans . . . Get clear by 0300 . . . Why? *Because they're going to drop some heavy-duty shit on Fort Leavenworth,* Victoria thought to herself. *Was one of the antimissile batteries located at the fort? Hell, yes.*

Suddenly, Victoria understood. Because the Union was deploying a system that could intercept conventional and nuclear weapons, the Confederacy was determined to inflict some pain while they still could. Assuming it wasn't too late. What was that her father had said down in Port St. Joe? "Victory always comes at a cost. And I think we should pay the price before the Union grows any stronger."

Shit, shit, shit! Her own army was going to nuke her ass! Victoria jerked the door open. "Clay! Radic! Grab your stuff . . . We're getting out of here. And I mean *now*!"

FORT RILEY MILITARY RESERVATION, NORTH CENTRAL KANSAS

Night exercises were a pain in the ass. But because a great deal of combat took place during the hours of darkness, such efforts were very important. And that was why Mac's Marauders had been sent 130 miles west to Fort Riley where they could play hide-and-seek with other armored units and get what Sergeant Major Price called, "their get-go juice back."

And that was important. Having lost half of Alpha Company, and with new people arriving every day, there was a need to strengthen unit cohesion. "Keep 'em busy," Colonel Lassiter had advised. "Work their asses off." And Mac had done her best to comply.

She found ways to test squads, platoons, and companies. How good were their leaders? How rusty were the soldiers who'd been in prison? And were their technical skills up to date?

Nor was the headquarters company spared. Wu and her people were expected to fight if it came to that, and had been tested along with everyone else.

So there the troops were, spaced out along the top of a steep embankment, waiting for an "enemy" convoy to pass below. But *would* it? According to the thermal images streaming in from one of the battalion's drones, it would.

But what about the convoy's drones? Their job was to spot concentrations of enemy troops so that the convoy's commander could call in an air strike. Mac had a solution for that, however . . . Or hoped that she did. Thanks to countless years of erosion, a rock ledge had been exposed, and it hung rooflike over the embankment, giving Mac's troops a place to hide. Hopefully, the partial "roof" would screen them from the convoy's drone. That's what Mac was thinking about when there was a bright flash of light, followed by a *second* flash, and overlapping explosions.

Mac's initial assumption was that the officer in charge of the exercise was throwing them a curveball . . . Something he did on a frequent basis. But before she could give the possibility much thought, her RTO offered her a handset. "Warlord is on the horn, ma'am."

Mac took the instrument and held it to her ear. The message

was for all COs, and Warlord was in midsentence. ". . . I repeat, *not* a drill. The rebs fired two short-range missiles at us. Both were intercepted by Iron Shield launchers and destroyed in midair. We believe that the enemy missiles were armed with nuclear, repeat *nuclear* warheads. That means there could be some fallout. Especially in the aftermath of an airburst. Those who can shelter in their vehicles should do so. Those who can't should seek whatever shelter is available and await orders. Decontamination units will be dispatched soon.

"We believe both warheads were relatively small and expect that the radiation will disperse in a week or two. In the meantime, monitor your troops for any signs of radiation sickness. Over."

All of Mac's people would fit into her Strykers, and all of the Strykers were equipped with a CBRN (chemical, biological, radiological, nuclear) warfare system, which would keep the crew compartments airtight and positively pressurized. So their course of action was clear.

After giving the necessary orders, Mac scrambled up the embankment and onto the flat area above. As troops hurried to board the trucks, Mac saw a flash of light off to the east. Fort Leavenworth? Mac hoped the interceptors had been able to protect that base as well. But were *more* missiles on the way? If so, one or more might get through.

Mac forced herself to wait next to the vic called **HELL ON WHEELS** until all of her personnel were accounted for. She ushered Tilly up the ramp before entering the Stryker herself.

The interior was crowded, and Mac felt a rising sense of claustrophobia as she sat down. Sergeant Major Price was seated across from her. He grinned. "I don't know about you, Major, but I could use a beer."

Mac nodded. "Me too . . . Put out the word. Off-duty personnel *will* assemble to complete mandatory beer training once we're off duty. I will buy the first round."

A cheer went up inside the vic. Mac's Marauders were on the mend.

CHAPTER 13

||||||||||||||||||||||||||||||||||||||

Speak softly and carry a big stick.

—WEST AFRICAN PROVERB

MCCONNELL AIR FORCE BASE, WICHITA, KANSAS

Sloan could have arrived in a black SUV or limo. But Press Secretary Doyle Besom was forever looking for ways to portray "the fighting president" as a man of action. So nothing less than a military vehicle would do. The flags flying from the Humvee's antennas snapped in the breeze as the vehicle rolled past a long line of KC-135 Stratotankers that were parked next to the main runway. Sloan's arrival would make a good picture when viewed from above, which it would be, since the TV networks had permission to fly camera drones over selected portions of the base.

An air force colonel was waiting to open the door and salute Sloan as he emerged from the vehicle. Sloan returned the gesture and shook hands with the officer. Cameras followed the two men up a flight of metal stairs to the top of a reviewing stand. Drones swooped in to capture tight shots of the president's face as a general stepped in to greet him.

Then, after a formal introduction from the general, Sloan stood in front of the microphones. His eyes swept the mostly military crowd. "My fellow Americans . . . The oligarchs who rule the Confederacy attempted to destroy this base using two missiles fired from Texas. Each weapon was armed with a tactical nuclear warhead packing explosive power equal to seventy-two tons of TNT. Or, put another way, the equivalent of seventy-two two-thousand-pound bombs.

"Fortunately, our newly deployed Iron Shield system kept one of the weapons from striking this base. Sadly, the other missile fell on the town of Belle Plain, where more than a thousand people died."

Sloan paused to let the words sink in. "Meanwhile, the Confederacy launched similar attacks on Fort Riley, Fort Leavenworth, and half a dozen other targets. I'm happy to say that all of those weapons, with the exception of the one that hit Belle Plain, were intercepted.

"Please remember that a significant amount of radiation was released into the atmosphere, however. So if you live in an area where one or more warheads exploded, be sure to follow the instructions provided by state and local authorities. Scientists assure me that so long as citizens take the right precautions, they should be fine. But if you, or someone you know, has symptoms of what could be radiation poisoning, see a doctor right away.

"Now let's ask ourselves some very important questions. Why was the Confederate government willing to use nuclear weapons? And how should we respond? What I'm about to say falls under the heading of conjecture . . . That's all we have to work with since the enemy hasn't seen fit to comment on their motivations.

"But to my mind, the sudden escalation from conventional weapons to nuclear weapons signals weakness and desperation. Having been unable to take more of our territory, it appears that President Lemaire and his flunkies are turning to a different strategy. What if their *new* goal is to lay waste to the North, in the hope that they can create a state of continual chaos and simply wall us off? If that's their plan, they might decide to fire nuclear-armed missiles at population centers. To counter that possibility, we will continue to expand the Iron Shield system *and* put appropriate civil-defense measures in place."

Sloan stared into the cameras. "Regardless of their reasoning, we need to respond. But *how*? After I heard what happened to the town of Belle Plain, I wanted revenge, and my first impulse was to launch a counterstrike, knowing that the Confederacy doesn't have an effective antimissile system. So our missiles were likely to get through.

"But as emotionally satisfying as that would have been, I remembered something very important. Who would die when our missiles fell? The oligarchs in their underground shelters? No, they would be safe. The casualties, and there would be thousands of them, would consist of the people who allowed themselves to be co-opted.

"Some might say that they *deserve* to die for supporting an evil government . . . And I can understand that view. Yet what about our *first* civil war? Reconstruction wasn't pretty, but it beat the alternatives.

"So," Sloan added, "the following message is for the oligarchs and the people who support them. *Do not use tactical nuclear weapons again.* If you do, we will intercept most, if not all of them, and retaliate in kind. There will be no further warnings and no negotiations. Just death raining down from the sky. And consider this . . . Rather than fighting a war you can't win, how about agreeing to a cease-fire in place? Let's exchange words instead of bullets."

There was no applause. Just jagged spears of lightning on the horizon, followed by the soft mutter of thunder. Rain began to fall, and Sloan looked up into the sky. Was a satellite staring down at him? Probably.

"Mr. President?"

Sloan turned to see that the general was getting wet. "Come on, General . . . I hope air force coffee tastes better than the sludge the navy serves. Let's get out of the rain."

NEW MADRID, MISSOURI

The Humvee slowed to a crawl as it followed a six-by-six into a traffic jam. Mac had never been to the river town of New Madrid before, which wasn't too surprising since it was a small community with a population of only three thousand people. She had looked it up, however—and been interested to discover that the Battle of Island Number Ten had been fought there.

Back during the first civil war, the Confederates had been determined to prevent the Union Army from using the Mississippi River as a path south. It took the Northern army a month to break through—but they did on April 8, 1862. And now, more than 150 years later, the town of New Madrid was about to play a role in the *Second* Civil War.

From what Mac could see, New Madrid was a pleasant place, or had been, before the military came to town. Now the streets were clogged with trucks carrying supplies for Flotilla 4. Whatever that was.

The orders had come down shortly after the attack on Fort Riley. Mac's Marauders were to pack up and drive to New Madrid. Once there, Mac was supposed to report to Colonel George Russell who, according to what she'd been able to learn, was a member of the Army Corps of Engineers and Flotilla 4's commanding officer. And that was the extent of what she knew. Her driver braked as an MP waved them down. He tossed Mac a salute as she opened the side window. "Where are you headed, ma'am?"

"We're Mac's Marauders," she told him. "I have twenty Strykers loaded with troops plus some support vehicles. Where do you want us?"

The MP consulted a clipboard and nodded. "Right. Follow the road into town. When you see the car wash, turn right and drive into the field beyond. It's all yours."

"Thanks. And where would I find Colonel Russell?"

"His office is on the *Mississippi*," the soldier replied. "Go down to the river. You can't miss her."

Mac thanked him, returned a salute, and turned to her driver. "You heard the man . . . Take a right at the car wash."

They didn't have far to go, but it still took fifteen minutes to get there. Once they arrived, Mac was pleased to see a hand-lettered sign with MAC'S MRDRS on it, plus a row of sanikans and a green Dumpster. The preparations were too good to be true! It appeared that someone was on the ball.

Roy Quick arrived a few minutes later, and Mac went over to speak with him. "We've got plenty of room, so spread the vehicles out and throw revetments up to protect them on three sides. And let's get a perimeter in place."

Quick nodded. "I like what I see . . . But we're going to need water."

"I'm about to check in," she told him. "I'll ask Colonel Russell about that."

As Quick left, Mac turned to find that Corporal Atkins was standing a few feet away. The ever-present RTO weighed no more than 110 pounds but never complained about the gear she was required to carry. Her eyes were huge behind the lenses of her army-issue "birth control" glasses. "Ma'am?"

"Come on . . . We're going to visit the man."

"Yes, ma'am."

The river was a block and a half to the east. The water had a greenish-brown appearance, and the eastern bank appeared to be relatively close. Or was that an island? Mac wasn't sure.

Mac got her first look at the vessels of Flotilla 4 as she passed a cluster of shiny storage silos. They were moored to the orange buoys anchored offshore. A white-over-red pusher boat was moored in front of Mac. And its blunt bow was in contact with the first of two empty barges, both of which were equipped with cranes.

But the pusher boat and its barges were dwarfed by the large motor vessel moored to Mac's left. It was well over two hundred feet long and a plaque bearing the name MISSISSIPPI was clearly visible on the ship's starboard side. Mac noticed that a gun tub had been installed on the boat's bow, where a group of sailors were gathered around an M163 Vulcan Air-Defense System. The weapon hadn't been designed for shipboard use but would probably work.

Mac led Atkins to the point where a couple of smart-looking soldiers were guarding the riverboat's aluminum gangplank. One of them saluted. "Good afternoon, ma'am . . . Can I help you?"

"Yes. I'm Major Macintyre, and I'd like to see Colonel Russell if that's possible."

The soldier nodded. "Yes, ma'am. We were told to expect you. Can I see your ID please?"

After showing their cards, both women were allowed to cross

the gangplank. It bounced under their boots. Once aboard, Mac stopped a passing sailor. "Where would I find Colonel Russell?"

"Deck three, ma'am," the man replied, as he jerked a thumb upwards. "A ladder is located just aft of here."

As she made her way toward the *Mississippi*'s stern, Mac saw that the "ladder" was actually a set of stairs. For some reason, the navy felt compelled to rename common items. She led Atkins up to deck three and through a varnished doorway. A private was there to receive her. "Name please?"

"Macintyre."

He consulted a clipboard. "Yes, ma'am. We are expecting you. Please take a number."

There was a dispenser on the table next to him. The kind normally seen in a bakery, or the Department of Motor Vehicles. The current number was seventy-nine. Mac frowned. "You're joking."

"No, ma'am. Except in the case of emergencies, the colonel sees people in the order they arrived. He says that keeps the process fair, and rewards promptness. Please have a seat."

As Mac entered the waiting area, she saw four civilians, two army captains, and an air force lieutenant. There were empty chairs next to the zoomie, so Mac sat in one and Atkins took the other. The lieutenant smiled. He had blue eyes and a boyish face. "Good afternoon, Major, and welcome to Colonel Russell's navy. Michael Hicks at your service."

"Robin Macintyre. You're a pilot."

"Sometimes, yes. But I'm serving as a combat-control specialist at the moment. When the colonel wants the rain, it's my job to bring it."

"So we're going to get shot at?"

Hicks grinned. "Oh, yeah . . . From *both* sides of the river and on a frequent basis."

Mac was going to interrogate Hicks further when a male voice called the number 73. Hicks stood. "Wish me well, Major . . . The colonel beckons." And with that, he was gone.

Nearly thirty minutes passed before Mac's number was called, and a private ushered her into Russell's office. The officer was seated behind an oak table with his back to a large window. Mac could see the pusher boat and the barges beyond. She came to attention and popped a salute. "Major Macintyre, sir . . . Reporting as ordered."

Russell returned the salute and gestured toward one of two guest chairs. Both were made of oak, lacked any sort of padding, and had straight backs. Like a restaurant that wants to move customers through. "Welcome aboard," Russell said. "Have a seat."

As Mac sat down, she saw the sign on Russell's desk. It was made of brass and turned her way. The inscription read: BE BRIGHT, BE BRIEF, AND BE GONE.

The tools of Russell's trade were laid out like instruments on a tray. Mac saw a pen, a mechanical pencil, a complicated calculator, a protractor, and a rectangular magnifying glass all positioned with the precision of soldiers on parade. The rest of the table was bare except for an in-box/out-box combo to her right. The out-box was full to overflowing.

Russell's eyes locked with hers. He had thinning hair, gray eyes, and a straight nose. "You arrived in New Madrid twenty-six minutes early and immediately went to work settling in. I like promptness, Major. And I like efficiency. So based on what I've seen so far, you and I are going to get along. How much do you know about Flotilla 4 and its mission?"

"Very little, sir."

Russell nodded, as if that was to be expected. "As the Union Army pushed south across the New Mason-Dixon Line, and the rebs were forced to retreat, they began to blow bridges along the Mississippi. Not all of them, mind you . . . because they had an ongoing need to move troops and supplies east and west. But they dropped enough spans to block the river and slow us down. We had no way to respond at first."

Russell made a steeple with his fingers. "But," he added, "things have changed. Something big must be afoot at Fort Knox because we have orders to head south and clear obstructions. The kinds of obstructions that would impede barge traffic.

"I've been working on this river for seven years, so trust me when I say that ours would be a difficult task under normal circumstances. But now, with people shooting at us, the job will be even more challenging.

"Each time we pause to clear underwater wreckage, it's likely that the enemy will attack. To counter that threat, you and your battalion will go ashore and provide the flotilla with security. Do you have any questions?"

Mac had plenty of questions but, in light of the sign on Russell's desk, forced herself to focus. "Not about the basic mission, no. But I have twenty Strykers and more than two hundred troops. How do you plan to accommodate them?"

Russell hooked a thumb back over a shoulder. "See the pusher boat? And the barges in front of it? Your Strykers will be loaded onto the barges. As for the troops, most of them will be billeted on the *Mississippi*, where, I might add, a cabin has been assigned to you. Is there anything else?"

"My officers and I appreciate the preparations that were made for us," Mac said. "But we need water."

"I think you'll find that a water tanker is in place when you return," Russell told her. "There's no need for anything more permanent since I expect all of your vehicles and personnel to be aboard the barges by this time tomorrow. We're scheduled to depart at 0600 the following morning."

Atkins was waiting when Mac left the office, and they returned to the unit together. After some quality time with Russell, Mac wasn't surprised to discover that a water tanker had arrived during her absence. It was parked between two supply trucks. What was she supposed to do with *them*? There were lots of details to take care of and no procedures to work from.

Mac worked until 2200 hours that night, slipped into her sack, and awoke seven hours later. The sun was little more than a pus-colored smear behind a screen of gray clouds as Mac entered a temporary enclosure and suffered through a cold shower before getting dressed. Breakfast consisted of an MRE Sloppy Joe and a cup of coffee.

Then it was time to head down to the river and get things rolling. It took the better part of twenty minutes to find the pusher boat's captain, and when she did, he was sitting in the *Mississippi*'s well-appointed dining room feasting on free food. His name was Foley. And he was dressed in a ball cap and dirty khakis. "My name's Macintyre," Mac told him, as she took the seat across from him. "Your crew is supposed to load my Strykers this morning."

Foley eyed her over a forkful of hash browns. He had beady eyes and purplish lips. "I have a contract with the government," he said. "And according to the terms of that contract, we begin work at nine. So, when nine o'clock rolls around, we'll load your vehicles."

Mac frowned. "What are you going to do when we're down-river, and the rebs attack before nine o'clock?"

Two rows of yellow stumps appeared when Foley smiled. "I'll do whatever I'm told . . . But it will cost the government time and a half. Now go find someone else to bother."

Mac was seething as she returned to the unit. Thanks to Quick's leadership, Mac's Marauders were packed and ready to go. The first Stryker in line was called the IRON LADY, and Mac rode her down to the river.

It was 0837 by then, and Mac could see the crane operators standing on Barge 1 shooting the shit. But, in keeping with Foley's contract, she forced herself to wait until 0900 before crossing the gangplank and stepping onto the barge. Mac could tell that Foley had warned the men about her because both of them had shit-eating grins. "Good morning, gentlemen . . . We're ready to load. How should we proceed?"

The next fifteen minutes were spent discussing how the Strykers would be positioned ashore, who would attach the slings, and how to secure the vics once they were hoisted aboard.

When the discussion was over, the crane operators climbed up into their cabs and went to work. The IRON LADY was the first to be plucked off the ground, swung out over Barge 1, and deposited on the rusty deck. And that was when Mac realized something important. The Stryker was positioned facing *forward*. That wouldn't do.

Mac hurried to board the barge. A sergeant and a team of three privates were there to secure each vic as it touched down. Mac asked the sergeant for his radio and held it up to her mouth. "Hey! Up in the cab . . . We need to reposition that Stryker. I want to place them back-to-back, facing out."

"No can do," came the reply. "Our deck plan was approved by Colonel Russell. And a colonel outranks whatever you are. Right?"

"That's correct," Mac said tightly. "Please stop loading while I speak with Colonel Russell."

That was when Mac heard Foley's voice on the radio. "Belay that bullshit . . . We have our orders. Continue loading."

Mac keyed the radio again. "Captain Quick?"

"Ma'am?"

"Don't bring any additional vehicles into the pickup zones until you hear from me."

"Roger that."

"That's a violation of our contract!" Foley shouted. "I'll have your ass for that!"

Mac sighed. The whole thing was out of control, but she couldn't back down, not without sacrificing authority that she might need later. So she left the barge, marched past Foley's pusher boat, and stormed over the *Mississippi*'s gangplank. One of the sailors objected, but she kept on going.

Once Mac arrived on deck three, a distraught private sought to intercept her but without success. And when Mac entered Russell's office she saw the source of the private's distress. Captain Foley was standing with hands on hips. "And that ain't all!" he proclaimed loudly. "The bitch refused to load her vehicles!"

Russell looked at Mac. "What's the problem?"

"The problem," Mac replied, "is that I asked the crane operator on Barge 1 to load my Strykers back-to-back, facing out."

"And that," Foley said, "violates the load order that *you* signed! It specifies that the vehicles will be loaded facing forward."

Russell's eyes looked like twin gun barrels as they swiveled back to Mac. "Captain Foley is correct, Major . . . I did specify that the Strykers be loaded facing the front. Is this how it's going to be? Are you going to waste my time by questioning each order I give?"

Mac regretted the whole thing by then. But there was no going back. "Sir, no, sir. But with all due respect, it doesn't make sense to load the Strykers facing forward."

Russell's voice was cold. "Really? Why not?"

"Because if vessels were to attack us from the side, or if we take fire from the riverbanks, the Strykers won't be able to return fire as effectively. I have twenty vics, sir . . . Some are armed with .50s, some with 40mm grenade launchers, and some with 105mm tank guns. That's a lot of firepower, sir. But my vehicles will be more effective if they're facing the enemy, and there will be less chance of a friendly-fire incident."

Foley opened his mouth to speak, and Russell told him, "Shut up."

Then, with his eyes on Mac, he spoke again. "You told Captain Foley what you told me?"

"No, sir. I never got the chance."

Russell turned back to the civilian. "The major is correct, Captain Foley. The notion of using the Strykers to protect the flotilla while it's under way never occurred to me. You will comply with the major's request, and with any other suggestions that she makes. Is that clear?"

"The change order is going to cost you five hundred bucks," Foley said triumphantly. "I win!"

"Get out."

Mac was about to follow Foley through the door when Russell spoke. "Major Macintyre . . ."

"Sir?"

"Try to resolve such conflicts on your own in the future."

"I will, sir."

Russell nodded. Then, for the first time since she'd met him, he smiled. "Good thinking, Major. Dismissed."

The loading process went well after that, but using cranes to swing the vics aboard took a lot of time, and Mac began to worry. What would happen when the flotilla ran into trouble? Would the enemy wait while the crane operators put the Strykers ashore? Hell no, they wouldn't. What she needed was a faster way to get the job done.

And that wasn't all. As Mac stood on the deck and looked up at the crane on Barge 1, she was struck by how exposed the crane operator was. He was sitting in a small box protected by little more than Plexiglas and some sheet metal. The moment the rebs got in close, they would realize that and target him. And once he was dead, her Strykers would be stranded.

In an effort to solve the loading problem, Mac sent Captain Amy Wu and a team of scroungers into town with instructions to find ramps or the means to make them. Then she turned her attention back to the cranes. An old barge was sitting on the riverbank. So Mac sent some wrench turners over to cut it up and ordered the crane operators to swing the steel on board.

Foley claimed that welding the sheets of steel to his cranes would damage them and promised to file a lawsuit. Mac chose to ignore him and went a step further. The wheelhouse perched on top of Foley's pusher boat was extremely vulnerable. And if the helmsman was killed, the barges *and* the boat would run aground. So Mac ordered her soldiers to bulletproof that, too.

The whole project involved a lot of work, and the barely visible sun was setting by the time Wu and her crew returned. The supply officer was riding in an army six-by-six with a big rig following along behind. It was towing a flatbed trailer loaded with what looked like a pile of aluminum scrap.

There was a smile on Wu's face as she came over to report. "We got lucky, Major . . . An aluminum plant is located south of town . . . And they fabricate stuff, including barge ramps! They only had one that could handle a Stryker, but it's extendable and takes five minutes to deploy. That's the good news."

Mac's eyebrows rose. "And the *bad* news?"

"The bad news is that you'll have to unload two Strykers so we can install it."

"That sucks," Mac said. "But the effort will be worth it. How complicated is the installation process going to be?"

"The extension-system bridge uses hydraulics," Wu replied. "So installation will take about eight hours. I brought two of the company's techs back with me."

"They were willing?"

"Semiwilling."

"Watch them. And, Amy . . ."

"Yeah?"

"You rock."

If Mac needed to put *all* of her Strykers ashore, she would still have to use the crane on Barge 2. But with any luck at all, the first ten would be able to fight the rebs off while Bravo Company deployed. The knowledge made her feel better. A lot better.

Crews worked throughout the night to remove the two vics and install the self-extending bridge on Barge 1. Once the work was complete, the Strykers were driven onto the barge. The first truck went up front end first, while the second had to back up the bridge, so its weapons would be pointed at the right bank.

As the sun rose in the east, Mac gave final orders to the lieutenant who was in charge of the Stryker crews. Then she hurried ashore and jogged back to the point where the *Mississippi*'s crew was preparing to pull the gangplank. No sooner was she aboard than the ship's horn produced a blast of sound, and the engine noise increased.

Mac made her way up to the bow. From there, she could see the so-called Spud barge, which the *Mississippi* was pushing out into the main current, and Foley's pusher boat beyond. Water churned at the smaller boat's stern as it guided Barges 1 and 2 downriver. Flotilla 4 was on the move.

By that time, Mac had been working so long that it was difficult to disconnect even though she knew the flotilla was 120 miles from Memphis and the rebel-held territory that lay beyond. She forced herself to visit the crowded dining room, discovered that she was hungry, and was eating a large breakfast when Lieutenant Hicks sat down. While they were chatting, Hicks revealed that rebel drones were monitoring the flotilla's progress, and it didn't take a genius to figure out that would mean trouble later.

After finishing her meal, Mac went looking for her cabin and was pleased to discover that it was equipped with a window, a desk, *and* a tiny bath, in addition to the neatly made bed. Her gear was piled in a corner. Atkins's doing perhaps? She would find out and thank whoever the person was. But the first order of business was a hot shower and eight hours of sleep. It arrived quickly and pulled her down.

Mac awoke feeling reenergized. Based on the strength of the vibration under her feet, she knew the ship was still under way.

After a shower and a hot meal, Mac went looking for her troops, most of whom were quartered on the *Mississippi*. It turned out that Alpha and Bravo Companies were down on the main deck and sleeping four to a cabin. That meant the accommodations were crowded but still better than living in the field. Especially since the troops could access the twenty-four/seven dining facility.

Because Quick was on Barge 1, Overman was in command of the troops. Mac found Overman in a tiny cabin, where he was ass deep in paperwork. The door was ajar, so she walked in. Overman stood and was about to salute when she waved the courtesy off. "No need for that. How are we doing?"

"Everything is going well so far . . . But it's hard to do any PT. We don't have enough space."

Mac considered the possibility of using the spud barge for PT but pushed the thought away. "Let them rest. Odds are that they'll be very busy during the days ahead."

Overman nodded. "The colonel has been calling on us to supply work parties."

"That's his privilege. But if it starts to have a negative impact on combat readiness, let me know. Atkins will be with me most of the time, and I will carry a radio as well."

"Will do," Overman replied. "I'll keep you in the loop."

From there, Mac went up to deck three in hopes of getting a sitrep from Russell's adjutant. The waiting area was empty. The door to Colonel Russell's office was open though, and light spilled out onto the floor.

Mac went over to take a look, and sure enough, Russell was seated at his desk. When he looked up, Mac saw that he was in need of a shave. "Please come in, Major. I was going to send for you in an hour or so."

Mac entered the office and took a seat. "Thank you, sir. What should we expect today?"

"We'll pull into Memphis soon," Russell predicted. "That's where the Riverines will meet us."

"Riverines, sir?"

"Yes. The navy is loaning us a couple of thirty three-foot special operations boats. They're heavily armed and should be able to keep reb speedboats from getting in close. A lieutenant is in charge, and I want her to report to you. Once we reach Helena, Mississippi, I'll be too busy to deal with the swabbies."

"Helena, sir? What's the situation there?"

"The channel is blocked," Russell replied. "The Helena Bridge carries, or carried, US-49 east- and westbound, and the Confederates dropped one of five spans into the river. And, because the navigation channel was only eight hundred feet wide to begin with, nothing of any size can get through. So we'll have to stop, put divers down, and cut the wreckage into manageable chunks. Once that's accomplished, the crane on the spud barge will lift them out. We won't attempt to clear everything . . . just enough to restore traffic."

Mac's mind was racing. "How long will that take?"

"That depends on what the divers encounter," Russell responded cautiously. "But I expect us to be there for at least three days, working around the clock."

Mac remembered what Hicks had told her about the rebel drones. The bastards knew the flotilla was coming and would be well entrenched by the time it arrived. Would Russell's engineers be able to do their jobs while the enemy fired on them from the remains of the bridge and both riverbanks? Of course not. Mac cleared her throat. "I'd like to make a couple of suggestions, sir. I think there are some things we could do to limit our casualties and increase theirs."

Russell nodded. "Please proceed. I'm all ears."

NEW ORLEANS, LOUISIANA

After being forced to run for their lives from Fort Leavenworth, Victoria and her team had returned to Fort Hood. Then, while meeting with her father, Victoria had accepted a *new* mission. "Don't worry," Bo Macintyre told her. "You'll get a chance to deal with Robin. But there's something more urgent that I need you to take care of right now.

"Based on a number of intelligence reports, it looks like the Yankees hope to break the existing stalemate with a two-pronged attack. Efforts are under way to clear the Mississippi, so they can send troops downriver. And, we believe they plan to invade the Confederacy from the Gulf of Mexico. The most likely point of attack is New Orleans. I don't need to tell you how important the Big Easy is in terms of shipping. Especially now that we're importing so many things from South America. And, if the bastards manage to take control of the Mississippi, they will cut the Confederacy in half. We'll fight for the river, needless to say . . . But what if we lose? That's when Operation End Zone will come into play."

Victoria had been confused. "End Zone? I don't understand."

Bo nodded. "There's no reason why you should. After giving the matter a lot of thought, President Lemaire and his cabinet came to the conclusion that there's only one thing that would be worse than losing New Orleans—and that would be to let the enemy occupy it."

Victoria remembered staring into her father's eyes. "So we'll destroy it?"

"No," Bo had assured her. "Not unless the situation becomes hopeless."

Now, days later, Victoria was standing near the Bonnabel Boat Launch, looking out over Lake Pontchartrain. She was wearing a white hard hat, reflective vest, and jeans. Just like the power-company workers who kept the city's power grid up and running each day.

A stiff wind was blowing in from the north, and an endless succession of waves rolled in one after another to explode against the rocks lining the bottom of the embankment. And there, right in front of her, was the weapon Victoria needed. She knew that the average elevation of New Orleans was between one and two feet *below* sea level, while some areas were even lower. All Victoria and her teammates had to do was to place explosives near key floodgates and pumps and detonate them at the right moment.

And, because New Orleans was located *inside* the Confederacy, they could plant the charges with impunity.

And there was another advantage to the plan as well. The explosions could be timed to coincide with the moment when Union forces arrived—thereby making it seem that the enemy was responsible for the destruction. That perception would serve to rally the population behind the Confederate government. The thought brought a smile to her face. She turned away. It was time for a beignet and a cup of coffee.

MEMPHIS, TENNESSEE

The *Mississippi* and the rest of Flotilla 4 was docked at the Beale Street landing just blocks from what had been the downtown business district. But as the first Stryker rolled off Barge 1, all Mac could see was a lead-gray sky, pillars of black smoke, and mountains of rubble.

The Union Air Force had bombed the city and for good reason. The rebs had been using Memphis as a hub for the distribution of troops and supplies. Eventually, elements of General Hern's division managed to fight their way down Interstate 40 and, as they entered Memphis, the rebel air force bombed the city *again*. And the results were horrendous.

Mac was standing in the **ROLLER SKATE**'s forward air hatch. She looked back to make sure that the rest of Alpha Company's vics were clear of the barge. They were . . . And Quick was riding drag so that the force would still have leadership even if she was wounded or killed.

The **SKATE** bounced through a crater as Mac turned her eyes forward. The Stryker's TC was a very competent sergeant named

Hassan . . . And since he had all of the latest recon imagery at his disposal, Mac knew Hassan would be able to find his way to Highway 61, which would take them south to the junction with 49. They would turn west at that point. And, if her suspicions were correct, they would encounter Confederate forces just short of the Helena Bridge. The same bridge the rebs had blown.

What would happen next was anyone's guess. But Mac hoped to not only take the enemy by surprise, but to chase them away, so that Colonel Russell's people could work on clearing the channel below. Barring problems, the seventy-mile trip would take about an hour and a half. During that time, Alpha Company would be vulnerable to an air attack, and knowing that, Mac kept scanning the sky. Yes, she could call for air support immediately, but that could signal the company's presence.

The question hung over Mac as the convoy cleared the central business district and passed through the suburbs south of town. The highway was littered with what looked like the remains of a rebel convoy. It had been destroyed from the air and served as an excellent example of what could happen to her Strykers if an enemy A-10 happened along. The need to thread their way between the wrecks set Mac's nerves on edge, as any of the burned-out vehicles could conceal an IED.

Farther on, the convoy passed through Walls, Mississippi, and a place called Tunica Resorts. The small town was home to some large casinos that, strangely enough, were open for business! Mac decided that the war was a strange affair indeed.

Her thoughts were jerked back into the present when a bullet smacked into the **ROLLER SKATE**'s hull, and the distant crack of a rifle shot was heard. Mac spoke as she brought the M249 machine gun around to point forward. "This is Rocker-Six . . . We're taking fire. Over."

"You got that right," a male voice said. "I see a head up on the overpass!"

"This is Rocker-Seven," Sergeant Major Price said. "You will use the correct radio procedure, or I will rip your head off and piss down your throat. Over."

Mac couldn't help but grin as ROLLER SKATE's gunner fired her .50. But as the heavy weapon blew chunks of concrete out of the overpass, a question niggled at her mind. One shot . . . Only *one* shot. Where was the automatic-weapons fire? Where were the shoulder-launched rockets? She fired the M249 until the Stryker rolled under the overpass, and Price spoke. "This is Seven. Cease firing. The target is down. Over."

Mac released her grip on the LMG. "The target is down." *What* target? A reb sniper? On his own for some reason? Or a patriotic sixteen-year-old with a hunting rifle? She feared the latter. Damn . . . It seemed like the bad things would never end.

But it wasn't until the column made the turn onto 49 west that things got *really* bad. Because there, crouched a quarter of a mile away, was a Confederate LAV-AT missile carrier! The eight-wheeled vehicle was very similar in size and shape to the ROLLER SKATE, except that it was armed with two roof-mounted missile launchers. Either one of them could destroy a tank, never mind a Stryker.

For one brief moment, Mac thought the enemy vehicle commander might assume that he or she was looking at some friendlies, but no such luck. In the blink of an eye, the Confederate gunner sent a wire-guided missile down the highway. Mac waited to die.

CHAPTER 14

‖‖‖‖‖‖‖‖‖‖‖‖‖‖‖‖‖‖‖‖‖‖‖‖‖‖‖‖‖‖‖‖‖‖‖‖‖‖

Maxim I. The frontiers of states are either large rivers, or chains of mountains, or deserts. Of all these obstacles to the march of an army, the most difficult to overcome is the desert; mountains come next, and broad rivers occupy the third place.

—NAPOLÉON BONAPARTE

NEAR HELENA, MISSISSIPPI

Mac saw the blur out of the corner of her eye, heard the explosion, and felt a sharp pain as something sliced through the flesh on her left arm. The missile hadn't struck the **SKATE** . . . So which vic *did* it hit? *Focus,* the voice told her. *Get in close.*

Mac knew what the voice was referring to, and yelled into the mike. "Step on it!" And then, like a cavalry officer from the first civil war: *"Charge!"*

Hassan put his boot to the floor, and Mac was forced to brace herself as the Stryker took off. Two hundred and fourteen feet. That was the minimum range for a TOW missile, and once the **SKATE** got in close, the LAV-AT would be forced to rely on a single 7.62mm machine gun for defense.

The **SKATE**'s .50 was pounding away by then, and Mac was firing her LMG even though she knew the slugs couldn't penetrate the tank killer's forward armor. But she had to do *something*, and operating the weapon helped.

Meanwhile, the LAV-AT's commander was faced with a difficult choice. He or she could order the driver to throw the engine into reverse *or* launch missile two. Because the vehicle couldn't do both at the same time.

Mac saw a puff of smoke as the second weapon came her way. But it was high . . . And passed over her head. *Why?* TOW missiles were controlled by a joystick. Maybe the gunner's hand was shaking . . . Or maybe anything. The important thing was that the missile missed.

And as the **SKATE** rolled past the LAV-AT, the Stryker's remotely operated weapons system swiveled around to stay on target. It was only a matter of seconds before the .50 caliber slugs found thinner armor. Then came a single bang, followed by a BOOM, as the tank killer exploded.

There was no time in which to celebrate. Mac could see troops up ahead. They were running every which way in response to the unexpected attack. But, because of the gap in the middle of the bridge, they had no way to escape.

Beyond them . . . on the other side of the span, Mac could see more Confederate troops. But they were facing the other way as Captain Overman and his Strykers attacked the other end of the bridge. Mac hoped that the rebs directly in front of her would surrender . . . And would accept if they offered to do so.

The Confederate soldiers weren't ready to quit. An M40 recoilless rifle was mounted on the back of a pickup truck. It had been aimed at the river. But the reb behind the wheel was turning the vehicle in order to aim the gun at the Marauders. It was too late. The **POPEYE** fired its 40mm grenade launcher, and the truck was consumed by a series of overlapping explosions.

Hassan braked as Mac made use of the PA system. Her voice boomed across the litter-strewn surface of the bridge. "Cease firing! Lay your weapons down! Place your hands on your heads!"

Roughly twenty rebs were still standing, with nowhere to go. Slowly, reluctantly, they did as they were told. Mac was thankful. There had been enough killing.

Mac felt a stab of pain as she pushed herself up out of the hatch. Her left sleeve was soaked with blood and, as she slid down onto the road, she felt light-headed. Dozens of troops were deassing the Strykers by then, and one of them spotted the blood. "We need a medic over here! The major was hit!"

Mac sat with her back to an enormous tire as a medic cut her sleeve away, assured her that the wound was relatively minor, and wrapped a dressing around it. "Painkiller, yes or no?" the woman inquired.

"No," Mac replied. "Not yet . . . Not until we lock the area down. Help me stand."

With help from the medic, Mac made it to her feet. And that was when she heard the now familiar moan of the *Mississippi*'s horn. "There she is!" someone said, and as Mac looked upriver, she saw the flotilla round a bend in the river.

Two smaller boats were dashing about. Their hulls were covered with camouflage paint, and they bristled with weapons. The Riverines that Russell had mentioned? Yes . . . The first battle was over. But how many still lay ahead?

Once Mac was confident that Overman had control of the west end of the bridge, and Quick's platoon leaders had secured the prisoners, she made her way east. Atkins followed a few steps back.

The LAV-AT was still burning, and machine-gun ammo continued to cook off as a daring soldier scooted in to hook a cable onto one of the vehicle's hard points. Were the reserve missiles inert? Or could they blow? Mac didn't know for sure but felt a sense of relief as the enemy vehicle was hauled away.

Mac continued on to the point where the first missile had detonated. What remained of **MAMA'S BOY** was still smoking. For some reason, the vic's TC had veered out of line. That made his Stryker visible to the enemy gunner, who had chosen to target **MAMA'S BOY** instead of the **SKATE**. That's how war was. Split-second decisions were made, and people died. Or lived . . .

A voice broke into Mac's thoughts. "The colonel is on the horn," Atkins said, as she offered the handset.

Mac took it. "This is Rocker-Six. Over."

Russell was all business. "Give me a sitrep."

Mac forced her eyes off the **MAMA'S BOY**. "We're in control of the bridge. An LAV-AT and a force of about thirty rebs were waiting for the flotilla on this side of the break. An equal number were on the west side of the span. We lost eleven people and have approximately twenty prisoners. Over."

"They might try to retake it," Russell replied. "Don't let that happen. Over."

"No," Mac said. "We won't. Over."

Mac let her eyes swing back to the wreck. "There are bodies in that Stryker, Atkins. Tell Captain Quick that we need a squad, cutting tools, and eleven body bags."

"Yes, ma'am."

Mac turned and began the long walk back. She was crying . . . But no one could see the tears.

ABOARD THE AIRCRAFT CARRIER *GEORGE WASHINGTON*, IN THE GULF OF MEXICO

Tropical Storm Ernesto was sending fifteen-foot-high rollers toward what had once been the United States of America as if determined to attack it. Sheets of spray flew away from the carrier's bow as it broke through a wave, and the hull shuddered. Sloan's stomach felt queasy, and he wanted to hurl, but that wouldn't look right to the people on the *George Washington*'s bridge.

The carrier, and her sixty-five warplanes, were at the center of a group that included seventy-five hundred navy personnel, plus transports loaded with three thousand Marines, a flotilla of eight destroyers, and a screen of five hunter-killer submarines. This was it . . . Or Sloan hoped so, as the contents of his stomach threatened to surge up and into his throat.

Month after month had passed while armies fought each other to a slow-motion standstill south of the New Mason-Dixon Line. The standoff was what Secretary of Defense Garrison referred to "as a nonstop meat grinder," which had already transformed a broad swath of the country into what looked like a postapocalyptic wasteland.

In an effort to open a new front and cut the Confederacy in two, Sloan's advisors recommend that he authorize an amphibious attack on the port of New Orleans. And after months of planning, Operation Swordfall was under way. The bow plunged, and Sloan had to grab a plotting table for support. "How long before we make contact?"

Admiral Carrie Moss was tall, slim, and had a smile on her face. The kind of smile that suggested that she, as an admiral, knew things a mere civilian couldn't understand. And Sloan figured that was true. "We made contact ten minutes ago, sir . . . They shot down one of our P-3 Orion antisubmarine aircraft, and we destroyed one of their attack submarines."

People were beginning to die as spray hit the glass, and wipers cleared it away. All because of orders that *he* had given. It was going to be a long day.

NEAR HELENA, MISSISSIPPI

More than twenty-four hours had passed since the fight on the bridge, and about half of the battalion was still up there, guarding against the possibility of a Confederate attack. Meanwhile, Mac was standing on the *Mississippi*'s top deck, just forward of the wheelhouse. Her arm ached but was going to be fine. Or so Dr. Halley claimed.

As she looked out over the ship's bow, Colonel Russell explained the process. "The spud barge, which is to say the one directly in front of us, has so-called spuds, or metal columns located at all four corners. They're down now, resting on the bottom of the river. That's what makes the spud barge stable.

"My divers have been working in shifts to clear the tangle of metal down there. Think about it, Major . . . Think about trying to work in almost zero visibility, with a two-mile-an-hour current trying to push you downriver and jagged metal all around! It takes skill, and it takes courage.

"Here we go," Russell added, as the crane's engine began to roar—and black smoke jetted out of its exhaust stack. A cable led down into the murky depths, and Mac watched it tighten. A cheer went up from the people assembled on the spud barge as the first chunk of dripping metal was hauled up to be deposited on the deck.

Russell smiled. "We're starting phase two now . . . By late afternoon tomorrow, I hope we'll be able to move on. How are we doing where security is concerned?"

"I think we're in pretty good shape," Mac replied. "I'm not so sure about the situation downstream, though . . . Lieutenant Hicks is coordinating airborne reconnaissance via the air force—and they sent a drone down toward Ferguson early this morning. The rebs shot it down. And they did so with considerable speed."

"They were waiting for it."

"Exactly. So Lieutenant Lasser is going to take me down for a look-see."

"I've seen her people," Russell said. "They look like a pig's breakfast."

"They're navy, sir."

Russell laughed. "Good point . . . Give me a report when you get back."

Mac made her way aft to the point where a set of metal stairs led down to the landing platform that had been rigged for the convenience of small workboats. That's where Lieutenant Lasser and her four-person crew were waiting. The special operations boat was thirty-three feet long, powered by two 440hp engines, and armed with a deadly array of weapons.

"Good morning," Lasser said as she rendered a salute so casual that it resembled a wave. The navy officer was wearing a faded baseball cap, a gray sweatshirt with a silver bar pinned to the collar, and a pair of army-style camouflage pants. Her footgear consisted of retro high-topped sneakers decorated with pink laces.

Lasser's crew wasn't any better . . . And that raised a question: Was Mac looking at a bunch of screwups? Or some hard-core special ops types with special privileges? Time would tell. "Good morning," Mac replied as she stepped into the boat. "Are we ready to go?"

Lasser had beady eyes and an angular face. "Yes, ma'am. Please hang on. Percy has a need for speed."

The sailor who was stationed at the controls was wearing a helmet, goggles, and a tac vest up top. The rest of his outfit consisted of board shorts and flip-flops. He grinned and threw Mac a Boy Scout salute. She nodded in return. Then they were off . . . And even though Mac was already hanging on, she had to reposition her feet in order to remain upright. The crew of the second SOC-R boat had orders to remain with the *Mississippi*, and they waved as the first boat roared past.

Because the special ops boat required only two feet of water, Percy was able to drive it under the bridge without hitting the wreckage hidden below. The SOC-R boat was fast, but the engines were noisy, which meant people would hear it coming. "How far do you want to go?" Lasser shouted.

"Assuming the rebs don't drop any more bridges, the next clearing operation will take place in Vicksburg."

"That's more than two hundred miles downstream," Lasser replied. "Fuel would be a problem, and we'd be sitting ducks for an Apache."

"Understood," Mac shouted. "We'll go as far as Ferguson and turn around."

The next fifteen minutes passed uneventfully, and Mac was eyeing the scenery, when Lasser shouted a command, and Percy pulled the throttles back. A wave surged away from the boat's bow as it slowed, and Lasser brought a pair of binoculars up to her eyes. Mac could tell that the navy officer was examining a grungy-looking barge. It was made out of wood and at least a thousand yards away. "Here," Lasser said, as she offered the glasses to Mac. "Take a look . . . Tell me what you see."

Mac could hear the challenge in Lasser's voice and knew she'd have to pay close attention. During the first pass, all Mac saw was the stack of old lumber on the barge's deck, lots of white bird shit, and the old rowboat that lay bottom up on the stern.

But Mac knew there had to be something more. Something she'd missed. So she looked again. And that's when she spotted the camera. It was attached to the short mast at the stern, and so small that it was barely visible at that distance. "The bastards are watching us!"

"Yes, they are," Lasser agreed. "And any other boats that happen past. But if my guess is correct, there's something more to worry about. Hey, Luther, light that sucker up!"

Luther had dreadlocks, was wearing a sleeveless Levi's jacket, and standing behind an automatic grenade launcher. As it began to chug, a series of explosions marched across the barge. Then BOOM! The whole thing went up in a massive explosion. Thousands of ball bearings churned the surface of the river and, had the boat been closer, would have destroyed it.

Did the Confederates have the capacity to detonate the charge remotely? Of course they did. And that meant the rebs could have triggered the floating bomb as the *Mississippi* motored past it. Mac looked at Lasser with a new sense of respect. "You have a sharp eye, Lieutenant . . . Well done."

Lasser shrugged. "I don't deserve any credit. Most of what we know was learned the hard way . . . Which is to say after someone died." And with that, Lasser signaled Percy, who pushed both throttles forward.

During the next hour, Lasser and her crew spotted a subsurface cable that was intended to rip the guts out of a ship like the *Mississippi*, two tethered mines of the sort normally used to defend harbors, and an explosive charge concealed underneath a railroad bridge. Was it supposed to bring the bridge down or damage any vessel passing below? Both perhaps.

Lasser's crew took care of the mines by blowing them up, but had to leave the cable and the railroad charge for Russell's engineers to deal with. After returning to the *Mississippi*, Mac reported to Colonel Russell, who made a face when she told him about the underwater cable and the bomb. "Please convey my thanks to Lieutenant Lasser. Her people may *look* like hell, but they certainly know what they're doing. I'll send a work party down to clear the obstacles."

"I'll ask Lasser to provide an escort," Mac told him.

"Excellent," Russell replied. "We're about finished here, so I hope to depart early tomorrow morning."

The boats left shortly after that, and Mac went up to visit the troops on the bridge. Quick was there, along with Overman, which meant Mac could brief them in person. "We're pulling out in the morning. So get everyone off the bridge by 0230 and load Bravo Company onto the second barge, using the crane. Then I'll have Foley move the barges to the east side of the river so that Alpha Company can board Barge 1 via the ramp. And please pass the word . . . Based on what I saw downstream, the enemy will be waiting for us. I expect everyone to be ready."

Mac went back to the ship after that, took a shower, and went to dinner. Some of her troops were in the dining room, and Mac asked for permission to join them. Most had been in Leavenworth and clearly liked the fact that she'd been there, too, if only for a brief time. The conversation centered around how bad the food had been, which guards were the most overweight, and the nature of the journey ahead. "How 'bout it?" a private wanted to know. "Are we going to see action?"

"I'd put money on it," Mac told him. "So get a good night's sleep. Odds are that we'll be up to our asses in it tomorrow."

But it didn't turn out that way. In spite of problems with the crane on Barge 2, and the difficulties associated with bringing

Barge 1 in close enough, all of the Strykers were loaded by the time heavily filtered sunlight washed over the land. A single blast from the *Mississippi*'s horn signaled the flotilla's departure.

The special ops boats went first, followed by Barges 1 and 2, and the pusher boat. The *Mississippi* was last in line, and her engines were barely turning over as she ghosted through the low-lying mist.

As the day progressed, the gray clouds produced big drops of rain. And as Mac stood on Barge 1's bow, she could see the thousands of interlocking circles that the droplets made as they hit the surface of the river.

But there wasn't any gunfire . . . No rockets . . . Nothing. Just the steady thump of the *Mississippi*'s engines, the sound of water gurgling away from the blunt bow, and an occasional burp of noise from her radio. The whole thing felt spooky.

After passing Friar's Point and Ferguson, they anchored north of Rosedale. And that was a dangerous place to be. They were well within the reach of rebel aircraft.

Mac decided to sleep on Barge 1 just in case. And that's where she was, snoozing in **COWBOY**'s cargo compartment, when the shit hit the fan. No one had to tell her. The steady rattle of gunfire said it all. Flotilla 4 was under attack. But by *what*?

Mac was fully dressed. All she had to do was roll off the bench-style seat and grab her gear as she rushed outside. Atkins materialized out of the gloom. "We're under attack from speedboats, ma'am. The Riverines have engaged them, but they need help."

An explosion lit up the night as Mac put her vest on. One of the attackers? Mac hoped so. "Give me the handset."

Atkins gave it over, and Mac thumbed the key. "This is Rocker-Six . . . Strykers will fire on enemy boats independently, but be careful! We have two friendlies out there . . . So make dammed sure you know who you're aiming at."

The battle was a sight to see. Tracers cut the darkness into abstract shapes as .50s opened up from both sides of both barges. Explosions marked hits as the 40mm grenade launchers fired, and the cacophony of sound was punctuated by an occasional boom as one of the battalion's 105mm guns went off.

The broadsides lit up the night, allowing Mac to see what appeared to be two dozen speedboats dashing in and out. Most were little more than glorified speedboats armed with machine guns. But there were some larger craft as well, one of which mounted a minigun, and Mac had to duck as 7.62mm rounds clanged, banged, and buzzed all around her. Someone screamed, and someone else yelled, "Medic! We need a medic over here!"

Under normal circumstances, the swarm-style attack would have been successful. But the massed firepower provided by the Strykers was too much for the thin-skinned pleasure boats. Those that could fled downstream, with the Riverines in hot pursuit. Mac called them back, fearful that an ambush could be waiting.

It was about 0430 by then, and Mac kept her troops at their battle stations until the sun rose, and it seemed safe to let half of them stand down. Then she went down to inspect Lasser's boat. It had taken a lot of small-arms fire, but the ballistic armor had done its job, and none of the sailors had been hit.

As the boat circled the flotilla, a great deal of damage was revealed. Foley's pusher boat was all shot up, and the spud barge's crane was blackened where a rocket had struck it, but it was the *Mississippi* that had suffered the most. Not only was she the most important target, she was the *biggest* target as well. Her formerly pristine superstructure was peppered with thousands of holes, shattered planks marked the spot where a rocket had punched through the radio shack, and a blood-splashed pontoon boat was still moored alongside. It was filled with the bodies of the would-be boarders the Riverines had slaughtered.

As for the rest of the badly-shot-up assault boats, the current had taken them downstream, where they would serve as a potent warning to anyone with plans to attack Flotilla 4. Was that it then? Would they be allowed to reach Vicksburg without further combat? *Sure,* Mac thought to herself. *When pigs fly.*

NEW ORLEANS, LOUISIANA

The apartment was located in the basement of an old building in the French Quarter. Victoria was seated at a card table. And as she stared at a news feed, she could hear the muted thump of a bomb exploding nearby. The lights flickered, and chips of green paint drifted down from the ceiling to settle around her. Victoria was deeply disappointed. A decisive sea battle had been fought and lost. *And no wonder,* Victoria thought to herself, *since their ships outnumbered ours two to one.*

She knew that the numerical advantage stemmed from a number of things, including the fact that most of the navy's ships had been moored in Union-controlled ports on the day war was declared. Just as most of the army was stationed in the South.

It was more complicated than that, of course, since some military personnel fled from the North to the South, and vice versa, depending on their political views and cultural backgrounds. Still . . . there had been reason for hope, and that hope was gone.

More bombs exploded, and Victoria felt the floor shudder in sympathy. *You need to concentrate,* she told herself as she watched the news. *You have a job to do.*

Strangely enough, at least three TV stations remained on the air. *Why?* Their towers would make excellent targets. *Because the Yankees want the stations on the air,* Victoria concluded. *They're winning, and they want the locals to know that . . . And, once they're in control, they'll use the TV stations for propaganda purposes.*

But Victoria was grateful regardless of the reason. Her job, which was to simultaneously flood New Orleans and blame it on the enemy, was going to depend on good timing. And thanks to the local news teams, Victoria had a reasonably good understanding of what was happening.

After defeating the Confederate fleet at sea, the Yankees had been able to close in on New Orleans quickly. The final assault began with bombing raids that were still under way. Meanwhile, the enemy used amphibious landing craft to put Marines ashore at Port Fourchon, while Riverines surged upriver, shooting anything that moved.

And as those attacks went forward, three amphibious assault ships were standing offshore, where they were launching landing craft and helicopters loaded with Marines, some of whom had already landed near Chalmette and Meraux. From there, they would be able to follow Highway 39 into the center of the city.

Victoria turned to Sergeant James Clay. He was seated at a table piled high with electronics. "Hey, Jimmy, we're getting close. Run a check on those detonators."

The team had been able to place about two dozen satchel charges in key locations around the city. Each case was loaded with military-grade C-4 rigged for manual or remote detonation. And by sending a "check" signal to the charges, Clay could determine if the system was working properly. "Roger that," Clay responded as he began to type. There was a moment of silence, followed by a heartfelt, "Damn it!"

Victoria frowned. "What's wrong?"

"The signal isn't getting through."

"Why?"

"There's no way to be sure," Clay replied. "But I think we're being jammed."

Victoria felt a surge of frustration. It made sense. Even though the Yankees wanted to keep the local TV stations on the air, there were lots of functions they would try to suppress—voice communications and targeting systems being excellent examples. And all they would need to do the job was some properly equipped jammer drones. She stood. "Stay here, monitor the news, and be ready to come if I call for you."

Sergeant Radic had been lounging on the beat-up couch. Now he was up and on his feet. There was a look of concern on his face. "What about you?"

"I'm going to arm those charges manually," Victoria told him. "Then I'll come back, and we'll celebrate with a cold beer."

"No offense, ma'am, but that's bullshit," Clay put in. "All of us should go."

"Thanks," Victoria said, "but no thanks. My bike is the fastest way to get through clogged streets. And one person will attract far less attention than three would. You have your orders . . . Carry them out."

Victoria left her pack behind, knowing the team would take care of it for her. All she needed was her helmet, a jacket, and a pair of boots. A flight of well-worn stairs took her up to the ground level, where a shabby door opened onto a stinking alley. It was dark, but a flash of light lit the city as a bomb exploded, and the ground trembled.

Thanks to the length of heavy-duty chain that connected the BMW to an overloaded Dumpster, the bike was still there. Victoria hurried to free it, and the chain went into a pannier. Then she threw a leg over the seat, turned the key, and heard a satisfying roar.

Victoria didn't need a map because she'd been present as each charge was placed. The plan was to blow key pumping stations first. Then she would turn her attention to certain floodwalls. An extraordinary amount of rain had fallen since the meteor impacts, which meant that Lake Pontchartrain was higher than it should have been. So once the walls went down, and without enough pumps to counteract it, water would flow in. Lots of water. Victoria smiled as she put the BMW into gear and took off.

There were twenty-five main pumping stations in New Orleans, and Victoria hoped to blow ten or twelve of them, knowing that destroying them all would be next to impossible given the situation. As Victoria turned onto a main street, she found herself surrounded by panicked refugees. An aid unit was trapped in the fleshy tide, a frustrated police officer was shouting orders, and a street vendor was selling popcorn.

And the chaos was good from Victoria's perspective because she'd be free to make her rounds. The explosives were concealed inside the ubiquitous metal service boxes that belonged to the power company. The C-4 was contained in locked cases. Each one was marked AUTHORIZED PERSONNEL ONLY and bore a toll-free number that would channel callers into an office at Fort Hood.

Once a fiberglass case was exposed, all Victoria had to do was enter a three-digit code into the combination lock, insert a special key, and give it two complete turns. Then she had ten minutes to get clear. As for any civilians who happened to be present when the charge went off, well, they were soldiers of a sort. And would have to die for their country.

Everything went smoothly at first. But as the sun started to rise, and the streets emptied, the situation started to deteriorate. Victoria had just blown the second floodgate on her list when the Apache helicopter attacked her.

Rockets flashed over her head, and explosions blew chunks out of the street, as the chopper roared over. Victoria's mind was racing as she turned to the right and raced away. What was going on? Were the Yankees firing on anything that moved? Or had a sharp-eyed drone operator spotted her and seen the pattern? Wherever the woman went, things exploded. Yes, it was always best to assume the worst.

No sooner had that thought occurred to her than the Apache appeared four or five blocks ahead. It was flying straight at her. Victoria saw a puff of smoke, and knew that the helicopter's 30mm chain gun would eat her up if she stayed on the street. So she wrenched the handlebars to the left and entered an alley. Shit, shit, shit. There was no way in hell that she was going to escape, unless . . .

Victoria opened the throttle, weaved in and out of the mazelike streets, and took a right on Bonnabel Boulevard. She ran the bike north, straight toward Lake Pontchartrain, but had to slow for a last-minute curve. After that, it was full speed ahead out onto a narrow finger of land. Then she was airborne. But not for long. The bike fell like a rock. Cold water consumed Victoria as she felt the impact of a shock wave and heard the muffled thud of an exploding rocket. Then, weighed down by her clothing, she began to drown.

JUST NORTH OF VICKSBURG, MISSISSIPPI

Rather than wait for Flotilla 4 to reach Vicksburg and begin work on the fallen bridge there, the rebs sent an armada upstream to attack the Union vessels. And the wave of attackers consisted of what Mac feared most, which was helicopters. She was standing on Barge 2 as the first helicopter attacked Barge 1 and drew blood. Rockets struck **OL' SLAB SIDES**, which was sitting on the deck of Barge 1. The Stryker was destroyed, and its two-person crew was killed as the Apache flashed overhead.

The helicopter was firing its chain gun by then, and as Mac turned to watch, hundreds of slugs struck the pusher boat. They couldn't penetrate the bolt-on armor, however—thereby saving Foley's mostly worthless life.

The sailors had brought the 20mm Vulcan mounted in the *Mississippi*'s bow into action by that time. It could fire six thousand rounds a minute, and the swarm of slugs ate the first helicopter alive. Mac watched the Apache stagger, fall, and crash atop the *Mississippi*'s superstructure. A fire broke out, crew people rushed to respond, and the ship's horn produced what sounded like a moan of pain.

The *second* chopper was making its run by then. Rockets hit the spud barge's crane, and it seemed to fall in slow motion. There was a loud crash as it hit the deck, and some of the wreckage fell into the river. That produced drag and caused the barge to swerve.

Mac was forced to turn away as half a dozen jet skis surged upriver, and the special operations boats went to meet them with guns blazing. A jet ski exploded, and someone shouted, "They're carrying bombs!"

Mac yelled, "Kill them!" into her handheld radio, but not before one of the extremely agile watercraft slammed into SOC-R 1. Mac watched in horror as Lieutenant Lasser and her crew vanished inside the explosive waterspout that lifted the front half of the boat twenty feet up into the air.

The Strykers were firing by then, and Mac had the satisfaction of seeing explosion after explosion as the twin broadsides blew the suicide bombers to smithereens. It should have been enough. And

Mac thought it *would* be enough until Quick spoke. "We have two, make that *three*, gunboats inbound at twelve o'clock."

After acknowledging the transmission, Mac issued orders to the Stryker crews. "Open fire on the gunboats the moment they appear . . . Meanwhile, I want all of the truck commanders to get on machine guns. The remaining helicopter will be back . . . Let's blow that son of a bitch out of the sky!"

Mac's words proved to be prophetic, as the Apache made a gun run from the north. Bullets tore into the *Mississippi*'s still-burning superstructure and killed some of the civilians who were fighting the fire. As the chopper swept over the already damaged spud barge, Mac was standing between the rows of Strykers, firing her pistol up at the Apache, when Atkins threw her down. Bullets clanged as they hit the spot where Mac had been standing.

"Sorry, ma'am," Atkins said as she let go. "But shooting at an Apache with a nine is just plain stupid."

Mac couldn't help but laugh. There was a hysterical quality to it. "Yeah . . . That wasn't my brightest moment. Thank you."

By the time the women were back on their feet, the Strykers were firing on the gunboats. Mac got a look at them as she peered through the gap between two vics. The forty-five-foot response boats had been Coast Guard property originally. Now they had been pressed into service as gunboats. Each carried a minigun up front and twin LMGs in their cockpits. Bullets raked the barge as the rebs fired.

But the Strykers were nearly impervious to small-caliber stuff . . . And when *they* fired, a metal hailstorm hit the boats, tore them to shreds, and triggered a series of secondary explosions. That part of the battle ended before it truly began.

But, after turning around, the Apache was back! As Mac watched, a man with an AT4 rocket launcher made his way up to the front of the barge, where he flipped the remains of a cigar into the river. It was Sergeant Major Price who, true to his notion of how senior noncoms were *supposed* to behave, was about to go *mano a mano* with an enemy attack ship.

Mac saw a puff of smoke as the rocket left the tube. Then, in a beautiful piece of timing, the missile hit the helicopter head-on. The resulting explosion tore the Apache apart and threw chunks of metal every which way. One of them took the sergeant major's head off. Mac heard herself utter an animal-like cry as the noncom fell. *The best of the worst.* That was Price . . . And Mac felt as if her heart would break.

She heard a roar and looked up in time to see an A-10 flash by. The plane was a welcome sight, but it was too late for Price and all the rest of them. Vicksburg had fallen to Union forces on July 4, 1863, during the first civil war. Independence Day . . . Now it was going to fall again.

ABOARD THE AIRCRAFT CARRIER *GEORGE WASHINGTON*, SOUTH OF NEW ORLEANS

The sky was almost the same color as the aircraft carrier's haze-gray paint, and when the sea heaved, the ship did, too. Even after taking some seasick pills, Sloan was still looking for his sea legs as he followed Major McKinney through a hatch and down a corridor.

A dozen people stood as Sloan entered the wardroom, and he waved them back into their chairs prior to taking the one that was reserved for him. "So," Sloan said, as his eyes roamed the faces around him. "Give it to me straight. How are we doing?"

He knew the answer of course . . . But the discussion had to start somewhere. All eyes went to Admiral Carrie Moss. Sloan saw that the mysterious smile was still in place. "Operation Swordfall is a success," Moss said without hesitation. "We put our troops ashore, we pushed the enemy out of New Orleans, and we're in control of the city's infrastructure."

"That's nice," National Security Advisor Toby Hall said. "But are we in control of the city's *population?*"

As with all officers of her rank, Moss was part politician and had a ready response. "No, not entirely," she admitted. "The Confederates blew some floodgates and pumps as they left town. So some of the streets are under a foot or two of water. Criminal gangs and resistance fighters have taken advantage of that to slow our forces down. But the Army Corps of Engineers and navy Seabees are making repairs. And, once their work is complete, we'll have full control of the city."

"I believe that Admiral Moss is correct," Doyle Besom put in. "But in spite of winning the physical fight, we're losing the battle for the hearts and minds of Southern voters. According to the lies the Confederate propaganda machine is putting out, *we* were the ones who blew the floodgates as part of a plan to punish the citizens of New Orleans for supporting Lemaire. And that notion continues to get traction in Georgia, Florida, and Texas, where support for the Confederacy is growing stronger."

Sloan cleared his throat. "Unfortunately, Doyle is correct. And, as many of you know, there's another problem as well. Time continues to pass . . . And, based on the most recent intel, it looks like General Macintyre is making use of it to redeploy his troops, funnel supplies to them, and bring more mercenaries in from Mexico. That means we will have an even bigger fight on our hands once we break out of New Orleans."

General Hern broke the ensuing silence. "I know Bo Macintyre, and he's one tough son of a bitch. But, ready or not, he's going down."

Sloan heard the expressions of agreement, but his thoughts were with *another* Macintyre. Was Robin okay? He would find a way to check on her during the next couple of days . . .

And a way to get his ass off the fucking aircraft carrier.

CHAPTER 15

||||||||||||||||||||||||||||||||||||||

Sometimes we see the Civil War in movies and imagine these neatly aligned rows of men with muskets, walking in line to shoot each other. In reality the things that fascinated me were how absolutely ruthless and violent so many engagements were, how much suffering and how men were not prepared.

–SETH GRAHAME-SMITH

SOUTH OF BATON ROUGE, LOUISIANA

It was early morning, and the traffic was light. *And that makes sense,* Mac thought, as the **POPEYE** rolled past a shot-up tanker truck. *We control everything between here and Georgia. But the situation is in flux, and it doesn't make sense to hit the highway unless you have to.*

Mac was tired, but so was the rest of the battalion. After the river battle ended, the badly damaged *Mississippi* had been able to creep into the bombed-out city of Vicksburg and tie up at a dock. But the ship and the spud barge were going to require extensive repairs before they'd be operational again.

Initially, Mac thought that would provide the Marauders with a much-needed opportunity to get some rest and perform maintenance on their Strykers. But that hope evaporated when new orders arrived. The rebs had been able to flood sections of New Orleans, Operation Swordfall was stalled, and there was a need for reinforcements. Especially Strykers, which were well equipped to operate in an urban environment.

So Mac's Marauders were put ashore. And, after a brief burial ceremony south of town, the unit left Vicksburg on Highway 61. It took the battalion south through Port Gibson, Fayette, and Natchez to the city of Baton Rouge. The 146-mile trip should have taken about three hours, especially in light traffic, but took twice that long because of the backups at checkpoints and a skirmish with Confederate resistance fighters.

Once the outfit arrived in Baton Rouge, Mac decided to laager up for the night rather than enter New Orleans while it was dark. The night passed uneventfully. And now, with fifty miles to go, Mac was scanning the terrain ahead. It was rural. Exits led to towns she'd never heard of, cell towers gave the hawks something to sit on, and woodlots separated farmers' fields. The sky was mostly gray, but she could see hints of blue here and there and knew that fighter jets were battling to control the air over New Orleans. And that's what worried her most . . . What if an enemy plane spotted the column? The battle would be brief and very one-sided.

The convoy ran into a backup about twenty minutes short of the city. Mac didn't like that because her vehicles were especially vulnerable while standing still and hemmed in. Fortunately, there were marshes on both sides of the freeway. That made it impossible for infantry or armor to attack the battalion's flanks.

Meanwhile, over on the northbound side of the freeway, a solid stream of refugees was fleeing New Orleans. Some rode in heavily loaded pickups, and others were packed into buses. There were people on bicycles, too . . . And motorcycles. One woman passed them on a Segway. All of which suggested that the city was in rough shape.

Finally, after fifteen frustrating minutes, a pair of MPs arrived from the south. They were riding motorcycles. Their job was to force civilian vehicles over into the right lane so that the military would have exclusive use of the left lane. As soon as she could, Mac ordered the **POPEYE**'s TC to pull out and lead the column forward. Progress was slow, but it beat the heck out of standing still.

By the time the battalion entered the city, Mac could hear the dull thud of artillery rounds going off and the distant rattle of gunfire. There was a crater where part of the freeway had been, but one lane was open, and some MPs were there to keep it from clogging up.

Consistent with the instructions she'd been given, Mac kept her vehicles on I-610 as I-10 veered to the right. Minutes later, she ordered the driver to exit onto Canal Boulevard. That took them to Navarre Avenue, which led into City Park. Union forces had taken control of Tad Gormley Stadium, and a wild assortment of troops were camped all around it.

An MP directed the Marauders to the area where teams of navy Seabees were using bulldozers to carve revetments out of what had been a well-manicured lawn. Mac ordered her vehicles to park out of the way so that the swabbies could complete their work, told Quick to let the battalion eat in shifts, and went looking for the man or woman in charge.

That person turned out to be a cheerful Marine colonel named Natasha Walters. When Mac found Walters, she was sitting on a crate of ammo spooning peaches into her mouth. "Don't salute," Walters said, as Mac started to do so. "This park is *huge*, it's lousy with snipers, and they like to shoot officers. In fact, everything west of Wisner Boulevard is hotly contested. 'Hotly contested' being code for rebel-held territory."

Mac laughed. "Roger that."

Walters aimed her spoon at an adjacent crate. "Take a load off, Major Macintyre . . . And yes, I know who you are. Your Strykers will be a valuable addition to the menagerie we call Landing Force Sword. Based on what I've heard, your people eat bullets and shit fire . . . That's exactly what we need around here. Once you're organized, I want you to go out and sweep the streets. We've got plenty of trash to clean up, including criminal gangs *and* resistance fighters. Your job is to disrupt their operations, force them to keep moving, and kill as many as you can. Have you got any questions?"

Outside of "Roger that," Mac had yet to get a word in edgewise. But there was no need. With very few words, Walters had been able to provide a cogent sitrep *and* a clear set of orders. "Yes, ma'am," Mac replied. "One question. Where's the ladies' room?"

It was the Marine's turn to laugh. "I like your style, Major . . . Step out of the tent, turn left at the water buffalo, third and fourth sanikans on the right."

NEW ORLEANS, LOUISIANA

As Victoria looked into the telescopic sight, she was aware of many things. Included among them was the way the light breeze might affect the flight of her bullet, the fact that her heart was beating faster than was ideal, and how the Union soldier was standing. His back was to the buildings on the west side of Bayou St. John, his assault weapon was slung, and he was looking down. *Why?* Because he was taking a pee, that's why.

Victoria smiled, and the trigger seemed to pull itself. She felt the stock kick her shoulder, heard the sound of the report, and backed away from the edge of the roof. Clay had been watching through a spotting scope. "Target down," Clay said via Victoria's earbuds. "Nice shot."

Victoria knew that without looking. It would have been impossible to miss. "We're pulling out," she said into the wire-thin boom mike in front of her lips. There were two sets of double clicks by way of a response. Both men knew that Union soldiers would arrive soon, barge into the church, and search it. The key was to be elsewhere when they arrived. Something the three-person team was good at.

The fact that Victoria was there, and still alive, was something of a miracle. As Victoria followed Radic down a set of metal stairs, she remembered the shock of landing in the cold water, the way her clothing pulled her down. And Victoria's lungs had felt as if they were going to burst by the time the second boot fell away, and her body began to rise.

But the helicopter was still there, hovering over the spot where the motorcycle had gone into the lake, firing its nose gun. Slugs churned the water as Victoria surfaced, took a deep breath, and dived. When she surfaced again, it was well outside the circle of agitated water. After filling her lungs with air, she went deep.

Victoria had a plan by then. The marina was nearby. If she could get in among the boats, she'd be hard to spot. But Victoria was tired. Very tired. And cold. Hypothermia was her worst enemy, and it was winning. She wasn't going to give up, though . . . So Victoria was still swimming, and still kicking, when a hand grabbed her collar. Strong arms pulled her up over the side of a small RIB boat. "There," a male voice said. "The catch of the day."

As Victoria lay in the bottom of the boat next to a couple of recently caught trout, she heard a motor start and knew the boat was moving. "Don't worry," the man said. "The *Dee-Dee* is only two minutes away. You'll be warm soon."

It turned out that the *Dee-Dee* was a large pontoon boat. And, although she had a couple of outboards to push her around, she was more houseboat than runabout. The interior was not only furnished like a home but equipped with what Victoria needed most, and that was an electric heater. The old man cranked it up to full blast and ordered her to strip. "I have a daughter about your size," he said. "I'll get a towel and something for you to wear." And with that, he disappeared.

The clothes consisted of frayed jeans that were a size too large, a tee shirt, and a Levi's jacket. A pair of slip-on tennis shoes completed the outfit. Once Victoria was dressed and holding a mug of hot chocolate, she realized how lucky she'd been. Without the old man's help, she'd be dead. He was seated a few feet away. "I saw the whole thing . . . The Yanks were trying to kill you. *Why?*"

Victoria saw no reason to lie. "Because I blew up some pumps and floodgates. We need to slow them down."

"So you're in the military?"

"The Confederate Army . . . Yes."

The old man nodded. "Good girl. Becky is, too . . . You can stay here as long you like."

But Victoria *hadn't* stayed. She couldn't stay. There was work to do, and she was doing it. Radic raised a hand as he opened the door to the parking lot. Then, after a careful look around, he waved them forward. The day was young, and there were people to kill.

|||||||||||||

It would have been nice to settle in for a couple of days and get organized, but that wasn't possible. According to Colonel Walters, Mac's Marauders were required on the streets "yesterday."

So Mac and her people worked through the night to get ready—and sent the first patrol out at 0600. Now it was midafternoon, the first Strykers were back, and six more had gone out to replace them.

Mac was riding with a platoon leader named Gomez and two vics loaded with infantry. She planned to spend time with *every* platoon in order to assess how they were doing. No one had deserted yet . . . And that was amazing since so many of her soldiers had been in jail a few months earlier. There had been some fistfights, however, a case of thievery, and a sexual assault. None of which could be tolerated.

The patrol went easily at first. There were areas of flooding, including places where the water was a couple of feet deep, but the Strykers had nearly two feet of ground clearance and could plow through even deeper spots when necessary. Not many people were out and about. But of those Mac saw, most were openly hostile. And no wonder . . . The Northerners had not only penetrated the heart of Dixie, the locals believed that *they* were responsible for the flooding, not to mention the bombing raids. And who could blame them? That's what they'd been told.

Gomez's vics were on Gravier Street, not far from the Mercedes-Benz Superdome, as two squads of ground pounders deassed their trucks. The mission was to search for a sniper team that had been working the area all morning. And there were lots of empty buildings and parking garages for such a team to take advantage of.

Gomez was clearly nervous about Mac's presence but did a good job of positioning his vehicles to protect each other and dispersing his troops. He led squad one through a shattered door and into a five-story insurance building, while the second squad remained outside to provide security. Mac followed squad one inside. Two of Gomez's soldiers were armed with M24 sniper rifles, and she had chosen to carry one as well since it was possible they might have to engage the enemy at a distance.

Each floor had to be cleared, and that took time. There was evidence of looting but no sign of snipers. And a careful examination of the roof didn't turn up anything either. No spent shell casings, no empty food containers, and no piles of poop. Half an hour had been wasted.

Once they were back on the street, Mac told Gomez's RTO to report the building as clear. Then they were sent to a structure located three blocks away. This one was "hot." Or so the operations people claimed, meaning that they had a drone circling above and had eyes on some bad guys. But Mac had heard that story before only to discover that the "bad guys" were vagrants camped on a roof. But orders were orders, and off they went.

The target building was an old factory that had been converted into chic office space. And as the soldiers began to leave their Strykers, a shot rang out. One of the soldiers went down clutching her leg. A medic ran to help and took a bullet in the head. It went through his helmet and entered his brain. Soldiers returned fire and risked their lives to pull both of their comrades in behind a vic. "It came from up there," a corporal said as she pointed to a structure located across the street from the target building.

"Are you sure?" Mac inquired.

The soldier nodded. "Yes, ma'am. I saw a head and a puff of smoke."

Mac was angry. Very angry. And confused. Had the operations people been wrong? It could happen. Were *two* sniper teams working the area? Or were noncombatants on the roof of the old factory building? She turned to Gomez. "Clear that building, Lieutenant. And get some people up to the roof. In the meantime, I'm going to take a fire team up to the top of the factory building. We'll nail 'em one way or the other."

Gomez nodded. "Yes, ma'am."

Once a fire team had been assigned to her, Mac led the mad dash across the street to the factory building. A shot rang out as they rushed through the open door, but none of them fell. That seemed to suggest a sniper on the roof of building two. Although a person *could* be on top of the first structure, firing straight down.

Mac ordered the four-person team to gather around. A sergeant named Cochrane was in charge. "Here's the deal," Mac told them. "If we had a full platoon, we'd do this by the book. But we don't. And there's no way in hell that five people can clear a five-story building. So we're going straight up the fire escape to the roof. I will lead the way, and Sergeant Dean will take care of our six. That's important because we could pass some bad guys on the way up, and they could fill in behind us. So pay attention . . . This shit is for real. Do you have any questions?"

"I have a question," one of the privates volunteered. "What is the warm liquid that's trickling down my leg?"

That got a laugh, and Mac grinned. "Come on . . . Let's get going before Kowalski fills his boots."

A series of signs led Mac to the fire escape. She opened the steel fire door with care, peered up between sets of switchback stairs, and gave thanks for the slit-style windows. The power was off, and without the openings, it would have been impossible to see without night-vision gear.

Mac took her time as she climbed upwards. The stairway would be the perfect place for a booby trap, and sure enough, a very thin wire was stretched across the stairs just past landing two. Not being an EOD specialist, Mac didn't bother to look for the explosives the wire was connected to. Instead, she stopped and pointed before continuing upwards.

Mac was having second thoughts about climbing up to the roof by that time. Maybe she should have called for an airstrike, maybe she should have waited for reinforcements, and maybe she was going to die. The single-shot rifle was nearly worthless for the situation she found herself in. Mac pulled her pistol and held it ready. *I'll take someone with me,* she decided. *I hope it's quick.*

IIIIIIIIIIII

Victoria was in a jam. The plan was to take a couple of shots from the roof of the factory building and haul ass. But moments after they had arrived, a sniper shot Clay from across the street.

Victoria assumed that the sharpshooter was part of a Union Army countersniper team. But why would such a team fire on people in civilian clothes? Since Clay had been killed *before* they could set up. Maybe the shooter was a guy who enjoyed shooting people. That was the problem with urban warfare . . . All sorts of creeps began to wiggle out of the woodwork. Not that it mattered. Someone had a rifle and knew how to use it.

The obvious solution was to leave Clay's body and run. And that's what Victoria was planning to do when two Strykers arrived. She knew that because Radic was monitoring the radio and could hear an officer giving orders. One of which was to secure the factory building. Things were not going well.

They had an emergency escape plan. It consisted of the climbing rope inside Clay's backpack. But the sniper's building was higher than theirs, which meant he could shoot down at them as they tried to retrieve the rope and do so without showing anything more than his head. And even if they managed to rappel down the opposite side of the building, the Union soldiers would be waiting below.

Worse yet was the fact that she and Radic had been forced to take cover behind the boxy structure that housed the top of the stairwell. The side *opposite* the door. So to go through the door, and take their chances on the stairwell, they'd have to expose themselves to the sniper.

Suddenly, Victoria heard a noise, and smoke billowed all around. A grenade! Union troops were on the roof! Well, smoke cut two ways. "Come on," Victoria said. "It's now or never!"

Both Victoria and Radic opened fire as they rounded a corner, and entered the smoke. But there were no shouts or screams. And when Victoria tried to pull on the doorknob, there was no give. Somebody was holding on to it from inside! "Drop your weapons," a muffled voice demanded. "And put your hands on your heads!"

Fuck that. Victoria backed away. The sniper's rifle was slung across her back, and the carbine was leveled at the metal fire door. The Union soldiers would come out. And when they did, she would . . .

|||||||||||||

The breeze that blew the smoke away came from the north. That gave the sniper the opportunity he needed. His name was Thomas Penny, and he was a Confederate deserter. He had the woman in his crosshairs. All he had to do was squeeze the trigger.

|||||||||||||

What felt like a blow from a sledgehammer hit Victoria from behind and turned her around. It wasn't until she hit the roof that the truth dawned on her. She'd been shot! *No,* she thought to herself, *other people get shot. Not me. Not here. Not now.*

But when Victoria tried to rise, she saw the blood and knew the truth. Gunshots rang out as Union soldiers burst out onto the roof, and Radic took a bullet in his right leg. He went down hard. Victoria heard a familiar voice. "Gomez! Have you got him? Good! Well done."

A man knelt next to her. "This one's alive, Major . . . But just barely."

That was when her sister Robin appeared. The dark gray sky served as a backdrop, and she looked just like their mother. A look of shock appeared on Robin's face. "Victoria? Is that *you*?"

Victoria coughed. Something warm dribbled down her chin. Her voice was hoarse. "I won . . . He hates you."

Robin was removing a battle dressing from a pocket on her tac vest. "I know that," she said softly. "You're the one he loves."

Victoria felt dizzy. It was difficult to see. "Yes, he does, because I'm a good girl."

"You're the one," Robin agreed. "The *only* one."

Victoria tried to speak. "Tell him . . . Tell him . . ." Then the darkness rose to envelop Victoria, and the pain disappeared.

||||||||||||

"She's gone," Sergeant Dean said as he felt for a pulse. "Who was she?"

"She was a soldier," Mac answered, as tears ran down her cheeks. "And my sister. Please make sure that they take good care of her body. I need to check on the rest of the platoon." And with that, she left.

||||||||||||

As the rain fell, it dug little holes in the loose earth, turned it into the consistency of brown gravy, and made puddles wherever the ground was low. The sun was little more than a yellow smear up above the clouds—and a bitter wind skittered through the trees, looking for something to kill.

The graveyard was a temporary affair. A vacant lot where Confederate soldiers were buried until the war ended, and their remains could be sent home. There were no headstones, no crosses, no Stars of David. Just three-foot-tall metal stakes bearing barcoded stickers.

There were mourners sometimes. But not often. In most cases, the only people present were the minister who had volunteered to say a few words and a couple of gravediggers, both of whom were holding their hats.

But in this case there *was* a mourner. *Well, not a mourner,* Mac decided. *But a witness.* So she was standing there, listening to the minister talk, when a person appeared at her side. Atkins perhaps. With an incoming call of some sort.

But when Mac turned to look, she saw a man wearing a broad-brimmed hat and a trench coat. His hands were in his pockets, and his shoulders were hunched against the cold. Two SUVs and people in dark clothing were visible in the distance. "I'm sorry," he said. "This must be very difficult."

"It should be," Mac replied. "But it isn't. My sister was a bitch. You're *here*. Since when?"

"Since the beginning of the operation," Sloan replied.

"I see."

"I wish we could go somewhere. I wish we could talk. There's so much to say."

"I would like that."

Sloan removed the hat, let some raindrops hit his face, and put it back on. Their eyes met. "You're very beautiful. I think about you all the time."

"And I think about you. Be careful, Mr. President . . . And thank you for coming. It means a lot."

Sloan tipped his hat. "We'll meet again, Robin . . . Watch your six."

And then he walked away. There was moisture on Mac's cheeks as she watched them lower the coffin into the ground. Some of it was rain, and some of it wasn't. Thunder rumbled in the distance. The guns were calling.